Wrecked

Elle Casey

All names, places, and events depicted in this book are fictional and products of the author's imagination.

No part of this publication my be reproduced, stored in a retrieval system, converted to another format, or transmitted in any form without explicit, written permission from the publisher of this work. For information regarding redistribution or to contact the author, write to the publisher at the following address:

Elle Casey
PO Box 14367
N Palm Beach, FL 33408

Website: www.ElleCasey.com
Email: info@ellecasey.com

ISBN/EAN-13: 978-1-939455-03-1

First Edition

Dedication

This book is dedicated first, to my husband, who's been telling me for years to "write the damn book"; and then, while I was doing it, wrangled the family, did the laundry and cooked spaghetti. We did it, babe!

This book is also dedicated to my kids who, if they were ever shipwrecked, I know would do just fine. Love you nuggets.

Last, but not least, this book is dedicated to my mom, Maggie Joy. You believed in me when no one else did, way back in the day. You have shown me what unconditional love is, and that love has given me wings. Love, Your Favorite Child -- P.S. I told you I would finish it!

Other Books by Elle Casey

War of the Fae: Book One, The Changelings
War of the Fae: Book Two, Call to Arms
War of the Fae: Book Three, Darkness & Light
War of the Fae: Book Four, New World Order

Clash of the Otherworlds: Book 1, After the Fall
Clash of the Otherworlds: Book 2, Between the Realms
Clash of the Otherworlds: Book 3, Portal Guardians

Apocalypsis: Book 1, Kahayatle
Apocalypsis: Book 2, Warpaint
Apocalypsis: Book 3, Exodus
Apocalypsis: Book 4, Haven

My Vampire Summer
My Vampire Fall

Wrecked
Reckless

Wrecked

Elle Casey

Business is Business

"I CAN'T *BELIEVE* YOU ROPED us into this stupid cruise," Sarah said in a tone of voice that clearly carried her frustration with parents who never appreciated her very important social calendar. She stood in the middle of her parents' bedroom with her hands on her hips, chin stuck out for emphasis.

"Sarah, we don't want to hear another word about this. You're going, and that's final. Now go pack your bag." Sarah's father turned his back on her to walk into his large bedroom closet. She lost sight of him as he turned the corner. The closet, trimmed entirely in dark cedar, was larger than many of her friends' bedrooms.

Sarah's mom stepped over and took Sarah's hands in hers. "I'm sorry, sweetie, but your father is right. We're all going, and you can't stay behind. It's important for your dad's business that we all be there. But don't look so glum – it's going to be fun!"

Sarah knew her mother was trying to sell her on the idea by using her especially chipper, upbeat voice. The annoying one. She rolled her eyes and pulled her hands away. "Oh, please. Like being stuck out in the middle of the ocean with you guys and those loser Buckley kids could ever possibly be fun. Not in a million years,

Mom. I'm not in the damn chess club, you know." The thought of being on a cruise with the two Buckley nerds was too much. Sarah had a boyfriend and a convertible, neither of which was going on this cruise. What was so difficult for her parents to understand?

Sarah's mom sighed and walked over to the dresser without responding, putting her fingers up to her temples to massage them. Confrontation wasn't her strong suit, and Sarah used this to her advantage as often as possible.

Sarah's father, on the other hand, wasn't one bit shy about going head-to-head. He stepped out of the closet carrying an armload of things for his suitcase. Without even sparing her a glance he said, "Don't talk to your mother that way, Sarah. Just go pack."

"But ... "

"Not another word, or you're going to be very sorry." He caught her eye, giving her one of his famous warning looks.

Sarah knew what that meant. Either he was going to take away the keys to her car and turn her into a social castaway or forbid her from seeing her boyfriend Barry.

"Fine!"

She turned and stormed from the room in a huff. She tried to stomp her feet for emphasis, but they didn't make a sound on the heavily padded, ultra thick carpeting. It was very unsatisfying.

On her way down the hall she stopped off at her twin brother's room and leaned in the doorway. Her eyes scanned the sports posters on the wall, the thirty or so perfectly arranged trophies on the shelves, and the small modern metal and glass desk with a computer sitting on it. He was always so neat with his stuff. "Kev, can you believe this crap? It's total B.S., right?"

Sarah's brother Kevin was packing a duffle bag he used for

rugby. She watched him move back and forth, grabbing things from different places. He always looked so at ease with himself. His muscled arms and back showed how hard he worked out so he could excel at his favorite sport. He was like most rugby players – he laughed at football players because they had to wear pads and helmets. Rugby players had to worry every game about broken bones and ears being bitten off, or so he said.

He continued to open drawers, pulling out wads of clothes and shoving them into his bag as he responded. "Whatever. I'm gonna go to the all-you-can-eat buffets and put them out of business. Then I'm gonna drink beer until I puke. Then we come home. No big deal." He didn't bother looking up.

Sarah snorted in disgust, a look on her face as if she'd smelled something bad. "Is that all you ever worry about? Food and beer?"

"What else is there to worry about?" he asked, dead serious.

"What about Gretchen? She's not going to be there."

"But there will be other girls, and Gretchen isn't the only fish in the sea." He sniggered at his own poor cruise joke.

"I'll bet she wouldn't be so thrilled to hear you say that."

He looked up at his sister to fix her with his threatening look. "She's not going to hear anyone say that, or else."

He sounded just like their dad. Sarah was sick of being threatened, but she knew that Kevin meant either he would share one of her secrets or he'd tackle her and mess up her hair – totally not worth it.

Gretchen probably had no clue that her brother was just using her like he did all the girls before her. The only thing he really cared about was rugby – and food and beer, of course. When he went to rugby parties, there was always beer there, provided courtesy of the older alumni of the team who still came to watch matches and party afterwards.

Sarah continued, "Whatever. I'm not going on this cruise and pretending like I'm having fun. We're gonna be stuck with those Buckley idiots the entire time, I just know it."

She paused in her ranting to carefully admire her latest manicure. Her nails were a rosy pink with white tips – flawless. Her skin was already very carefully bronzed to match her summer outfits. Her hair was expertly highlighted. All of it was going to be wasted on this stupid business cruise.

Kevin paused in his packing to spare her a glance. "Don't worry about it. We'll ditch 'em as soon as Mom and Dad aren't around, and I'll make sure they keep it to themselves and don't rat us out."

Sarah stood up straight and took a step into the bedroom. "Ooh, are you going to threaten them? That should be entertaining."

"No, I'm not going to threaten the twerp or his sister. I'm just going to explain to them that they'll have much more fun doing things with other kids more their speed." He stopped, pointing a finger at his sister. "And don't take another step into my room, or I'm gonna tackle your scrawny butt and mess up your hair."

She gingerly stepped back, knowing her brother wasn't kidding. Then she continued, "Awesome. That's one issue out of the way, at least." Sarah was picturing Jonathan and Candace Buckley, who she saw from time to time at school in the hallways or at lunch. *What is it with those people who can't even look in the mirror and see what they're wearing, anyway?* she thought to herself.

"Consider it done." Kevin finished packing his duffle bag, zipped it up with one quick, practiced motion, and threw it over his shoulder.

"Sounds like a plan," said Sarah, holding her hand up for a high five as he came towards the door.

Their hands met with a loud crack. "I'm outta here. Tell Mom I'll be back before four."

"Tell her yourself. I have to pack for this disaster." She pushed off the doorframe, stepped around him, and went into her room across the hall.

"You're a serious pain in the ass, you know that?" he yelled after her, shutting his door behind him.

She didn't bother to answer, other than to slam the door in his face as he walked by. She could hear him muttering behind the door, walking down the hallway towards the stairs.

She reached under her bed, pulled out her Louis Vuitton suitcase and carry-on make up case and put them on the bed. She turned towards her huge closet, throwing open the doors. *So, what does a girl wear on a cruise from hell?* As her eyes landed on the short, black skirt her aunt had bought for her on their last shopping spree, an evil glint came into her eye. *Well, this little number for starters...*

Her parents were going to be sorry they forced her to go on this stupid trip. She laughed out loud thinking about her revenge.

*****

Thirty minutes later her bags were packed and sitting in the hall by her door. She knew either her father or brother would take them down to the car for her. In her house, the men did the heavy lifting. As far as Sarah was concerned, there was a time and a place to assert one's power, and when manual labor was needed, it was not one of those times.

She checked her watch and realized it was a lot earlier than she had thought. *I still have time!* She sped down the stairs, grabbing her car keys off the ring by the door as she went by. "I'm going over to Barry's house!" she shouted up the stairs, not waiting for a response. She ran out the door and got into her Volkswagen convertible, heading to the neighborhood nearby.

As she drove, she was thinking about how excited Barry was going to be to see her. Usually she called or texted him before she came over, but she wanted to surprise him before she left for the cruise. He had asked her to come over earlier, but she had told him she couldn't because she had to get ready for the cruise. Lucky for him, she had some time to spare.

She pulled up in front of his house, paying no attention to the cars in the driveway. She walked up the front path and rang the doorbell. Within a few seconds, Barry's younger brother Sherman was there to answer it. Sherman was wrestling with the beginnings of puberty. He was about a foot shorter than Sarah, covered in peach fuzz and freckles, with a voice that always cracked on every third syllable or so.

"Is Barry here?" she asked in a breathless voice, excited to see the boyfriend she'd worked all year to win over. She craned her neck to peer over Sherman's head, looking to see if Barry was maybe down the hall in the kitchen or in the family room to the left.

"Oh yeah, he's here." Sherman nodded his head up and down while slowly running his eyes over her body, his right eyebrow lifted in an obvious positive assessment of her short skirt and low-cut top.

Sarah huffed out a breath of impatience and put her hands on her hips. "Well? Are you going to let me in?"

"What's your hurry, babe?"

"Outta my way, little turd." She pushed him into the hallway to get past him and climb the stairs.

Sherman tripped over a potted plant just inside the front door, falling on his rear end. "Fine ... go ahead. Have fun!"

He sounded a little too enthusiastic for someone who was yelling from his butt on the floor, but Sarah brushed it off. She hated Barry's little brother; he was such a little creep. Barry wasn't like Sherman at all. He was caring and sweet, plus he really loved her and ...

Sarah reached the top of the stairs and eagerly threw open Barry's door, ready to see him smile in surprise and happiness. She was planning to give him a very memorable kiss goodbye.

She stood in the doorway, shocked, unable to comprehend at first exactly what she was seeing. The door had swung in to reveal her loving boyfriend, lying on his bed, tangled up with ...

"*Gretchen?!*"

"*Sarah!* What are you doing here?!" yelled Barry, trying to jump up off the bed and lift his pants at the same time. He failed miserably, falling to the floor with his jeans around his ankles.

"Oh, my ... oh my God ... Barry ... Gretchen ... you ... you ... ASSHOLES! You cheating, lying, complete *assholes!*" Sarah turned and ran down the stairs, past a smirking Sherman, out the front door and into her car. It was then that she recognized Gretchen's stupid Nissan sitting in the driveway, plain as day. The bitch wasn't even trying to hide her deceit.

Sarah heard Barry yelling after her. She started her car and threw it into gear, grinding them in her hurry.

"Sarah, *wait!*"

She stopped the car in the street at the end of his driveway. Barry reached her window with his pants still not zipped or buttoned, gasping for breath. "Sarah, just stop, I can explain ... "

She struggled with the ring on her left hand. "Explain it to *this*, asshole!" She launched the puny promise ring he had given her last month at him, watching it hit his chest and bounce off to the ground. "And you can tell Gretchen the first person I'm going to go talk to right now is my *brother!*"

She slammed her foot down on the accelerator, tearing off towards home. Tears were streaming down her face as she alternated between sobbing and feeling like she was going to throw up. Her whole high school life was passing before her eyes; she couldn't stop thinking of all the time she had wasted on worshipping that jerk – thinking he was so amazing and sweet and *honest*. He sure had her fooled. The more she thought about it, the madder she got.

She pulled up to the stoplight a few streets over from her house, waiting for it to change to green. Her face was hot from all the crying and tears, so she rolled down her window to catch a cool February breeze. As the window lowered, she heard the sound of a small engine coming near. She looked in her side mirror, seeing what looked like a large bug coming up next to her car. She squinted her eyes to focus better, and realized it wasn't a bug – it was none other than Jonathan Buckley, king of the nerd herd. She would recognize that stupid lime green scooter and helmet with orange flames anywhere.

Jonathan was riding his Vespa and wearing his really safe, really big flame-painted helmet. He pulled up next to Sarah and looked over at her. After a second, he lifted his gloved hand to push up the visor of said helmet.

For a moment he just stared at Sarah with his big, blue eyes and impossibly long eyelashes. He swallowed a few times – she could see his Adam's apple moving up and down with the effort. He was nervously squeezing the handle of his scooter. Tentatively, he asked, "Hey Sarah. Uh ... what's up? Are you okay?"

"Of course I'm okay, don't I *look* okay?!" she screeched back. All she could think was that it was a really shitty day when the king of the nerds, wearing corduroys and velour, asks you if *you're* okay. *Holy crap, my life sucks.*

"Wh ... well, yeah, you look fine. I mean you look great. I mean, you look sad too, and you look great." He was clearly flustered, trying to think of the right thing to say.

"Well, I'm not sad, I'm very *happy*, so thank you very *much* for pointing out that I look like crap!"

The light turned green, and without saying another word, Sarah raced off, leaving Jonathan behind.

*****

"I didn't say you look like crap," Jonathan said to the cloud of exhaust she left behind. He sighed as he revved up the engine of his Vespa, dropping his visor back down, and slowly pulling out into the intersection.

Well this cruise is going to be interesting, Jonathan thought as he tooled along towards home. He wasn't an expert on girls by any means, but he knew that when they got moody, anything could happen. Living in his house with his mother and sister had given him a certain understanding of the female species. Like, for example, the fact that they were totally unpredictable – so he'd stopped trying to figure out what they were going to do or how they were going to react a long time ago.

He pulled into the driveway of his parents' modest two-story house and got off his scooter. He pushed it into the garage, shutting it off at the same time. He took the grocery bag out of the little lockbox on the back and went into the house through the side door, hitting the garage door button as he went in.

"Mom! I'm back!" he yelled from the mudroom. He took his

shoes off and lined them up neatly next to the others.

A voice responded from upstairs, "Hi, sweetie! Bring the stuff up to my room, would you please?"

He ran through the kitchen and up the stairs, taking two at a time, managing to trip halfway up, knocking a framed family photo off the wall. Luckily, he caught it before it hit the stairs and broke. "Yessss ... cat-like reflexes, once again," he murmured to no one in particular.

"What, sweetie?"

Jonathan sauntered into her room with the bag of things he had bought dangling from his finger. "Oh, nothing. Just practicing some ninja moves out in the hallway."

"Oh, that's nice," she replied absentmindedly, pushing a few more items into the corner of her already full suitcase. She stopped and looked up to see her son standing in the doorway, staring at her suitcase with a serious, calculating look on his face.

She moved over closer to where he was standing and took the bag from his finger, putting her other hand on his shoulder, snapping him out of his trance. She was smiling, looking him right in the eye.

"Thank you so much for getting this for me, Jonathan. You know how easily we burn." She went back to the bed to resume her packing, a small smile playing on her lips.

Jonathan took a step forward to stand next to the bed, looking down at her open suitcase. "Hey Mom, you know, if you want I can re-pack that bag for you so you can fit more stuff in it while also remaining under the fifty-pound weight limit required by the airlines at check-in."

She smiled, knowingly. "No, that's not necessary. I've got it handled." She started digging through the grocery bag. "Oooh, boy ... wow, you got a few kinds here. Oh, and one of them has SPF 50 ... I didn't even know they made it that high."

Jonathan grasped his hands behind his back and began rocking up on his heels and then his toes, back and forth with a regular rhythm. "Well, you know SPF is really an imperfect measure of potential skin damage because invisible damage and skin aging are also caused by ultraviolet type-A light, you know ... 'UVA' ... which is on a wavelength of 320 to 400 nanometers, by the way, and does not cause redness or pain; conventional sunscreen blocks very little UVA radiation. These broad spectrum sunscreens that I bought are designed to protect against both UVB *and* UVA light." He smiled, very satisfied with his product choices.

Jonathan's mom patted his shoulder absently as she looked at the sunscreen label. "That's nice sweetie." Her touch seemed designed to neither encourage nor discourage his factoids. If she acted more interested, which she sometimes did when he gave her the science behind his choices, he would elaborate; but he wasn't getting that signal right now.

Jonathan continued, "I bought some for Candi and me too. I'm going to go give it to her unless you need me to do anything else for you. Like ... re-pack that bag maybe?"

"No, no, that's okay. You go ahead and see your sister. I'm going to finish up here. Do *you* need any help with packing your things?"

"Nope, I'm all done." He smiled, proud of his organizational skills. He didn't want to hurt his mother's feelings, but it was obvious she had no idea how to pack a bag, so she would be the last person he'd ask for help. Her stuff was all wadded up with space around the edges. If she removed the air around her fluffy clothes and filled the spaces with smaller items and shoes, she'd have a much more efficiently packed bag, but it was useless trying to explain it to her because she would just brush it off. Jonathan was fully aware that not everyone shared his desire to be as efficient as possible, and he was okay with it.

"Good. Okay, be downstairs and ready to go at four o'clock. That's when the shuttle is supposed to be here."

Jonathan leaned in to give his mom a quick kiss on the cheek. "Love ya, Mom."

"Love you too, sweetie," she responded.

Jonathan took some sunscreen bottles his mother had put on the bed and left to go see his sister. He found her sitting on her bed, neatly folding a shirt to put into her suitcase. He noticed she had already taken care of the problem of small spaces around the clothes by shoving socks and sandals around the edges. He nodded in appreciation.

"Here," he handed her the sunscreen he'd bought for her, thinking it might work as a good space stuffer too.

"What's this for?" Candi asked, holding it in her palm, scanning the label.

Jonathan sat down on the edge of her bed, leaning back on his hands, staring at the posters of rock bands she had on her pink walls. "It's sunscreen, silly. I bought the broad-spectrum sunscreen that is designed to protect against both UVB and UVA. Did you know that ... "

"Yeah, okay, I don't need to know the details." She held up her hand in mock surrender.

"But, I was going to tell you that ... "

"Okay, yeah – that's great. You got me the best kind because you researched it and you know that this particular sunscreen will keep me from ever getting cancer *or* a tan. I get it. Thanks." She sighed as she threw it into her suitcase.

"What's wrong? You don't want the sunscreen?" Jonathan was confused. Usually she liked hearing his factoids.

She sighed aloud. "It's nothing. I'm just not super excited about this cruise is all."

Jonathan sat bolt upright, turning to sit sideways on her bed. "But why? It's gonna be fun! The ocean, pools ... ," he started gesturing with his hands in his excitement, " ... I mean they have like five pools on this ship – and all-night eating and dancing and drinks with umbrellas in 'em. What's not to like?" It sounded like heaven to him.

Candi shook her head in exasperation, her expression tinged with sadness. "Well, first of all, we have to go with Kevin and Sarah Peterson. What am I supposed to do about that?" She threw her hands up in frustration.

"Do? What do you mean, *do?* You don't have to do anything. Just go and have fun."

Candi's voice rose in frustration. "How can I have fun if *they're* there?"

"I'm sorry, Candi, I'm lost. How exactly do they stop you from having fun?"

"Jonathan, I love you but you are completely clueless."

"Well, explain this mystery to the clueless idiot then."

"Listen. I hate to break this to you, but they judge you. They judge *us*, Jonathan. You never notice, but I do. I can't stand being around someone who's looking at me, thinking I don't measure up." She put her head down and stared at her hands in her lap, obviously sad just thinking about it.

Jonathan leaned over and awkwardly patted her on the shoulder. "Hey, hey, don't be sad about that. I think you're just being paranoid. We just don't know them very well, they're probably really nice. We just need to give them a chance; you'll see. Once we're on the cruise and all this high school stuff is left behind us, they'll wanna hang out. I mean, who wouldn't want to hang with us? We're fun!" He put on his best smile and bounced up and down a little bit, trying to warm his sister up to the idea of relaxing.

She laughed at his goofiness, reaching over to push him off her bed. She laughed harder as he lost his balance and fell off the bed sideways, his legs flying up in the air.

"Whatever. You go off and live in your dream world. I have to live in the real world where people like Kevin and Sarah Peterson hate kids like us just because we're not as cool as they are."

He flipped himself over and jumped to his feet, taking a fighting stance like he'd seen Jet Li do once in a movie.

"God, you are such a dork. Dorky and funny. Now leave. I have to finish packing."

Jonathan transitioned back into his normal non-martial arts posture using loud, deep-breathing theatrics and lowering arm movements. "Wise move on your part – surrender before I have to seriously mess you up with one of my ninja moves." He stopped short as if he had just remembered something. He held up his hand and started ticking off items on his fingers. "Oh, I meant to tell you ... don't forget to pack your magnifying glass, compass, rain poncho, and Swiss army knife."

"What?" Candi responded, completely unruffled at both being granted a pardon from one of her brother's famous ninja moves and from his nonsensical switch of topics. "Are you serious? Are you packing all that stuff?"

"Of course I am."

"Um, okay, then maybe you can explain why to this dummy

here because I have no idea why I'd need a magnifying glass, compass and whatever else you just said, on a cruise. This isn't summer camp."

"Duh, in case the ship sinks, silly. If you wash up on a deserted island, you're gonna wish you had all those things, so pack 'em." Jonathan nodded his head in a confident way and continued, "Did you know that on this particular cruise, we're going to pass by no less than forty-two documented but uninhabited islands? And that there have been reports of pirates and ... "

"Okaaayyyy, that's enough of that. Thanks, Jonathan, but it's time for you to go bye-bye now." She stood up, taking him by the shoulders and spinning him around so he was facing the door. She pushed him out of her room and into the hallway.

"No, you really should listen to this stuff, it's very interesting, I'm also bringing my pocket telescope and my pocket knife and ... "

*****

The rest of his sentence was cut off as Candi shut her door and turned up the volume on her stereo.

That kid is totally in the weeds, she thought to herself. He was older than she was by only nine months, but sometimes it seemed as though he was a lot younger. She sighed. There was no hope for him – he was going to be a nerd for life.

She, on the other hand, had high hopes for her social life; and going on a cruise with the very popular and very beautiful Sarah Peterson could make or break Candi's next and last year in high school. If she could just get Sarah to like her, it could completely change her senior year.

She looked at herself in the full-length mirror and not for the first time lamented the baby fat that didn't seem to want to leave her belly or her cheeks. This cruise was not going to help – she couldn't imagine avoiding the buffets completely. She was a sucker for pecan pie and strawberry daiquiris. Her parents sometimes let her drink them without alcohol when they went out to dinner. *Maybe I'll get to try a real daiquiri on this cruise.*

She sucked in her gut and her cheeks, turning sideways to see what she might look like if she didn't have that extra five pounds. If she could just get Kevin Peterson to look at her one time, just once – and if that one time she was tan and her hair was just right, and she wasn't so darn puffy – maybe he'd notice her, and then ...

The fantasy was too far-fetched to continue. She let her gut back out and stopped biting in her cheeks. The day Kevin Peterson – the most perfectly formed, hottest guy in high school – noticed her as a dateable girl and not some weirdo with unruly hair, puffy cheeks and short legs, was the day she was the last girl on Earth. It was too depressing to even dream about.

She turned her attention back to her packing. *Should I pack the green bathing suit and the pink one, or just the green one? So many decisions to make and so little time. I wonder which color Kevin would like better.*

Her magnifying glass stayed in the drawer of her desk, the poncho only making it into the bag because it was sitting right next to the pink bathing suit that she finally decided to take. The rest of the items on Jonathan's list remained where they were. In their place went mint gum, sunglasses, eyeliner and waterproof mascara. A girl has to look her best on a cruise, and she only had this one shot to prove herself.

*****

Kevin was standing at the refrigerator drinking out of the milk carton when he heard the front door slam.

"KEVIN!!"

He choked as the word slammed into his eardrums. He quickly put the cap back on the gallon jug, practically throwing it back into the fridge. *How did she know I was drinking out of the carton?* She was at the front door; he knew she couldn't see the kitchen from there.

"What?!" he choked back, having hurriedly swallowed and wiped the small milk mustache off his top lip with the back of his hand. He leaned on the counter to make it look as if he was just hanging out in the kitchen for no reason – not drinking out of the milk jug without using a glass. That was a big no-no in the Peterson household.

Sarah rounded the corner from the front hall, and the first thing he noticed was her face. It was streaked with black stuff, from under her eyes to her jawline. Her eyes were blazing red and her nose was dripping snot. He quickly surmised that her current mood had nothing to do with his drinking-milk-out-of-the-jug infraction.

"What the hell happened to you?" was all he could think to say.

"What the hell happened to *me?* I'll tell you what the hell happened to me! I just found your slut girlfriend messing around with my asshole ex-boyfriend in his bed, that's what!"

"What the hell are you talking about?" Kevin responded, the words not yet completely sinking in.

"Yeah, you heard me right. I went over to Barry's house to surprise him, only I'm the one who ended up surprised – because your girlfriend was there *naked* with Barry and his pants half off!"

Kevin was dumbstruck. He jerked himself off the counter, grabbing his phone out of his pocket. He tapped out and sent off a furious text message.

"I ... " started Sarah.

"Don't say anything," he warned, menacingly, barely containing his rage. He stood there, staring at his phone, waiting for a response. The ticking of the kitchen clock and the humming of the refrigerator were the only sounds to be heard.

The beep of a return text reached their ears. Kevin took half a second to read the response and then punched the stainless steel refrigerator door, lightning-quick, leaving a dent in the front.

"Holy shit, Kev," said Sarah, staring back and forth between the dent and his face, her face showing surprise at his quick and violent anger.

He turned to leave the kitchen through the other doorway.

"Wait!" Sarah came chasing after him. "What are we going to do about this?"

Kevin continued through the butler's pantry, the dining room, and then down the hall and around the corner to the bottom of the stairs. "We're not going to do anything. It's over. They deserve each other. Move on." His voice was cold and heartless.

Sarah stopped at the bottom of the stairs, as Kevin to them up, two at a time. "Move on? How can I move on? My heart is broken into a thousand pieces!"

He laughed bitterly, not looking back. "Please. That guy's a complete ass, he didn't deserve you anyway. I don't want to talk about it anymore. Story's over. I'm gonna go on a cruise and find me a new piece of ass."

Sarah ran up the stairs behind him. "But ... "

"But nothin', I told you. I'm not talking about it."

He could hear her feet racing down the hall to catch up to him as he was entering his room. "But! ... "

His response was a door slammed in her face.

*****

The next thing Sarah heard was her brother's stereo being turned on and up really loud.

She leaned her head on the door and said softly, "But I really liked him a lot." The tears were burning her eyes, but she willed them not to fall. She hated feeling weak, and tears were a sign of weakness.

There was no response from Kevin – not that she had expected one. When her brother told her he wasn't going to talk about something, that was it. He wasn't the touchy feely type.

Sarah turned to go into her room. She planned to either cry where no one could see her until it was time to leave, or, if that didn't make her feel better, to come up with a suitable means of revenge against her cheating ex-boyfriend and his slut. Entering her room, she looked around and couldn't help but notice the tons of Barry mementoes all over the place – the photos, the stuffed animal he'd won for her at the school fair, the valentine flowers he had given her this year that she had hung and dried, the empty box of chocolates from her birthday. She felt a well of anger begin to build. *How could I have been so blind?*

*****

Kevin planned to stay in his bedroom until he was sure his sister was gone. She could be a serious pain in the butt when it came to talking about 'feelings' or 'emotions'. She didn't get that even though they were twins and pretty close, nothing and no one was going to get him to talk about that crap.

He sat down on the bed and took his phone out of his pocket, looking at the text messages that had just been sent and received.

I HEAR YOU WERE WITH BARRY JUST NOW. IS IT TRUE?

YES ... SORRY

He flipped open the keypad and texted back: *SCREW YOU.* Then he went to her contact and deleted it – and all the pictures he had on his phone of her, even the one of her tits that he'd taken just last weekend when they were making out in his car near the park. For him, there was no going back, no forgiveness. Like he had said to Sarah earlier, there were plenty more chicks where this one had come from, and they were all the same too – worried about their hair, makeup and clothes, pretending that they enjoyed sports to get guys to like them back. Fun to party with but annoying after more than a few hours.

Deleting Gretchen off his phone made him feel better. She was a fun girl, but he really didn't care that she had cheated on him. Sure it pissed him off – no guy likes that feeling that someone else was more attractive to his girl than he was, but he really didn't like her that much. She was cute and had a hot body, but she really didn't have anything else going on. It got old really quick listening to her talk. He usually tuned her out after about ten minutes and then grunted or 'mmm-hmmed' every once in a while when it seemed like she was waiting for a response.

As he looked back on his past few girlfriends, he realized that this pretty much described all of them. He tended to go for the Barbie Doll look, not paying much attention to personality. If the chemistry started flowing when he checked her out, she was a possible candidate. His sister had once accused him of purposely picking the dumbest, shallowest girls to go out with. At the time he'd disagreed, but making a more honest evaluation now, he thought there might be more than a grain of truth to that statement.

He shrugged his shoulders at this thought. *At least they aren't too complicated. I've got too much going on with rugby and potential college scholarships to worry about this chick garbage. I've got plenty of time to get serious with the marrying kind.*

Kevin had a theory. There were girls who were the dating kind – like Gretchen – and there were girls who were the marrying kind. So far, he hadn't bothered to get to know any of those. They were dangerous, in fact; they could distract him from what was important – his goals. Besides ... there was no point in hooking up with the marrying kind of girl, since he didn't plan on settling down until he was done with college. He had some serious wild oats to sow before then.

He fell back onto his bed and laced his hands behind his head, imagining all the gorgeous single girls who were going to be on this cruise. That instantly made him feel much better. *Lookout ladies, Kevin is back in business.* He smiled. That shithead Barry and airhead Gretchen really did deserve each other – he hadn't been lying to Sarah or just trying to make her feel better when he said Barry didn't deserve her.

Still, even though his sister was better off without Barry, she didn't deserve to have her heart crushed. Kevin knew how much she really liked the guy. Her problem was she couldn't see people for who they really were. She kept her thoughts and her interests shallow so she didn't have to feel too much. They were very much alike in that way.

He thought that he was probably the only person in the world who knew how intelligent and sensitive his sister really was. Maybe someday she'd let someone else see that side of her. The problem was that she'd been spoiled by their parents and ignored way too much. Their parents let her get away with murder because they felt guilty about how much time they spent away, plus they were mostly clueless anyway. His dad was pretty harsh and his mom was addicted to pills that made her sleep all the time.

When Kevin was in his psychoanalyzing mood, he'd say that Sarah acted shallow because she was afraid no one would like the real her – the smart, sharp-witted one. Instead, she focused on things she knew her parents valued – looks, style, attitude. And it wasn't the nicest attitude in the world either. They'd both been raised to be arrogant and selfish. Their father was the epitome of self-indulgence and self-importance. Their mother wasn't so much, but she was so weak, she went along with whatever their father wanted – when she wasn't sleeping.

Right now, their father wanted to get into some business deal with the Buckleys' father. Supposedly, this cruise was going to mean big changes in their lives in the near future. Kevin thought about that and some of the other things he'd heard his father say, both to his face and to other people. His father didn't know that Kevin listened to all of these conversations with interest. Frank Peterson thought his son was a dumb jock who had nothing on his mind but sports and girls. It suited Kevin to let people think that about him. Being underestimated gave him the upper hand.

He had pieced together that the Buckley kids' dad had made some software or program that was going to revolutionize the telephone relay service world, and his dad wanted to somehow get involved. This cruise was something his dad had put together to convince the Buckley guy to work with him and not some other company. Buckley was some kind of goofy genius who had no idea of the true worth of his invention. Kevin's dad was going to get this guy signed up with him and then take it from there. Kevin got the impression that what his dad was doing was legal, but not exactly right. He gathered this from some of the offhand comments his father had made and the level of stress Kevin was feeling in the house lately. He could tell his dad was really counting on this deal going through. He'd heard his dad say that he didn't want Buckley to figure out the real value of this program before he was locked in by contract.

The Petersons lived the high life – drove nice cars, lived in a big house, wore all the cool designer clothes – but Kevin knew that all was not as perfect as it seemed. He'd heard his parents up late at night arguing about money. He knew his dad had recently taken his mom's credit cards and cut them in half.

A lot was riding on this trip. Kevin didn't share this information with his sister. He knew she would only try to use it to manipulate their dad into letting her stay behind – and if he had to go on this stupid cruise, so did she.

He let his mind drift over to the things he remembered reading in the cruise brochure. There were five swimming pools, one of which was open all night, seafood buffets, breakfast buffets, lobster dinners ...

It wasn't long before he'd fallen asleep. The next thing he knew, his sister was pushing his shoulder saying, "Wake up, dumbass, the shuttle is here."

He opened his eyes and noticed right away that she'd cleaned herself up and almost looked happy. No more crazy black streaks running down her face or snot dripping out of her nose.

"Well, you sure got over your heartbreak pretty quick."

She smiled knowingly. "Yep. Like you said, he's not worth it."

Kevin got up to follow her down the hall but stopped when he caught a glimpse of her bedroom. "What the ... ?"

All over the bed and floor were little tiny pieces of what looked like confetti and possibly an exploded pillow.

"I did a little redecorating," said Sarah casually.

"Uh, it looks like a friggin' bomb went off in there. What'd you do, blow up a teddy bear?"

She turned around casually, showing no sign of emotion, other than personal satisfaction. "Nope. Just cut up all of Barry's pictures and shredded the stuffed animal he won for me at the fair."

Kevin got a big smile on his face, nodding in appreciation. "Nice."

Sarah smiled back. "Thanks."

"I deleted Gretchen's contact and photos off my phone."

"Sweet."

They shared a smile, bonding over lost love and heartache. Or maybe revenge. Either way, it felt good.

They both went downstairs and out the front door to get into the airport shuttle that was waiting to take them to the plane for Miami. Their bags were all stacked behind it, ready to be loaded by the driver. That was a sure sign that their dad was anxious to go. He hadn't even asked Kevin to help him with the bags.

"Tell me again why we have to go *now*, the night before the cruise?" Sarah demanded of her mother as she approached the shuttle van.

"Because the ship leaves in the morning, and we want to be sure we don't miss it." She was searching through her purse, anxiously as she answered.

"Yeah," responded Sarah, sarcastically, "we wouldn't want to miss the boat, would we?" She sniggered at her joke. "Get it? Miss the boat?"

Kevin rolled his eyes. He knew she was purposely egging on their mother. If their father heard, she was going to get in trouble. Again.

His mother responded distractedly. "Just keep your little comments to yourself, please, and don't let your father hear you.

He's very stressed out right now." She pulled her passport out of her purse. "Here you are. Why are you in here and not in my other bag?"

"Uh-oh, Mom's talking to herself again," said Sarah.

"Yeah, Sarah, whatever, give it a rest," said Kevin, tugging on her hair as he walked by to get into the shuttle.

*****

Sarah shot her mother a dirty look and slapped her brother's shoulder as he walked by, but kept her retort to herself. The sooner this was done, the sooner she could get back and plan her revenge on Barry The Bastard. She got into the shuttle and buckled herself up, settling in and staring out the window.

After everyone was in and all the bags were loaded, their dad gave the driver directions to some address several blocks over.

"I thought we were going to the airport," said Kevin, confused.

"First we have to pick up the Buckleys," said Sarah's mom.

"Are you *kidding* me? We have to go to the airport with them too?" asked Sarah.

"THAT'S ENOUGH, SARAH!" her father yelled, loud enough to make their ears ring.

The van suddenly got very quiet. Sarah had never heard her father lose his cool like that in front of other people. The driver just sat there as if he'd heard nothing.

Frank Peterson was seriously stressed out. In a quieter voice, he continued, jabbing his finger at Sarah's face for emphasis, "You are going to be *nice*, keep your comments to *yourself*, and *get along* with these people, Sarah, or so help me ... " He dropped his hand and turned around to look out the front window. He gestured to the driver to start driving.

Kevin nudged her in the leg to get her attention and then shot her a knowing look.

She stuck her tongue out at him. *As if* she needed him to tell her to shut up.

They continued on in uncomfortable silence to the Buckley house. Three minutes later they pulled up in front of a small, slightly shabby, two-story house. Within seconds, the Buckleys started spilling out of the front door, accompanied by their baggage. Sarah barely suppressed a groan. Kevin smiled and laughed quietly as they both watched the show unfolding. These people were unbelievable.

Jonathan Buckley led the pack, wearing fluorescent green swimming trunks that went down to his knees, a white undershirt, goofy sunglasses and an orange baseball hat. Behind him was his sister, what's-her-name, with her frizzy hair sticking out in all directions and her ninety-nine cent flip-flops flapping around all over the place. The last person out the door was obviously their mother, since she was the spitting image of her daughter, only taller.

Great, thought Sarah, *I'm going on a cruise with the crew from Sesame Street. All we're missing is Big Bird.* She watched as Jonathan's mother said something to him; he dropped his suitcase on the sidewalk and ran back to the door, tripping in the front entry.

"Daaad!!" he yelled into the house, as he righted himself. "Daaadd!! Shuttle's here!"

He must have heard an answer because he turned around and ran back to his bag. He picked it up and disappeared behind the van. A minute later the man of the house appeared in the doorway.

Kevin snickered.

Sarah saw what looked like a mad scientist, fiddling with his keys, trying to lock the front door. The guy's hair was greasy-looking and standing on end. He looked like he had slept in the outfit he was wearing – a large yellow shirt that didn't even come close to matching the blue shorts he wore with it. He dropped the huge key ring twice before he could get the key into the hole and lock the door.

Oh, goody. Now our Sesame Street crew is complete. Welcome to the cruise, Big Bird. Sarah turned away from the spectacle to look out the opposite window. She knew it was going to take all her concentration not to let her frustration show when her father was around.

Mr. Buckley started down the pathway to the van.

"Honey, did you get your bag?" shouted Mrs. Buckley.

"Oh, darn it, no I didn't."

"Don't worry, Dad, I'll get it for you!"

Sarah watched as Jonathan ran up to his dad to take the keys and then skipped to the front door, dropping the key ring twice before managing to unlock the door.

Sarah shook her head in pity. *Like father like son.*

Jonathan disappeared and then reappeared moments later with an old, worn faux-leather duffle bag.

Sarah couldn't help but stare at the father-son duo. "Hopeless," she whispered under her breath.

Kevin nudged her with his foot, signaling her to be quiet.

Sarah could see that he agreed with her Buckley assessment, but he gestured with his chin towards their dad, indicating he didn't want Sarah to upset their father. Frank was definitely on a hair-trigger – it wouldn't take much. As tempting as it was, Sarah didn't want to bear the humiliation of her father going off on her in front of these dorks, so she decided to keep her opinions to herself. For now anyway.

All the bags were finally piled up in the back of the van and the two families buckled into their seats – the Petersons in the front and the Buckleys in the back. Mr. Peterson gave the driver the instructions to head to the airport, and then an uncomfortable silence fell over the group. No one knew what to say.

As the van started down the street, Mr. Peterson turned around from the front seat with a thousand-watt smile and said, "Hey, Glen! Nice to have you on board here with the family! This is my wife, Angela and my kids, Sarah and Kevin." He tipped his head in each of their directions.

Glen picked up his hand and made a weak wave with it. "Hello, Frank, and everyone, heh, heh, nice to meet you all. Um, this is my wife Candace and our two children Jonathan and Candace." He paused for effect, as if waiting for them to catch up to the introductions he'd just made and to realize his wife and daughter shared the same name. Then he continued, "We like candy so much, we decided we needed more than one gumdrop in the family, didn't we, sweetie?" he nervously looked to his wife for support and then to his daughter – the other gumdrop, apparently.

*****

Candi closed her eyes in pain and groaned inwardly. *Please, God, make it stop.*

Mrs. Buckley gamely joined in. "Yep, that's right honey, she's Candace also. Sometimes I'm Candace Number One and she's Candace Number Two." She giggled nervously.

"You're Candace Number *Two?*" Sarah turned around and asked Candi with disdain. "Your family calls you *Number Two?* Are you serious?" Her tone said everything Candi had feared. Apparently "Number Two" meant the same thing in the Peterson household as it did everywhere else in America. Candi was now being compared to something people did in the bathroom. On the toilet.

"Um, no, not really. It's just a joke. You can just call me Candi." She could feel her face becoming flaming red. She was hoping the ground would open up and swallow her whole.

"Candi's cool. Hey Candi, nice to meet you. You can call me Kevin Number Two if you want." He laughed at his own lame attempt at chivalry. Candi saw him frown at his sister and then look back at her, smiling again.

"Okay ... " she responded, tentatively, not sure if he was making fun of her or if he was really just trying to be nice. His attempts felt more like pity than anything.

Jonathan chimed in, oblivious to his sister's shame. "You can call me Jonathan or Jon if you want. I don't care. Maybe Jon is better. It's faster. It has one syllable instead of the three." He yanked his hat off his head and held it in his hands. He was nervous – Candi could tell. Earlier he had told her that Sarah and Kevin were probably really nice; but now in the car, it was clear that he wasn't so sure about Sarah. He kept glancing at her nervously. Candi wasn't sure if his attraction to Sarah was fear or the fact that she really was beautiful close-up like this.

Sarah rolled her eyes.

Candi pleaded with Jonathan with her eyes, begging him not to say something too horribly dorky.

"Hey, Jon. I've seen you around school," said Kevin. "Play any sports?"

"Uh, no. No sports. I played baseball when I was six, but that's it. I got hit in the forehead with a fastball one time, so my mom didn't want me to play anymore. Now I mostly play games on the computer, you know, video games. I'm pretty good, though."

"Computer games, huh? Where you kill stuff and shit?"

"Kevin!" his mother squeaked, "Language! Please!"

"Oh, yeah. Sorry, Ma. Where you kill stuff and crap like that?"

"Uh-huh. Mostly aliens though or monsters. I prefer killing those kinds of things to killing people."

"Well that's a relief," said Sarah.

Candi got the distinct impression Sarah was thinking that Jonathan could be the kind of kid who snaps one day and takes out the whole school with some sort of homemade bomb. That made her mad, since nothing could be further from the truth.

Sarah's father turned around to fix her with a stare.

"What? What'd I say?" she asked innocently.

Frank didn't respond and Sarah eventually turned to look out the window, ignoring any more of the conversation in the van.

Mrs. Buckley decided to try to change the subject, "So, is everyone as excited about this cruise as I am?" She smiled shyly at the kids and then at Mrs. Peterson.

"Oh, of course we are, aren't we, kids?" Angela said with what looked like a fake grin plastered to her face.

"Yep," said Kevin, "I can't wait to hit those buffets."

"Oh, me too," said Jonathan. "Did you know that this cruise has eight different buffets, and at each buffet they have a minimum of forty-three different items, so that means at any given time on this ship there will be three hundred and forty-four types of food available?"

Kill me now, thought Candi silently.

"Seriously, dude?" asked Kevin.

"Yeah. Um, seriously. It's not a joke. I wouldn't joke about that."

"Huh. So, how do you know all this stuff, anyway?" Kevin

sounded genuinely interested.

"I did some research online. I read all the company's brochures. Plus I read some tour guide sites and blogs." Jonathan smiled, obviously proud of the thoroughness of his research.

"Did those guides tell you how many single chicks there usually are on this cruise line?"

"Kevin!" his mother admonished.

"Well, yes, actually – there should be approximately four hundred and forty-eight on this cruise, give or take."

Kevin's face broke into a big grin. "Sweet. Guess we have our work cut out for us then, don't we, Jon?"

"Uh, yeah, I guess so."

With that, Kevin plugged his mp3-player earbuds in, tuning out the rest of the conversation that had started going on between the parents. Sarah was staring out the window, seemingly oblivious to everyone else. Jonathan contented himself with reciting the periodic table in whispered tones, explaining to Candi when she complained that he was going to be facing a test in chemistry class when he returned. Candi started reading a book, trying to block out the sounds of science and boring adult prattle.

The shuttle van arrived at the airport with only thirty minutes to spare. The two families checked their bags at the curb, ran through the airport, passed through security and sprinted up to their gate. As soon as they got on board, the door to the airplane closed. The two families weren't seated together on the flight since the reservations had been made very close to the departure date, so they said goodbye and agreed to meet again at the baggage claim in Miami. They quickly found their seats and sat down, frazzled and out of breath.

Candi spent the first hour reading her book, but it was hard to concentrate. She knew Kevin was on the plane somewhere, and she wished she knew where, so she could sneak a peek at him. The plane was too big, though, so she settled for the memory of him sitting near her in the van earlier.

An hour before landing in Miami, Candi got up to use the bathroom. It was just a few rows back from her seat near the tail of the aircraft. She had to stand in the flight attendant's galley area to wait for it to become available. She was looking at all the different cabinets and drawers that were back there when someone bumped into her from behind.

"Oh, sorry, excu ... ," she started to say, but stopped when she looked up and realized it was Kevin who had bumped into her.

"Hello, Gumdrop," he said, smiling at her with his adorable grin.

Candi stood there staring at his beautiful white teeth, momentarily stunned and unable to speak. *How could a person have such a perfectly gorgeous face? And look at those teeth!* She'd never been this close to him before, but even up close, she couldn't find a single flaw. His jaw was showing a bit of a dark shadow coming in, but all that did was make him more gorgeous.

Oh my god, he just called me Gumdrop. I'm going to kill my father. What am I supposed to say?! She was panicked at the idea of the most beautiful guy in the school talking to her in a space no bigger than her closet. And it was dark, too.

"Um, what?" *That's it. Stall for time. Be cool.*

"I said, 'Hello Gumdrop.' What's up? How's the flight so far? Did you like your peanuts?" He smiled again, staring in her eyes.

She had to shake her head a little to clear it so she could respond like a normal person. "Hi, Kevin. Kevin Number Two. Yes, I liked my peanuts. All four of them."

"Ha, that's funny. Bummer for you, though, 'cause I got five peanuts. They must like me more."

She smiled shyly back at him and then looked down at the floor. "I'm sure they do."

The door to the toilet opened and a very large man came out, momentarily squeezing the two of them together. Kevin was much taller, so his face was pushed into her hair – the hair that was sticking out in a cloud around her head, as usual.

Sniff. "Hmm, your hair smells good." He got a curious look on his face, as if her hair shouldn't smell good. Or maybe he was just surprised that he'd actually said it out loud.

"Uh, thanks. I think." She stepped away to enter the bathroom.

"See you later, Gumdrop," Kevin said with a grin, as Candi stood in the tiny bathroom compartment looking out at him.

"Yeah, bye." She shut the door and locked it. Then she dropped her face into her hands. *I am the world's biggest dork of all time. Kevin Peterson calls me Gumdrop, tells me my hair smells nice, and then I open the door and step into a stinky bathroom stall and say goodbye. The most inglorious exit. Ever.*

When she came out, Kevin was gone. Candi breathed a sigh of relief. As much as she thought he was the hottest thing since, well, anything, she didn't think her heart could take any more of these close-quarter encounters with him. She was not prepared to function in that league. She was going to have to work on some cute one-liners and things she could say next time – assuming there would be a next time. She knew she'd never get an opportunity like this at school, and she was determined not to blow it if she got another one. She hadn't really thought about what would happen if she did win the social lottery and actually got Kevin to like her back. Probably because it *would* be like winning the lottery – the chances were just too remote.

*****

The plane landed in Miami forty minutes later. The two families gathered their luggage and took another shuttle van to a hotel near the cruise ship's port. They checked in at the reception desk and then gathered in the lobby, surrounded by all of their luggage.

"So, who's up for some dinner?" asked Frank, rubbing his hands together. "Anyone?"

Kevin still had his earbuds in, so he didn't hear or respond. Sarah just stood a few feet away saying nothing.

Jonathan and Candi looked at each other. Candi shrugged her shoulders at her brother.

"I'm in," said Jonathan.

"Yeah, me too," said Candi shyly.

"Actually, I have a bit of a headache, so I think I'm just going to go lay down, if that's okay with you, kids?" said the older Candace.

"Sure, Mom, no problem," answered Candi.

"I'll stay with Candace," said Glen. "I have some things with the program that I'd like to work on tonight, anyway. You kids go ahead with the Petersons – if that's okay with you Frank. Do you mind if my kids tag along?"

"No, not at all! The more the merrier!" Frank turned to his wife, "So, Angela, where should we go?"

"How about the restaurant here in the hotel?" she offered.

Frank turned to the group. "All in favor?"

"Aye!" said Jonathan, enthusiastically.

"Aye," said Candi.

"Whatever," said Sarah, while admiring her fingernails. She nudged her brother.

"What?" said Kevin, taking one earbud out.

"It's settled, then. Let's go." Frank gestured to a bellhop who was standing nearby. "Hey, buddy, can you give them a hand with the luggage?" The bellhop hurried over, dragging a rickety cart with him, ready to load all the bags and deliver them to the rooms.

"Frank, wait, let me give you some money for my kids' dinner," said Glen.

Frank held his hands up in front of him, "Oh, no, no – don't be silly. I've got it covered, it's not a problem at all, my pleasure."

Kevin looked at his sister and they exchanged questioning looks. Kevin knew their dad didn't have a bunch of extra cash lying around. He was obviously trying to act like money was no big deal, and he was definitely sucking up to Glen Buckley. If the Buckleys hadn't been here, they would have eaten at some fast food place instead of an expensive steak restaurant. It made him feel weird to see his father acting so strangely. It's almost as if he was nervous; and Frank Peterson was *never* nervous. Especially around guys like Glen Buckley.

The Buckley parents went up to their room while their kids and the Petersons went to the restaurant. Once they were all seated around a big round table together and had ordered some drinks, Frank began to talk.

"So, Jonathan, your dad tells me you've been helping him with his computer software program. That's pretty impressive." He waited expectantly for Jonathan's response.

Kevin started feeling uncomfortable. His dad was trying to act casual when he obviously had an agenda.

"Oh, not really. Just little things here and there. Sometimes I just check his code for errors. Sometimes you get so bogged down in your own work you miss the little things."

Kevin watched as Candi frowned at her brother, seeming like she wanted to say something but decided not to. She glanced over at Frank, her expression telling Kevin that his father made her nervous.

"Candi, do you do any of the work with your dad? Are you a computer expert too, like the men of the house?" He smiled at her really intensely.

Looking at him, Kevin was reminded of the Cheshire cat. It embarrassed him.

"No, not really. I don't really get into all the computer stuff like Jon does. Sometimes I help my dad with the artwork, but that's it."

"Hmm, artwork, huh? What kind of artwork?" Frank tilted his head to the side to show how interested he was. It was so overdone as to look comical.

"Well, sometimes when my dad or Jon is working on a part of the program that has a graphic component, they ask me to draw some things on the computer they can use. It's no big deal, really, just small stuff."

Kevin looked over at his mother, to see what she thought about her husband's second degree questioning. She just stared absently at her menu, ignoring him. Nothing new there.

"Give us an example of the kind of graphic work you've done, say, on this latest project of your dad's." Frank licked his lips and stared at Candi, waiting to hear her answer.

Kevin couldn't take it anymore – watching his dad act so weird, Candi getting more and more nervous by the second. "Dad, she already said it's just little stuff, no big deal."

"Quiet, Kevin. I want to hear what the girl has to say."

"Dad, are we going to talk about business all night, because it's giving me a headache," snapped Sarah.

Candi smiled first at Kevin and then Sarah, looking relieved.

Jonathan's head was moving back and forth, following the conversation being batted around the table, a confused look on his face.

"No, no ... this isn't business, I was just making conversation." Frank picked up his menu. "Why don't we just figure out what we're going to eat? Anyone interested in the sampler appetizer platter? We could share it ... "

Sarah put her menu up in front of her face, refusing to answer. Jonathan looked around the table, moving only his eyes now. Candi stared at the menu lying in front of her on the table, not knowing what to say. She looked like she felt nauseous, the way she kept swallowing.

"I'm up for it, and some of those stuffed mushrooms too," said Kevin, rubbing his stomach under the table. "I'm starving. Those five peanuts I had on the plane just didn't cut it." He winked at Candi.

She glanced up just in time to see it, blushing furiously.

Kevin smiled at her extreme embarrassment. It was kinda cool how she blushed so easy like that.

*****

Jonathan caught the exchange between Kevin and his sister and wondered about it. He wasn't used to his sister being so shy all the time. Usually by now she would have opened up and started talking away. When he saw Kevin wink at her, he decided she must be extra shy because of him.

Jonathan had to admit, he wasn't his usual gregarious self either. Kevin seemed pretty nice, even if he was built like an NFL football player; but Sarah Peterson intimidated the heck out of him.

She was beyond beautiful and so sure of herself. In his wildest dreams, he couldn't have imagined her even acknowledging his existence – and so far she really hadn't, so there were no surprises there. He'd never had a girlfriend before, but he didn't think Sarah Peterson was his type. She seemed angry all the time and probably didn't like science or computers like he did. He knew when he fell in love someday, it would be with someone who shared his interests.

But then again, he had to admit – Sarah Peterson was one of the most beautiful girls he'd ever seen. She was the most popular girl in school, and guys like him didn't normally get the chance to eat dinner with someone like her. He smiled to himself as he pictured the look on his friends' faces when he told them he went out to dinner with Sarah Peterson.

"What are you staring at, you little creep?" said Sarah angrily, glaring at Jonathan.

"Umm ... nothing ... uh ... I mean, *you* ... but not like a creep ... I was just thinking about telling my friends I had dinner with you ... " Jonathan's face started burning immediately, realizing he'd revealed too much.

"Ew, I'm not eating dinner with *you*, I'm eating dinner with my family and you just happen to be here." Her face showed something akin to disgust.

"Sarah!" yelled her father, his own face a fiery red that matched the color of Jonathan's.

"What?! He's sitting there staring at my cleavage, what am I supposed to do?" Sarah reached up to her blouse, buttoning it up two more places.

Jonathan watched her, feeling humiliated. "Sarah, I wasn't looking at your cleavage ... um ... I wasn't really, I ... "

"Jon, just let it go," said Candi, using a short, clipped tone. She looked over at Sarah with narrowed eyes, obviously not appreciating anyone calling her brother a little creep. She had always claimed he was a gentleman and so unlike all the boys at school in that way.

Jonathan didn't know what to say, so he just sat there, wondering what had just happened. He had been staring at Sarah, that part was true. But he wasn't thinking anything bad at the time, nor did he even really notice her cleavage. At least, not at that particular moment. He had noticed it earlier, but then again, so had the rest of the world.

He wondered why girls wore their shirts unbuttoned like that and then got mad when someone looked. It didn't add up for him, and since he didn't know enough about girls like Sarah, it was a puzzle that was going to stay with him until he figured it out. Jonathan liked solving riddles. Maybe later on the cruise he could ask Sarah why she did it. Since his sister didn't wear shirts like that, he wasn't sure Candi would know the answer.

*****

Kevin watched everything playing out at the table, smiling to himself. *This cruise is going to be awesome.*

His dad was busy trying to gather intel without anyone figuring out what he was doing.

Jonathan was completely clueless about women and was therefore going to annoy the ever-loving shit out of his sister whenever he was around.

Sarah was just waiting for a chance to lash out at anyone, and Jonathan was the perfect target since he would never know when it was coming.

And last, but certainly not least, Candi – the little mouse who was afraid of her own shadow – shows that maybe she has a little bit of backbone in her, at least when it comes to defending her brother.

Yep, this cruise is definitely not going to be boring.

Appetizers and dinner passed without further incident. The table was quiet except for discussions about the cruise schedule and amenities. After a dessert of ice cream sundaes, they all went up to their rooms, agreeing to meet for breakfast at seven the next morning.

All Aboard!

CANDI WAS ONE OF THE first ones down for breakfast the next day, preceded only by Jonathan. They were followed shortly by their parents, Frank, Kevin, and Candi. The group waited a few minutes outside the restaurant, eventually deciding to go in and start breakfast without Sarah and Angela.

"If we wait for them, we'll be late to the cruise, and I don't want to miss it or be the last in line," said Frank.

"Yeah," agreed Kevin, "they're never ready on time – they gotta pack on the makeup before they let their adoring public see them."

"That's enough, Kevin," said Frank without anger.

Candi and her mom shared a secret look. Neither of them was big on makeup, and they both had hair that was nearly impossible to tame, so they didn't even try most of the time; they just washed it, conditioned it, and let the curls do what they wanted.

Everyone ate breakfast from the buffet. They were joined in the last ten minutes by Sarah and her mother, both of whom had only a piece of dry wheat toast and coffee.

Candi looked down guiltily at the remnants of her scrambled eggs, bacon, and pancake breakfast. She had no control over her eating habits; she saw something that looked good and she ate it.

Luckily she was young and had good metabolism. She knew she wasn't going to win any swimsuit model awards, but she wasn't fat either. She looked over at Sarah and sighed.

Sarah was fully capable of winning a swimsuit model award. Life was so unfair sometimes. Candi thought if she were as beautiful as Sarah, she wouldn't spend so much of her time being so rude, like Sarah did. Candi didn't know her very well, but so far she wasn't impressed with what she'd seen. She decided to give Sarah the benefit of the doubt, though. Maybe she was nervous about the cruise. Candi had seen Sarah at school being cheerful and laughing with her friends, so she knew Sarah could be a happy person, at least sometimes. Maybe when they got together on the cruise without their parents around, they could start to build some sort of friendship.

Looking down at her plate again, she realized this might mean eating less at breakfast time. *If that's what I have to do, then so be it. Goodbye pancakes and goodbye bacon.* She pushed the uneaten portions of her breakfast away, even though she really wanted to eat them.

She looked up and caught Kevin watching her with amusement. He looked over at his sister, who was sitting there with her sunglasses already on, looking bored over a piece of dry toast. Then he looked back at Candi again, sitting in front of a plate she wished wasn't there. She was embarrassed to think he was noticing that she'd laid waste to the buffet.

He smiled and nodded his head, frowning as if impressed at how much she'd eaten. Then he looked over at Jonathan's plate.

Jonathan looked up with his mouth full of food to see Kevin staring at him.

"Whaffs wong?" He swallowed with some effort and then

tried again. "What's wrong? Did I do something?" He looked from Kevin to his sister and then back to Kevin again.

"No, dude, nothing. I was just looking at how much you're eating. I know guys on the football team who can't eat that much for breakfast." He wasn't being rude – he sounded fascinated.

Candi wanted to die. Here was her brother, the skinniest kid in their grade at school, eating his normal gigantic breakfast, oblivious to the fact that everything they did on this vacation was potential ammunition to be used against them later at school.

"Oh, he normally doesn't eat this much," explained Candi, "He's just excited about the buffet."

Her brother looked at her, confused. "That's not true. I eat pancakes and bacon and eggs almost every morning. Sometimes I have a waffle instead of the pancakes, or sausage instead of the bacon, but the fat and calorie count is virtually equivalent."

"Seriously?" asked Kevin. "How do you stay so skinny?"

"Oh, I run and do other stuff."

"What do you mean, you run? Like track?"

"No, I'm not on the track team. I just run around the neighborhood. Sometimes I just have a lot of energy, especially when I'm studying and I'm trying to work out a calculation or a piece of code or something; I get a little antsy, so I go running and come up with the answer while I do it. Then I can calm down and finish my work."

"Interesting," was all Kevin said in response. He seemed to be mulling over the answer in his head.

Candi couldn't tell whether Kevin thought this response was normal or completely crazy, which is what she thought. Her brother was telling the truth, though. He had lots of energy. When it wasn't spent coming up with answers to complex mathematical equations, it was spent burning up the pavement. He probably ran thirty miles a week ... more during finals.

Sarah looked up from her coffee and toast to join in the conversation. "So, you eat a million calories, run, and do math while you burn every calorie you ate?"

"Yep, I guess so," answered Jonathan, a wary look on his face.

"Does it help? The running I mean?"

"Well ... yeah ... it helps me. It clears my mind so I can just let it do the work for me. I kind of just stop thinking at all, and my mind works behind the scenes and comes up with the answers I'm looking for."

Kevin joined in. "I've heard about that kind of thing – you know, letting your subconscious come up with answers to questions. Like you have to stop thinking about a problem so the solution will just come to you from your subconscious."

Candi knew the look on her brother's face and wished she could stop the train of thought that she knew he was forming in his head – but there was no stopping one of her brother's freight trains of useless facts.

"Did you know that 'subconscious' is the layperson's word for what Dr. Sigmund Freud called the 'unconscious mind'? He said it's a place where socially unacceptable ideas, wishes or desires, traumatic memories, and painful emotions are put out of the mind through psychological repression."

Oblivious to the blank stares that greeted him from around the table, he took a quick breath and continued, "Unconscious thoughts are not directly accessible, but are supposed to be capable of being 'tapped' and 'interpreted' by special methods and techniques such as meditation, random association, dream analysis, or things like running, like I do."

He finished by clasping his hands together, waiting to hear the comments he was expecting to come from his rapt audience. This topic was obviously fascinating to him; Candi knew he could talk about it for hours.

No one said a word. Jonathan raised his eyebrows, still waiting for someone to comment. He looked over at his sister.

She was stared at him, wanting to kill him.

"What?" he asked.

Candi didn't answer. She just shook her head slowly, rising up out of her chair.

Kevin was the first to break out of the trance. "Dude, how do you know all that stuff? You sound like you're reading out of one of our school textbooks or something."

"I read it in various treatises on the subject. I find the topic of the subconscious mind fascinating. I remember most of what I read."

Sarah stood up to leave. "Well, I think a kid who reads about that science stuff just for fun has some serious issues."

"Sarah!" said her mother sharply, before standing up to join her daughter. "Excuse us, please – we're going to go wait out in the lobby. I'm sorry for Sarah's rudeness, Jonathan."

Jonathan just smiled. "Oh, don't worry about it Mrs. Peterson. My sister says I have issues all the time. I know not many people my age like to study like I do. See you later."

Kevin laughed. "You're alright, Jon, you know that? I'm impressed that you know all that stuff. Who knows when it might come in handy? Hey, maybe one of the chicks on the ship will need to know the molecular weight of copper or something."

"The atomic mass of copper is 63.546, actually," responded Jonathan, eagerly.

"Well, there you go then. It's in the bag, dude. You'll have the ladies all over you by the end of the cruise." He stood up and clapped Jonathan on the back, throwing him up against the front of his plate.

"*Ooof*. Um, thanks. Yeah. Hopefully." He glanced at Sarah's retreating form trying not to be obvious about it – but Candi saw through his pitiful attempts at casualness.

She watched as he shook his head a little but continued to stare at Sarah's back. Candi prayed he wasn't entertaining the idea of falling in love with that viper. She was so far out of her brother's league, they weren't even on the same planet. She'd eat him alive.

Candi hooked her purse over her shoulder, leaving the restaurant for the lobby. She couldn't watch her brother be a dork anymore. At least Kevin seemed to be okay with it. He was laughing, but he wasn't really making Jonathan feel bad. He seemed to look at Jonathan like he was amusing more than anything else. Candi decided this was better than having Kevin see Jonathan as a target of harassment or bullying. Kevin didn't seem the type though. Good thing, since Jonathan was an easy target. He always had been, and he'd been teased often enough; but it didn't seem to bother him overly much.

Once, when a kid at school punched him, Jonathan came home and spent three hours researching bullying and the psychology behind kids who use violence against other kids. Later, he told Candi that he just felt sorry for the bully, now that he knew the problem wasn't really him, per se. That was when Jonathan was ten years old.

Jonathan was still a kid in some ways, but in others he was amazingly mature beyond his years. Candi wished she could be that nonchalant about high school life. Maybe it was a guy thing or whatever, but she couldn't be that unaffected.

She entered the lobby thinking about ways she might be able to start up a conversation with Sarah. *What can I talk to her about? What do we both like that would be interesting to her? Oh, I know ...*

Candi walked up to Sarah who was standing in the lobby next to her bags, examining her fingernails. "So, um, Sarah, hey. Whatcha doin'?"

Sarah dipped her head, looking at Candi above her sunglasses. "Standing here, waiting for the stupid shuttle to bring us to the cruise."

"Oh, yeah. Me too. Um, I was wondering ... what kind of bathing suit did you bring?"

Sarah sighed. "Suit? As in singular? I didn't bring just one, I brought five, one for each day of the cruise. Didn't you?"

"Um, no. I just brought one." Candi was so embarrassed. The cruise hadn't even started, and she'd already apparently committed a fashion faux pas.

"Well, I guess you could buy some in the gift shop on the ship."

"Oh, yeah, that's what I planned to do. I didn't have time to shop before we left." The lie came easily to her lips, as she tried to impress Sarah.

"Well, I have all bikinis, of course, all hooked in the back so I can unhook them to avoid tan lines. I hate tie-backs, don't you? A couple of them have Brazilian bottoms too. My father is going to hate them." She smiled coldly. "So, what type of suit did you bring?" She looked Candi up and down, not bothering to conceal her critical evaluation.

Candi didn't want to answer. She didn't know what a Brazilian bottom was, but she was pretty sure it wasn't something she would wear, especially since she knew it was something Sarah wore to make her dad angry. Candi hadn't worn a bikini since she was seven years old. She was pretty conservative and a bit self-conscious about her body.

"I have a one-piece. It's pink."

"A pink one-piece? Are you kidding me? Does it have one of the Disney princesses on it or something? How are you going to get tan in a one-piece?" She lifted up her glasses, resting them on the top of her head, and stared at Candi incredulously. "Hello! We're going on a cruise ... you don't wear a one-piece on a cruise, dummy, didn't you know that?"

Candi felt like shriveling up and dying right there on the spot. How was she supposed to know these things? "No, I didn't know, actually. I've never been on a cruise." Her face was burning red.

"Well, I have, and I can tell you that the only people who wear one-pieces are old ladies and fat people; and you're neither of those." She put her sunglasses back down over her eyes and opened up a magazine she'd been holding under her arm.

"I'm not? I mean, I know I'm not fat, but I really didn't think I had a bikini body, I mean, like, at all." *I can't believe I just said that. How pitiful can I be?*

Sarah didn't seem to notice. "You do. You're just too afraid to show it. You're repressed. All you have to do is lay off the pancakes for a week and you'll be fine for bikini season." Then she stopped reading her magazine to look Candi in the eye. "Maybe you can use the cruise to come out of your shell, live a little bit. I plan to." She smiled smugly at Candi, which only made Candi more nervous than she already was. Sarah seemed to have some sort of plan formulated in her mind, and if Candi had come to know her at all in this very short period of time, it probably involved doing something that would give Frank Peterson a stroke.

"Yeah, maybe," Candi replied, noncommittally. She didn't really enjoy annoying her parents. That usually resulted in being grounded, and she hated being grounded. It meant no after-school activities and no television for a week. It was like a jail sentence where the only thing she could do was go to school or sit in her room.

Without looking up, Sarah said, "I'll help you shop for a suit on the ship if you want."

Candi seized the opportunity, "Okay, that would be great! Thanks! When?"

"I don't know. Whenever."

Candi couldn't help but smile hugely. "Okay, good. Whenever. That sounds great."

"What sounds great?" The voice came from just over her shoulder, causing Candi to leap up and squeak in surprise. She turned around to find Kevin standing right behind her, listening in on their conversation. Thank goodness he'd only heard the tail end of it.

"We were just talking about going shopping together on the ship."

"Oh, god, you're going shopping with Sarah?"

Sarah didn't even look up from her magazine. "We're going to get her a hot bikini so we can get all the little boys drooling around the pool."

Candi's face started burning again. "Well, I don't know about that part."

"Oh, I believe it. I could picture you in a bikini." Kevin backed up to appraise her more frankly. "Yep, no doubt. You could get them drooling." Then he winked at Candi and reached out to pinch her cheek.

Candi stood frozen in place. Her stomach had about a thousand butterflies flying around in it. *Is he flirting with me? Oh my god, quick! Think of something witty to say back!*

"Um, thanks."

Oh crap, what is wrong with me? Why can't I talk? He's going to think I'm a brainless idiot!

"Speaking of drooling, somebody get me a napkin." The girls followed the direction of Kevin's gaze and saw a beautiful Latina girl walking by, looking like she'd just walked off the cover of the Sports Illustrated swimsuit edition. She turned her head, catching Kevin's eye, smiling at him with her perfectly straight, brilliantly white teeth.

Kevin wasted no time taking off, leaving the girls standing alone again in the lobby. They watched him go over, pick up her bag, and walk out the front door of the hotel with her hanging on his arm.

"Typical," said Sarah.

"Yeah," was all Candi could say, dejectedly. To dream that this guy would actually notice her when he was really only interested in women who were so beautiful they made your eyes hurt was a complete waste of time. What had she been thinking? She and Kevin were never going to happen. She was just going to have to crush on him from afar and hope that someday, life would be different for her.

"What's your problem?" Sarah asked, picking up on Candi's sad vibe.

"Oh, nothing."

"You sound depressed."

"I'm not. Really."

"Huh. Whatever you say. I know depressed when I hear it." She let Candi get away with her little white lie, and went back to her magazine. A couple seconds later, she smiled, somewhat deviously. Candi looked away, not wanting to see anymore. She was afraid Sarah was going to figure out her deep, dark secret – her crush on Kevin.

Sarah reached out and casually hit Candi on the shoulder with the back of her hand. "I wouldn't waste my time on him. He doesn't get serious with girls, and he never goes out with the smart ones, even if they are cute."

Candi stood there in horror, realizing that Sarah was on to her, somehow having figured out that Candi was in puppy love. *How embarrassing.* She couldn't think of anything to say so decided to go with denial. "Who me? Kevin? Don't be silly. He's totally not my type."

"Oh, yeah? So who is your type then?" Sarah asked, a challenge in her voice.

"Well, smart. Of course Kevin is smart, I'm not saying that he isn't or anything ... "

Sarah raised her eyebrows. "And?"

"And, well, he would be strong and athletic ... which I know Kevin is also, but I'm not talking about Kevin ... "

"Continue ... "

"And he would also be nice and serious, too," she finished lamely, knowing she'd pretty much just described Kevin to a T.

"Alright. Let me get this straight. Even though you just described a person exactly like my brother, he's not your type. Okay. I get it." She went back to ignoring Candi and reading her magazine.

Candi stood there, alternately staring down at the floor and up at the ceiling. Her strategy to engage Sarah in conversation hadn't gone exactly as she'd planned; now she was roped into buying a bathing suit that was going to take half of her savings to pay for and probably going to make her feel practically naked – and Sarah knew she had a crush on Kevin. *Shoot me now.*

*****

The shuttle dropped the Petersons and Buckleys off at the port where the cruise ship was docked. The air was already starting to get heavy with the Miami humidity. All of their baggage was piled in front of them. The men found some carts and loaded the bags, as the women headed towards the check-in area.

It was like a huge cattle call. There were hundreds of people – families, couples, singles – all standing in one giant room that had several agents checking people in at counters on the far side of the high-ceilinged space. After people checked in, they left their bags with the agents and walked up a ramp that led them out of the reception area, presumably to where the boat was waiting.

The Petersons and Buckleys stood in a group, staring at the mass of people in front of them.

"Okay, everyone, let's get in line!" said Frank enthusiastically, a big grin plastered on his face.

Sarah rolled her eyes, watching as her brother grabbed a cart of luggage and started pushing. Jonathan tried to do the same, but he wasn't making much progress. His cart was really loaded down. Candi moved over to help him, and together they wrangled it over to the nearest line. Angela and Candace followed directly behind them. Glen had his nose buried in a cruise brochure and didn't realize he was being left behind. Sarah strolled behind the group, wishing she wasn't with them.

"Dad, come on!" yelled Jonathan.

Sarah looked back and saw Glen glance up at the sound of his name, lost. Seconds later, realization that he was alone dawned on his face.

He hurried over to join them in line. "Oops, sorry about that. I was just reading the technical brochure. Did you know that this ship was recently retrofitted with new Wärtsilä diesel-electric generators to reduce fuel consumption?"

Everyone but Jonathan stared at Glen with empty looks. "Oh, yes, I did read that. It's exciting. I wonder if we'll be able to tell any difference."

Glen chuckled. "It's not likely, son, since we've never been on a cruise ship before."

"Yeah, I guess you're right." Father and son shared a smile.

Sarah couldn't help but stare at them. They were like aliens in her world. A kid who got along with his dad like that? The look on her face said it all – *that is just not natural.*

Sarah looked over at Candi and noticed a mutinous expression on her face. She'd been watching Sarah carefully. Candi looked over at Sarah's father, barely disguising her dislike before looking back at her father.

"Cool, Dad."

Mr. Buckley smiled at his daughter. "So, Gumdrop, what's the first thing you're going to do when we get on board?"

"I don't know. Maybe explore a little bit?"

"Actually, Gumdrop," interrupted Kevin, "you have to stick around your room and get ready for the muster." He wiggled his eyebrows up and down at her and smiled.

"Muster? What's that?"

Jonathan jumped in to answer. "The muster drill is when all of the people who are onboard the ship respond to the call, which is seven short blasts of the ship's horn followed by one long blast, to report to their lifeboats with life jackets on. It's like a practice run for a sinking ship situation. International law requires that it be conducted within twenty-four hours of departure. The captain of the ship is required to instruct the passengers on the escape routes and use of life vests," he paused a millisecond to take a breath, "and you have to stay totally silent during the drill so you can hear what the captain is saying." He smiled at the group that was now standing around him with their eyes glazed over.

"Okaaaay," responded Candi. "Thanks for that very complete answer."

"You're welcome," responded Jonathan cheerfully.

Kevin chuckled under his breath.

Sarah pressed her fingers to the bridge of her nose, as if she were fighting off a headache. "Seriously, Jonathan, you need a hobby or something." He couldn't be more textbook nerd than he was. She didn't know whether to be fascinated or irritated.

The adults turned their focus to checking in the families, their turn finally coming up. Once that was done and all the bags identified and stowed away with the agents, they followed the crowds walking to the ship.

Candi kept glancing back towards the bags with a concerned look on her face.

"Don't worry – they'll deliver them right to our rooms. When we're done with the muster, they'll be there," said Kevin.

"Oh, yeah, okay. That makes sense."

"Why'd you look so worried? Are you carrying some contraband in there or something?"

"What?! Oh, my god, no." She was all flustered.

He started laughing at her, but not in a mean way. Sarah was intrigued by the look on her brother's face. It's almost as if he was ... charmed or something.

"Oh, you were joking."

"Yeah, I was joking. I'll bet you've never even touched anything remotely considered contraband in your entire life, right?"

Candi looked down as she walked, not answering right away. Sarah could tell she was embarrassed and wrestling with some inner demons. She wished she could read the mouse's mind.

"Yeah, you're right. Never."

Kevin patted her shoulder. "Good for you. Don't get mixed up in that stuff. Stay straight. It's not good for the body or the mind – and you've got a good thing going on there." He smiled lecherously.

Sarah saw it as a chivalrous attempt to take Candi's mind off of whatever was making her frown right now. She couldn't figure out why he kept flirting with Candi, though, since she definitely wasn't his type. Maybe he was just trying to make her blush. The girls he usually ran with weren't the blushing type, and Candi's face was on fire now – like it usually seemed to be whenever Kevin was around.

"Yeah, okay. And thanks. I think." Candi looked at the ground, refusing to meet his gaze.

Just then they reached the door to the inside of the ship. The interior looked dark compared to the outside where they were nearly blinded by the bright Miami sun reflecting off the side of the dazzlingly white ship.

Frank took charge. "Okay everyone, get your ticket and your IDs out. And let's make a plan for meeting up later."

Sarah looked down at her ticket, frowning. She looked over her mom's shoulder to see her ticket.

"What the hell, Mom? You guys have an ocean view with balcony and you have us on the inside without windows? Are you friggin' kidding me?"

Frank stood there with a fake smile frozen in place. He spoke carefully through gritted teeth. "Yes, that's right. Kids below decks and parents above. Someday when you're buying the tickets, you can spring for a balcony. Until then, deal with it. Okay, sweetie?"

Sarah huffed out a breath of air and stormed off, knocking a couple of guys out of her way, ignoring the catcalls that followed her.

*****

If Sarah had turned back she would have seen Candi and Jonathan sharing a look. They had no idea what the big deal was. Who needs a window in a room you're just going to sleep in anyway?

Frank continued as if the tantrum hadn't just happened. "Let's meet up after the muster drill for dinner. We'll do the first seating at the Nautique Restaurant at six o'clock."

Candace and Glen nodded at one another. "Sure, Frank, that sounds great. We'll see you later, then." Glen turned to Candi and Jonathan. "Kids, just get settled in and do the muster drill, then we'll see you for dinner, okay?"

Candi and Jonathan agreed immediately. Candi knew they were both thinking the same thing – freedom! She was happy to be getting away from their parents. Not that she was planning to get into trouble, but it wasn't often that she and Jonathan did things with other teenagers and no adults around outside of school activities.

"It's party time, guys, let's hit it." Kevin clapped Jonathan on the back as he walked by. Jonathan stumbled forward, catching himself before he fell into his father.

They all entered the dimly lit interior, using the map given to them to find their rooms.

Candi noticed that Sarah and Kevin were traveling down the same hallway as she and Jonathan. Eventually, they stopped at the door directly next to her and Jonathan's door.

"Oh, shit, they actually have us rooming together, Kevin," said Sarah, looking down at her ticket.

"That's lame," he responded. Then he looked up at Jonathan and Candi. "You guys rooming together too?"

They looked at their tickets, comparing them. Jonathan responded, "Yep, looks like it."

Kevin and his sister exchanged knowing looks. Sarah shrugged her shoulders. Kevin looked at Jonathan and said, "How 'bout this Jon ... you change tickets with Sarah and come room with me. Then the girls can be roommates next door. That way, we don't have to deal with hair stuff and makeup all over the bathroom, and we can take a dump with the door open."

Jonathan just nodded his head, a stunned expression on his face. Candi was pretty certain he was trying to picture a situation where he'd want to go to the bathroom with the door open and another guy in the room.

Candi was grateful that her brother seemed temporarily speechless. "Yeah, that's fine with me," she agreed. This way, she could have some more quality time with Sarah. If they roomed together, maybe they could become friends and ...

"Well, it's fine with me, but I'm going to be the first one in the shower every morning, and I call the table inside for my makeup area. You can put your stuff somewhere else," said Sarah. She held her hand out to Jonathan.

He stood there looking at it, confused as to what she wanted.

Elle Casey

"Hello, McFly, key please."

"Oh, yeah, sorry!" He handed her the plastic card key and took the one she offered.

Candi looked at her brother. "See you later, Jon."

"Yeah, okay. We'll come and get you and go to the muster together. We'll be in the same lifeboat area."

Candi nodded her acquiescence. Now all she had to do was figure out what she and Sarah could possibly talk about that wouldn't be humiliating, unlike her super crush on Sarah's brother or her lack of proper cruise attire.

Making Waves

SARAH USED THE KEY CARD to open the door. She stood staring at the inside of the cabin. "Holy shit, this sucks. I can't believe there's no window in here." She casually gestured towards Candi. "If I vomit on Sugar Lump here, it's not going to be my fault."

Kevin took a quick look inside their cabin while saying absently, "That's Gumdrop, idiot, not Sugar Lump."

"Whatever." Sarah brushed off her brother's correction and went into the room.

Candi followed, trying not to think about being vomited on by someone who wouldn't care one bit about doing it. She could probably ask her brother for a seasickness remedy. If she knew him, he had one in his backpack somewhere.

Candi shut the door to the cabin, leaving the guys standing out in the hall. She looked around and realized there wasn't much room to move around. Candi saw that there was a small table with a mirror in front of it off to the right, opposite the bathroom door, which she guessed was the makeup area that Sarah had claimed for herself. Candi didn't much care since all she wore for makeup was some occasional eyeliner and mascara, if that. Lots of the time she went without any at all.

There was a knock at the door. Candi turned around to open it expecting Jonathan to be there, but it was a man in a white uniform with their bags. He left them on the bed and then continued on his rounds of bag delivery.

After he left, Candi watched Sarah open up one of her bags and start rummaging around, mumbling under her breath. "Where is that thing? I know I packed it ... A-ha! There you are!" She pulled out a small piece of material in a leopard print. She was humming as she reached to open another, smaller bag, pulling out a pair of very high heels from inside.

"What are you doing?" asked Candi. She looked at the material and shoes, thinking Sarah was putting on some kind of negligée and heels, which didn't make sense since they were going to be leaving the room soon.

"I'm getting ready to muster." And with that, she started pulling off her clothes.

Candi stood there speechless, not used to strangers just stripping down in front of her. Sarah was wearing a really sexy, lacy bra and matching g-string panties. Candi thought about the serviceable white cotton underwear and flesh-colored bra that had zero lace anywhere on it that she was wearing, feeling embarrassed that her things were so plain. She looked at the bathroom to gauge whether it was big enough for her to change in so maybe Sarah would never know.

She turned back to watch as Sarah took the leopard print thing, which turned out to be a very thin mini dress made out of something shiny, and slipped it on over her head. She kicked off her sandals and slipped her feet into the delicate, black, strappy heels, bending down to secure the tiny buckles that rested above her ankles.

Sarah stood up to see Candi standing there with her mouth hanging partially open, too stunned to say anything. "What's the matter? Cat got your tongue?" Sarah asked, waspishly.

"Uh, no. I'm just ... "

"What?" Sarah demanded, bristling at the naked disapproval coming from her roommate.

"It's just that ... I mean ... aren't we going to the muster?"

"Yes, of course we are. I don't see your point," said Sarah, being deliberately obtuse.

"Well, I don't know, I mean, maybe it would be easier in ... other shoes ... or something?"

"What? These things?" She lifted her foot up to the side, twisting her leg around a little bit, showing off her long, shapely, tan and very exposed leg. "I walk around in shoes like this all the time. They're as comfortable as those horrible shoes you're wearing."

Candi glanced down to look at her flip-flops. "I doubt that."

"Yeah, well, whatever. This is what I'm wearing and *nobody's* going to tell me I can't."

"I wasn't trying to tell you that you can't wear them, Sarah." Candi felt bad that Sarah felt censured, even though she had just criticized her and her flip-flops.

"I wasn't talking about *you.*" She fixed Candi with a stare that carried a lot of meaning.

Candi caught on right away. "You're talking about your dad, aren't you?"

"So what if I am?" Sarah answered nonchalantly, shrugging her shoulders.

Candi was curious. "Why do you try so hard to make him

mad?" It seemed counterintuitive to her. If you want to get along with your parents, you don't work overtime to make them angry.

"Why does he work so hard to be such an asshole? I don't know. Maybe because it's fun." She zipped her bags back up in sharp motions, then grabbed her makeup case from the bed. "Watch out. I need to freshen up my makeup and you're standing in front of my mirror."

Candi stepped to the side. She ran out of room in the tiny cabin to go any farther, so she climbed up on the bed. It was a very small double bed, which she was just realizing might be a problem when rooming with a bossy space hog.

Sarah sat in front of the mirror, putting on makeup that would have been more at home on someone going out to a nightclub, not a person on a cruise ship in the middle of the day.

Candi sighed, not looking forward to the altercation that was sure to erupt between Sarah and her father.

"I hear you sighing at me. You'd better watch out, or I'm going to put some of this on you, too. Then we'll see what *your* precious daddy has to say about that."

Candi didn't like Sarah talking about her family like that. It gave her a little extra courage she normally didn't have. "Listen, Sarah, I appreciate that you have some sort of thing going on with your dad or whatever, but that doesn't make it okay for you to say crap about my dad or my brother, okay?" The adrenaline was pumping through her veins, making her feel shaky. Her fight or flight instinct was kicking in, and at this particular moment, she was choosing *fight*.

Sarah put her makeup brush down and a slow smile broke out across her face. "Easy now, killer, no harm meant. Relax." She turned back towards the mirror, picking up an eyebrow brush. "My father's an asshole, and yours apparently isn't. Poor me, yay for you. That's life. I'm over it."

Candi stood up and squeezed past her, heading towards the door. "If you were so over it, you wouldn't be wearing that outfit." Candi opened the door, stepped out beyond it, and slammed it closed before Sarah could respond.

Apparently now she was in the flight mode of the fight or flight instinct. She leaned against the hallway wall and exhaled loudly. Confrontation with Sarah was nerve wracking and not fun.

*****

The door next to hers opened and Kevin stepped out. He stopped short when he saw Candi standing there, just a couple of feet away. "Hey there, Gumdrop, what're you doing out here?" He took a look at the high color and frustrated look on her face, guessing instantly what had probably happened. "Did you tangle with the tiger in there?"

Candi smiled back. "I think so, if by tiger you mean Sarah."

"That's the one. Don't worry about her. She's all snarl and no bite."

"I'm not so sure about that."

Kevin took her gently by the upper arm, steering her down the hall away from the rooms. He continued, "Trust me – just don't give in to her shit, she'll back down. She's really a nice girl at heart – but don't ever tell her that I told you that because I'll deny I said it."

Candi said nothing in response. She was too busy alternatively staring at his hand on her arm and looking up shyly at him.

"Aren't you wondering where I'm taking you?" he asked, finding it amusing that she didn't have a quick comeback for him this time.

"Um, yeah, I guess."

He stopped walking and looked down at her, with only a trace of his earlier humor on his face. "You shouldn't be so trusting of guys, Candi. You can't let some guy just grab you by the arm and drag you through the ship. You could get hurt that way."

She looked confused. "Are you saying I shouldn't trust you then?"

Now it was Kevin's turn to be uncertain. He stopped for a second to think about what he had been trying to say, momentarily flustered. "No, you can trust me. I'm talking about other guys."

She smiled, seemingly amused by the fact that he was a bit unsure of himself. "But you're a guy who just grabbed me by the arm and is dragging me through the ship." She was teasing him, flirting back.

He recovered quickly, now on the solid, familiar ground of flirting with a girl. He was an old pro at seduction, and this little bit of sweetness didn't have a chance. "You're right about that, but I'm not just *any* guy, now am I?" He leaned a little closer to her while keeping his eyes locked on hers.

Her breath started coming more rapidly. He could see a slight sheen of sweat breaking out on her upper lip. Her face began to glow a pretty pink.

"Please let my deodorant be working," she whispered, before her eyes nearly bugged out of her head.

He smiled, bemused. "What did you just say?"

"Nothing!" she squeaked.

They heard a door slam down the hall and the sound of approaching footsteps. "Hey, guys! What's up? Where're you going? Mind if I go with you? I was thinking about going to ... "

Jonathan stopped short when he reached Candi and Kevin.

"Hey, Candi, are you okay?"

The trance broke. Kevin watched as Candi stepped back and quickly pulled herself together.

"Yeah, I'm great. We're just getting some air. Where are you going?"

"You're getting some air? Here in the hallway?" Jonathan looked around at the enclosed space, trying to figure out what she was talking about. Kevin could practically see his mind working, wondering if there an air vent hidden somewhere he wasn't seeing.

"Hey, buddy, whaddya say we go up to the bar and get us a beer?" Kevin put his hand on one of Jonathan's shoulders to steer him down the hallway away from his sister. They both started walking down the hall together, leaving her behind.

"Oh, I'm not drinking age yet."

"Don't worry about that. We're in international waters now, and I have a fake ID. I'll get us both a beer."

"Actually, the fact that it's international waters is irrelevant. Each cruise line has its own drinking age, and usually it's twenty-one. I'm not twenty-one yet."

Kevin stopped walking for a second, forcing Jonathan to also stop since Kevin's hand was still firmly on his shoulder. "You know, Jon, there *is* such a thing as too much information. Has anyone ever told you that?"

"Oh, yeah, Candi says that to me aaaaalll the time. T-M-I Jonathan, T-M-I!"

Kevin glanced back at Candi and winked at her, causing her to blush all over again. "Your sister is a sharp one. I think we need to be careful of her, I'm pretty sure she's not exactly what she seems."

Jonathan was completely oblivious to the undercurrent of

flirtation present in that statement. "Oh, I agree, totally. Wait 'til you really get to know her. She acts totally different at home than she does at school."

Candi's feet immediately went into motion, closing the distance between them and her, her expression telling Kevin she meant to try and stop her brother's motor-mouth.

"Oh, I'm looking forward to it – getting to know more about her, maybe over that beer I mentioned. Are you up for it, Mister I'm Not Twenty One Yet?"

Jonathan hesitated only for a second. "Yeah, okay, that sounds good. My dad said we should relax and live a little on the cruise; I guess having a beer qualifies."

Kevin released his shoulder and clapped him on the back a couple of times. "Yes, Jon, my man, it sure does." He glanced back over his shoulder at Candi, who was now standing right behind them. "You comin', Gumdrop?"

"No thanks, I'm going back to wait for Sarah." She stared at her brother hard before turning and walking back toward the cabin, while the boys continued to the stairs at the end of the corridor.

Kevin shouted, "Suit yourself!" already forgetting about their exchange.

*****

Candi stood in front of her cabin door. She knocked, then used her key to go in.

Sarah was still sitting at the makeup table. "Back so soon?" she asked sweetly, as if nothing had happened.

"Yeah," Candi responded quietly. She stood there for a moment, weighing the pros and cons of dealing with Sarah head-on, deciding eventually that it would be better to fix it and move on than to let it fester. "Listen, Sarah, I'm sorry I said that stuff about your dad or whatever. I don't want to fight with you; I just want to hang out and have a good time. I'd prefer to do that with you, but if you don't want to hang out with me, that's fine too. I'll understand."

Sarah stopped with her makeup application and turned to look at Candi, sitting on the edge of the bed. "What is it exactly that you would understand?"

Candi started playing with her cuticles nervously. "Well, that hanging out with me might not be what you would want to do, I guess."

Sarah continued to push her, "And why wouldn't it be what I want to do?"

"I don't know – maybe I'm not like your other friends at school and so maybe since I'm not like them, the things I do might not be your idea of fun or whatever." She was frustrated trying to explain this concept that was floating around in her head, which was essentially: *I'm not cool enough for you.*

But Sarah was hearing something totally different. "So what you're saying, basically, is that you're too goody-goody for me and you don't want to hang out ... is that it?" Her tone was getting bitchy, a barely controlled temper simmering beneath the surface.

"What? No! Of course not, don't be silly! I don't think that at all. It's just ... it's just that ... well ... you and I travel in different circles. I mean, your friends are more sophisticated than mine are, wear fancier clothes and shoes, go to parties and stuff. I wish I could do those things, but I can't – or I don't – I don't know which, actually, but it doesn't matter. What I'm trying to say is you're cool and I'm not, so if you don't want to hang out with me, I totally understand, okay!"

Candi stood up and walked quickly to the door. She didn't

wait for a response; she turned the handle, jerked open the door, and rushed out into the hallway, letting the door slam shut behind her again. *Great*, she thought, *this is the second time in ten minutes I've run out of the room. I'm such a wuss. Sarah's going to think I'm a total drama queen.*

She wasn't sure if Sarah had purposely goaded her into it, but somehow she had figured out Candi's deepest thoughts and got her to say them out loud. Running away was the only escape from her humiliation.

As Candi walked quickly down the hallway towards the stairs, all she could think about was how Sarah was probably going to go back to school and tell all her friends about how much of a loser Candi Buckley is. The thought was just too depressing to dwell on. *So much for moving up the social food chain.*

*****

Back at the cabin, Sarah sat staring at the door that had just closed with a bang. She carefully reviewed the exchange she'd just had with Candi, turning mindlessly back to the mirror to finish up her makeup. As she went through the motions of putting on blush, she put it all together, finally figuring out what Candi had been trying to say.

So, the little Sugar Lump thinks I'm cool. That's nice. And the poor thing didn't think she was worthy of Sarah and her friends. Sarah laughed out loud at that. The irony was that Sarah's friends were only interested in being with Sarah because they thought she was rich and well-connected, or because Kevin was her brother and they wanted to be his one and only true love. And truth be told, Sarah was jealous of the relationship Candi seemed to have with her parents. It was so open and loving. They didn't care what anyone thought of them. Life would be so much easier if it was really that way.

Well, if she had any hope at all of having a good time on this cruise, she definitely needed something to keep her occupied. Since Candi seemed to be worried about being cool, maybe there was something Sarah could do to take care of that. She got up from her ministrations and headed to the bed where Candi's bags were sitting.

Without any regard for Candi's privacy, she opened them up, one by one, examining their contents. *Tsk, tsk, we have a LOT of work to do here. This girl dresses like I did in sixth grade. No, make that fifth grade.* As she lifted up different outfits and pulled them in at different points in the fabric, mentally pairing them with pieces of jewelry she knew she had with her, she realized that maybe she could help Candi pull off something cute with this pitiful selection of clothing.

She threw everything back in the bags without folding any of it, just as she heard an announcement come over the loudspeaker. A garbled, disembodied voice said that the muster was going to take place in thirty minutes and that everyone had to attend. They were going to check cabins to make sure they were empty; the muster wouldn't end until every passenger had checked in.

Even without this threat, Sarah didn't plan to miss the muster for anything. She had a show to put on. She was a little disappointed that her parents would likely be in a different muster line on a separate deck, but she knew if she didn't see them now, she would at dinner. She sat down with her magazine and waited for her roommate to come back. They needed to show up with their life jackets, and Candi's was still in the room, she knew it wouldn't be long.

A few minutes after muster horns sounded, Sarah heard

muffled sounds coming from the hallway and some banging around in the room next door where Kevin and Jonathan were staying.

The door to the cabin opened and Candi stood in the entrance.

"I guess we have to go to the muster now. I'm here to get my lifejacket."

"Here." Sarah threw it to her from the bed where she had been sitting and waiting. She stood and walked over to join Candi in the hallway, shutting the door behind her.

The boys' door opened and Kevin and Jonathan came out into the hallway. Sarah smelled alcohol.

"Have you guys been drinking already?" she smiled in approval. Her parents were going to hate that.

Jonathan's hair was sticking out on the side making him look just slightly adorable. Sarah frowned, and without thinking, reached out to smooth it down.

Jonathan stood stock-still, looking as if he were afraid to move, his mouth hanging open. Just his eyes followed her hand as it went up, smoothed the hair down, hesitated for a second, then dropped back down to her side.

"Yeah, we ... " Kevin had started to answer before he was struck speechless, watching his sister's tender gesture.

Candi looked horrified, probably worried that Sarah was going to smack him or something. Her expression transitioned into shock at the realization that it wasn't violence being meted out, but kindness.

Jonathan appeared completely awestruck. His mouth hung open, and it was clear that the drink he'd had with Kevin had gone straight to his head. Sarah surmised from his current state that he probably never drank; plus he was skinny, so he was probably already buzzed.

Candi reached over and pushed up on Jonathan's chin, closing his mouth. "Please ... you're going to drool on someone."

Kevin broke out with a confused laugh. "Okaaaay, so, everyone got their lifejackets?" Then, for the first time, he noticed what his sister was wearing. "What the hell are you wearing, Sarah?" His good mood soured immediately; he sounded angry.

"I'm wearing clothes," she answered stubbornly.

Jonathan snapped partially out of his reverie by shaking his head and then looked at Sarah more closely, squinting his eyes at what she was wearing. He was still in some sort of trance though. He responded to Kevin's question as if he was under some kind of mind control. "Yeah, Kevin, can't you see? She's wearing clothes. Leopard clothes."

"Okay, so we've established that Sarah is wearing clothes," said Candi, in an annoyed voice. "Can we please go to the muster now?" She turned and started walking down the hall.

Kevin ran his fingers through his hair. "You know Dad is going to have a shit fit when he sees you in that."

Jonathan just stood and nodded as if in agreement, his eyes still in a daze.

Sarah saw the nodding, and it sparked her anger, making her even madder than she already was with her brother. "If I was one of your floozies, you'd like this muster outfit, *Kevin*."

"Yeah, well, you're not one of my floozies, you're my *sister*, and I don't like to see my sister dressed like that!"

Jonathan started shaking his head slowly from side to side, appearing as if he agreed with Kevin.

Sarah turned on him, "Stop agreeing with him, and *stop staring at my boobs, Jonathan!*"

*****

That snapped Jonathan out of his daze.

"I ... I ... I wasn't! I wasn't staring at your ... you know ... your ... whatevers! I was just staring at nothing! And you smell good."

"Nothing? Now you're saying I'm nothing? And you're smelling me now, too?! *Weirdo!*" Sarah shot him a dirty look and took off, storming down the hall, following the direction Candi had recently taken.

"No! Not nothing! You're something! You're something!" Jonathan started walking quickly after her with this finger raised to emphasize his point, trying to figure out where he'd gone wrong and realizing he really didn't have a point. *Why do I get so confused whenever she's around?*

"Yeah, you're something all right," echoed Kevin, following all of them at a slower pace.

Jonathan reached the top section of the stairs at the same time Kevin did. Candi and Sarah were waiting on the top landing for them to catch up, not because they wanted to hang out with them apparently, but because they had no clue where to go.

"Where's the muster spot?" asked Sarah, not looking at anyone, instead staring out the window across from the foyer where they were standing.

"Don't worry," said Candi, "Jonathan will know."

"Of course he will," replied Sarah snidely.

"What's your problem now, Sarah?"

"Nothing. I don't have a problem, I'm glad your brother knows everything about everything."

"Well, it's coming in handy right now, since neither of us bothered to figure out where this muster thing is."

"Whatever." Sarah turned her back on Candi and looked down, examining her fingernails.

Candi just sighed in response.

Jonathan was so busy taking this in, that he missed the last step of his climb. He tripped and landed on his face at the top of the stairs, just next to Sarah's feet. He rolled over onto his back, bumping up against her leg.

Slowly he opened his eyes, mentally checking at the same time to make sure his legs, feet and arms were still movable. As his eyes focused, all he could see at first was a bunch of leopard print, a beautiful tanned leg, and then some pink lace.

Pink lace? What the ... ?

"Stop looking up my dress, you pervert!!" yelled Sarah. She kicked Jonathan in the shoulder with her toe.

"Ow! No! I wasn't looking up your dress! I fell! I fell!"

Kevin stood next to them, laughing his butt off and holding his ribs.

"Yeah, *right*. How convenient." Sarah backed up to get away from him, bumping into Candi who was standing behind her.

"Watch out, Sugar Lump."

"Watch out, yourself, *leopard lady*," Candi replied in an angry tone. "Jonathan just tripped. He didn't look up your dress intentionally."

"Okay, okay everyone," said Kevin, holding up his hands, still laughing. "Everyone, calm down now."

He offer his hand to Jonathan. "You okay buddy?"

Jonathan stood up with Kevin's help. He started brushing his pants and arms off, afraid at first to look at Sarah. "Yeah, I'm fine." He gave himself a quick inner pep talk, telling himself to man up. He looked cautiously over at Sarah and sighed heavily.

"Sorry, Sarah, I really didn't mean to look at your pink underwear."

"Aaaargh! That's *it!*" She made a move to come at Jonathan, who surprised himself with how fast he could move, running around behind Kevin.

"I'm sorry! I'm sorry! I'm sorry!" was all he could think to say.

Kevin grabbed his sister as she tried to get around him. He wrestled her while he continued to laugh at the mayhem.

"Come on, Sarah, let it go. It's time to go to the stupid muster. Let's just forget about the pink panties, forget about Jonathan being a pervert, and go to the lifeboat area."

"I'm *not* a pervert!" Jonathan yelled, just as a group of people came to the top of the stairs. They walked by, snickering.

Jonathan's face turned beet red. He looked down at the carpet muttering, "I'm not a pervert. It's not my fault she's wearing pink underwear and I fell under her dress."

Jonathan looked back over Kevin's shoulder tentatively and noticed his sister's face slowly relax to reveal a sweet smile. Kevin must have winked at her or something. He was glad she wasn't mad at Sarah anymore.

"Watch it, Kevin, or *you're* gonna get it next," threatened Sarah, pointing a manicured fingernail in his face.

Kevin turned around. "Don't worry about it, dude. Consider it your lucky day. Free peep show. Now, tell us – where are we supposed to go for this muster thing? Do you know?"

Jonathan brightened up immediately, his face going back to its normal color. "Yep! Just follow me. I've memorized the layout of the ship, we're on deck C."

He was going to force himself put the underwear incident out of his mind, intent on capitalizing on the time he had taken studying the ship's floor plans. Ship specifications were a much safer thing for him to be thinking about than Sarah's underthings, anyway. He walked across the foyer and out the doors that led to the outside deck area.

The others followed him out. Within two minutes they were standing in a line with a group of other people out on the deck, just across from where their lifeboat was secured to the side of the ship. There were twelve passengers in their line.

They stood there for about twenty minutes in a huge, boisterous crowd of people holding life jackets, before they were told they could leave.

"Is that it?" asked Candi. "I'd kind of expected more."

"Yep. Now what? Anyone feel like having some cocktails?" Kevin put his lifejacket under his arm, rubbing his hands together in anticipation of the fun he was obviously envisioning.

"What time do we need to get over to dinner?" asked Candi.

"We're supposed to meet in the Nautique dining room at six for the first seating," answered Kevin.

Jonathan checked his watch that had a big calculator on it. "That's still a few hours away."

"Yep. Time to hit the bar. You in, Jon?"

"Sure. That's fine, but I'm just going to drink soda since that beer made me a little clumsy." His face reddened just thinking about his earlier run-in with Sarah.

"Suit yourself," said Kevin as he started walking away, expecting Jonathan to follow him.

"Are you guys coming?" Jonathan asked Candi. He was afraid to speak directly to Sarah and she wasn't acknowledging his existence now anyway.

"I'm not sure, just go ahead without us, I'm sure I'll catch up with you later. Want us to take your lifejackets?"

"Sure," said Jonathan, going over and taking Kevin's before handing them over to Candi. "See you later."

*****

Candi stood there awkwardly, wondering if she should suggest that Sarah come with her or just go back to the room and let Sarah decide what she was going to do. Before she could make up her mind, Sarah spoke up.

"Let's go back to the room and do your makeup and hair."

Candi hadn't been expecting this. "Um, I'm already wearing my makeup and my hair's done."

"No, you're wearing an eight-year-old's makeup. I'm going to put some grownup makeup on you. And as for the hair ... well ... no comment."

Candi looked at her with suspicious eyes. "I don't want to wear a ton of makeup, Sarah."

Sarah put her hand up to her chest in mock offense. "I didn't say I was going to put a *ton* of makeup on you – I'm just going to update your look a little. Or a lot." She started walking away, but said over her shoulder, "You want to look cute for the boys on the ship, don't you?" She smiled slyly before continuing on.

Candi wanted to impress Kevin. She had a feeling Sarah was using this to get Candi to let her play dress up. She wasn't sure how she felt about that. Deciding that over-analyzing wasn't going to get her any closer to understanding, Candi shrugged her shoulders and followed Sarah back to the cabin. *I could always wash it off if don't like it.*

Minutes later, Candi was seated in front of the mirror in their tiny cabin while Sarah stood over her, giving her a play-by-play makeup lesson, transforming her face into one she barely recognized.

"You see, you have great eyes, so you should really emphasize them. You don't want to use any crazy colors because that green color in your irises just speaks for itself. Just bring in some natural looking shadows with these browns and give your brows and eyelids the outline they need to really frame your eyes. Finish off with a light gloss and *voilà!*"

She gave Candi one more stroke with the blush brush and said, "So, what do you think? If you don't like using the blush you could always just pinch your cheeks."

Candi was speechless. The person staring out at her from the mirror was a stranger – a really pretty one. And the funny thing was, she really couldn't see all that much makeup on her face. It's like Sarah had performed some sort of crazy magic on her.

"I ... I really like it. I really do, I just ... can't believe it's me." She reached up to touch her face, but Sarah smacked her hand away.

"Don't touch! This is my work of art; I don't want you smearing it. I know you don't usually wear it, so don't forget you have it on. I don't want you reaching up to rub your eyes, smearing mascara all over the place. I don't do emergency makeup repair after I leave this room."

She started putting her makeup brushes away, packing up her little pots of shadow, foundation and blush into her Louis Vuitton makeup case.

Candi stood up and without thinking, grabbed Sarah from the side in a big hug. "Thanks, Sarah!" She dropped her arms suddenly to her sides, a little surprised at her show of affection.

Sarah was surprised too, but tried not to let on that it pleased her. She erased the smile that had appeared on her face, unbidden.

"Hands off. You're gonna wrinkle my dress."

Candi smiled. Sarah tried so hard to be prickly, but she had just spent half an hour not only making Candi beautiful, but giving her lessons so she could do it herself when she got back home. She was starting to think that the bitchy Sarah was a front used to hide a pretty nice person – *a nice person who was buried verrry deep inside.*

Sarah finished packing up her makeup case and turned back to Candi.

"Now, what are we going to do with that hair of yours?" She was eyeing the cloud of frizz that surrounded Candi's face.

Candi's eyes followed Sarah's up to the top of her head where she could just see the edges of her bangs standing out above her forehead.

Sarah reached out and took a lock of Candi's hair in her fingers. "Ugh. Awful. Don't you condition? Your hair is like straw."

Candi pushed her hand away. "Hey, be nice. That *straw* happens to be my hair, and it's naturally curly okay? It's been a frizz bomb since I was a baby. There's nothing you can do with it, so don't even bother trying." Candi tried to move away, but Sarah wasn't having it.

"Not so fast, Sugar Lump. I think I have something that can help you."

She walked over to her suitcase and started digging around inside.

"Not make it perfect, mind you, it's much too far-gone for that. But I can improve it, at least."

"Wow, thanks. Thanks a lot," said Candi sarcastically, as she took a clump of hair in her hands, trying to examine it next to her face. It wasn't very long. All she could see were a few inches of the ends – they were dry and split.

"Ah-ha, here it is!" She popped open the top of the green tube that had emerged from her bag and squeezed some white goop from it out into her hand. She started smooshing and rubbing it between her fingers.

"What *is* that? Glue?"

"Shush. And sit." Sarah gestured to the chair in front of the table with her elbow. "And don't look in the mirror; I want this one to be a surprise." She smiled wickedly.

Candi didn't like the evil smile, but she figured Sarah wouldn't go to all this trouble with her makeup only to ruin her hair by gluing it all together. She walked over to the chair, sitting down as instructed, facing the door so she couldn't her reflection.

"That stuff better wash out of my hair."

"Don't you worry your frizzy little head about that. Having to shave your hair off wouldn't be the worst thing that could happen to it, trust me." She started working the cream through Candi's hair, starting at the ends and moving up towards the roots. "You should just shave it all off and start over – treat your hair right from the beginning."

"Well, I guess I don't know how to 'treat my hair right.' It's not my fault my hair is impossible."

"Don't feel bad. Lots of girls with hair like yours don't know what to do with it. I'm going to show you some tricks. Don't you have any black friends? See, you just need to work with the natural curl instead of fighting it. You're not a straight hair person, so you should stop trying to be one."

Candi sighed, "I don't try to be a straight hair person, and yes, I have black friends, but we don't share hair tips. I just wash and brush my stupid hair."

"That's what I mean. Someone with hair as curly and frizzy as yours shouldn't *be* brushing her hair."

"What? I'm supposed to have dreadlocks?"

"No, stupid, you should use a very wide-toothed comb like *this one* and only comb it once, when it's wet. Let it air dry. Put product in it so the frizzies don't rear their ugly heads. Fluff later with your fingers as necessary, but never, EVER brush. Sheesh. You'd think your mother would have told you this stuff."

She was pulling chunks of Candi's hair and Candi was trying like heck to sit still. She let the comment about her mother go by because the pain was too distracting.

"*Ouch!* You're pulling!"

"Shut up, I'm almost done." Sarah walked around to take a look at Candi from the front. She reached out and pulled a few more chunks of hair around Candi's face.

"Okay, Sugar Lump, behold my magic."

Candi turned in her chair and faced the mirror. Again, she was speechless, but this time, she felt tears burning her eyes.

"Hey!" yelled Sarah, pointing at Candi's face, "No tears! You are going to *ruin* my makeup job!"

Candi immediately started laughing, and then hiccupped a cry. She jumped up, hugging Sarah fiercely. All these years of her life spent with horrible hair she thought was hopeless, only to find out after five minutes with Sarah that she could have pretty hair she actually liked.

"Thank you so much, Sarah! Thank you!"

Sarah awkwardly patted Candi's back. "You're welcome." All this affection was obviously uncomfortable for Sarah, but she didn't detach Candi from her shoulders. "Go ahead, get it out of your system."

Candi stepped away to look back at the vision in the mirror. She reached up, gently touching her hair.

What used to be a frizzy, puffy, dried mess of, yes, straw-like hair, was now a mass of strawberry blond curls, falling gracefully around her face, surrounding her beautiful, sparkling green eyes that had been perfectly highlighted by Sarah's expert makeup job.

"Who is this person?" asked Candi, breathlessly.

"It's the new you. Now we just need to find you something to wear to the ball, Cinderella." Sarah was already digging through Candi's suitcase.

"Hey! What are you doing? That's my stuff!"

"Yeah, I know. Sad. I already went through all of it. You have practically nothing suitable for this cruise in here, you know."

"What? What do you mean you already went through all of it? Those are *my* things." Candi was irritated knowing Sarah had snooped through her stuff. "You have absolutely no personal boundaries at all – has anyone ever told you that?"

"Oh, don't get your panties in a bunch. Boundaries are for wussies. You've got nothing to hide from me, we're all girls here." She smiled cheekily. "You just need to update your wardrobe a bit. Lucky for you, you've got me as your roommate."

Candi quickly glanced at Sarah's outfit and her face broke out in a look of horror. "Um, no offense, Sarah, but I'm *not* wearing any leopard print dresses."

"Don't be such a snob. I'm not going to dress you in anything like this, it's not your style anyway – too sophisticated. No, you need something a little more on the cute side. I think we can make this work."

She held up a long green blouse that Candi had packed to wear with her white capri pants.

Candi breathed a sigh of relief. "Oh, sure, okay, I can wear that."

Sarah turned around, grabbing something out of her bag. "Aaaand *this!*" She was holding up a black, spandex mini skirt.

Candi looked at it suspiciously. "I'm not so sure that I can ... "

Sarah cut her off. "Shut up. Take your clothes off. Put it on – the whole outfit. I don't want to hear another word."

Candi stopped trying to talk, slowly reaching down to pull up her t-shirt. "Aren't you going to turn around? A little privacy here ... "

"Are you kidding me? What am I going to see that I haven't already seen? I've got boobs too, you know."

Candi just looked at her with eyebrows raised.

"Oh, for chrissakes, whatever, Miss Prude." She turned around in a huff.

"I'm not a prude," said Candi as she quickly undressed.

She grabbed the blouse that Sarah had flipped behind her back, putting it on in a rush. Sarah turned back around to watch her finish the buttons.

"Now the skirt."

Candi stepped into the skirt, pulling it up to her waist. The blouse hung halfway down to the bottom of it.

"I look pregnant or something."

"Patience, Prudy. I'm not finished with you yet."

"Don't call me Prudy. I'm not a prude, I'm just shy."

"Shy, my ass. Now come here so I can put this belt on you."

Candi stepped forward allowing Sarah to secure a black, wide belt around the blouse at Candi's waist. This pulled the green blouse in so it wasn't hanging so low, letting it emphasize Candi's narrow waist and curvy hips.

"Yes! I have once again created a masterpiece. Men of this cruise, you are welcome." Sarah then bent over at the waist and took some bows to her imaginary fans.

Candi turned to look in the mirror. She was surprised to see that she really liked the look Sarah had put together. Usually, she just wore the green blouse hanging down over her pants; it did a good job of hiding most of her body, which she tended to do because she was embarrassed about her curvy figure.

Candi put her hands on her butt, turning left and then right, admiring the view from different angles. Without thinking about what she was saying, she wondered aloud, "Do you think Kevin will like it?"

Sarah jumped in the air and landed next to Candi, pointing her finger in Candi's face. "A-HA!!! I KNEW it! You like my brother." She raised her eyebrows at Candi, daring her to deny it.

"I do not like your brother. I was just wondering if a guy *like him* would like this outfit. You know ... a guy who's like our age and everything." She was trying like heck to deny it, but her stupid face was giving everything away. Her skin was a bright, burning red and she was starting to sweat again.

"Uh, uh, uh, little prude, I know your big secret now. Don't try to lie to me. I can see right into that fuzzy little head of yours." She was smiling huge and looking dangerous.

"Okay, whatever, just please don't say anything to him!" Candi begged, desperate not to be totally humiliated. All she needed was Kevin to know she was crushing on him. It would ruin this cruise completely. He'd probably feel sorry for her and avoid her, which would make her feel like a complete idiot loser.

"Don't worry, your secret is safe with me. And a little word of advice for you ... I love my brother and everything, don't get me wrong ... but he's not exactly very good boyfriend material."

"You don't have to beat around the bush, Sarah. I know what you're really trying to say."

"No, seriously, that *is* what I'm trying to say – he's not a very good boyfriend."

Candi started to get mad. She was offended Sarah didn't think she was good enough for Kevin. Of course, Candi didn't think she herself was good enough for Kevin, but that was a different issue.

"Yeah, okay, so I know I'm not good enough for your amazing brother, I get it. Let's just drop it." Candi stepped over to the bed so she could try to re-pack her messy suitcase.

Sarah reached out, touching Candi's shoulder. "Um, no, Candi, that's not what I'm saying." She sighed in frustration. "What I mean is that my brother usually goes out with girls who are stupid – girls he won't fall in love with because they have nothing going on upstairs." She tapped her temple to emphasize her point. "He uses them. He sleeps with them. And after a while, when he gets bored, he dumps them. So like I said – he really isn't a very nice boyfriend."

"Oh. I guess I had no idea about that." Candi smiled tentatively, seeing that Sarah was actually trying to be nice. "Thanks for looking out for me, Sarah."

Sarah brushed off her gratitude. "Yeah, that's me. Always looking out for the little people. Come on, let's get out of here. It's getting too misty in here for my taste." She sniffed as she grabbed her small bag and headed towards the door.

Candi kept smiling to herself. Sarah had a hard time taking thanks from people and accepting gestures of friendship and she hid her uneasiness with sarcastic or mean remarks. Candi could see now that this was just a defense mechanism, not meant to be personal. She wondered what kind of life Sarah must have had to decide she wanted to have relationships like this with people. It made Candi feel sorry for her.

"Are you coming or not? I want to show off my masterpiece if you're up for it."

Candi smiled, brushing off her feelings of pity. Sarah was tough – she didn't need pity. "Yep, I'm ready. Let's go meet some boys."

"No, dahhling," Sarah corrected her, using her upper crust, sophisticated voice, "let's go meet some *men*."

Candi laughed, tentatively. She wasn't so sure about the men thing, but she was definitely sure she wanted to go strut her stuff. She'd never felt so beautiful before, and soon she would be having dinner with Kevin. She wondered what he would think of her new look.

"Let's go to the club lounge that's on the same deck as the dinner place. That way we won't have too far to walk to meet the parents."

"Fine, lead the way."

The girls left the cabin, heading off to the lounge.

*****

Sarah realized shortly after entering the lounge that Candi was no longer next to her, and stopped. She turned around to see Candi still standing in the entrance, looking like a deer caught in the headlights. Sarah walked back and grabbed her by the elbow.

"Come on, little girl. Time to go to the big girl party."

"What?" mumbled Candi, obviously panicked.

"Never mind, just follow me."

Sarah led her over to the bar.

"We'd like two margaritas, please."   She smiled at the

bartender and leaned a little towards him at the same time, giving him a nice view of her cleavage.

The bartender smiled back. "How old is your friend?" he said, gesturing with a slight tilt of his head towards Candi.

"Old enough," answered Sarah, still smiling, with very enticing promises in her eyes.

Candi nudged Sarah with her toe. Sarah kicked her back. Luckily the bartender couldn't see what was going on down below the bar top.

"Here you go," he said a minute later, putting two very large margaritas on top of the bar in front of Sarah.

"Thanks, sweetie. What time do you get off tonight?" Sarah asked, flirtatiously stirring her drink.

"Not 'til three," he responded with a playful frown.

"That's too bad. Maybe I'll still be around then."

"I hope so."

Sarah turned to Candi who she caught rolling her eyes. "Come on, Sugar Lump, let's go find us a seat."

"I really wish you'd stop calling me that," Candi said to her back.

Sarah just ignored her.

They walked over to a dark corner where a comfortable couch and a couple of tables were gathered together. They dropped down onto the couch, setting their drinks on the table in front of them.

"So, what kind of meat is at the market today?" asked Sarah, scanning the room slowly from left to right, her eyes locking onto two guys who stepped away from the bar and began heading in their direction.

"A-ha, yes. I thought so. Tits out, Sugar Lump. Incoming."

"What?" was all Candi could get out before two really hot guys were standing in front of them. She looked over at Sarah who was mouthing the words 'tits out' at her and throwing her shoulders back at the same time.

Candi leand in and whispered, "What is this, Animal Kingdom?"

"Yes," deadpanned Sarah.

The big blond guy on the left spoke first. "Hey, what's up? What are you girls drinking?"

"Margaritas, of course," answered Sarah, evenly. She didn't seem flustered at all, just really sexy.

"Mind if we join you?" asked the other one, looking at Candi.

"Sure, sit ... for a little while, anyway," answered Sarah, knowing instinctively that Candi would be too tongue-tied to respond properly.

"Uh-oh, Jack, we have a dangerous one here," said the blond, smiling. They moved some nearby chairs so they could sit across from the girls.

The guy named Jack got comfortable, setting his drink down across from Candi's. "So, I'll break the ice ... we're Jack and Mason, I'm Jack, he's Mason, and we're from New York. What are your names, and where are you from?"

Sarah answered for both of them since Candi seemed to have been struck dumb. "I'm Sarah and this is Candi; we're both from North Carolina."

Candi looked over at Sarah, looking as if she were trying to send a silent message, her eyebrows raised.

"What?" asked Sarah, looking directly at Candi.

"What?" responded Candi, acting innocent, while also raising her eyebrows again and giving a nearly imperceptible shake of her head.

Sarah deliberately ignored her and turned back towards the boys. "Is this your first time on this ship?"

"Yep," answered Mason. "How 'bout you guys? This your first time?"

"Yes, it is," answered Sarah as she reached out, lifting her drink off the table and taking a big drink through the straw before she continued. "We haven't really seen anything here yet. Is there a dance club on this ship?"

"You bet. Up on B-deck, just down the hall from our rooms, in fact."

Sarah got a sour look on her face. "B-deck. Isn't that near the top? With the ocean view balcony rooms?"

"Yeah, how'd you know? Is that where your room is too?"

Candi blurted out, "No! I mean ... no. We're down below that area. Our room doesn't even have a window," she finished sheepishly.

Jack jumped in, trying to bring the mood back to a happier place, "I've stayed in those rooms before, they're not bad. You hardly spend any time in them anyway, if you're lucky." He lifted his eyebrows encouragingly at Candi. His message was clear. Sarah could tell he was more than willing to give Candi a personal tour.

Sarah smiled. "I like that idea ... spending no time in the room." She looked over at Candi. "See? We just have to stay out dancing all night. Problem solved."

Candi smiled back nervously.

"The club opens at nine, but Jack says it doesn't really get going until ten or so. We were going to go over there later ourselves," said Mason. He lifted up his drink, holding it up in front of him. "Here's to having a good time, staying out all night, and dancing and drinking until the sun comes up!"

The others reached for their drinks, clinking them together across the table, toasting to a night of revelry. Everyone finished their drinks with big, long gulps.

*****

Candi put her glass down on the table a little too hard, laughing nervously at her own clumsiness.

Jack looked into her eyes and grinned. He had the cutest smile. Candi took a minute to really look at him. His eyes were the brightest blue she had ever seen; paired with his dark hair, broad shoulders, and trim waist, they made him look like some sort of underwear model or something. He had a really manly jaw, square with a hint of beard shadow. She didn't know what to say to a guy this cute. He was almost as cute as Kevin. She wondered how old he was. He looked at least nineteen, maybe older.

Sarah nudged her and whispered in her ear, "Stop staring, dork."

Candi laughed self-consciously and looked down for a moment at her hands, trying to force herself not to twist them nervously.

"How old are you, anyway?" Mason asked Sarah.

Candi looked up to see what Sarah's response would be.

"How old do I look?" She started at him with a dare in her eyes.

"Old enough to get into a little trouble," was his flirty response.

"I guess you're right about that." Sarah turned to Jack. "What about you, Jack? Are you old enough to get into a little bit of trouble?" She smiled sweetly, acting as if she was oblivious to the game she was playing, making Mason jealous by acting like she cared about Jack. Candi could tell she really didn't care about either one of them.

"I guess so," he answered, smiling gamely, buying into her flirtatious manner. Then he looked over at Candi, winking at her.

Candi's face went red. She was confused with the games. First Mason flirts with Sarah. Then Sarah flirts with Jack. Jack flirts with Sarah and then with her, right there at the same time. In front of his friend. Was this normal?

Mason and Jack were both staring at her now. Candi started to squirm under their attentions, completely paranoid that she had a booger or something on her face. She casually reached up to wipe at her nose. Hopefully whatever they were staring at was now gone.

"Who needs another drink?" asked Mason, breaking the spell.

"All of us," said Sarah. "Come on, Mason, let's go get a round together."

Mason held out his hand for Sarah who took it and stood up.

"Be right back!" she said to Candi, waving at her with her fingertips. "Don't do anything I wouldn't do."

Candi tried not to squirm. She knew that there were probably a whole lot of things she could do and not run afoul of that directive.

"Have you ever been on a cruise before?" Jack asked, back to staring at her again.

She tried not to let it creep her out with its intensity. "No, never. Have you?"

"Yeah. Several actually. They're all pretty much the same – partying, eating, getting no sleep. Then you go home and back to the real world."

"Sounds like fun," was all she could think to say, even though it didn't.

"Yeah, it's fun, but it can get old. Buuuuut I think this one holds promise."

Candi smiled at his obvious innuendo out of courtesy, but she couldn't keep the misgivings from rising up in her mind. Something about him was off. Or maybe it was just the alcohol taking over her good sense.

"Why have you been on so many cruises?" she asked, before she realized how stupid that sounded. "Sorry, that was a dumb question."

"No, no, not at all. Well, my parents work a lot, so I guess they feel bad about me being stuck alone at the house all the time. So sometimes when they go out of town, they send me out with my uncle on these cruises. This time I took Mason with me instead. We go to school together."

"Oh, well, that's cool, I guess. I mean, my parents would never send me off on a cruise without coming along, so you're lucky."

"Yeah, well, it's fun; but like I said, it gets old. At least this time I have a room to myself. If you feel like checking it out later, just say the word."

Candi shrugged her shoulders noncommittally, reaching over to grab her empty glass. She sipped some of the melted ice water. She wasn't used to talking to totally hot strangers in bars, especially ones who were very possibly flirting with her if she wasn't mistaken, so she didn't know what to do or say. She was praying Sarah would hurry up and get back with their drinks.

"Are you going to the dance club later?"

"I'm not sure. If Sarah wants to, probably."

"What Sarah wants, Sarah gets, is that it?"

Candi laughed. "Yeah, pretty much. I don't bother telling her no anymore."

"You guys are pretty close friends, huh?"

Candi was surprised at this question. "I guess so. I mean, we don't know each other that well, but we get along okay."

"Huh. That's surprising. I saw you two earlier when you came in. You seemed pretty close."

Candi thought about this, realizing that she and Sarah had actually hit it off, even bonded a bit. She was happy about it and decided not to over-think it too much.

"We are, pretty close I mean. She's fun."

"I'll bet." Jack looked at her and smiled. "I'll bet you are too."

Oh my god, he's totally flirting with me, thought Candi. *I can't believe a guy this hot is actually flirting with me!* She couldn't stop the totally goofy smile that broke out across her face. Jack saw it and smiled back. Both of them just sat at the table grinning at each other – Candi because a cute boy found her interesting and Jack for reasons she didn't want to analyze too much. The alcohol was starting to make her feel a little fuzzy, and she didn't mind it at all.

"Okay, what's so funny?" asked Sarah, approaching the table with a drink in her hand.

Mason followed, balancing three glasses. "Here you go everyone. Drink up." He set them down on the table, grabbing the nearest one and taking a long drink from it.

Candi and Jack took sips of their drinks, looking at each other over the rims. Candi was so nervous, she just kept drinking. Within thirty seconds she had drained her glass. Her loud bottom-of-the-glass slurp brought her back to reality.

"Oops, my bad," she said, then hiccupped.

"Oh boy, we have a lightweight here," said Mason, laughing.

Sarah rolled her eyes. "Slow down, Sugar Lump, we need to

last all night. Pace yourself." She had only taken one sip of her drink so far.

Jack winked at her, gallantly trying to make her feel better.

"So, what time are you girls going to dinner? The second seating?" asked Jack.

"No, we're going to the first seating," said Sarah absently as she played with her straw.

Jack looked at his watch and his eyebrows went up. "Well, if that's the case, you may want to drink up and get going, because it's six thirty right now."

"Oh, crap, are you serious?" exclaimed Candi.

"Yep."

Candi stood up quickly. "Come on, Sarah, we have to go!" She could just picture the look on Mr. Peterson's face when they walked in a half hour late.

"I have to finish my drink," said Sarah.

"No, we don't have time!"

"I'm not leaving until my drinks is finished." Sarah sat stubbornly, and Candi knew she meant it.

"Fine!" Candi grabbed her drink and sucked the straw so hard the drink was gone in five seconds flat. She burped as she let out the little bit of air she'd also drank. "There!" She slammed the glass down on the table.

"Thatta girl!" said Mason.

"Not now, Mason, they're late for dinner," said Jack, wryly.

"Oh, that sucks. Well, hopefully we'll see you later at the club."

"Will we see you there?" asked Jack, addressing his question to Candi.

"I don't know, we'll see."

"Yes, definitely. See you guys later," said Sarah as she stood to go. "Thanks for the drink, hot stuff. See you soon." She leaned over and kissed Mason right on the mouth.

Candi stood there, frozen in place. Then looked at Jack with a panicked expression on her face.

He laughed and leaned down to kiss her on the cheek. "I hope I see you later, Candi. Have a nice dinner."

Sarah grabbed Candi by the upper arm. "Come on, Cinderella; time to go to dinner. We'll see the boys later."

Candi snapped out of her reverie, letting herself be led away. "Bye!" she said over her shoulder.

She couldn't believe it. Jack had kissed her on the cheek. It was her first kiss from a guy who wasn't playing spin the bottle at a junior high birthday party. Well, okay, so it wasn't on the lips – but it was still a kiss and it counted. She sighed with contentment as they walked towards the doors to the dining room.

Sarah laughed. "So, what do you think of the cruise so far?"

"So far, so good," responded Candi, smiling.

"Excellent. Now let's go to dinner and see how much we can piss off old Frank."

Candi grabbed her by the arm to stop her from going into the dining room. "Do you really need to try so hard to do that – piss your dad off, I mean?" Candi didn't want to see her new friend get hurt. She also didn't want to have to sit through what was surely going to be a very uncomfortable meal after Mr. Peterson flipped out.

"Oh, don't worry. I won't have to try hard at all." She gave Candi a hard look and then opened the doors, stepping through them, without worrying about whether Candi was following.

The room was full of people sitting at round tables covered in light cream-colored linen. Waiters and waitresses in uniforms were hurrying from table to kitchen and back again in what looked to be a carefully synchronized operation designed to get everyone fed in two hours and then out again so the second seating could begin. The far wall was mostly glass, with a view out to the ocean beyond. The sun was setting and the rays of red and orange light streaking across the sky made a perfect backdrop for the formal dining room.

Candi saw that Sarah had spied her parents at a far table and was making her way over. Kevin was facing her, as were Mr. and Mrs. Buckley. Candi knew when Kevin saw her because he rolled his eyes in greeting. The Buckleys both stopped doing what they were doing, frozen in place, staring at Sarah as she approached.

Frank didn't notice anything was amiss and kept right on talking. As Candi approached, she heard him saying something about the current software market and blah, blah, blah. Mrs. Peterson's seat was facing away from Sarah also, so she had no idea what was coming either.

*****

Jonathan was looking at his parents' faces. He turned his head to see what had caught their attention so completely. It was then that he noticed Sarah coming across the dining room towards their table.

She was practically prowling across the room, taking long strides in her impossibly high heels, looking like a leopard-spotted man killer after its prey. She was stalking something... but what?

Uh-oh. Too late Jonathan realized that it wasn't a *what*, but a *who*. Mr. Peterson, specifically. She was homing in on the table, looking like she was on a mission. Her long hair was blowing back away from her face; she looked like she was on one of those fashion runways. Her legs were so tan, he could see the definition in her thigh muscles as each leg came forward, bringing her closer and closer to her victim.

He swallowed hard, his Adam's apple moving slowly up and down as he struggled to get the swallow to finish. She was so beautiful, it took all the spit out of his mouth. It was fascinating really, when he stopped for a split second to think about it. He was going to have to research this phenomenon when he got home.

Sarah reached the table, standing behind the empty seat next to her father. "Hello, everyone," she said with a purr in her voice.

Frank stopped in mid-sentence and looked up. Everyone else at the table looked first at her, then at Frank.

Frank had been talking and eating at the same time. His fork now floated midway between his plate and his mouth, a leaf of lettuce dangling from its end. The knife he was holding in his opposite hand dropped, making a clattering sound on the plate as it landed.

Frank slowly lowered his fork down to the table.

"Hello, *Sarah*. Nice of you to show up." He paused to look her up and down. With barely contained anger, he continued, "I thought I told you to *dress up* for dinner."

She smiled sweetly back at him. "Thank you, I'm *so* glad to be here. And as you can see, I did dress up for dinner. I wore this for you." She spun around in a flirty circle, which had the unfortunate effect of causing her dress to twirl up a little, revealing even more of her tanned thigh than was already showing.

"That's *it!*" Frank said loudly, as he struggled to get up out of his chair.

Just then, Candi arrived at the table, jumping to Sarah's side, grabbing her upper arm in the process and squeezing it – effectively blocking the back of Frank's chair and halting his attempt at getting up.

"Hi guys! Are we too late? We rushed to get here. It's my fault we're late! Sarah was helping me get dressed and do my makeup. We didn't realize what time it was. She didn't have time to change, did you Sarah?"

She didn't even look at Sarah, just continued on, "So what do you think? Do you like the hair, Mom? I just love it." She paused to look over at Sarah's mom. "You see, Mrs. Peterson, I have the driest hair, and I've never been able to work with it. Sarah took one look at it and within seconds had it all fixed; I'm so excited because I think now I can figure out how to make it look nice and maybe not so frizzy all the time because, you know, my hair is so frizzy, it's like straw, isn't it Sarah?" She had to suck in a loud gulp of air since she had been babbling without taking a second to breathe.

She looked expectantly at Sarah, almost frenzied in a way.

Sarah sighed loudly. "You are a complete freak, you know that?" Then she smiled, despite herself. Candi was wigging out, and apparently Sarah found it pretty entertaining.

"Candi," started her mother, "what's wrong with you? Have you been ... drinking or something? You're acting very strangely ... "

Kevin stood up all of a sudden, distracting the parents with the unexpected movement. "Well, I for one think you look amazing, Candi, beautiful in fact. Here – have my seat." He gestured for her to sit in the place he had just vacated which was across from Candi's parents.

This was probably the best place for her, since this way, Mrs. Buckley wouldn't be able to smell what Jonathan thought was probably going to be alcohol breath whenever Candi started talking.

"Well, thank you, Kevin." Candi walked over and took his seat. Now she was sitting close to the still steaming, but slightly mollified Mr. Peterson.

"Come on, Sarah, you can come sit over here between me and Jonathan. Maybe you can share some of your hair-do know-how with us guys," Kevin said sarcastically.

"As long as the pervert promises to keep his hands *and* his eyes to himself," Sarah said, staring pointedly at Jonathan. She had lost her predatory look and didn't seem happy about it.

Mrs. Buckley looked over at her son, a big question mark on her face, probably horrified to think about what Sarah could possibly be referring to.

Mr. Buckley just frowned, looking at his son as if confused about what Sarah was saying and trying to figure out the meaning behind the mysterious words.

Mrs. Peterson looked over at Jonathan with her right eyebrow raised, making him feel like he'd been accused of doing something terrible to her daughter.

Frank just gritted his teeth and stared at the ceiling of the dining room. It was taking all his self-control to keep his rage in check, that much was obvious. Jonathan feared that Sarah was going to be very sorry she provoked her father tonight; he didn't look like the type that forgave and forgot.

Jonathan was frustrated by all the suspicious looks being pointed in his direction. He couldn't let her words go unanswered. "I'm *not*. A. *Pervert*. I told you, I fell."

Kevin stood by the chair next to Jonathan's and reached over to pat him on the back. "We know, man, we know. Just eat your burger."

He pulled the chair out for his sister to sit in.

Jonathan looked down at his half-eaten meal and frowned. How did he end up being the bad guy here? *That Sarah is trouble and that's a fact.* He wished she didn't make his heart beat faster and his pulse start racing. She'd be a lot easier to dislike if she wasn't so beautiful.

Sarah sat down, and a wave of her perfume washed over him. He tried not to, but he couldn't help it – he closed his eyes and inhaled deeply. He'd never noticed that a girl could smell so good. His mother and sister didn't smell like this at all. They just smelled like, well, nothing.

Sarah, on the other hand, smelled like, like ... he couldn't think because the blood was not only pounding in his ears, it was pounding in other places now, too. *Oh god, please don't make me have to get up from this chair right now!*

Sarah leaned over casually and whispered in his ear, "Stop. Smelling. Me. You. *Perv.*"

Jonathan gripped his fork really hard, slowly turning his head to look at her. He stared her right in the eye, answering her in a tightly controlled voice. "I am *not* a pervert."

He was completely disarmed when she smiled at him and said, "Gotcha."

He turned back to look down at his plate. *Holy crap.* She was totally screwing with him, and he was now just figuring it out. *This girl is wicked tricky.* He was going to have to be on his toes around her for sure. The thought made him smile. He was super good at chess. Once he knew the game, no one could out strategize him. He turned to her then and said, "You think you do, but you don't." *Ha. Let her stew on that for a while.*

A loud squeak leapt out of his mouth at the exact moment he felt her squeeze his thigh – high up ... like *really* high up. Then he choked. It wasn't on food, since he didn't have any in his mouth at the time. It was probably on spit or drool or something. Whatever it was, it had him gasping for air.

Kevin reached around his sister's chair and started clapping Jonathan on the back. Jonathan grabbed his glass of water and started chugging it.

Sarah looked at him sweetly. "What's the matter, Jonathan?"

"You ... ! You ... !" Words were failing him. He couldn't very well accuse her of grabbing his leg in front of their families.

"I what?" she asked sweetly, lifting her hands above the table and spreading them out in an act of innocence.

Jonathan stopped trying to talk, shaking his head in silence and lifting his eyes to stare up at the ceiling. He thought maybe he was feeling a small measure of Frank Peterson's pain, and felt less inclined to judge him harshly in that moment. Sarah knew how to get under a guy's skin. Somehow, she'd honed her skill to levels he'd never experienced before.

Kevin looked at Jonathan with questions in his eyes and then his eyes went to his sister. Jonathan could see him doing the math. A smile broke out across Kevin's face as he bit into his dinner roll, finishing half of it in one bite. He looked over at Candi and winked. Jonathan wasn't sure if he was happy that Kevin was obviously on to his sister's games or not.

Kevin leaned over to talk to Jonathan behind his sister's back.

"Dude, you're gonna be my wingman tonight, right?"

"What?"

"My wingman. My sidekick? My Robin?"

"Robin? What are you talking about?"

"I'm Batman, you're Robin. We're going out tonight to pick up some chicks."

Jonathan kept on eating and talked while looking at his plate. "I'm not going to wear any tights or a stupid cape if that's what you're talking about. I don't know what Sarah's been saying to you, but I am *not* a pervert."

Kevin laughed and shook his head. "No tights, no cape, man. Don't be a cheese brain, just shut up and eat. We leave in thirty minutes."

"Okay, fine." Jonathan didn't really know what he was supposed to do as a wingman, but whatever. He had nothing better to do anyway. He didn't feel like studying for his chemistry exam, even though he knew he probably should.

Making Friends

THIRTY MINUTES LATER, KEVIN PUT his napkin on the table next to his plate and stood up. "We're outta here. Come on, Jon."

"Where do you think you're going?" asked his mother.

"Oh, I don't know, maybe go do the rock climbing thing or shoot some pool."

Jonathan interrupted, "But I thought you said ... "

Kevin clapped him on the back, making him fall forward against the table. "Yep, I did say we were going to go to the putting green too, didn't I, Jon? Thanks for reminding me. We're also going to play a little golf if we have time." He gave the parents his best toothpaste commercial smile.

Frank looked at his son suspiciously, but Kevin's mother was easily fooled by her son's charm. "Okay, sweetie, that sounds like fun. Remember though – no alcohol."

"Of course not, Mom. You know I don't drink that stuff."

"But ... ," said Jonathan, pointing to Kevin's chest and then pointing at the table, obviously confused.

"We'd better hurry up before all the reservation slots are taken." Kevin grabbed Jonathan by the upper arm and started pulling him from the table.

"Bye, Mom and Dad. Bye, Candi." Jonathan was shouting from two tables away since Kevin was intent on getting him out of there before he blew the lid off their plans.

Sheesh, this kid doesn't have a clue. If he had told his parents they were going to the bar, it would have ended their cruise freedom and fun for sure.

"Dude, what is your problem? You know you can't tell them we're going to the bar."

"Why not?"

"Because we're not supposed to do that; we're underage."

"So why are we doing it then? I'm not really used to lying to my parents, Kevin. I'm not sure that's something I'm comfortable doing."

They continued walking down the passageways that would take them to a bar that was not the one Frank had mentioned the parents were going to after dinner.

"Well, it's done, so don't worry about it. We're going to go have some serious fun."

"That rock climbing thing sounded fun ... "

"Yeah, you can do that tomorrow afternoon if you want. I'll be in the pool."

"So did the golf. I'm really good at putt-putt, actually."

"Tomorrow."

"Why can't we do it now?"

Kevin stopped and faced Jonathan, frustrated that he had to practically force this kid to have fun. "Listen, dude, do you want to have fun tonight or not?"

"Well, yeah."

"Do you want to meet some girls tonight and maybe get a little action?"

"I don't know, I guess."

"You guess? You *guess*? What are you, gay? Because if you are, that's cool, I don't care – but you should tell me so I stop trying to hook you up with girls."

"No, I'm not gay! I'm straight. I like girls. I'm just not sure that I need your help hooking up with one, though."

"Trust me, dude, you need my help."

Jonathan sighed in defeat. "Okay, whatever. Lead on, once more into the breach, my friend."

"Into the *what?*"

"'Once more into the breach my friends.' It's a quote from the 'Cry God for Harry, England, and Saint George!' speech of Shakespeare's Henry V, written in 1598. Specifically, it's in Act III. The breach in question was the gap in the wall of the city of Harfleur, which the English army held under siege. Henry was encouraging his troops to attack the city again, even if it meant lots of English would die."

"Holy shit, Jon, you really need to chill on the T-M-I stuff."

Jonathan laughed. "Oh, yeah. I know. Sorry about that."

"Don't worry about it." Kevin stopped outside some smoked glass doors. "Okay, we're here now. Just chill with the T-M-I and you should be fine."

He opened the doors, and they went in. Kevin led them over to the bar where they sat down and ordered drinks. Jonathan may have been skinny, but he was tall enough that the bartender didn't bother to ask them for I.D. This crew didn't seem to care much about any drinking age issues.

"Okay, take a look around and tell me if you see any girls that look interesting."

Jonathan picked up his drink and grabbed the straw with his

lips, maneuvering it around with his tongue until he could start sipping from it.

"Dude, stop making out with your drink."

Jonathan dropped the straw immediately. "I'm not making out with my drink! Geez."

"Guys don't use straws. Take the straw out and just drink from the glass normally."

"But straws are more efficient. They keep the ice from dropping down due to the effects of gravity and hitting your mouth."

Kevin fixed him with a death stare. "Take. The straw. Out. Or I'm gonna hit you."

"Geeeez, take a chill pill. Easy on the 'roids – they can cause heart problems and testicle shrinkage, you know."

Kevin put his drink down slowly. "Did you just accuse me of using steroids?"

Jonathan was oblivious to Kevin's simmering anger. "Not really, but it's not out of the realm of possibility, is it? I mean, look at you." He gestured towards Kevin's chest, arms, and legs. "Your pectoral, biceps, and quadriceps muscles really aren't in proportion to your underlying skeletal structure, which suggests either very intense eating and exercise regimens that are adhered to with an almost religious intensity or some form of chemical enhancement."

Kevin responded with a very low and even voice, which belied his offended fury. "I could snap your little twig neck with one hand for saying that."

"See, that's exactly what I mean. You have the strength in one hand to literally end a person's life; you can't argue that steroids couldn't make that possible."

He reached down and wrangled his straw with his tongue one

more time and started sucking away at his drink, oblivious to Kevin's anger.

Jonathan perked up when his eyes locked onto something across the room. "Oh look, there are some cute girls. There are two of them. Maybe we should go say hi."

Kevin just looked at Jonathan and shook his head. He realized that Jonathan had no idea how insulting he had just been. Kevin worked hard to sculpt his muscles and keep himself in top shape for rugby. If he didn't, he could get seriously injured out on the field; it was a very rough sport. Nobody ever appreciated that fact, outside of the guys on his team and his coach.

He ran his fingers through his hair and let his anger fade out. Since the kid didn't mean anything by it, Kevin didn't need to turn it into a big deal. Later he'd explain to Jonathan that it wasn't a good idea to tell guys twice your size that they're 'roid ragers.

He looked over to where Jonathan was staring. There were two girls sitting there, one really beautiful one and one who looked like her younger, plainer sister, maybe.

"Now, there you go, Jonathan, that's more like it. Okay, obviously I'll take the blond, you go for the brunette." He stood, preparing to walk over.

"Hey, I had my eye on the blond," said Jonathan, in an offended and slightly proprietary tone.

"Dude, she's totally not your speed, you're better off with the little one."

"Nope, I like the blond. You take the little one. She looks like my sister, so you should get along fine with her."

Kevin hesitated. "What's that supposed to mean?"

"Well, I can see that you kind of like my sister, so that smaller girl is a good substitute."

Kevin was shocked that this guy could be so far out in left field. He held his hands up, palms out, in front of his chest. "Dude, no offense, but I have no interest in your sister, whatsoever."

"Well, that's not what it looked like to me."

"What are you *talking* about?"

"I've seen you, the way you're looking at her all the time, the flirting. It's obvious."

Kevin started sputtering, "You're ... you're nuts, man. She's cute and all, but she's definitely ... not ... definitely *not* my type. Not at all. I mean, *at all.*"

Jonathan put his drink down and stopped looking at the girls. He turned his head to meet Kevin's eyes. "What's wrong with my sister?"

"Nothing's wrong with her, dude, she's just not my type."

"In what way? Explain it to me." Jonathan rested his right elbow on the bar, folding his hands in front of him, waiting expectantly for Kevin's response.

"Well, first of all, she's too young."

"She's your age or maybe a year younger."

"Yeah, well, she's also pretty shy."

"That's only because you don't know her very well, and besides, that didn't stop you from flirting with her. Try again."

Kevin sighed loudly in frustration. "She's ... she's ... not experienced!"

Jonathan smiled. "I'm sure you could remedy that problem." He hesitated for a minute, looking down at his hands. "Is it because she isn't pretty enough or smart enough for a guy like you? She says she could never go out with someone like you because she isn't popular enough. But you see, that's what I can't figure out. Why isn't she? Because as far as I can see, she has it all – looks, brains, personality. So you explain it to me, what is she missing? Why isn't she your type?"

"Jesus Christ, Jon, you sure know how to put a guy on the spot. But let me put your mind at ease. Your sister is beautiful, really, she is. I mean, I thought she was cute before, but tonight at dinner, I mean, she really is pretty hot. And as far as being smart is concerned, she's probably smarter than all of my past girlfriends put together, so it has nothing to do with her brains. I don't know her very well, but she seems to have a nice personality."

Kevin ran his fingers through his hair, agitated that he was being forced to explain something he didn't really understand himself.

"Why isn't she popular? I don't know, maybe because she's too nice. I don't know if you noticed, but the popular kids in our school can be serious assholes."

"But you're pretty popular."

"Yeah. Exactly. Trust me, Jon, you don't want me dating your sister. I don't have the best track record with women."

"Oh, don't worry about that. I don't want you dating my sister either, I was just curious. When something doesn't make sense to me, I try to figure it out."

"Now, wait a minute. What do you mean you don't want me dating your sister?"

"Well, you said it yourself. You don't have the best track record with women. I don't want some guy dating her just to use her and then dump her when he's done."

"Who the hell says I'd do something like that?" Kevin was kind of offended that this little geek was judging him, captain of the rugby team and lady killer extraordinaire.

Jonathan patted Kevin on the shoulder and picked up his

drink off the bar. "Don't worry about it, Kevin, you don't like her anyway, right?"

"Yeah. Right," answered Kevin, confused now, not sure at this point whether he liked her or not. Jonathan had gotten him totally turned around.

"So, what about those chicks over there ... do I get the blond one or what?"

Kevin shook off his confusion, smiling. "Sure, dude, go for it. See what you can do."

"And you'll be my wingman?"

"Sure, Jon, I'll be your wingman." Kevin would be there for him when he crashed and burned, poor, clueless kid that he was.

The two walked away from the bar, heading over to where the girls were sitting. Jonathan stopped in front of the blond, looking a little awkward.

Kevin couldn't wait to see what he was going to say. *This should be interesting.*

"I see you have the newest version of the iPhone that hasn't even been released yet. How'd you manage that?"

What? Kevin never saw that pickup line coming.

"Uh-oh, busted." The blond smiled at him. "My dad works for Apple. He's one of the employees in charge of testing new products, figuring things out, what the bugs are, how to fix them. Basically check the phone for usability, human factors, that kind of thing."

Human factors? What is this girl talking about?

"Cool. I've studied human factors design in computer keyboards but never cell phones. I'll bet it's really interesting. Can I take a look?" Jonathan held out his hand for the phone.

She hesitated. "I'm really not supposed to let anyone else use it."

"Oh, don't worry, I just want to take a look at the apps you have on it. I've written a couple for the iPhone in my spare time."

"Really? Which ones?"

"Have you ever heard of Tick, Tack, Blast? That's the most popular one."

"Oh my god, of course I have! I love that one! Look, it's here on this phone actually, and I was just playing it before we came out. That is so *weird*, isn't it Millie?" She looked over at the girl sitting next to her who was rolling her eyes.

"Yeah. Weird all right."

Kevin just stood there, stunned. How could this be happening? The prettiest girl in the bar, who by all rights should be his conquest, was sharing geekspeak with Jonathan.

"Why don't you guys sit down and join us? My name is LeeAnn by the way, and this is my cousin, Millie."

Jonathan sat down right next to LeeAnn on the couch and they immediately began debating the pros and cons of the iPhone operating system versus its popular competitor, Android.

Kevin sat down in a chair next to Millie. *Oh well, might as well go with it.* "So, Millie, where are you from?"

"Chicago."

"Oh, Chicago, that's cool. Do you go to school there?"

"Yes."

"Okay, so, um, what do you like to do for fun?"

"Not much."

"Alright, not much. Interesting." *Or maybe not. Geez, trying to talk to this girl is like pulling teeth – painful.*

"I'm going to go get myself another drink, do you want anything?"

"No."

"Okay, then."

Kevin had never been so thoroughly dissed in his life. He'd been a good-looking guy since he was, like, five. Even the girls in kindergarten couldn't get enough of Kevin on the playground and in class. What was this chick's problem anyway? *Oh well, at least Jonathan is hitting it off.* And who would have guessed that would happen? Beneath the exterior hotness of this girl beat the heart of a nerd. She didn't seem to notice Jonathan's awkwardness. Actually, now that Kevin thought about it, Jonathan didn't seem awkward around this girl at all – probably because they spoke the same language.

Kevin went to the bar and ordered himself two shots. *Might as well get this party started.* He downed those right away and then ordered a Long Island Ice Tea. *What's not to love about a drink that had five types of alcohol in it? Great, now I'm having a conversation with myself.*

A few minutes later, Kevin glanced over and noticed that Millie was nowhere to be seen. Jonathan and his girl were deeply engrossed in conversation, sitting very close together on the couch.

Kevin ordered six shots and brought them over. "It's ten o'clock. Time to do some shots."

Jonathan and LeeAnn looked up in a daze. They appeared as if they had forgotten where they were for a little while, lost in their world of operating systems, iPhone apps, and JavaScript programming.

LeeAnn looked at Jonathan and shrugged her shoulders. "If you say so." She took one of the shots and held it up in front of her. "What are we drinking to?"

Jonathan took his shot glass and said, "Here's to bug-free

operating systems!"

Kevin laughed. "Here's to Millie! The girl who broke my heart and left me to wither away at the ship's bar."

They all threw back their shots and then struggled to breathe.

In a slightly strained voice, LeeAnn said, "Yeah, I'm sorry about that. She has a hard time having fun."

"What do you mean she has a hard time having fun?" Kevin's mind didn't compute something that strange.

LeeAnn shrugged. "Seriously. I've known her all my life. She hates going out and having fun; she's morose and gloomy, all the time. It's a pain in the ass, but she's family. What am I going to do?"

"Boy, that sucks," said Jonathan. He looked over at Kevin who just lifted his shoulders indifferently.

Kevin picked up another shot and quickly drank it.

Jonathan leaned over and took another one of the shots and got ready to chug it down.

"Are you sure you want to do that?" asked Kevin.

"Of course. If you can do it, so can I." He quickly threw back the shot and immediately began choking as the burning fire raced down his esophagus.

Kevin laughed. "Yeah, that's what I thought. I'll be right back, I'm going to get you some water."

LeeAnn reached over and patted Jonathan's back, trying to help him stop choking.

Kevin came back as Jonathan was pulling out his cell phone and saying, "Give me your number, and I'll text you the details. It's not that far away, you know."

"What's not that far?" asked Kevin.

"Comic-Con. A convention we both go to."

After Jonathan put her number in his phone, he sat there looking awkward. It seemed like they'd run out of things to talk about.

"Oh, no!" LeeAnn said with dismay, looking alarmingly at the door to the bar.

Jonathan started to turn towards the door to see what was bothering her so suddenly.

"No! Don't look! I don't want him to notice me!"

Kevin caught sight of two guys walking into the bar, one with blondish hair and one with really dark hair.

"Why, what's wrong with them?"

"Well, one of them, Jack, is a real jerk. He was harassing me earlier, and he kind of creeps me out. One of the waitresses told me he's bad news. Oh, crap, they're coming over here." She was wringing her hands in her lap. "I hate confrontation like this. Quick! Kiss me!"

"Wha ... ?" was all Jonathan could get out before he found himself crushed into a major lip lock.

"Mmm ... fmmm ... dmmm," he tried to speak, but she wasn't letting him go.

While LeeAnn was kissing him, she kept one eye out for the duo that had walked in. Once she saw that they had turned and left the bar, she let Jonathan go.

Kevin sat there speechless, watching the whole thing unfold as if in slow motion. It was like a bad movie.

"Phew, that was close. Um, thanks for the rescue."

Jonathan sat staring at her, stunned into silence. His mouth hung partway open, as if he was still in the middle of the kiss.

Kevin laughed. *I've been shown up by Jonathan Buckley. Awesome.* He wasn't mad. In fact, he was proud of the kid. He didn't think Jonathan had it in him, but obviously he was wrong. Wait until Sarah heard about this. She was gonna be more surprised than he was.

Thinking of Sarah, he wondered what the girls were doing right then. This bar was getting boring. There was hardly anyone there. There had to be another place where people their age were hanging out. "I'll be right back," he said.

He went over to talk to the bartender. "So where's the happening place to be tonight, anyway?"

"That would be Club Neptune."

"Thanks, man."

"Yeah, no problem."

Kevin went back over to the lovebirds. "Hey, are you guys up for some dancing at Club Neptune?"

They nodded their heads yes, so the three of them finished off the shots on the table and left. They followed Jonathan's perfect directions, finding themselves standing in front of Club Neptune within minutes.

"Well, here goes nothin'," said Kevin, pulling open the heavy wooden door.

The room was dark except for the flashing disco lights that lit up the ceiling and walls with flashing colors in pink, green, and blue. The bass was really pumping, and the crowd on the dance floor seemed to be moving as one big mass of arms, legs, and asses. They could feel the beat coming up through the floor and filling up the air all around them.

"I'm going to get a drink!" yelled Kevin, trying to be heard above the noise.

"We're going to go find a place to sit down!" yelled Jonathan, moving away, holding LeeAnn's hand.

Kevin worked his way slowly through the crowd standing at the bar and ordered another shot. All this alcohol was going to mess up his training regimen. He was going to have to work out extra hard and long tomorrow. The thought cheered him up; surely there would be some hot girls at the ship's gym.

He scanned the crowd while he waited for his drink. As his eyes reached the dance floor, he caught a glimpse of leopard print and flashes of green. *Is that ... ?*

He watched as his sister did some sort of dirty dancing hip gyration thing with some big blond-headed guy. Then just to the right of her was Candi, dancing with a tall, dark-haired guy who was making sure everyone knew she was there with him. He couldn't seem to keep his hands off her. She didn't seem to mind too much; she had a big smile on her face.

Kevin muttered to himself in annoyance. *Shit.* Even little Gumdrop was getting action on this cruise.

He couldn't stop looking at her. She wasn't dancing like his sister, but her more reserved moves were sexy anyway. It's like she was holding back, like she had some sort of inside secret she wasn't sharing; and that tight black skirt she had on was really doing a good job of emphasizing her curvaceous hips. He'd never paid much attention to a girl's hips before, but he found hers to be mesmerizing for some reason.

He'd never noticed her body before because she always wore big shirts or baggie pants. *Why would a girl who looked like this go to such lengths to hide herself? It's stupid.*

He got his drink and finished it in one gulp. Enough of this crap, he was going to ask her to dance. He walked over to the dance floor, just as the song ended and a new song started – a slow one. It was too late to turn back since Candi had already seen him approaching. *again. Tonight is just not my night.*

"Um, hey there, Gumdrop, got a dance for me?" He looked at the dark-haired guy standing opposite her and realized for the first time that it was the guy who had scared LeeAnn. Kevin watched as he put his hand on Candi's back, up near her neck, his eyes never leaving Kevin's. This guy was being unapologetically possessive, and Kevin didn't like it one bit.

Kevin lifted his head in a subdued gesture of greeting. "What's up, man? I'm Kevin."

"Jack." He nodded back, but his body language made it clear he wasn't interested in releasing Candi into Kevin's hands.

Candi smiled, a little flustered. "Sure, Kevin. You don't mind, do you, Jack?"

"Well, actually I do, but if it's what you want ... "

Candi lost her smile for a second. "Yes, it's what I want. I'll see you after the dance is over, if you want."

Jack made room for Kevin on the dance floor. "I'll see you in a few minutes then." He bent to kiss her on the cheek. Then he stood and looked Kevin in the eye. "Keep her warm for me."

Kevin didn't respond. Instead, he stepped up to Candi and gently took her in his arms. Jack walked off the dance floor to the bar where he could keep an eye on them while he drank.

*****

Candi was immediately overwhelmed by the totally male scent of Kevin, filling her nostrils. *Oh my god, he smells so amazing.* She inhaled deeply. It was kind of woodsy and spicy and, well, manly. She'd never smelled anything quite like that in her whole life. Her dad used Aqua Velva aftershave, which had its own distinct smell that was totally unlike what she was experiencing right now.

Her heart started racing, and she felt herself starting to sweat;

but her hands were ice cold. Her body was in full freak-out mode. She felt Kevin lean down and put his nose in her hair. She hoped he didn't notice how full of sticky stuff it was.

"You smell so good," said Kevin, softly by her ear. It sent tickles down her spine.

"I was just thinking the same thing about you."

He pulled away just a bit to look in her eyes. "You were?" He smiled at her.

She smiled back. "Yes. Like the woods or like something spicy ... like a man."

He put his head back and laughed. "Well I guess that's a good thing."

Her faced turned pink with embarrassment. She was glad it was too dark for him to see it. "Sorry, I know that sounded stupid."

He took his hand off her back and gently took her chin between his thumb and first finger. "Don't apologize. It wasn't stupid, it was nice." Then he put his hand back around her and pulled her to him a little closer.

Candi could feel her ears ringing. She didn't really hear the music anymore. She was completely enveloped in the smell and feeling of Kevin Peterson. *Kevin Peterson! I'm actually slow dancing with Kevin Peterson right now. Holy crap!*

Why wasn't he dancing with one of the ten supermodels who were here right now? And why didn't she feel this overwhelmed when she was dancing with Jack? Certainly he'd tried to hold her like this, a few times at least, even in just the short time he'd been in the bar; but each time she had pulled away. He didn't smell like Kevin, he wasn't as solid as Kevin; he just wasn't Kevin, period.

Sooner than she wanted, the song ended, and Jack came back immediately to claim the next dance. It was a fast one, so Candi didn't think she'd have to worry about not getting too close to Jack and feeling uncomfortable, but Jack had different ideas. As soon as Kevin started walking away, he grabbed her and pulled her in close.

"What are you doing? Stop that." Candi put her hands up on his chest and pushed a little bit, but he wasn't letting her go.

"I want to dance closer with you, come here." He kept pulling her to his chest, wrapping his arms around her, imprisoning her there.

Candi struggled to get free. "But it's a fast song, I don't want to slow dance. Let me *go!*"

Still he didn't listen. "SShhhh, just calm down. I know you like to dance like this, I just saw you do it with that guy, Kevin. We were having fun before he got here, let's just keep doing that."

"I told you, I don't *want* to. Now let me *go!*" She stomped on his foot and his sharp intake of breath told her that she'd hit her mark – but still he refused to give in.

He gritted his teeth in determination. "Just relax, I'm not going to hurt you. You just need to ... "

He wasn't able to finish his sentence because Kevin showed up at his elbow and started talking.

"She said to let her go, Jack. I suggest you do it."

Jack stood up straighter, and without releasing Candi, said, "This is none of your business, dude; why don't you just get the hell out of here?"

"No can do, buddy. Candi says let her go, so you need to let her go. Or I'm going to have to help you."

Jack immediately dropped her, except that he kept a grip on one of her wrists. He was squeezing pretty hard.

Candi tried to pry his fingers off, but he was obviously determined to keep a hold of her.

"You got a problem with me, *Kevin?*"

"Only if you continue to man-handle Candi. Let go of her wrist."

"Fine. Let's you and me take this outside, then."

Jack let Candi go, and Sarah wrapped her arm around Candi's shoulder, leading her away from the dance floor. Once Kevin saw that she was several feet away, he said, "No thanks," and turned to walk away. Candi held out her hand hoping he would come and take it, but Jack had other plans for Kevin.

Jack grabbed him by the shoulder and pulled back hard, causing Kevin to spin around halfway back towards Jack. Candi watched in horror as Jack let loose a punch that caught Kevin right on the side of his face, near his left eye, snapping his head back about eight inches with the force of its blow, causing him to stumble.

Kevin jumped back up into fighting position so fast, Candi didn't have time to think about it, before he executed a quick jab right into Jack's nose. Candi heard a sickening crunch. Jack's nose had broken and blood started pouring out.

"You bwoke by dose! You fuggin bwoke by dose you azz-ole!" Jack grabbed the bottom of his shirt, trying to use it to staunch the flow of blood.

Everyone on the dance floor who saw what had happened started yelling. Some tried to run away, while others jumped in, ready to either join the fight or keep the two guys apart.

Candi ran back to Kevin, followed closely by Sarah and Jonathan. She was wild-eyed and frightened. "Oh, my god, what happened?! Kevin!! Your face! Oh, my god, and your hand!"

Kevin looked down to see that he had a large bleeding gash on his knuckles.

Mason grabbed Jack by the shoulders and guided him off the dance floor towards the bathrooms. The manager of the bar came over and told Kevin to leave.

Jonathan looked over at the statuesque blond who had been standing off to the side, watching the scene anxiously. "LeeAnn, I have to go. See you tomorrow?"

"Sure. No problem. How about at the pool for breakfast? On the B-deck?"

"Yeah, that would be great. See you then."

Candi watched in shock as this gorgeous girl leaned in and gave her brother a pretty deep kiss on the mouth. She released him and walked away. Jonathan waved at her retreating form, absent-mindedly reaching up and touching his lips. She had left her lip prints in pale pink lipstick smudged on the edge of his mouth.

"Who the hell was that?" Sarah asked, gesturing over to the place where LeeAnn had been standing.

Candi was equally shocked. "Yeah. Who *was* that? And what was she doing performing CPR on you, Jonathan?"

Kevin laughed. "Welcome to my world, ladies – where Jonathan bags the one of the hottest babes on the ship, and I get my ass kicked by a womanizer with a sweet tooth."

Candi frowned at him, looking at him through slitted eyes. Yes, Jack had turned out to be quite the a-hole, but what was this about the sweet tooth?

Kevin winked at her, or at least tried to wink at her, before he grimaced in pain. He had obviously forgotten that he had an injury to his winking eye.

Oh, she thought, *the Gumdrop thing again.* She sighed and took Kevin by the arm.

"Come on, let's go get you cleaned up, Galahad." She looked

over at Jonathan. "Come on, Romeo; we have to get Kevin back to the room. Party's over."

Sarah just stood by silently, watching Jonathan very closely. She seemed to be wrestling with something in her mind.

Candi didn't have time to figure out what Sarah's problem was. She was worried about getting ice on Kevin's face and hand. After all, he had been defending her honor when he got hurt. She felt somewhat responsible for his current situation.

Jonathan and Sarah led the way, leaving Candi and Kevin to trail behind. Candi could hear Jonathan and Sarah talking, but not what was being said.

She looked out of the corner of her eye a few times, trying to figure out if Kevin was mad. She felt really stupid that he had gotten mixed up in her situation. She had no idea Jack would become so possessive. He seemed so nice all evening; then he kind of turned on her. Probably the drinks they'd had hadn't helped. She felt pretty dizzy herself, actually. She'd never been drunk before, but she was pretty sure she was now. She didn't notice it so much in the loud, dark club – but out in the quiet hallways, it became apparent she wasn't totally sober. She wished she could read Kevin's mind, but all he did was stare straight ahead as they walked slowly back to their rooms.

*****

Sarah kept up a stream of conversation with Jonathan from the moment they had left the club. Now she was getting to the subject she really wanted to talk about.

"So, what's with the blond chick at the club?"

"Nothing. Her name is LeeAnn, by the way. She's not just a chick."

"Well, I could see that. You practically sucked her face off before we left."

"I did not."

"Did too. And frankly, Jonathan, I have to tell you that I didn't really think you had it in you."

"What's that supposed to mean?"

"Oh, I don't know – I thought you'd be afraid to kiss a girl in public like that. You don't strike me as the make-out type."

"Well, you were wrong about me then, I guess, weren't you?" He smiled to himself.

Sarah could tell that it was alcohol that had emboldened him. His speech was a little bit slurred and he wasn't walking a very straight line. She was frustrated, but she didn't know why. Even with the courage from a bottle, he still should have been acting shy and embarrassed; but he seemed perfectly at ease with himself. She hated it when people surprised her.

"I wonder what else I've been wrong about where you're concerned." She looked at him with her eyebrows raised, sure this suggestive statement would get him all flustered. This would put her back on solid ground with him and stop this silly game he was trying to play.

Jonathan stopped walking and took her by the upper arm. He pushed her gently towards the wall of the hallway they had been walking down. They were well ahead of Kevin and Candi who were still around the corner, now totally alone.

"Sarah, you know what your problem is? It's that you judged me before you took the time to get to know me. I'm pretty sure you think you have me all figured out, but trust me, you don't." He paused to consider his next words. "You can't get the right answer if you don't have the correct formula. You should remember that from eighth grade math."

He leaned in towards her face, breaking eye contact, staring at her lips as he moved closer.

Sarah's heart stopped beating for a second, then raced to catch up. She was breathing faster, frozen in place against the wall as Jonathan's face got nearer and nearer to hers. She couldn't pull away and didn't want to. It was complete madness.

She wondered what he was going to do. *Is he going to kiss me? Am I okay with that? Yes, I think I am. Why? He's a total dork!* She closed her eyes and waited expectantly anyway, her lips just slightly parted, her sweet breath passing gently between them.

She felt his cheek next to hers, his lips near her neck. She heard him inhale deeply, the air rushing by and tickling her ear. *What the ... ?*

He whispered, "You smell nice." Then he stood up straight, released her, and started walking down the hall again.

Sarah opened her eyes, remaining against the wall for another second, her brain trying to compute what had just happened. She had thought he was going to kiss her, but instead he'd smelled her. *What in the hell was that all about?*

"Did you just *smell* me?" she demanded of his back as he walked away. She hurried to catch up to him.

"Yes, I did, and like I said, you smell nice. Really nice, actually."

"What kind of a weirdo traps a girl in a hallway and then sniffs her neck?"

"I don't know. A kind of weirdo who likes the way you smell, I guess. And for the record, I didn't trap you anywhere, you went willingly."

"I did *not* go willingly, as you put it. You forced me against the wall."

"Sarah, please, don't delude yourself. I didn't force you to do anything you didn't want to. You liked it when I smelled you; admit it."

"God, you are so *weird*. Normal people don't admit to purposely smelling other people, Jonathan." She shook her head in annoyance. Didn't he know anything about how to act around girls? How did he get that pretty blond to hook up with him like that when he acted so strange all the time?

"Maybe they don't admit it, but they do. I'll bet you notice when a guy smells good."

"I do not."

"Do toooo."

"Do NOT!"

"Do too!"

"Fine! Come here!" Sarah grabbed Jonathan by the shirtsleeve and pulled him against her hard. Their bodies slammed together in the hallway, knocking them both off balance. Sarah fell against the wall, but her contact was only light, since Jonathan for once in his life didn't fall but managed to grab her by the waist and hold her steady. He did lean over in his efforts to break their fall, and she found her face buried in his neck.

She inhaled deeply. *Holy shit. He does smell good.*

"So?" Jonathan waited, tipping his head back and starting at her with totally guileless eyes.

"Like I said," she shrugged her shoulders. "Nothing."

Jonathan's eyes narrowed. "I don't believe you."

Sarah pushed him away and brushed off the front of her dress, removing non-existent dust particles.

"Believe what you want; I smell nothing. Like I said – normal people, Jonathan. That would be me. Abnormal people, that would be *you.*"

Kevin and Candi came around the corner, immediately breaking the spell that Jonathan had somehow woven between them. Sarah caught sight of Kevin's eye. "Oh boy, that's one hell of a shiner you're going to have there, Kev."

"Yeah, thanks for noticing."

"I'm going to go grab some ice," said Jonathan, racing down the hall to the cabin to open the door and get the ice bucket.

Candi and Sarah helped Kevin get into the room and lie down on the bed.

"You guys can go now. I'll be fine."

"No. This is my fault. I'll stay and at least help clean you up."

"Ew, not me. I'm going to bed." Sarah left, saying, "Feel better, bro," as she walked out the door.

*****

Candi and Kevin heard Sarah settling in next door. They heard one bang against the wall, followed shortly by another.

"That would be her shoes that she's kicking off her feet and into the wall," predicted Kevin.

Candi sighed. "She's not the neatest roommate in the world." She stood up to get a washcloth out of the bathroom and wet it at the sink, coming back to sit next to Kevin on the bed.

Kevin had laughed and now was grimacing with the pain it had caused in his swollen eye. "You got that right. You should see her bedroom at home right now; it looks like a bomb went off in it."

Candi started cleaning the cut on Kevin's hand. "Oh, is she messy like that all the time?"

"Ouch, careful there ... No, actually, she's not messy at all, normally, but she caught her boyfriend Barry cheating on her the day we left to come on the cruise, so she cut up all the things he had given her, their pictures and stuff, and then threw it all over her room."

"Wow," was all Candi could think to say.

"Yeah, it wasn't pretty."

"Well, that might explain her attitude on the cruise, I guess."

"Yeah. She took it kind of hard. I mean, I don't blame her. He was in bed with my girlfriend, now ex-girlfriend. Sarah literally caught them in the act."

Candi put her hand to her mouth. "Oh, my god, that's terrible! I'm so sorry, Kevin, I had no idea. No wonder you were alone tonight, you must be devastated."

"Hardly. I was alone because I struck out. No chicks wanted the Kevster tonight." He smiled bitterly and closed his eyes.

Candi suddenly felt shy again. "I don't believe that for a second. Any girl would have been psyched to be with you tonight. You obviously didn't try very hard."

"No, I did, seriously. Jonathan got the girl in the club. Jack obviously thought he had you all sewn up in his web. I tried to dance with you and got my ass kicked. I struck out big time." The side of his mouth lifted in a self-deprecating grin.

Candi took a second to think about what Kevin had said. Had he purposely included her in his list of potential conquests? *He's just messing with me.*

Jonathan came through the door with the bucket of ice. He put some into a washcloth and handed it over to Candi. She gently placed it on Kevin's face.

"I'm afraid this is going to swell a lot more."

"Yep," Jonathan agreed, "you're going to have a pretty significant hematoma there by your orbital bone. I should probably check it for you to see if it's cracked." He made a move towards the bed. Kevin opened his good eye, lifting his uninjured hand and holding it out.

"Hold it right there, Dr. Jon. You're not touching this orbital bone or the hemawhatever you just said. Just stay back."

"But ... "

"Jonathan, he said no," said Candi, firmly. "Just go over to my room with Sarah and go to sleep. I'm going to stay here with Kevin for a little while to make sure he's okay and finish cleaning his hand."

"What?! No way am I going over there with that she-devil. She'll eat me alive. I'm staying right here. You go over there and *I'll* take care of Kevin."

"Hey, stop talking about me like I'm an invalid. I play rugby, remember?"

Candi and Jonathan looked at each other and shrugged. Apparently Kevin's sports status was supposed to mean something to them, but they weren't making the connection.

Kevin sighed. "Rugby players get injured all the time. This will be my fifth black eye in two years. I broke my shinbone in a game last year. This is no big deal."

He looked at Candi and took her hand. "Seriously, thank you; but go ahead and go to bed, I'll be fine."

He let go of her hand and looked over at Jonathan. "You don't have to go over with my sister, but you seriously do have to stay the hell away from my face. Touch me, and I'll kick your ass."

"Okaaay, fine. Whatever, I won't touch you."

Jonathan turned to his sister. "'Night, Candi, see you tomorrow. Good luck over there with you-know-who." He rolled his eyes in the general direction of her room and the 'she-devil' that was now sleeping in it.

"Thanks. G'nite guys, see you tomorrow." Candi stood up, yawning. She took one last look at Kevin and walked out the door, stepping into the hallway and stumbling as she neared her room. The ship was really moving a lot. Either that or she was still drunk. She put her hand on her stomach and didn't like the feeling she was having. She hoped she wasn't getting seasick.

Candi entered the cabin and saw that Sarah was in bed, sound asleep, still wearing her dress. She was laying spread eagle over the top of the covers, which meant Candi was going to have to move her. She took her time getting dressed into her pajamas, since she didn't relish the idea of arguing with Sarah over personal space.

As she put on her pajama bottoms, she fell to the floor. The ship was rolling back and forth so much, it was impossible to keep her balance. She wished they had a window so she could see what was going on with the waves. They must be going through some seriously bad weather for her to be able to feel the rocking of the boat this much.

She crawled over to the bed and climbed in, shoving Sarah over as far as she could, and closing her eyes. Sarah didn't offer any resistance. *Man, she sleeps like the dead.* Within seconds, Candi drifted off into a dream-filled, turbulent sleep.

All Hands on Deck

JONATHAN STOOD IN THE BATHROOM washing his face and brushing his teeth with his legs spaced far apart to counteract the movement of the ship. He'd never been on a boat this big before, but he was pretty sure this much movement wasn't normal. Not a lot of people would do cruises if that were the case – seasickness would be a major issue. He didn't feel sick now, but thinking about it started making him feel funny.

He checked his watch; it was just after one in the morning. He wondered if he'd be able to see anything if he went up on deck. He decided to just give it a try. There were no parents here to tell him it was too late to be wandering around; might as well take advantage of it. He put his shoes on very quietly and checked on Kevin. He seemed to be asleep, breathing even and slow.

Jonathan opened the door and stepped out into the hallway. He closed the door as quietly as possible before continuing down the hall, grabbing the walls on either side to steady himself as the boat rocked back and forth, up and down. He didn't see anyone on his way to the upper deck.

He reached the foyer area that had doors leading out onto the main deck. Outside it was pitch-black; rain was slashing against the glass of the doors and windows. Jonathan hesitated, wishing he had thought to put on his poncho.

Oh well, I can always take a shower and dry off if I have to. He pulled on the doors, trying to wrestle them open. The wind began whipping through the foyer once it was given access through the open door.

Jonathan stepped outside onto the deck, and after another wrestling match, succeeded in getting the door closed. He turned, immediately going into shock at what he saw. The boat was leaning to one side – the side he was standing on. The waves were incredibly high, hitting the side of the ship and blowing up several feet into the air, washing the decks with their salty spray. There was a wall of blackness surrounding the ship, like a blanket of gloom.

Just then, the boat tipped even more on its side. A huge wave that had been rolling out in the distance started moving towards the ship. It seemed to be sucking the water away from the boat to build itself into a wave from hell.

Jonathan stared at it wide-eyed, not believing what he was seeing. It was like that *Perfect Storm* movie, where the wave was as big as a building. It was going to hit the boat, right where Jonathan was standing.

He felt like his feet were mired in quicksand. He turned to go back inside, but when he grabbed the door handles, he couldn't get the doors to open. The difference in pressure between the inside and outside was sealing them closed.

His scientific mind jumped into overdrive. He turned to look over his shoulder at the approaching rogue wave. It was less than fifty yards away and even bigger than it had been three seconds ago. He struggled to cram his hand in his pocket, searching for the pocketknife he always carried there.

His hands made contact with the metal; he struggled with his wet fingers to get it out and then open.

"Come on! Come on! *Come on!!*" he yelled out into the night. "Open you mother effer!"

Finally the knife popped open.

Jonathan didn't hesitate.

He jammed it in between the doors and wrenched it sideways, breaking the seal; it was enough to equalize the pressure between the two spaces and release the door's hold. He pulled the door open just enough to squeeze through. He quickly slid it closed behind him, just as the wave crashed into the side of the ship.

Jonathan heard the sound of the outside railing breaking under the stress of the water pressure. He backed quickly away from the foyer doors that were now completely covered in water. He felt like he was looking at an aquarium just outside the door, as if the whole deck were underwater. He unconsciously folded his knife blade back in and put it in his pocket.

Without waiting to see what was going to happen next, he spun around, ran down the stairs, and sprinted back to the cabin. He struggled to get his key to work in the lock. As soon as he heard the click of the lock mechanism releasing, he burst through the entrance and started yelling.

"Wake up, Kevin!! Wake up!!"

Jonathan ran next door and pounded on the girls' door. "Wake up, Candi!! Let me in!!! We have to get ready to muster!!"

He ran back to his room before the door had time to shut and saw Kevin still sleeping on the bed. He didn't think, he just ran and jumped. He landed square on Kevin's stomach with his knees.

"WAKE UP, I SAID!!! THE BOAT IS SINKING!!"

Kevin let out a huge burst of air as Jonathan's thrown weight emptied his sleeping lungs. With the bit of strength he could gather from his half-sleeping state, he threw Jonathan off of him and onto the floor.

Jonathan scrambled to get up, momentarily tangled in the covers that had dropped to the floor, breaking his fall.

"I'm serious, Kevin, GET UP NOW!!! Do you hear me?!!" He started running around the cabin like a crazy person, yelling things out, not knowing if anyone was listening but doing it anyway. "We need to pack one backpack each. Put everything in it that could be of use. Make sure you include at least one bottle of fresh water." Then he ran out of the room again to go pound on the girls' door.

*****

Kevin put his hand up to his head, trying to make sense of what was going on. It was difficult to do with the headache that was pounding away in his brain. He wasn't sure if the pain was from the cold cocking he had received earlier, Jonathan's yelling, or the one hundred and fifty pounds of weight that had just dropped on his chest. Jonathan was skinny, but he was tall, and apparently his bones weighed more than Kevin had thought possible.

He could hear Jonathan out in the hallway. "I know you're in there! Open up!! We have a HUGE problem, Candi. HUGE!! You need to get up!"

Jonathan came back into the room, frantic. He had tears starting to well up in his eyes. "Kevin, please HELP ME! Our sisters are sleeping. The ship is sinking, and I CAN'T WAKE THEM UP!"

Kevin held up his hand, moving himself towards the edge of the bed.

"Slow down, little man, just relax. What the hell are you

talking about now?"

Jonathan took a deep breath and put his hands on his chest in an effort to stop his heart from beating out of it.

"I went out on the deck to see what the problem was with the ship. Can't you feel it leaning to the side? There are some huge rogue waves out there. They crashed into the ship and damaged it. I just know this ship is going down, we have to prepare!"

Kevin tried to wrap his head around the idea of a cruise ship sinking. "Jonathan, it's not like this is the *Titanic* or anything. Don't you think they would sound the muster alarm if there was a problem with the boat?"

Jonathan looked momentarily confused. "Of course, I don't know why they haven't, but I know a listing ship when I see one. This ship is turning on its side; you have to agree that's not normal!"

Kevin thought about it for a second. The ship was tipping to one side. "No, you're right. I can feel it leaning. So what should we do?" He was waking up out of his sleep stupor now, hearing some really eerie sounds coming from inside or outside the ship somewhere – some kind of groaning or moaning. Like the ship wasn't feeling good.

"I think we should get backpacks, one each, and fill them with supplies. Fresh water, food, and rain covers or clothes. Sunscreen. Anything like that."

Kevin looked confused. "Anything like what? You just described supplies for a day at the beach."

Jonathan looked Kevin right in the eye and said in a deadly serious voice, "No, I just described supplies we will need if we are set adrift on a lifeboat in the middle of the Atlantic Ocean."

Kevin got serious immediately. "What the hell, Jonathan ...

you're serious, aren't you?"

"More serious than I've ever been about anything in my entire seventeen years and forty-one days of life."

Kevin stood up and sighed. The kid sounded crazy, but he was also smarter than anyone he knew. *What's the worst that could happen, anyway?* They could miss some sleep running around like chickens with their heads cut off, which he could easily remedy by sleeping it off on the pool deck. "Fine. I'm in. What do you want me to do?"

"Get me your backpack. Go wake the girls up. Break their door down if you have to, but don't hurt yourself. I don't have much in the way of medical supplies, and in our worst case scenario, there won't be a hospital or doctor around."

"Sheesh, Jonathan, you really know how to stay positive, don't you?" He headed out the door with Jonathan yelling after him.

"I'm a realist, especially when a ship is sinking!"

Apparently, Jonathan's worst-case scenario was a little different than the one Kevin had considered. Kevin brushed it off without giving it any thought. *No need to go nuts.*

Kevin knocked forcefully on the girls' door. "Open up, Sarah, Candi, seriously, you have to get up."

A few seconds later the door cracked open. Looking out was a green eye with black streaks under it. "This had better be good."

"How about this: the ship is sinking and you need to get your asses out of bed ... is that good enough for you?"

The door flew open to reveal Candi standing there in pink flowered pajamas and fuzzy purple slippers. "What did you just say?"

Kevin's eyebrows raised in surprise. The sexy gumdrop had turned into an eight-year-old at a slumber party, except that she also had black makeup smeared all around her eyes and her hair looked like some rats had made a nest in it.

"I said, Jonathan thinks the ship is sinking. He wants us to get ready for the muster."

Candi looked like she was still half asleep. "Why aren't they sounding the alarm?"

"Jonathan doesn't know, but he said the ship is sinking, and until I hear different, I'm going with him. You can feel the boat leaning to the side, so it's not totally crazy. He wants you and Sarah up now. Pack your backpacks with water, food, and other supplies."

"What supplies?"

"Like you're going to the beach, kind of supplies."

Sarah decided at that minute to sit up in bed and join the conversation. "Will you guys shut the hell up, please? I'm trying to get some beauty sleep here."

Kevin looked at Candi and smiled. "I'll leave you to get Sarah up." He quickly moved back to his cabin.

"Chicken!" yelled Candi at his back.

*****

Candi turned to face a sleeping Sarah.

"Get up, sleeping beauty, the ship is sinking."

"Go to hell."

"No, I'm serious, the ship is sinking. We have to pack supplies."

"Says who? I don't hear any horns."

"Says Jonathan, who is almost never wrong."

"Yeah, well, call me when the alarm goes off. In the meantime, I will be sleeping here, in this bed, ignoring you." With that, she rolled over onto her stomach and fell back to sleep.

Candi went next door to talk to Jonathan. She found him scrambling all over the room, opening drawers and muttering to himself.

"Jonathan, what's going on?"

"I don't have time to explain, Candi. You need to pack. Remember all those things I told you to bring before we left? Get those and put them into your backpack. We're going to need them if we're lucky."

Candi felt a shiver move up her spine. "What do you mean, 'if we're lucky'?"

"I mean, if we don't drown when this ship goes down."

Candi felt vomit rising up from her stomach and a sense of dread. She worked her throat convulsively to keep it down.

"Um, Jon ... I didn't pack that stuff," she said weakly.

Jonathan immediately stopped what he was doing and whipped around to confront her. "WHAT?!"

Candi started to cry. "I'm sorry, I wasn't thinking. I just figured there was no point. I mean, cruise ships don't sink, right?" She looked desperately from Jonathan to Kevin.

"HAVEN'T YOU EVER HEARD OF THE TITANIC?!" Jonathan yelled in her face. "It was one of your favorite movies, Candi!"

"Hey, hey, Jon, there's no need to yell at her; she didn't know. She's right, it's like a chance in a million this would happen, right?"

"No, more like a chance in two million three hundred twenty thousand, give or take, but that's not the point." He looked at Candi again. "How much room would a magnifying glass have taken in your bag, huh? You couldn't do that for me? Just that little thing?"

Candi was shaking from nerves and sadness. "I'm so sorry, Jonathan. I really am. I'll go find anything I can to bring, just tell me what to do, and I'll do it."

Jonathan looked chagrined. "Don't felt bad. I'm sorry I yelled at you. I'm not perfect either. I'm kicking myself right now for not thinking about putting in a bigger knife, water purification tablets and about fifty other things that I'm afraid we're going to need."

Kevin laughed mirthlessly. "Jonathan, you're nuts. No one on this ship brought anything like that. No one expects a cruise ship to sink."

"Whatever," said Jonathan, obviously not ready to forgive himself. "It's too late for regrets now. Just go pack whatever you can find. Make sure you have at least one bottle of sealed water per person. More is better, but it all has to fit in the backpack, zipped up completely. Bring anything that could be made into a shelter, food in closed containers or packaging, any plastic bags you have. If you have any aspirin or other medicine, bring it. And don't forget your sunscreen."

Candi smiled weakly. "I have that."

Jonathan grabbed her and took her in a surprisingly strong hug. "Don't worry, Candi, I'll take care of you."

Candi could see Kevin watching with grudging admiration.

Candi went back to her room and started gathering supplies, shoving them into her backpack. *Water? Check. Sunscreen? Check. Candy bar? Check. Windbreaker? Check.* That was about all she had that was useful. She couldn't believe that was all she had to contribute. On a whim, she pulled the thin sheet off the bed and threw it into the sack too. Next, she filled Sarah's backpack with water and a few other things she found lying around, including airplane peanuts that she found in her purse.

*****

Sarah continued to sleep, snoring lightly as she dreamed of being with Barry on a sailboat. Her eyebrows screwed up in confusion. *Why am I dreaming about Barry on a sailboat?* She could feel the gentle rocking of the boat in her dreams. She could hear yelling and banging too. *Why was Barry making so much noise? Why is Barry even here, that cheating bastard?*

The muster horn started sounding across the boat. Sarah stayed asleep, incorporating the sound into her dream. Now Barry was playing the saxophone very badly. He couldn't keep a tune going at all. He just kept blasting the same note, over and over and over ...

"Sarah, get up NOW!!" yelled a voice in the back of her mind. It sounded like that annoying girl, Candi.

Then a few seconds passed before she heard Kevin's voice, saying, "Sorry kid, I hate to do this to you, but you leave us with no choice."

The sound of water splashing reached her ears, then immediately after, the sensation of something very cold and very wet ...

"AAACCCCKKKK!! What the ... I'M GOING TO KILL YOU!!"

Sarah jumped out of bed, soaking wet from the freezing cold water dumped on her from the ice bucket. She was soaking wet, her leopard print dress clinging to her body. Her makeup was smeared down her face; her hair had seen much better days.

"What in the hell is your problem?!" she yelled at the three faces that were staring at her with determination.

Kevin spoke first. "Sarah, the ship is sinking. The muster alarm has gone off. Get your frigging life vest on and come with us. Bring whatever you can't afford to live without."

She noticed for the first time that they were all wearing life vests and carrying backpacks. Candi was fully dressed in her long green shirt and some white capris and sneakers. The guys were wearing windbreakers, t-shirts, and shorts. Her brain was not computing. Why was everyone dressed? Why did they have backpacks on? What time was it?

"What?" It came out weakly, missing the venom that had so recently laced her words.

Candi stepped forward and took her hand. "Come on. We have to go. Get your shoes on."

Sarah looked around the room in a daze. She sat down on the edge of the bed, reaching over to grab her heels and put them on.

"You can't wear those shoes, Sarah," said Jonathan, impatiently.

"Why?"

"Because they are unsuitable. Don't you have any sneakers or flip-flops at least?"

"No, I only have heels."

Jonathan threw his hands up in the air. "What kind of person goes on a trip with only high heels?!"

"I thought I was going to be dancing every night, *Jonathan*. Excuse me for being a complete idiot who didn't plan on a sinking ship like you apparently did!"

Jonathan left the room in frustration. "Come on, we have to leave," he said from the hallway.

Candi took Sarah's heels away from her and put some of her own flip-flops down on the floor by Sarah's feet. "Here, wear these for now."

"But they're way too small. You have oompa loompa feet."

Candi rolled her eyes in exasperation and responded sternly. "Well, you can't afford to be choosy right now. Put 'em on and let's go."

Sarah cooperated woodenly. Half of her heels were hanging off the ends of the stupid rubber shoes, but she had lost her will to fight. This whole thing was probably just a nightmare, and she was going to wake up from it very soon. She couldn't wait. The first thing she was going to do when she woke up was take these stupid flip-flops and throw them off the ship.

Everyone but Sarah finally exited the room, all of them wearing their life jackets. They could see that the people in the neighboring cabins were taking the warning seriously too. People were moving towards their muster stations, some quickly and some very slowly, obviously reticent about going out into the wild night that was still full of rain, thunder and lightning. The doors at the end of the hall at the top of the stairs were open; through it they could hear the stormy night that raged above their heads.

Sarah grabbed her makeup valise on her way out the door. Jonathan didn't notice until they were in the foyer, getting ready to head out towards their lifeboat.

"Holy crap, Sarah, you can't bring that!"

Sarah got a stubborn look on her face. "Yes, I most certainly can."

Jonathan stepped over to stare down at her. "No, you can't. Put it back."

Sarah stared right back at him, mutiny in her eyes. "I will do no such thing, and if you so much as make one move towards my Louis Vuitton, I will *take you out*, do you understand me?"

"Louis Vuitton? What the heck is that? I'm talking about your makeup suitcase."

"Then we understand each other perfectly. Now step aside. I'm going to my lifeboat."

Jonathan spun on his heel, leaving her standing there holding her makeup case in a kung-fu grip Everyone followed Jonathan, walking up flights of stairs until they got to the main doors that led outside. Lots of people were milling around, nervous about going out into the wild night.

Jonathan looked at Kevin and nodded as they reached the doors that were only partway open. They grabbed them together and pulled them open wide enough so they could all get through.

The rush of rain and saltwater hit them in the face. Already there were several people on the deck, all of them staying clear of the area that had the broken railing.

Jonathan yelled to the others, "Watch out for the railings! They're not secure! I saw one of them break earlier!"

Candi looked at her brother in horror, hoping she had misunderstood. "What do you mean you saw one of them break earlier?"

"I came out here before I woke you up to see what was wrong. I wanted to be sure we had a real problem before I did anything else."

Candi looked like she felt sick to her stomach. "You could have been washed overboard! You could have died! Why did you do that?!"

Jonathan just shrugged and shouted to be heard over the waves, "I don't know. It just seemed like the thing to do at the time!"

Kevin just shook his head, along with Sarah. Jonathan either had nerves of steel or a complete lack of appreciation for his mortality.

They arrived at their muster station and looked around them. Half of the passengers weren't wearing their lifejackets. None of them were carrying supplies. Some were still in their pajamas. A few looked like they had come directly from the bars.

The muster horns were still going off. The ship's crew was running back and forth, trying to get everyone organized. It was hard when the railing wasn't safe.

Sarah looked out towards the lifeboats that were secured to the side of the ship. She could barely see them because the night was so dark, and the rain obscured everything. She couldn't believe she was possibly going to be getting into one of those. This was the most realistic nightmare she had ever had. She felt completely wet and could taste the salt of the sea on her lips.

Just then a guy in a ship's uniform came over to their area and started yelling, "Okay, we need all of you to get on your designated lifeboats! They are numbered. You are on lifeboat number eighty-four. Everyone in muster line eighty-four must get on lifeboat number eighty-four *now!*" And then he moved on to another row, repeating his instructions with the next boat number.

The four of them looked at each other and then at the couple behind them in line. There should have been twelve people there but there were only six. The couple took one look at each other, shook their heads and took off.

"Where in the hell are they going?!" yelled Sarah.

"Who cares? You heard the guy, we have to go get in!" responded Jonathan.

"But I wanna go where they're going ... ," wailed Sarah.

"Get in!" yelled Jonathan and Kevin together.

Sarah jumped and started moving towards the lifeboat, sullenly, grumbling to herself.

Kevin and Jonathan reached the lifeboat first and lifted up the edge of the cover that was on top of the boat. It was held there with heavy-duty snaps and straps. They lifted up the edge high enough so the girls could climb in under it, passing in the backpacks behind them. Kevin was the last one in, holding onto Sarah's makeup bag. He knew better than to leave it behind. Hell hath no fury like Sarah and no makeup supplies.

They left the lifeboat cover in place since it sheltered them from the rain and kept the water from filling up the boat.

They all sat in the dark of the lifeboat, listening to the rain slash against the cover over their heads. They could hear men yelling in the distance but were unable to make out any actual words.

"So, now what do we do, boy genius?" asked Sarah, her teeth starting to chatter. Kevin handed her his windbreaker which she gratefully put on.

Jonathan sighed in annoyance. "We wait. They should cast us off soon. We don't want to be anywhere near this ship when it goes under."

"Why?" asked Candi.

"Because it will create a huge whirlpool vortex that will suck anything nearby down with it."

"Holy shit, dude, are you serious?" asked Kevin.

"Totally serious."

"Does this thing have an engine?" asked Kevin as he felt around in the dark.

"No."

"Hey! Watch the hands there, buddy," squeaked Candi.

"Oops, sorry 'bout that," responded a not very apologetic-sounding Kevin. "What about oars at least? Does this thing have any oars?"

"Yes, I think so."

"Okay then, we know what we have to do Jon. We're gonna

row this mother like we've never rowed before."

"Actually, it will be like I've never rowed before, since I haven't," said Jonathan frankly.

Kevin laughed. He couldn't help himself. "Jonathan, you are hilarious."

All of a sudden, their lifeboat jerked. The girls screamed. Everyone reached out to try and steady themselves. The girls found each other and the guys found things on the inside of the boat to hold onto.

"You girls hold onto one of us!" yelled Jonathan.

Sarah grabbed onto Jonathan, digging her manicured nails into his arm.

"Youch! Holy crap, watch the talons, woman!"

"Sorry! You told me to grab you!"

"Not with your nails, just your fingers!"

"Okay, sorry! Geez!"

The boat jerked again and then tipped partway on its side. All four of them screamed together as they were thrown towards the edge of the lifeboat.

From outside on the ship they heard someone yelling. "What the hell is going on?! Who's releasing those boats? I didn't authorize that yet!!"

Then the sound of a high-pitched whirring reached their ears and the boat righted itself.

"Phew! I think that was a close one!" said Jonathan.

No sooner had he spoken, then the whirring sound started up again and the boat was set completely free of its moorings. Sarah felt for a few seconds as if they were airborne, floating up ever so slightly off their seats as the boat made a quick downward journey towards the sea. They were completely at the mercy of gravity.

The boat slammed into the water with a huge bang, jarring their teeth and skulls. Immediately the boat started spinning and rocking. They were thrown against each other violently, their bags and other items in the boat hitting them in the faces, chests and heads.

"Aahh my friggin' eye!" yelled Kevin.

"Hold on everyone!" yelled Jonathan.

"Please God, please God, please God," was the chant that Candi took up.

"My dress is completely ruined now," yelled Sarah. "I hope you're happy, Jonathan!"

They all felt a slight lull in movement, and soon after a gradual lifting up of the boat. It felt like it was going up, up, and up some more, like it was on an elevator.

"Oh crap, hold on tight, everyone!" yelled Jonathan.

"What's happening?!" yelled Kevin.

"We're on a wave! We're gonna get thrown! Hang on!!"

The wave reached its peak and started its deadly descent, the small lifeboat perched at its crest.

They heard the roaring of the wave. It sounded like an out of control freight train.

"I love you, Jonathan!" yelled Candi.

"I love you too, Gumdrop!" yelled Jonathan.

And then the wave crashed. It threw the boat and slammed into it, sending it spinning out of control, tossing it out over the ocean, far away from the cruise ship. Water rushed in beneath the cover, as snaps and straps came loose. The boat was quickly filling up.

"We have to take the cover off!" yelled Jonathan, trying to be heard over the roar of the storm.

"Are you crazy?" yelled Sarah. "We'll die! We'll drown!"

Kevin understood immediately. "No, we'll drown if we leave it on. The boat is filling up anyway. The best we can do is either try and drain it as it fills or turn it upside down and hang on to it somehow."

"I think we need to try and stay inside if we can," said Jonathan. "If we get out and turn it upside down, it will be almost impossible to turn back over. We won't have the strength to hold on for long. Make sure we hold onto the cover because it will shelter us in the day ... assuming we make it to daylight."

Sarah was terrified. The fact that Jonathan had actually said the words out loud made it all the more real.

Kevin took the lead. "Okay, I'm going to hold onto this cover thing. Jonathan, you go around and unsnap each part. Candi, I need you to tie us all together. Use the rope over here behind me. If one of us gets washed overboard, I want to be able to pull 'em back in. Does everyone agree to this?"

Everyone looked around at each other, trying to pick out faces in the dark. Three of them nodded and said, "Yes."

Sarah, the one who had not yet committed, clarified, "That also means if one of us drowns, the rest of us will drown too, right?"

Kevin shrugged and answered honestly, "Probably."

Sarah thought about it for a second and nodded her head. "Do it."

Candi got the rope, and between her and Sarah, they were able to feel their way and wrap it around everyone's waist and tie it firmly to a ring attached to the side of the boat.

"What if the boat sinks?" yelled Sarah, knowing that the rope was attached to the boat with four knots.

"Even if it fills with water, it probably won't go more than a foot below the surface," yelled Jonathan in reply.

"How is that possible?" she asked.

As he continued scrambling around the boat, hunched over in the dark, undoing snaps and straps, he answered, "I checked out these lifeboats online before we got on the ship. They're made of fiberglass on the outside, but on the inside they have foam-filled flotation chambers built into the hull. The foam can't sink, so it might go beneath the surface of the water a little, but it won't sink entirely. If we start having a problem with it, like a hole or something, we can flip it over and sit on top of it."

Sarah smiled tentatively. "I guess that makes me feel a little bit better."

"You're welcome," Jonathan said as he finished the job.

"Ready?" asked Kevin.

"Ready!"

Together the boys pulled the heavy tarp off the top of the boat and pushed it to the center. All four of them worked together to get it somewhat folded up, piling it up near the middle of the boat. It was thick and bulky, making it hard to maneuver.

Now that the cover was off, they were able to see around them a bit. The boat was being tossed all over the sea's surface. The rain was coming down very heavily, but the moon was visible through the clouds from time to time, making it possible to see that they were in a very dark and very lonely place. They could barely make out the lights of the cruise ship way off in the distance. Even this far away, they could see that the ship was listing to the side. It was weird seeing such a big thing looking so ... well ... wrong.

They started scooping up handfuls of water, throwing them overboard as fast as they could; but no matter how fast they scooped, it seemed the rain kept coming in to fill up the bottom of the boat. The skies showed no signs of clearing. There were clumps of black clouds as far as they could see.

After nearly an hour of scooping, they were all exhausted. Sarah stopped scooping altogether, followed shortly by Candi.

"I just ... can't ... anymore. I'm exhausted," said Sarah.

"You have to keep trying," said Jonathan, focused on scooping and tossing; scooping and tossing.

Candi's gaze was fixed on a spot just over Jonathan's shoulder. Sarah looked over and caught the expression on her face. Sarah could see she was terrified.

"What? What's wrong? Other than the obvious of course."

Candi couldn't answer; she could only point.

Everyone turned to look and Sarah felt the blood drain from her face.

It was a huge building-size rogue wave. It looked like a tsunami, and it was heading right for them.

"Oh, shit!" yelled Jonathan.

"Oh, shit is right!" agreed Kevin. "What should we do?"

"I don't know! Just hold on and pray!! And put your backpacks ON!! We can't lose our supplies!"

Everyone scrambled to grab a totally soaked backpack and put it on. Sarah put her backpack on and grabbed her makeup valise. She put it in her lap and held onto it with one hand, holding onto the side of the boat with the other.

"Would you get rid of that thing?!" yelled Jonathan.

"No! Leave me alone!"

Candi glared at her brother. "Just leave it, Jonathan; we have bigger eggs to fry."

Sarah felt the boat rising up and up and up again – just like last time – only last time, they had the cover on the boat. This time the boat was wide open and already half-full of water.

The boat started to spin as it reached the crest of the wave, which was just starting to break at the top. Sarah began to feel dizzy and sick, losing track of where they were.

The only thing they could hear was the roar of the wave and their screams. The only thing they could see was spinning, spinning, spinning and a great yawning, foaming whiteness. The water rushed over the boat and filled their mouths, trying to force its way into their lungs. Sarah gagged on the salty seawater, holding on to her brother and the boat as tight as she possibly could.

The wave seemed to be pounding around them over and over. Just when she thought it was calming down, it would rise up again. It was like a series of vicious waves, growing and climbing, with the specific purpose of destroying their little boat and sending them to the ocean floor to become food for the sharks that were certainly waiting for them below the turbulence of the surface waves.

One last wave, bigger than all the rest, rose up out of the black sea. All four of them looked up, and the last thing any of them remembered seeing was a wall of black water, coming to claim their lives.

Adrift

JONATHAN WAS THE FIRST ONE to wake up, slowly at first. Then enough that he could taste the dried salt water covering his chapped lips. The inside of his mouth felt wrinkled and salty. He sensed the heat of the early rays of the sun, already burning his salt-damaged skin. He moved his fingers and felt the skin crackling, as if they were coated with dried glue.

He tried to move his legs but they were pinned in place. He had a momentary panic attack until he opened his eyes and realized he couldn't move his legs because someone was lying across them. He wiggled them a little bit and managed to rouse Candi.

Candi sat up all of a sudden, quickly leaning over to the side of the boat to vomit into the water.

"Uuuuhh. What the hell happened? I feel so sick. Oh no ... here it comes again ... " She leaned over and vomited a second time.

She wiped her mouth off with the heel of her hand and laid back down in the boat, arched uncomfortably over the pack that was still strapped between her shoulders.

The noise woke Sarah up. She lifted her head off the tarp where it had been resting. Her hair looked like it hadn't been brushed or washed in a month. Jonathan was afraid of what she might do if she saw it, doubting that she'd ever seen herself look this bad before. He wisely kept his mouth shut about it.

"What? What's happening? Are we rescued yet?" She looked around and her face dropped.

All Jonathan could think was, *water, water, everywhere, nor any drop to drink.* Funny that *The Rime of the Ancient Mariner* would pop into his head right now. Hopefully their little boat would have better luck than the one in that story. He shivered to himself thinking about it.

Kevin stayed put, giving a slight moan as an indication that he was still alive.

Sarah looked over at her brother, frowning in concern.

Jonathan saw that Kevin's eye was swollen shut and looked pretty gross. His lips looked as chapped and dry as Jonathan's felt.

"I need some water," croaked Sarah. She started shrugging off her backpack to get a bottle from within.

"No! Wait!" yelled Jonathan.

Sarah shot him a dirty look. "Why? I'm thirsty."

"Yes, I know. We all are. But we have very limited supplies, and we don't know when we're going to be rescued. We have to take stock of what we have and then ration it. We have to use as little as possible."

Sarah thought about what he said and nodded slowly.

"Everyone take your backpacks off and empty them here on the tarp. Let's see what we have," instructed Jonathan.

Slowly they all sat up, Kevin more slowly than the rest, and wrestled with their backpacks to get them off. It was easier said than done, since the saltwater had started to dry into a stiffness that made the straps difficult to bend and pull off.

They each opened up a backpack and started putting things

out on the tarp. Kevin and Jonathan organized it all into separate piles and tallied it up.

"Okay, Kevin, how many ounces of water do we have?"

"Well, we have six, eight-ounce bottles, so that makes forty-eight ounces, give or take."

"Okay, so there are four of us, that makes twelve ounces each. Maybe a little less for us and a bit more for you, since you have a bigger body mass than us. Now, how much food do we have?"

Kevin answered, "We have three protein bars, one bag of airline peanuts, two melted candy bars, and a mini bag of beef jerky." He held up the bag of beef jerky and smiled. "Who's the genius who brought this?"

Candi smiled mirthlessly and raised her hand. "That would be me."

She looked around at everyone looking at her like she was crazy. "What? I like to eat beef jerky when I go on road trips! I figured I'd like it on a cruise, too."

"Hey, it's good protein, Candi, don't worry about it. We just have to be careful because of the salt. We can't afford to make ourselves more dehydrated than we probably are already going to be. We'll save that one for last," said Jonathan.

"Okay, what else do we have with us?"

Kevin held up a sopping wet hunk of white cloth and some other miscellaneous things. "One bed sheet. One pocketknife. One black thing I don't know what it is. Two rain ponchos. Two pairs of sunglasses. One compass. One baseball hat. One tiny scope thingy ... aaaaand ... that's about it."

"Don't forget the tarp," said Candi weakly.

Jonathan frowned at the file of rations on the boat cover. "That black thing is a flint, for starting fires. So, let's start with water. I think we're all pretty thirsty. Only two ounces each, though." Jonathan looked each person in the eye and they all nodded in agreement.

As she drank, Sarah looked around. "Don't we have some stuff on this boat from the ship? I mean, it's not like they'd send people out on a lifeboat with nothing in it, would they?"

Everyone started looking around them at once. It was then that they realized the lumps they were leaning against actually were hard, covered boxes with latches on them.

They each hurried to open the box nearest them. Kevin got his opened first. "Ha! Water! A big container of it, probably ten water bottles' worth or more. Plus some vacuum-packed foil packets that might be food ... Yes, I think these are meals. There are twelve of them."

"I have a flashlight with batteries! Hey, and it works! There's also a mirror in here, a hatchet, and ... um ... dynamite sticks," said Candi.

Kevin and Jonathan looked at each other with confused expressions on their faces. *Dynamite?*

"Flares!" they both yelled at the same time, grinning at each other.

"My box has a first aid kit in it. Should I open it?" asked Sarah.

"Yes, open it," said Jonathan.

Sarah flipped the latch. "There are band-aids, some scissors, some white tape, some iodine looking stuff, rubber gloves, some foil packets with antibiotic cream, and tweezers. Oh, and some gauze pads."

"What about your box, Jon? Anything good?" asked Kevin.

"Well, I think so. This looks to me like ... ," he pulled out a black box, "some sort of radio!"

"Does it work?" Sarah asked, desperately.

"I don't know, there's a switch here. If I can figure out how to turn it on ... " He flipped it back and forth, but nothing happened. "Hmmm, it doesn't seem to be working."

"Hand it to me, Jon, let me see what I can do." Kevin reached his hand out for it.

"No, just wait, I want to look at it first."

"Give it to him, Jonathan," said Sarah, a dangerous tone in her voice.

Jonathan disregarded it. "In a minute."

Sarah got up on her knees and reached over to take it from him. "Give it up, Jonathan, you don't know what you're doing. Kevin is very good with electronics."

"Back off, Sarah, I'm not done yet," Jonathan warned, keeping a strong grip on the black box.

Sarah had obviously had enough of Jonathan's arrogance. She grabbed the box and hauled back hard on it, yelling, "Give it!"

Jonathan lost his grip suddenly, and it slipped out of his hands.

Sarah wasn't expecting to win it so easily, and fell back with it in her hands held high above her head.

Jonathan watched the scene as it played out in what seemed like slow motion – Sarah tumbled backwards and the box flew out of her hands, over the back of the lifeboat and into the water.

"Holy shit, Sarah!" yelled Kevin, an instant before he got up and jumped into the water after it. Unfortunately, he had forgotten they were all still tied together.

Jonathan felt the tug on the rope first. A burst of air and a loud painful groan flew out of his mouth as he was dragged towards the edge of the lifeboat.

With the combined weight of Kevin in the water and Jonathan connected to him on the same side, the entire boat started leaning sideways and began taking on water.

"Jonathan!! Kevin!! Oh my god, get back in the boat!"

Sarah threw herself to the opposite side, trying to counterbalance the weight.

Candi reached over and tried to help Kevin get back into the boat. He was finding it difficult with his swollen hand and only one eye to work with. Being fully clothed in wet canvas shorts and cotton made his body a lot heavier than normal.

Kevin was finally able to drag himself back into the boat with Candi's and Jonathan's help. He didn't have the radio in his hand. It was made of metal and had sunk too fast.

Everyone just sat there for a minute, Kevin trying to get his breath and Jonathan wrestling with the knot in the rope around his waist. He didn't want to get dragged overboard like almost just happened. He decided that the idea they'd had of everyone drowning together earlier was a stupid one.

Sarah sniffed and looked down at her nails, saying nothing.

Kevin looked at his sister, a frustrated look on his face.

Sarah looked up and saw her brother staring at her. "What? I'm sorry, okay? Sheez, how was I supposed to know Jonathan was going to let the thing go like that?" She looked over and shot Jonathan a dirty look.

"Wha ... ? Me ... ? You're blaming this on *me?* You're nuts, you know that?" He shook his head in disgust, mumbling under his breath. He kept himself busy packing their supplies evenly into the four backpacks, putting items like the flares and flashlight in his and Kevin's packs. Sarah had already proven she couldn't be trusted to be responsible; he wasn't about to have her holding their life-saving supplies.

"Come on, guys, let's not fight. We're going to be out here for at least part of today, so we should make the best of it."

"I'm sorry to break this to you, Candi, but I think we're going to be out here a lot longer than just today," said Jonathan bitterly, without looking up.

Candi started feeling sick to her stomach again. "Why do you say that?"

"Because that storm blew us really, really far away. I'm no expert at navigation or anything, but if I were searching for the passengers from the ship, I probably would limit my search to the area *near the ship*. They might not even know about those rogue waves that kept throwing us farther and farther away from the standard search grid area."

"What is a rogue wave, anyway?" asked Kevin.

"Rogue waves are really large and spontaneous ocean surface waves that occur far out at sea; a threat even to cruise ships, let alone little lifeboats like we're on. Maybe that's what caused the problems with our ship, I'm not sure. Technically, rogue waves are waves whose height is more than twice the significant wave height, which is the mean of the largest third of waves in a wave record."

"Holy, blah, blah, Jonathan, what are you actually saying?" asked a frustrated Sarah.

"Therefore," Jonathan continued, not even glancing at Sarah, "rogue waves are, in a nutshell, surprisingly large waves for a given area of the ocean."

"So, you're talking about a tsunami, then?" said Kevin.

"No, rogue waves are not tsunamis. Tsunamis are triggered by earthquakes that happen out at sea, which cause a wave to travel at high speeds and build up strength as it approaches a shoreline.

Rogue waves, on the other hand, occur in deep water or where a number of physical factors such as strong winds and fast currents converge, but not earthquakes. Some think a rogue wave is a bunch of smaller waves that join together to make one, large wave; and based on what I was feeling last night, I'd agree with them. The biggest rogue wave ever measured was something like ninety feet high."

"Which is ... " said Kevin, trailing off as if he were trying to calculate the size of a wave like that.

"About as big as the one that threw our boat last night – the height of a ten story building."

"You act like you're not really sure, though," said Candi.

"The problem with rogue waves is that they're rare. Hardly anyone has ever seen one. They have almost never been measured. So the fact that last night there wasn't just one, but several, is some sort of crazy anomaly that no one could have predicted or planned for. It's entirely possible that we're the only ones who even knew they were there!"

Sarah started putting it all together. "So that means that if someone comes to look for us, they're probably not going to look out this far, and if they don't find us near the ship, they'll probably assume we drowned."

"Yes," answered Jonathan, sighing deeply and sadly. "That is exactly what I'm trying to say."

Everyone on the boat went quiet. The only sound they could hear was the gentle lapping of water against the sides of the boat and the sea breeze blowing against their dry, chapped faces. They sat there, absorbing the news that they were probably completely doomed. Each of them was doing the calculation in their heads. Enough water for a couple of days. Food for a couple of days. And an endless expanse of salt water and burning hot sun.

"Hey, I don't want to add more gloom to our doom," said Sarah, "but shouldn't we do something about this sun? I'm starting to bake. I may be dying soon, but I don't want to go down prematurely wrinkled."

Candi nodded her head. "Yes, I agree, who has the sunscreen?"

"It's in this bag." Jonathan handed it to his sister. "I think we should all wear the backpacks, so nothing goes flying overboard again." He looked pointedly at Sarah, who refused to meet his eyes.

"Should we worry about rogue waves anymore, do you think?" asked Kevin.

"Who knows? I guess we should be ready for anything."

"Um, what about sharks, should we worry about them?" asked Candi, nervously.

Kevin shook his head. "I doubt that. I mean, we're out here in the middle of nowhere. I think sharks stay mostly near the shallower waters, don't they?"

Candi pointed over Kevin's shoulder and said, "Well, maybe you can tell me what that thing is right over there, then."

Jonathan followed Kevin's gaze out to where Candi had pointed.

"Holy shit!" yelled Kevin. "That's a fucking shark! Shit, there's more than one!" He backed slowly away from the edge of the boat, being careful not to rock it.

All of them stared fearfully at the group of fins that were slowly making their way over to the boat. Jonathan, Sarah, and Candi moved very carefully to join Kevin in the center of the boat, until they were all sitting nearly on top of each other.

There were at least five sharks now, slowly circling the boat and swimming under it. They felt one of them gently bump the side. One of the girls screamed.

"Jonathan, what do you think about getting out the oars and whacking one of them on the nose?" asked Kevin.

"I think that's an excellent idea. I saw a shark documentary that said that's their most sensitive spot."

"I think I saw the same one. Hand me an oar."

Jonathan struggled to release one from the oarlock on the inside of the boat. Once he had it freed, he carefully handed it over to Kevin.

"Be careful with that, we only have two."

"Roger that. Okay everyone, get ready."

Kevin scooted over to the side of the boat and peered over the edge. He was looking down into the deep blue water when Candi screamed, "There's one coming from your right ... your RIGHT!"

Kevin looked to his right and had less than a second to prepare. This shark was a little more curious than the others and actually opened its mouth as it came nearer, as if it wanted a taste of the fiberglass.

Kevin raised the oar up high and slammed it down on the nose of the shark as hard as he possibly could.

The force of the downward movement threw him off balance. He pitched forward and tried to grab the edge of the boat, but it was with his sore hand that wasn't working like it normally did.

The pain caused his arm to buckle under him, sending the top of his body into the water, while the rest of his body stayed mostly in the boat.

Everyone including Jonathan screamed and grabbed onto Kevin's bottom half, pulling on him for all they were worth. Critical seconds went by when he was submerged.

All Jonathan could think about was the shark Kevin had just bonked on the nose who was probably royally pissed off right now.

Kevin finally came up out of the water, sputtering, and Candi, for one, looked immensely relieved to see he still had his face and head attached.

"Watch out!" yelled Jonathan, who noticed another shark coming over to investigate.

Kevin rolled over and landed on his back in the bottom of the boat. He was breathing heavily, the pulse in his neck visibly beating rapidly. Other than his puffy eye, he seemed to be okay, though.

"Well, that didn't go as well as I'd planned," said Kevin after catching his breath.

Sarah and Candi still hadn't let his legs go.

Jonathan watched as the fins seemed to be retreating. "Well, I think you did something, because they're leaving now."

Sarah pointed to the other side of the boat. "Not so fast, Jonathan. Here come some more."

Kevin lifted his head off the floor of the boat so he could see what the others were looking at. "Holy shit, please don't tell me I have to body slam another shark." He closed his eyes as if trying to block out the recent memory of almost becoming shark food.

"Ummm, I don't think so!" said Candi in a cheery voice.

Sarah looked at her in horror. "Oh crap, Sugar Lump has lost it. She's happy to see a group of about ten sharks coming to eat us for lunch."

"They're not sharks! Look!" She pointed gleefully out to the group of animals in the water – animals that were swimming towards them and occasionally blowing water spouts out of the top of their heads.

Sarah clapped her hands together in glee before she realized what she was doing and stopped. "They're dolphins!"

Jonathan's face broke out in a smile. "Cool, dolphins. Dolphins hate sharks if they have babies around. Look! That one is a baby for sure."

"Really?" Sarah asked, turning to him, flashing him a million-watt smile. Then she looked at a mini-dolphin that came right up to the side of the boat. "Oh, he's so sweet!"

Jonathan couldn't help but smile back. "Yep. Sharks don't want to mess with dolphin families that have babies in them. Dolphins have been known to head butt and tail thrash sharks to death to protect their young. That's probably why the sharks took off."

"You mean it wasn't my mad skills with the oar?" asked Kevin in mock offense.

"Oh, I'm sure that had something to do with it," Jonathan assured him.

"My god, there have to be about thirty of them," said Candi, fascinated, her voice full of awe. "I've never seen a real, live dolphin in the ocean. This is totally different than the aquarium."

The dolphins stayed with them for nearly an hour, swimming around and occasionally even leaping out of the water. For some reason it made them feel better – infinitely more so than being surrounded by sharks.

After the dolphins left, they decided to save the sunscreen and hide under the shade of the sheet from the cruise ship bed. They thought about using the tarp, but it was too heavy and unwieldy, making it difficult and hot to stay sheltered. They each held a corner of the sheet over the back of their shoulders and sat across from each other. Their heads propped up each corner, creating a canopy effect.

"Yuck. I feel positively disgusting – like I have a coating of salt covering every square inch of my body," said Sarah.

No one answered. They were all feeling the same way.

Jonathan and Candi handed out rations. Each of them was allowed to drink only two more ounces of water and have one of the meals in the foil packets.

"Well, I guess I've been saying for a while that I need to go on a diet." Candi laughed half-heartedly. "I guess I should be careful what I wish for next time."

"What are you talking about? You don't need to lose weight," said Kevin, as he scooped out bits of what might have been beef from his foil packet.

"Kevin's right, Candi, you don't," chimed in Sarah.

"Thanks, guys, that's nice to say. I guess I've always thought of myself as kind of baby-fat fat."

"Nope," said Kevin matter-of-factly, "you're curvy, not fat." Then he realized what he was saying and shut up, looking out around the sheet at the sea.

"Uh-oh guys, you'd better take a look at this." They all pulled the sheet down, looking out to where he was pointing. "There's a storm coming."

"Oh, no, not again," moaned Candi.

"What's next?" said Sarah, instantly angry. "Haven't we been through enough yet?"

"Okay, we have to get prepared. It could be just like last night with the waves and all. I think we should tie the tarp down as tight as we can and try to keep it on. That way we don't have to bail so much water out of the bottom," said Jonathan.

"Um, just one more little thing," said Candi shyly. "I, um,

kinda hafta go pee."

"Oh, thank god you said something, so do I," said Sarah.

Kevin got a big grin on his face. Jonathan screwed up his eyebrows, obviously trying to figure out the mechanics of an on-board toilet for the girls.

"Just squat over the edge," suggested Kevin, smirking.

"Yeah, right, like I want a shark jumping up and biting my hoo-ha off while I'm taking a piss. I don't think so," said Sarah.

"Here, do what you can to squat over this." Jonathan handed Candi the plastic lid that used to be over the radio that was now at the bottom of the ocean.

Candi rolled her eyes in disgust. "Fine. I'm probably going to pee all over my ankles, but I'm with Sarah on this one. I don't want a shark anywhere near my privates."

Sarah and Candi took turns using the plastic bin, managing to only pee on themselves a little bit. They threw the pee overboard and rinsed the bin out for their next on-board toilet adventure.

"Yuck, I smell pee, and it's *on* me. This is so *sick!*" Sarah was disgusted. She grabbed some seawater and splashed it over her ankles.

"I choose to remind myself that things could be worse. Pee on my ankles is better than doggy paddling without a boat under me."

"Well, when you put it that way," said Sarah, rolling her eyes.

The business of peeing done, they all finished up their rations and got to work tying down the tarp as best they could, leaving two opposite corners unsnapped and lifted to let in air. It was already getting stiflingly hot underneath.

They agreed to be tied to each other again and to the metal oar loops on the boat. After seeing a rogue wave up close, they decided that being attached to an unsinkable lifeboat was their best bet for survival if the boat capsized.

They each strapped on a backpack and used the extra shoulder strap lengths to tie them around their waists too. They locked down the boat hatches with all the precious equipment inside. They finished off another foil packet of food each and took two more ounces of water apiece before stowing the bottles of water away in their backpacks.

Then they waited. They passed the time avoiding all talk of their parents' possible fates, instead trading easy, lighthearted stories about school and different teachers. They were in unanimous agreement about Mr. Feldman, their biology teacher – the guy had a very unhealthy attachment to his class pets. They all agreed that he probably slept with his pet snake over the vacations. *Ew.*

They discovered each of their favorite colors and favorite foods. Jonathan and Kevin had a debate about which restaurant in town had the best burger. Candi sided with Jonathan, insisting it was the Brass Ring Pub because their burgers were the biggest and juiciest. Sarah said she didn't like burgers so she wasn't a good judge, but that the Brass Ring also had a killer veggie burger. Kevin and Jonathan agreed – there was no such thing as a killer veggie burger and that 'veggie' and 'burger' should never be used in the same sentence.

As the winds picked up and the boat started rocking, they talked about what they'd do if they won the lottery, to keep their minds off the motion sickness they were all starting to feel. Everyone laughed when Sarah said she'd buy a damn motor and some gas for the lifeboat. Still, none of them broached the subject of their parents. They were nearly going crazy worrying about their own survival; thinking of their parents on the sinking cruise ship was too much to handle right now.

When the storm finally came, it hit hard – and poured what seemed like hundreds of gallons of water on top of their tarp. They became quiet, since it was nearly impossible to hear each other over the roar of the storm, anyway. They tried to find comfortable spots where they could lay down in the bottom of the boat, next to each other. Each of them found the hand of another, holding on in shared desperation. None of them had the time or inclination to consider the fact that they were cuddling and holding hands; they were just worried about whether they would survive the night. They were about as far from the hallways of high school as they could possibly be, physically and mentally.

The motion of the boat constantly being tossed around and the roar of the storm and rain eventually became too much to bear, and each of them gave in to the exhausted sleep they could no longer avoid.

Land Ho

THE FLIES WERE BUZZING IN Jonathan's ear. He kept lifting his hand up to brush them away. He was hot and sticky and his lips tasted salty. They were beginning to crack and bleed. He felt the stinging as the salt entered the broken skin. It was still dark and incredibly humid – and these flies were making him crazy.

Flies?

His mind started to compute what his body was experiencing. *How can there be flies out in the middle of the ocean? Unless ...* He immediately sat up. His head hit the tarp that was stretched across the top of the boat, yanking out some pieces of his hair with the friction.

"Ouch. Hey! Wake up, guys, I think we might be near land!"

Everyone started moving around, but it was dark and hard to see. Bits of sunlight penetrated cracks around the edge of the tarp, but it wasn't enough to see clearly. Several inches of water had settled in the bottom of the boat, so they were all soaked through, the skin of their hands and feet wrinkled deeply like salted prunes. The heat that was coming from outside the boat had turned the inside into a sauna – a hot, salty, watery sauna.

Jonathan started to feel like he was suffocating.

A mad scramble started, everyone trying to get some fresh air at once.

"Wait, stop! Try not to push up on the tarp. I think it has rainwater on it that we could drink," said Jonathan.

"Holy crap, I need some air," whined Sarah.

"Just wait a second, I'm working on it," said Jonathan. He turned to start unfastening the snaps and straps behind him. "Candi, help me get this tarp off on the edges. Try to save any water that's up there though."

He and Candi carefully crawled around the edges of the tarp, releasing it from its fastenings, bending the tarp towards its center. They folded up the edges trying to capture whatever water was on top, channeling it into the middle. They took a couple of minutes to add that water to the water bottles they had emptied earlier while handing out water rations.

"This water may have a little ocean water in it, but maybe not. We might as well save it now and check it later," explained Jonathan as he screwed the cap on the last bottle.

The first thing they noticed was the sun. It was out as if it had never left – as if the storm that had tossed them around like a cork on the sea for eight hours had never come; but the liters of water that had been centered on the tarp told a different story.

Then they noticed the cloud of flies that was buzzing around their heads. They were smaller than regular flies and bit their exposed skin. The bites felt a little like mosquitos, only sharper.

"Ouch! Those bugs are annoying!" said Candi, slapping her arm. "I can barely see them, they're so tiny."

"Mother fu... " shouted Sarah, as she swatted her legs with both hands.

Kevin let out a low moan. "Where are we?" he asked weakly.

Jonathan was surprised to hear him sounding so frail and looked down at him for the first time since they had the tarp opened up.

"Oh crap, Kevin, look at your hand."

The split on the knuckles from hitting Jack's nose was bright red and swollen, with puffy white-looking skin around the edges. His eye didn't look much better. It was swollen and bluish-greenish in color.

"It's infected," said Jonathan. He looked at Candi, and noticed fear in her eyes.

"What does that mean? I mean, what should we do?" she asked.

Sarah sat up and rubbed her eyes, and before she stopped to think said, "We need to get him some antibiotics."

Candi looked at her with an exasperated expression, silently scolding her.

Sarah had the grace to look chagrined. "Sorry. What I meant to say is that we need to clean it really good and do what we can to get the infection out." She nodded her head to add some affirmation to her words.

"Oh, shit, I don't feel so good," moaned Kevin, holding his stomach. He sat up and vomited over the edge of the boat.

He heaved over and over again, making Jonathan only slightly worried that Kevin's guts were going to come out and float away. He'd never seen anyone so violently ill.

Candi leaned forward and patted him on the back, clearly at a loss.

"Kevin, what's going on?" asked Jonathan. This wasn't normal for a hand wound as far as he knew.

"I don't know," gasped Kevin. "I think I ate something bad on the ship at dinner." He gulped uncomfortably. "Did anyone else eat those ... god, I don't even want to say the words ... raw oysters?"

Everyone looked at each other, shaking their heads. Jonathan answered for all of them. "Nope."

Kevin wiped his mouth off with his hand and dipped it into the water. Then he fell back into the boat, landing on his back, moaning. "Fuck me. I've been poisoned."

Candi's eyes bulged out of her head. This was not good.

"Kevin, you need to drink some water. You're going to get dehydrated quickly if you do have food poisoning and keep vomiting like that." Jonathan turned his attention to Candi. "Candi, get the water bottle and get at least four ounces of water in him over the next thirty minutes."

Candi nodded her head, moving to follow his instructions.

Sarah just sat there numbly, looking worried, nodding her head at nothing in particular. Then she stopped nodding and started squinting at Candi, examining her, as if seeing her for the first time.

"What?" said Candi.

"What do you mean 'what'?"

"I mean, why are you staring at me?"

Sarah shrugged. "No reason. I was just thinking that you look like total crap."

Candi got immediately offended. "Well, thank you very much, Miss Thinks She's Perfect, and may I say that you don't look so hot yourself!"

Sarah reached up to touch her chapped and salty lips. Her fingers glided over the skin of her face, which pulled tight every time her mouth moved. It had a layer of salt coating it that Jonathan knew from his own face, felt like a fine, dry crust. She shrugged. "I probably do look less than my best, but at least my hair doesn't look like there's a family of rats living in it."

Candi laughed bitterly. "I wouldn't be so sure about that, if I were you."

Sarah frowned and then reached up to touch her hair. She pulled some of it forward and stared at it, obviously surprised to see that a light salty coating had come to rest all over it, making it go from blond to nearly gray. She reached up with both hands to feel her entire head of hair. "Oh. My. God. It feels like teased cotton candy. What the hell ... ?"

Jonathan wasn't paying any mind to what they were saying. Something he saw off in the distance was grabbing his attention.

"I think I see land!" yelled Jonathan, suddenly.

"What?! Where?" said Candi, twisting around as far as she could, to see where Jonathan was looking.

"There!" answered Jonathan, pointing off in the distance. "It has to be. Otherwise there wouldn't be flies."

"I thought it was seagulls that flew around land," said Sarah sarcastically.

"Yeah, but flies too," said Jonathan, ignoring her attitude.

Kevin sat up with obvious effort.

"Land. Cool." He laid back down and closed his eyes.

Jonathan began rustling through one of the boat's storage bins behind him.

"What are you looking for?" asked Candi.

"I think we have my small telescope here, don't we?"

"I don't think you need one – it's definitely land, I can see it from here. We're getting closer."

Sure enough, the current seemed to be driving them towards the land at a rapid pace.

"Sweet," said Jonathan, a smile breaking out across his face as he confirmed Candi's assessment. "I guess we can just sit here then and wait until we wash up on the shore."

"What shore is it, though?" asked Sarah, trepidation in her voice. "I mean, where in the hell are we?"

"I have absolutely no idea," said Jonathan, "but we're about to find out. Do you have any idea how lucky we are right now? To have run into an island like this?" He couldn't stop himself grinning from ear to ear.

"Are there any, like, wild cannibal tribes out here that eat people and shrink heads and stuff like that?"

Jonathan frowned at her. "Don't be silly. We're in the Caribbean. You'd have more trouble with pirates and drug runners than cannibals out here."

"Ha! Pirates! That's a good one," said Sarah, looking out at the island with a smile. "Johnny Depp can come after my treasure any day of the week. I'll barely even put up a fight, I promise."

Jonathan broke into her daydream with his serious response. "I'm not joking. There are modern day pirates out here that hijack and steal from unwary boaters and do all kinds of other things that we probably don't want to know about."

Sarah was instantly pissed again. "Are you serious? Because that's just great, Jonathan. Great. *Pirates!* And I thought sharks were our biggest problem."

"Sharks are definitely a problem; but there are also poisonous jelly fish, barracudas, venomous snakes ... "

Sarah's face grew more and more alarmed with every word that came out of Jonathan's mouth.

"Okay, Jonathan! That's enough, we get it now!" said Candi.

"Did you hear that, Kevin? We're getting out of the frying pan and heading right into the fire," said Sarah, bitterness lacing her voice.

"Mmmph, fire ... " was all they heard in reply. Then Kevin started singing, very out of tune, " 'Come on baby light my fiiiirrre, try to set the night on fiiirrre ... ' " He petered out at the end and went quiet again.

"Kevin?" asked Candi, tentatively. He sounded so out of it.

Jonathan reached over and put his hand on Kevin's forehead. "He has a fever. I don't know if it's that hand or the food or what, but he's burning up. Seems kind of soon after the injury to have an infection that bad. We need to get him to that land over there and cleaned up and hydrated. Let's put the tarp up over his part of the boat to give him some shade. Sarah, you see if you can get him to drink some more water."

Candi began securing the tarp over Kevin to give him some shade.

Sarah wasn't registering Jonathan's orders. "Are my eyes fooling me, or are we moving *away* from the land now?" asked Sarah.

Jonathan looked up at the horizon and saw that she was not mistaken. "Oh crap, the current is moving us parallel to the shore. If this keeps up, we're going to miss the shore completely!"

He got up and shook off his backpack. "Come on, we have to start rowing!" There was no mistaking the panic in his voice.

The girls scrambled to help him lock the oars in place and put them out over the water. "I'll get this one; you two get the other and row together," ordered Jonathan.

This was one of those live or die moments. They were going to have to row their asses off and not waste any time arguing.

They got the oars locked in quickly and sat in position, side by side, preparing to pull back on it.

"Go!" yelled Jonathan, heaving back on his oar.

The girls rowed in tandem with him, meeting him stroke for stroke. Jonathan was able to take quick looks back every minute or so to check their progress.

"I'm going to need ... some serious paraffin treatments ... after this," grunted out Sarah.

"It's working! Keep it up! Don't stop!" Jonathan gasped out. They had cut the distance in half with twenty minutes of steady rowing. They could have been closer but they were forced to row diagonally to their goal to fight the push of the current. All of them were wishing Kevin were in shape so he could help, since it would undoubtedly have been a much easier chore with his strong back and arms; but he was out of commission for sure.

Kevin tried to sit up, but his head bumped up against the tarp that Candi had secured over him. "Lemme help, guys, you can't do it all by yourselves."

"Just save your strength, Kevin, you have a fever."

"Don't be silly, I don' hava feeve ... " The next thing they heard was Kevin slumping back down into the bottom of the boat.

"That's not good. We have to get him to land, guys, row harder!"

Sarah and Candi put their backs into it. Candi moved her hands to a different spot on the oar, and said, "Try to switch your hand position so you don't pop any blisters!"

Jonathan followed her orders. All they needed was more infections. He wasn't convinced this land they were seeing was inhabited. All he had seen was green, green and more green when he glanced back over his shoulder at the shoreline.

Finally, after thirty more minutes of rowing, they were within forty yards of the shore. Jonathan told them to stop and locked the oars in place. Sweat was pouring off his body and running into his eyes, stinging them and making them burn.

"Untie the rope, quick."

The girls did as he asked without question.

He jumped into the water, yelling to the girls, "Tie the rope to the front of the boat and hand me the other end with a loop in it!"

Candi rushed to do what he ordered. She threw the loop out to him so he could start pulling the boat in.

Sarah was staring out to sea with a look of heavy concentration on her face. Jonathan wrestled with the loop trying to get it around his body as Candi looked at her and asked what she was doing.

"Watching for sharks."

"Oh, good."

"Jonathan, if I see a shark, I'll yell 'Shark!' and then Candi will haul you back into the boat by the rope."

"Fine!" he yelled, turning to swim for shore.

*****

Candi smiled, a little bit relieved to have a plan. "Good idea, Sarah. Okay. Cool." She felt a tug as Jonathan began dragging the boat behind him.

Candi kept an anxious eye on him, while simultaneously watching the shore come closer and scanning the water's surface for the gray triangles of death. As her eyes passed over her brother's swimming form, she wondered how he could possibly have the energy to do this. He'd had hardly any water or food, and was as exhausted as she was. She decided the first thing she was going to do when they reached shore was give him the biggest hug of her life.

"Shark!!" yelled Sarah from the back of the boat.

The fear raced up into Candi's throat and threatened to choke her. "No!" she gasped, as she leaned over to take the rope that was connected to her brother.

"Yes, look!" yelled Sarah, pointing off to the side of the boat.

Candi's hand was on the rope, ready to use the adrenaline coursing through her veins to haul her brother back into the boat like Superwoman.

She hesitated a moment. She looked to where Sarah was pointing. "Wait, that's not a shark ... " She peered through squinted eyes at the movement of the gray body under the water.

"It's another dolphin!"

She had noticed it swimming in an up and down motion and not the side-to-side, zigzag motion of the sharks from the day before; plus the fin was rounder or more curved. She took a split second to silently thank Mother Nature for including this telltale difference so right now she didn't have to be overwhelmed with visions of her brother being eaten while she tried to rescue him using strength she didn't have any more.

The dolphin chose that moment to leap out of the water and flash them a trademark dolphin grin.

Sarah let out a whoop and shot her fist in the air. "Yes! That is a friggin' DOLPHIN, ladies and gentlemen!" She turned and shot Candi a huge grin and put her hand up for a high-five.

Candi smiled and slapped her palm. Things were looking up. She checked on Jonathan and saw that he was no longer swimming, but was standing in the water on some sort of sand bar, walking the boat closer to shore. The shallow spot went pretty far out into the water that was now a beautiful bluish green and clear enough to see all the way to the bottom. Candi looked back to see the dolphin again, but it had disappeared.

Now that the shore was so close, the girls could see it in detail for the first time. There was a vast expanse of white sand that ringed what looked like an island about the size of two football fields. The beach was about fifteen yards wide, met at its far edge by a line of palms and other kinds of trees with medium sized, roundish leaves. They were growing together so closely and were so thick with foliage, it was impossible to see too far into them. The left side of the island, which was probably the south side, if Candi's navigation wasn't completely off, had some rocks she could see above the treetops. She saw no signs of houses or hotels or anything she was used to seeing on beaches.

Candi felt a little bit sick to her stomach. She looked down at Kevin, wondering how they were going to help him if there wasn't anyone there with medicine. He was sleeping; she could see his chest rising and falling as he breathed. His lips were crusty and cracked with dried blood on them. His face was coated in fine, white salt. She could see the skin underneath was burned pretty badly from the sun. There were little tiny pieces of shell and sand all through his hair, and she could see it in one of his ears too. It must have been churned up by the terrible storms and put on their bodies with all the sea spray. She felt her own face to see if she felt the same things there. Sure enough. She tried to brush it all away, but it hurt the sunburn that she just realized was also there.

A small piece of her was jealous of Kevin's unconsciousness. She wished she could be sleeping through this day like he was and then be able to wake up when it was all over.

But that was stupid – she knew Kevin felt terrible and was in very real danger without medicine or enough water. *Be careful what you wish for. Look where it's gotten you so far. You wanted to be better acquainted with Sarah and Kevin Peterson; you dreamed of someday having some alone time with Kevin. Well, here you go.* That was a very sobering thought. Wishing was dangerous business.

*****

"Man, am I glad to get back to civilization. I'm going to go have the longest, most relaxing shower I've ever had in my entire life," exclaimed Sarah.

"Uh, Sarah ... "

"Shush!" yelled Sarah, holding up a finger at Candi, not bothering to open her eyes. "Don't mess with the fantasy, okay, Sugar Lump? I'm five seconds away from a cool cucumber facial and a hot oil massage given to me by a man-boy named Juan."

"Okaaaayyy ... "

Sarah heard Candi jump in the water and sighed, opening her eyes. She watched as Candi walked in slow motion through the small waves until she reached Jonathan, grabbing the rope that was still around his chest.

"Let me take it now; you can rest. I think you're overdoing it, Jonathan."

Sarah strained her eyes to see Jonathan's face, wondering at the concern she heard in Candi's voice.

Jonathan didn't answer. He just took the rope off and continued trudging through the water until he reached the shore. Once there, he dropped down in exhaustion, his face landing sideways in the sand.

"Jonathan!" yelled Candi. She couldn't move fast enough to get to him because she was still hauling the boat.

Sarah didn't think – she just jumped into the water and started swimming, cutting a clean line through the surface, swimming freestyle towards the shore.

As soon as she reached the shallow water, Sarah stood up and ran over to Jonathan, dropping down beside him and turning him over.

"Hey! Are you okay? *Jonathan!* Say something!"

Jonathan squinted his eyes, trying to open them, the color slowly returning to his face.

"What do you want me to say?" he asked innocently.

"Oooh, you ... *idiot!*" said Sarah, flinging sand on him as she stood up quickly and moved away from him.

Sarah saw that Candi was nearly to the dry sand now. She was trying to figure out how they were going to get Kevin out of the boat so they could start taking care of him. They weren't going to be able to pull it up very far because it was so heavy.

"Here, let me help." Jonathan had stood up again and got behind the boat where Sarah had already gone, and began pushing along with her.

The boat made contact with the sand and stopped abruptly. They heard Kevin groan as his body was jerked to the side.

"Errrh! I can't. Push. This. Thing. Any. Farther!" grunted Sarah.

"Just do your best ... a couple more inches," said Jonathan, putting his shoulder against the back of the boat and pushing with all his might.

They got two more inches of movement before the boat dug itself into the sand. It wasn't going any farther today, they decided.

Jonathan and Sarah dragged themselves around the side of the boat to stand on the beach next to Candi.

"How are we going to get him out of the boat?" asked Candi, concern marring her features.

"First thing we have to do is prepare a place for him to be

taken to." Jonathan looked at Sarah. "Can you manage that?"

"Of course I can," responded Sarah indignantly. "What do you want me to do?"

"Just make some sort of shelter up there in the trees. Use the tarp and the sheet – put the sheet on the ground and the tarp in the tree as a canopy of some sort. We need to protect him and us from the sun as best we can." He looked up and squinted at the sky.

Sarah could feel her face burning. She looked at Candi and Jonathan and saw that they had pretty bad sunburns too. All she could think about was the skin cancer that was probably being created on her face as she baked under the sun.

He turned to Candi. "Let's go see if we can wake him up enough to get him out of the boat."

Sarah climbed into the boat, taking the sheet from the puddle in the bottom and the tarp from above Kevin's head. She headed up to the tree line with the two items to begin making their shelter.

*****

After Sarah was gone, Candi and Jonathan got back into the boat, studying the situation. Jonathan was the first to speak.

"Wake him and try to get him to sit up. When he does, I'll try to get him on his feet. Watch his hand."

Candi bent down over Kevin's face. "Kevin. Wake up. Kevin, we need you to wake up." She started shaking his shoulder as she continued. "Keeeevin, wake uuuuup. We're home! Look, Kevin, we're home! Time to get up!"

"Mmmph, home. Good. Tired."

Candi looked up at Jonathan. "He isn't budging."

Jonathan sighed, making his decision.

"I'm sorry to have to do this to you, Kevin, but it's the only way."

He reached down and squeezed Kevin's sore hand.

"HOLY FFFFFRIG WHAT THE HELL ARE YOU DOING? ... I'M GONNA KILL YOU!"

Kevin sat bolt upright, cradling his hand, his eyes ablaze with pain and fury.

"Grab him!" yelled Jonathan.

Brother and sister each grabbed him under an arm and lifted with all their might. Kevin's body didn't budge.

"What the hell are you doing? Getting rid of the dead weight?" asked Kevin indignantly, thinking he was being offed by the Buckley kids.

"We're trying to get you out of the boat!" yelled Jonathan, frustrated that he had no upper body strength.

"I can't swim like this ... I'll drown!" yelled Kevin.

"Kevin, we're on an island right now. Look." Candi gestured towards the shore.

Kevin sat up straighter, looking out over the bow of the boat. "Hey. We're not moving anymore. And there's trees. Lots of 'em. Holy shit, Jon, you did it, man!" A beaming smile broke out over his face, now that he realized he wasn't being fed to the sharks. He looked over at Jonathan. "Way to go, dude. You're the man. Help me get out of this shitty boat, will ya?"

"Yeah, like I haven't been trying to do that for the past five minutes," he said wryly, as he bent over to grab Kevin under his arm again.

With Kevin helping, they were able to get him over to the side of the boat. After a few seconds of calculating and debating the best way to get him onto the shore, Kevin managed to roll himself over the side to land on the sand below. He yelped in pain, but it seemed to wake him up a bit and made it easier to get him stumbling up the sand to the tree line.

When the three arrived at Sarah's camp, they were pleasantly surprised to see that she had been very busy setting up a temporary shelter for them. "Wow, this is nice," said Jonathan.

The sheet was laid out over the sand and the tarp had been tied at three corners to nearby trees with some sort of vine. Sarah was nowhere to be found.

Candi and Jonathan got Kevin settled on the middle of the sheet, then worked on carrying the supplies out of the boat and over to their shelter.

"We might as well bring it all over here for now, just in case there's another storm and our boat gets pulled away."

"I hope that doesn't happen. We want to keep the boat, right?" asked Candi.

"Of course, but I'd rather keep our supplies close. Those rogue waves scared me." Jonathan looked at the boat stuck in the sand. "Honestly, though, I don't know that we're going to get that boat moved at all. I'm afraid we're going to have to leave it there."

Candi nodded in agreement. "Yeah, me too. It's already sunk into the sand a little bit, even after just thirty minutes."

Four trips later they had everything around the blanket. Candi started unpacking the first aid kit, laying out the items she thought they could use for Kevin.

"There's antiseptic here, and some gauze and tape. Also, I think this is antibiotic ointment." She held up a small, foil packet.

"That's good. First, though, we need to scrub the cut and clean it out – get all that pus and stuff out of there."

Candi went a little green. "Ew, are you sure?"

"Yes. Can you do it, or should I?"

"I think you'd better do it."

"Okay, fine." Jonathan moved so he was next to Kevin's hand. "Kevin!" he yelled.

"Dude, you don't have to shout, I'm lying right here."

"Oh, sorry, I thought you were sleeping. I'm going to clean your hand now. It's probably going to hurt a lot. Don't hit me."

Kevin opened his one good one eye. "Don't worry, I can take it. I play rugby."

Jonathan took Kevin's hand and pulled it towards him, muttering, "Playing rugby is not the same as having surgery without anesthetic."

He took a deep breath and began.

His plan was to use the gauze and antiseptic to wipe off the goop that had hardened on top, but as soon as he started, he noticed his heart rate starting to climb. Then several droplets of sweat broke out on his upper lip. He started feeling dizzy and queasy ...

"What the ... ?"

Jonathan sat up, looking around in confusion. Sarah was sitting nearby, smirking at him, and Candi was packing up the first aid kit, casting glances his way.

"What's going on? What happened?" He was completely bewildered.

"You passed out, that's what happened," laughed Sarah. "Your little sister had to clean up after you and take care of our patient without your help."

Jonathan looked over at his sister for confirmation, then looked at Kevin's hand. Sure enough, it was neatly bandaged with gauze and tape.

Jonathan looked sheepish. "Sorry, Candi. It must have been a vasovagal response."

"Don't worry about it. I'm sure that's what it was – the vasowhatever thingy. I took care of it, and I think I did a pretty good job, if I do say so myself." She smiled, proud that she hadn't passed out or puked when that gooey pus had come out of Kevin's poor hand.

"Yeah, Candi's like Florence Nightingale over there. I vote she's in charge of the island hospital from now on."

Candi looked up from her packing. "And I vote Sarah's in charge of shelter arrangement on this island from now on." She smiled over at the girl who had single-handedly made a pretty nice field hospital for her to operate in.

Sarah smiled back. "I don't mean to brag, but I also managed to find these for us." She pulled out a bunch of bananas from behind her back.

"Holy crap, bananas!" exclaimed Candi.

"Yep!" said Sarah, as she ripped one from the bunch and started peeling it. "There are trees full of 'em on this island." She took a bite of it and continued, "They're kinda little, but they taste fine. I also saw some coconuts, but they were up too high to get. Plus I have no idea how to open one."

Jonathan sat up slowly, holding his spinning head gingerly. "I think we could figure out how to open them. I'm glad to know they're here, because we only have a little bit of water. Until we find other fresh water, we could survive on coconut water."

"Isn't it called coconut milk?" asked Candi.

"No, not really. What we call coconut milk that people make daiquiris out of is actually the juice squeezed from the white meat of the coconut, not the liquid that swishes around inside the round nut."

Sarah looked at him with exasperation on her face, like she

couldn't figure him out. "How do you know all this stuff? I mean, the difference between coconut water and coconut milk? How esoteric can you be?"

Jonathan shrugged his shoulders. "I don't know. Discovery Channel, National Geographic, Bill Nye the Science Guy. A variety of sources, really."

"Yeah, but, how do you *remember* all of it?

"I don't know. I just do."

Candi nodded her head. "He's like an elephant. He never forgets anything. He's still mad about a lollipop I stole from him when I was three."

Sarah rolled her eyes. "How annoying."

"Well, people shouldn't steal other people's candy. That's just not right. Anyone would remember that."

Candi laughed at him and reached over to play-slap him on the arm. "Sorry, Jonathan. I'll buy you a new one when we get home."

The group fell silent as they thought about the idea of going home and being able to just walk into a store and buy a lollipop. It seemed so simple, purchasing candy. Now, it was something they couldn't do and maybe would never be able to do again. It was a sobering thought that no one wanted to say out loud.

"Mmmph ... wanna lollipop ... " Kevin's head moved from side to side.

Candi, Jonathan and Sarah all shared a look and then burst out laughing. Leave it to Kevin to rein them all in again. Even when he was passed out, he was still keeping it real.

"No ... notta lollipop ... wanna gumdrop ... heh, heh ... " He smiled in his delirium.

Candi's eyes bugged out of her head, afraid she had just heard what sounded like Kevin saying he wanted a gumdrop. Her face turned burning red.

Sarah got a wicked look on her face. She leaned in towards her brother. "What's that Kevin? What do you want? Tell us again." She looked over at Candi's face and lifted her eyebrows twice, signaling that she had heard the same thing Candi had heard – and now she was going to torture Candi with it, just for fun.

Jonathan leaned in curiously. "What is it? What does he want? Maybe we can give it to him."

Sarah rocked back on her heels laughing her head off. "Jonathan, you are hilarious, you know that? I love it. I agree – maybe we can give it to him. Candi, what do you think? Can we give it to him?" She snorted at her own teasing.

"What? What'd I say? What's so funny?"

Candi stood up and patted Jonathan on the back. "Nothing. Nothing at all. Sarah's just insane. We're going to need to build a cage to put her in later. We'll call it the coconut house." She looked over at Sarah and glared at her.

The girls spent the next couple of hours forcing water down Kevin's throat while he yammered on and on about gumdrops and rugby. His fever seemed to be dropping which made them all feel a little bit better. He hadn't vomited anymore which was definitely a good sign.

Jonathan did a little nearby exploring, bringing back a coconut that he had found on the ground and proceeded to examine it in great detail, before laying it in the sand near the blanket.

They ate only a small amount of their food and water. Not wanting to risk being discovered by who knows what, and the night being pretty warm, they vetoed building a fire and went to bed early. They agreed to come up with a plan of action when they woke up the next morning – no use trying to figure anything out now in the dark when all of them were too exhausted to think straight.

They opened the ponchos and laid them out as covers for all of them to share. Each one was almost big enough for two people. Kevin was still a little hot, but he was shivering. Sarah and Candi positioned themselves with their backs up against him to keep him warm.

One by one, they drifted off to sleep, left alone in their thoughts of home and being lost in the middle of nowhere, none of them hearing the distant sound of a powerful motor slipping past the island, far out in the ocean waves.

Getting Acquainted

KEVIN WAS DREAMING. HE WAS in a burning bed. The house was on fire around him and he was trapped in his sheets. He had to get out!

He started thrashing around. If only he could get the covers from around his legs. It's as if they were tied around him, intent on making sure he would never escape the flames.

"Kevin, what the hell! Stop it!"

In his sleep-induced haze, he heard his sister's voice. *Is she trapped in the house too? I have to save her, but where is she?*

"Kevin, cut it out or I'm gonna slap you."

Huh. Well, those aren't the words of someone who should be grateful they're about to be rescued from a blazing inferno. She'll be sorry if she gets stuck in this fire.

"What are you mumbling about a fire for? There's no fire. Just you, kicking everyone who's trying to sleep here, you idiot."

Kevin's mind started to clear as his sister's words began sinking in.

"Give him a break, Sarah, he's still sick."

Sick? Who's sick? Me? Who was that?

Kevin struggled to open his eyes. Only one was obeying his

command.

"What's going on?" he mumbled, "Where's the fire?"

Candi sighed and sat up, giving up on the idea of any more sleep. "Good morning, Kevin. There's no fire. You used to have a fever. I guess you're dying of the heat now because you've got a rain poncho on you and no more fever."

Kevin sat up slowly, looking around him. "Don't forget the two hot butts that are pressed up against me too, Gumdrop."

Candi looked down at herself and then over at Sarah. "Okay, so you have a point. Wow, is it ever muggy here with that humidity and heat."

"You said it," agreed Kevin, using his shirt to wipe his face off.

"Well this butt is getting up now. Sorry about getting you all hot."

Kevin lifted up his bandaged hand, waving it weakly. "No, don't get up on my account. I'm sure at some point I was appreciating your butt being here." Then he looked over at his sister and nudged her awake. "You, on the other hand, can take your butt on over there, if you don't mind."

Sarah reached back and slapped his hand away, as if she was going to ignore him. But the flies had other ideas.

"Son of a BITCH!" she yelled, as she slapped at her neck. "You have got to be frigging *kidding* me. What is it with these goddamn flies anyway?"

She sat up, rubbing her neck and arms, trying to get the flies to go feast on something else.

"They aren't bothering me at all," said Kevin.

Sarah shot him a stink eye and mimicked him, "They aren't bothering me at all. Eewwwmew mew mew mewwww."

Kevin laughed.

Jonathan sat up and rubbed the top of his hair, which made absolutely no difference to its totally unkempt state, except maybe to add another teaspoon of sand to it.

"Studies have shown that blood-sucking insects are attracted to some people more than others. One recent study I read suggested that they were attracted to people who were more stressed. People who were able to manage their stress levels more effectively attracted less bites than others who weren't."

Kevin watched Candi send a worried look over to her brother and then turned to see Sarah's reaction.

Sarah very carefully stood up, and calmly brushed the sand from her legs and arms. She walked over to where Jonathan was innocently sitting on the edge of the sheet, with no idea that Sarah was coming closer.

"Stressed?"

Jonathan looked up, surprised and instantly looking a little wary.

"Stressed?!"

Jonathan got a very worried expression on his face.

"Stressed?!! Do you think I'm stressed, Jonathan?!"

Jonathan's mouth dropped open; he froze in place, unable to move even a finger. Only his eyes followed her movements.

She was looming over him, her crazy, knotted and salty hair sticking out on one side; remnants of her black makeup still stuck under her eyes; chapped and crusty lips, thinned into a white line ... an angry, sunburned, scary woman face like Kevin and Jonathan had never seen before.

Kevin was pretty sure she was going to attack Jonathan. He didn't know if he should rescue him or let it play out.

"Um, yes?" Jonathan answered meekly, ducking his head a

little and hunching his shoulders – keeping an eye on her lunatic face, waiting for the physical attack he was wisely expecting.

"Well, isn't that very *astute* of you, Jonathan, resident brainiac. You are, indeed, correct. I am very stressed. I am *more* stressed than I have ever been in my entire *life*, in fact." She paused to catch her breath and then continued, counting off complaints on her fingers.

"Let's see ... two days ago, I caught my boyfriend cheating on me with my brother's girlfriend. *Then*, I was forced onto a cruise ship with the brother and sister tweedle-dumb and tweedle-dee team from hell. *Then* that stupid cruise ship *sank*, sending me into the bowels of *hell* where my brother has laid near death for twenty-four hours. I got to watch him almost get eaten by a shark. Oh, and my hair has knots in it that will probably never come out, which will force me to have a very short, very ugly haircut that will make me look like a very manly lesbian, not that there's anything *wrong* with being a manly lesbian if you are, in fact, a manly lesbian, which I am *not*. *And*, I have just started my period, and I don't have any tampons or pads with me. So *yes*, I am just a little bit stressed out. *AND I THINK I'M ENTITLED TO THAT, THANK YOU VERY MUCH!*"

She finished her tirade by storming off into the jungle, leaving the three of them in stunned silence.

"Well, that explains it. She's on her period." Jonathan stood up and brushed himself off, oblivious to the daggers his sister was sending him with her eyes and the silent laughter shaking Kevin's shoulders.

"*You* are an inconsiderate *oaf!*" yelled Candi, getting up and storming off in the direction Sarah took.

Jonathan looked after her, confused. "What? What'd I say?

It's true, you know!" he yelled after her. "The hormonal instabilities present during a woman's menses make women act unreasonably emotional!"

Kevin held up his hand, gasping for air. "Dude, stop. You're killing me." He kept laughing while he was talking. "Who says that shit, seriously? You're hilarious. Thanks, man, I needed that."

"Yeah, well, I don't think Sarah or Candi appreciated my medical information or research findings," said Jonathan, looking around their shelter site. "Should we go after them?"

"No way, dude. That's like hunting jungle cats. Wait 'til they cool down and come back, then we'll figure out what's what."

*****

"Wait up, Sarah. Wait! You have longer legs than me." Candi could hear Sarah crashing through the trees ahead, still muttering to herself.

"Asshole. Asshole, asshole, *asshole*. They have *no idea*. None! Assholes."

Candi caught up to Sarah and reached out to grab her shoulder and slow her down. "You're right. They're assholes. Now slow down before I barf from all this exercise and humidity."

Sarah stopped in the middle of the path she was following. "Seriously, Candi, what am I supposed to do with a friggin' period in the middle of the jungle?" Sarah swept her arms around her, gesturing to the trees that rose up high above their heads, some of them leaning together so close they blocked out the sun. The sounds of birds calling out to one another filled the air around them.

Candi looked at the surrounding wildness and threw up her hands too. "I don't know, but we'll come up with something. Look, I have all the incentive in the world to help you. My period is coming any day. Come on, don't look so sad, we'll work it out. We'll tear up the sheet or something and stuff our underwear like they did in the olden days."

All of a sudden, Sarah started crying. She stood there looking so pitiful with her awful hair and destroyed makeup, ruined leopard print dress still clinging sadly to her dirty, sandy, and sunburned body, wearing flip-flops that didn't fit.

Candi couldn't help herself. She reached out and hugged Sarah.

Sarah grabbed onto her and started crying even harder. "I'm sorry I called you tweedle-dumb. I'm just so pissed right now, I can't see straight."

Candi chuckled into her shoulder. "I thought I was tweedle-dee."

Sarah laughed and quickly pulled away, embarrassed by her weakness, swiping at her eyes. "Whatever. I didn't mean to say it. I'm not mad at you or Jonathan, even though sometimes he can be a total pain in the ass. No offense." She hesitated and wiped at her eyes again before saying, "If it hadn't been for you two, I don't even want to think about what might have happened to Kevin and me. We would probably be in a shark's stomach right now or something." She looked up above them and then gestured all around her with her arms open wide and a tremulous smile on her lips. "Instead, we have all this!"

Candi and Sarah smiled at each other and then laughed. A little at first, and then more, until they were both hysterical.

"Oh my god, stop, stop – I'm gonna pee on myself," gasped Candi.

"Go ahead, you couldn't possibly look or smell worse than you do right now!" laugh-screamed Sarah.

"Oh, y-y-yes I could ... I could b-b-be on my p-p-period!!"

They both fell to the ground, laughing like hyenas. All of their problems were temporarily forgotten as they held their sides, laughing like they'd never laughed before.

After a couple of minutes, their merriment petered out and they were able to get their breath back. They were both exhausted, but enjoying the endorphins that their laughter had released into their bloodstreams.

"Man, I needed that," said Sarah.

"I guess I did, too." Candi looked around them. "Where in the heck are we, anyway?"

Sarah looked up into the trees. "I have no idea." She looked down at the ground. "But this seems to be some sort of trail we're on."

"Trail? Well, that's weird, should we follow it?"

"Yeah, maybe there's a Wal-Mart at the end of it, and I can buy some tampons."

"Did you bring any money?" asked Candi, a sparkle of remaining laughter in her eyes.

"Honey, when you look like I do, you don't need to bring money," said Sarah, saucily, flinging her knotted hair over her shoulder and walking down the path like she was on a Paris fashion runway, except her flip-flops kind of ruined the effect with their sound and the sand they were spraying up behind her.

"That's the spirit!" said Candi happily. Now they just had to find something that could be like a period pad and everyone would be permitted to live through the night unscathed by her majesty, the queen of menstruation.

*****

The girls made it back to the campfire just in time to see Kevin stumble off into the bushes to vomit.

"Ew."

"Sarah, that's not very nice," scolded Candi, walking over to where Kevin was leaning his hand on a tree.

"Are you okay, Kevin?" she asked tentatively.

"No, I feel like shit. My stomach is in knots."

Candi looked back Jonathan who had a contemplative look on his face.

"Kevin, if you did get food poisoning from those oysters, I expect you're gonna feel sick for a couple of days. You're probably going to get diarrhea too."

"Dude, if you say that word again, I'm gonna come over there and bust you up."

"What word? Oysters?"

"That's it!"

Kevin turned around as if he was going to head towards Jonathan, but his legs had other ideas. He fell to the ground on his knees, moaning as he went down onto his side in the sand, landing at Candi's feet. He looked up at her and said, "Hey, sand fairy, can you get me some water?"

Candi moved quickly to get him some water from their precious stores.

"We need more water," said Jonathan, worriedly. "I'm going to go do some exploring, see what I can find."

"I'm going to stay here with Kevin. Maybe I'll be able to get him to eat something," said Candi as she lifted his head to help him drink.

Kevin stopped midway and fixed his gaze on her eyes. "If you say a food word, I'm gonna have to bust you up, too."

"Yes, well, I'm very worried about that, for sure." Candi

looked over at Sarah and Jonathan and rolled her eyes. "Sarah, why don't you go with Jonathan and help him look. I'll stay here and look after the tough guy. See if you can find any more b-a-n-a-n-a-s for d-i-n-n-e-r later."

Sarah shrugged her shoulders and started walking into the trees. "Come on, Jonathan, I don't have all day to wait on you."

Jonathan shot his sister a weary look before he got up to follow her into the jungle.

The last thing Candi heard was Sarah singing, "'This shit is bananas, B-A-N-A-N-A-S! I said this shit is bananas, B-A-N-A-N-A-S!'"

Candi couldn't help but laugh. They were a million miles away from Gwen Stefani on the radio and everything else they used to think was normal.

She looked down at Kevin who seemed to be asleep again, his head resting directly on the sand. She looked around and decided to spend some time trying to create a more comfortable place to put him. She started by grabbing a nearby fallen palm frond, stripping it of its leaves, trying to figure out how to weave them into some sort of mat he could sleep on.

*****

"I said this shit is Bananas, B-A-N-A-N-A-S! The B is Bananas, B-A-N-A-N-A-S!"

"What in the heck are you saying, Sarah? Is that some kind of cheer or something? What do bananas have to do with football?"

They had been pushing their way through the trees for half an hour, and so far, everything looked the same. Trees, trees, sand, and trees. Birds chirping. Sun. Humidity. Trees.

"It's not a football cheer, dork, it's a song by Gwen Stefani. I'm surprised you don't know that. The song only got played about a million times on the radio."

"Don't call me dork."

"Fine. How about doofus."

"No, as a matter of fact, I don't like being called doofus either. Nobody would. Why do you always have to be so rude, anyway?"

"Because, you annoy me. When I'm annoyed, I'm rude. Deal with it."

"No."

Sarah stopped tromping through the underbrush and turned to face Jonathan.

"What do you mean, 'No'?"

"I mean *No*. I'm not just going to deal with your rudeness or act like it doesn't matter. Words can hurt, Sarah; what you say means something. Even if you think it's nothing, it's not nothing to me – or anyone else for that matter. Just because you *can* say rude things, doesn't mean you *should* say them."

Sarah thought about what he said for a second. Her first instinct was to tell him to go get bent. He sounded like a parent or something. But then she started warring within herself. On one hand, this 'take it or leave it' attitude kind of defined who she was; but on the other hand, Jonathan seemed to be suggesting that her words had some kind of power, which was a concept she hadn't really considered before.

She shook off the philosophical points that had started swimming around in her brain and opted for the standard Sarah response. "Whatevs."

"Yeah. Whatevs yourself." Jonathan, obviously disgusted with her complete lack of respect for anyone's feelings, pushed around her to continue through the trees ahead. He kept up a fast pace, forcing Sarah to have to hurry to keep up. And she was wearing

Candi's flip-flops that were two sizes too small.

"Wait up, Jonathan, you're going too fast!"

Jonathan ignored her. His attention was elsewhere. Soon he disappeared in the trees ahead of her.

*****

The sound of the water got louder. As Jonathan pushed through a particularly thick stand of bamboo, he reached an outcropping of rock that rose up above the jungle floor at least thirty feet. They had reached the southern end of the island. This was the big outcropping of rock they had seen from out in the ocean when the boat was still a hundred yards offshore.

Coming from a crevice in the rocks was a stream of water. It dribbled over the edge and fell to the jungle floor, disappearing quickly into the sandy loam.

Jonathan approached the rock and held his hand out under the water. It wasn't cold, but it was cooler than the air around him. He hesitantly put a drop of the water on his tongue from this finger and found that it wasn't salty.

"Whoo-hooo! I found it! I found some water!" He looked around to share his enthusiasm with Sarah, but she was nowhere to be seen.

"Sarah?" he called out, confused. *Now where the heck is she? God, what a pain in the butt she is sometimes.* He thought about that for a second and then amended his thought. *All the time. She is a pain in the butt every second of the day that she's not sleeping.*

Jonathan headed back in the direction he had come, finding Sarah sitting on a fallen tree.

"Hey, come on, I found something seriously cool."

"No."

"What do you mean, 'no'? Come on!"

"No. I'm not going anywhere with you. You are rude and you are not a gentleman; all you do is insult me, so I'm finished. Continue, Christopher Columbus, I'm staying here." She folded her arms and refused to budge.

Jonathan was flummoxed. What was she going to do? Sit in the jungle by herself all night? Besides, she was the rude one, not him. He considered leaving her there, but he knew his sister would kill him if he did. Plus he could never do that. His parents raised him to take care of weaker people. Only thing was, she didn't seem very weak. That's why a piece of him still wanted to leave her there.

"Okay, listen. I'm sorry. I shouldn't have been so honest with you back there. Next time, I'll just keep my comments to myself. Now can we go, please?"

"No."

Jonathan grabbed his hair in frustration. "What do you want me to do? I can't just leave you here!" He threw his arms down at his sides in disgust.

"Sure you can. You left me in the dust just a minute ago, might as well do it again." She stared off into the distance, refusing to meet his eyes.

Jonathan sighed, the fight going out of him. "Yeah, about that. Sorry. It's just that you really frustrate me sometimes, and I'm not used to that. Candi is more level-headed than you are, and she's really the only girl I've ever been around, other than my mom – and she doesn't really count."

Sarah turned to look at him with her eyebrow raised. "Seriously? You're a junior in high school, and you've never been around another girl? Had a girlfriend?"

A sarcastic puff of air escaped Jonathan's lips. "Yeah, right,

Sarah. Me? A girlfriend? Get real."

"I saw you with that girl on the ship. Sucking face. Don't tell me you don't know your way around a girl's panties."

"Sucking face? Who says that anymore? And anyway, she grabbed me and kissed me to keep some other guy away from her, so it wasn't a real kiss." He turned to go back in the direction of the water. "And I don't think I want to talk to you about this anymore, so let's go."

"Oh, poo, just when things were getting interesting." Sarah stood up to join him. "I'll come with you, but *only* if you agree to slow down and wait for me, and *only* if you agree to be interrogated by me until I am satisfied with your answers."

This girl was nuts. He just shook his head no.

"I'm dead serious. Either you agree to my terms, or I will stay here all night and you can explain to level-headed Sugar Lump why her perfect brother left me out here to die with the vipers and the cannibals."

"Fine. Whatever. But there are no vipers or cannibals here that I've seen, and you probably should stop calling Candi Sugar Lump, because if she ever gets really mad at you, you'll be sorry."

"Oooh, I'm so scared," laughed Sarah.

"You should be. She might be little, but when she finally gets mad, look out. I know some karate, but she's sneaky, and she doesn't fight fair." He shivered inwardly as he remembered her last kick to the family jewels.

The pair continued through the trees, Jonathan in the lead.

"So, what did you find?"

"I found water."

"No, you didn't!"

"Yes I did!"

"Oh, my god, I could just kiss you right now Jonathan."

Jonathan felt his face go red. He was trying not to picture that kiss, but it was impossible. Sarah was the biggest pain in the butt girl he'd ever met, but for some reason she got under his skin, and not always in a bad way. Or maybe it was in a bad way. He was so conflicted.

They reached the stand of bamboo and pushed through. Sarah saw the splash of water coming off the top of the rock. She let out a squeal of delight and clapped her hands.

"Holy mother of all things holy, it's a shower! It's not just water, it's a friggin' *shower!* Jonathan, you are the king of the island!" She grabbed him in a bear hug and planted a big kiss, right on his lips, before running over to the water and letting it flow across her hand and then down her arm.

Jonathan watched her as he felt the warmth from her kiss travel down to his chest and into other regions of his body. The kiss didn't seem to affect her at all, but it was definitely affecting him. He turned around so she wouldn't see exactly how much.

*****

As the water ran down to her elbow and then dripped off onto the top of her foot, Sarah reached up with her other hand to touch her lips. The enthusiasm of the moment had caused her to throw that kiss out there – but she was still feeling the effects of it, even when the discovery of the water should have washed it all away.

She turned to look at him, but his back was to her. She snorted in disgust. *Typical.* He was probably looking for bugs or something.

"So, what's next, Magellan?" she asked with feigned casualness.

Jonathan looked sideways, up to the top of the rocks where the water was coming from. "I'm going to climb up there to see where the water source is."

Sarah followed his eyes and saw a pretty steep rock face that disappeared up and over to its other side, out of sight.

"I'm not so sure that's such a good idea."

"I'll be fine."

"No, seriously, Jonathan, what if you fall?"

"I'm not going to fall."

"Well, how about if we get a rope just in case?"

"No, I don't want to take the time to get a rope, I'm going now."

Sarah sighed in frustration, but she was too happy about the water discovery to let his know-it-all-ness get to her. She followed with her eyes as he started making his way up to the highest point of the rock pile.

As Jonathan reached the top, Sarah heard him gasp. Then she heard some sliding sounds. He disappeared in an instant, yelling out as he fell.

Then there was silence. Even the birds had stopped chirping.

Sarah ran over to the rocks and scrambled up to get higher so she could see better. Jonathan's head had disappeared over the edge somewhere, and she had no idea what was on the other side.

"Sarah!"

"Jonathan, are you okay?!"

"No!" he grunted out. "I slipped. I need a rope or something, quick!!"

"Holy *shit*, Jonathan, you told me NOT to get a rope! Hold on, I'll be right back!"

"You'd better hurry up. I don't know how much longer I can hang on!"

Sarah scrambled down the rocky slope as fast as she could in flip-flop-covered feet.

"Ohmygod, ohmygod, ohmygod ... shitshitshit."

She continued her litany as she stumbled back to the stand of bamboo. She scanned the ground for a loose piece, and luckily found one that felt pretty solid, sitting among the stalks. She wrestled it out of the pile and then rushed back to the rock. She kicked off her flip-flops, climbing up to get back to where she had last seen Jonathan.

"Jonathan!"

"Yes, I'm here."

"Okay, I got a stick. There wasn't any rope."

"Well, I don't think a stick will work," he said weakly.

"The stick is going to work, Jonathan! Now shut up, and for once in your life, *listen* to me."

Sarah inched out on her butt across the top of the hard surface. She could see where Jonathan had slipped. There was a small pile of sand with a sliding shoe print in it. She scarcely noticed the amazing view of the ocean and jungle below, although she did feel the refreshing cool breeze since it was now blowing across her hot and sweaty face. All she could see was the top of Jonathan's head and the rest of his body trying to cling to the other side of the rock. He had hold of a thick, dangling tree root that was growing out of the boulder in front of him. It was the only thing keeping him from falling about fifty feet into the tops of the trees below.

"Okay, I'm going to lower this stick down to you, and you're going to take it and use it to pull yourself up to me."

"It won't work, Sarah! I'll pull you over the rock with me, and we'll both die!"

"No, you won't! I have two spots for my heels to hold on. I'm not going anywhere. Now grab the damn stick before I hit you with it and knock you down off this rock myself!"

Jonathan risked a look up at Sarah. She was staring at him determinedly. "Shit, Sarah, you sure are bossy."

Sarah smiled. "You just said 'shit'. I'm telling everyone when we get back."

"Okay," he said breathlessly, "here I go."

Jonathan grunted as he used what little momentum he could create by swinging his lower body out and then towards the rock, to transfer his right hand to the stick Sarah was holding.

His hand made contact.

He grabbed on as hard as he could.

Her body lurched forward with the weight of Jonathan now holding onto the stick, but her heels dug in and she didn't let go.

"You sure about this, Sarah?"

"Sure as I'm gonna be. Now shut up and grab the stick with your other hand. My heels are killing me." She could feel her bare feet bruising with the pressure.

Jonathan took one last look at Sarah's face and said, "Try not to let me go."

"Not a chance." She gritted her teeth, ready for the pull of Jonathan's full bodyweight.

*****

Jonathan let go of the tree root and grabbed onto the stick with his other hand. He felt the stick go down, as his weight pulled Sarah forward even more. He couldn't risk looking at her face. He focused on using the leverage she provided to get a foothold on the side of the rock.

Finding a small bump with the edge of his sneaker, he used it to push himself up a foot. He moved his lower hand up the stick, above his other hand. He tried not to think about how his lower hand was being crushed between the stick and the rock. There was blood dripping down his wrist.

He felt around for another foothold with his other sneaker. He touched another bump on the rock and secured his toe to it as best he could. He pushed up and was able to transfer his left hand to a place on the stick above his right, scraping the skin off his knuckles and the back of his hand.

He risked a glance at Sarah, and it gave him renewed energy.

Her face was bright pink, sweat running off her in rivers. She was focusing all of her energy onto holding that stick. For him. For the first time since he'd met her, she had nothing to say.

He knew if he didn't get up there in the next few seconds, one of them was going to see what it felt like to fall from a very great height – very possibly it would be both of them. By now, he knew that look on Sarah's face. It meant she wasn't going to let go, even if it meant she was going down too. *Damn stubborn woman.*

The rock started to curve to a more flat surface, just a few inches above Jonathan's face. If he could just get one more foothold, he could probably get his arm on top of it and use it to bring himself the rest of the way up. He felt around with his foot, looking for another bump on the rock.

Just then the stick slid down. Sarah's hands were sweaty; she was losing her grip on the bamboo.

"Holy shit, Jonathan, the stick is slipping!" she screamed. "Grab my hand!"

"Do *not* let go of the stick, Sarah! You can't hold me with one hand!"

"I can't hang onto the stick anymore, you have to grab my hand. On three. You pull on the stick as hard as you can for leverage and then let go; then I let go and grab your hand at the same time."

"It's never going to work, Sarah! It's physically impossible!"

"DON'T GIVE ME ANY OF YOUR PHYSICS SHIT! IT'S GOING TO WORK! Now grab my right hand with your left hand on the count of three. One---two---*three!!*"

In that split second, when Jonathan pulled up on the stick and let go of it, using whatever grip he had on the rock to launch his hand up in the air, he knew that he had never been so vulnerable, never counted on another human being like he was in this moment, ever in his life. God help him, Sarah Peterson was going to determine his destiny.

He felt her hand in his before he saw it. The smack of their palms meeting jolted his fingers into action. He closed them around hers in a kung fu grip. Even if he had wanted to let go, it would have been impossible. He was on survival autopilot.

Sarah dropped the pole and leaned over as far as she could. She was folded completely in half. She stretched her open hand out towards the still prone and dangling Jonathan.

She grunted out, "Now grab my other hand. *Hurry!*"

Jonathan flailed around for a second before they could make contact. Then they were together, hand in hand – Jonathan hanging over the edge, Sarah bent in half, her bruised and bleeding heels stuck into grooves that kept her tethered to the top of the rock.

Jonathan dug his elbows into the unforgiving hard surface, instantly feeling excruciating pain. Blood begin to drip from his elbows now too. He had to ignore it. His feet kicked around in the air, looking for purchase.

*****

Sarah strained her already nearly exhausted biceps, trying to manhandle Jonathan back up to the top of the rock.

Inch by painstaking inch, Sarah's power and Jonathan's elbows and abdominal muscles pulled him closer and closer to their joined hands. Finally, he was able to throw one leg up, allowing the heel of his sneaker to grab hold of a bump on the top part of the rock. He used this leg to pull the rest of his body over.

Now that his full weight wasn't resting on her heels, Sarah was able to use her upper body strength to pull on him. She pulled one more time using all the strength she had left, at the same time Jonathan rose up on his knees, apparently intending to release her hands and crawl the rest of the way up.

His body flew forward and landed on top of Sarah. They both fell over, Sarah's back against the rock and Jonathan lying prone on top of her. Both of them were too stunned and in pain to move.

Sarah laid her head back against the rock, first feeling the burning numbness and then the pain that was shooting up from her heels. Next, she felt sweat dripping down her face and neck. Then she noticed her heartbeat and Jonathan's heartbeat mingling together to create a frantic melody. Last, she smelled Jonathan's B.O. as it quickly threatened to overwhelm her completely.

"Holy crap, Jonathan, you smell. Get off me."

Jonathan didn't move. His face was buried in her chest. His words came out muffled. "I'm sorry, but I can't move. Every ounce of energy I had is now gone. Wake me up in five minutes." Then he began to snore.

Sarah sat still for a second trying to figure out if he was really sleeping. "Jonathan? Are you seriously sleeping in my boobs?" she asked tentatively.

Then she felt his body shaking with laughter.

"Get off me, you idiot!" She pushed him to the side. He rolled over to lie next to her.

"Ah, that was awesome. I got you."

Sarah feigned brushing off his smell from her body. "Whatever. I knew you weren't sleeping." She sat up and tried to stand, immediately stopping and reaching for her feet. "Oh shit, that hurts. Holy crap, I think my feet are broken."

Jonathan sat up, quickly, all signs of mirth disappearing as his concern for her pain came to the fore. "Let me see them."

"No, get away, Stinky McSmellypits." She slapped at his hands.

"Seriously, Sarah, let me take a look. I'll sit downwind from you."

Sarah relented out of sheer desperation, she was in so much pain, letting him pick up her legs by the calves so he could look at her heels. His sharp intake of breath told her that it wasn't good.

"Well, they're pretty banged up. Cut and bruised too." He didn't let go of her leg – he set it down gently in his lap.

"Sarah."

"What." She was refusing to look at him.

"Sarah, look at me."

"Fine. What."

"Thank you. Thank you for destroying your heels to save my life. I'll never forget it."

"Whatever. You're welcome."

"Ever."

"Ever, what?"

"Never ever."

"Never ever, what?" Sarah was getting frustrated. He looked so earnest.

"I will never, ever forget, or let you forget, that you saved my life." Jonathan flashed her a huge grin.

Elle Casey

Sarah smiled back, despite herself. "Don't make me come over there."

"Give it your best shot." He issued the challenge, and it hung in the air between them.

She gave him her best cocky girl smile. "Maybe another time, when I'm not on the injured list."

"Whenever. Wherever."

Sarah laughed; she couldn't help it. "Since when did you get so big and bad anyway?"

"Since I nearly lost my ass over that rock, that's when."

Sarah grimaced as she tried to stand again. "You just said 'ass'. I'm telling."

"Don't you dare, or I won't help you walk back to the waterfall where you can have a shower."

"Oh, so now you play dirty, too. Okay, fine, I'll remember that. By the way, did you notice the breeze up here? It's amazing."

Jonathan stood, reaching his hand down to help Sarah up.

"Yep, it's awesome. And no bugs at all. Must be the breeze keeping them away."

"No bugs, holy crap. I wanna live on this rock."

"Well, first we have to get you *off* this rock and back into those flip-flops."

The two of them working together eventually located her shoes, which made walking around a bit easier, but not much.

Sarah stood under the trickle of water and shivered in delight at the feeling it gave her, working its way through her tangled, salty hair.

"Did you figure out where the water is coming from?"

"Nope. I couldn't see anything; of course, my exploration was cut short by my, well, you know, little mishap. It could be some sort of artesian well, but I thought those things had to be dug by someone. I guess it makes sense that there's fresh water under this island. I mean, how would anyone have ever settled in these places in the first place without fresh water?"

"Yeah, well, I hope it's a permanent thing and not just a rainwater thing."

"Me too, but I'm glad you said that. Just in case, we need to have other ways to collect water so we don't run out completely during the dry season, whenever that is."

Sarah nodded her head in agreement, but was too preoccupied to actually respond. She was looking at something just past the stand of bamboo next to the water. She finished her mini shower and walked over to check it out.

"Get a load of this tree, Jonathan. Is it a tree? What *is* this thing?" She was pointing at what looked like a large, gray elephant leg. It was a big, above-ground root that was connected to several others just like it, all part of a very large tree that had thousands of small, dark green leaves on it. The whole trunk was as big around as a car, but the roots spread out even farther than that. It was almost prehistoric looking.

"Pretty cool, huh?" Jonathan ran his hands over the smooth, gray bark. His eyes followed the path of the root. "Look how the root is part of this huge network that's all above the ground. It makes all kinds of small caves and tunnels under the tree."

"That is cool," agreed Sarah.

"And the branches above the root system are pretty substantial too. Wow."

"Yeah, and look! Some of them actually have roots coming down from branches, which have dug themselves into the ground below. I've never seen a tree this big before in person – only in photographs."

"Man, I would have killed to have a tree like this in my back yard when I was a kid. I mean, what kind of killer treehouse could you make in one of these babies?" said Jonathan, as if he were daydreaming.

"Hey, Jonathan, that's a *great* idea!"

"What's a great idea?"

"Building a treehouse here. Could we do it? In this tree, I mean?"

Jonathan thought about it for a second. He studied the roots and the branches above. "I don't know for sure, but maybe. I mean, we have all kinds of bamboo here, which is a pretty good building material, really. I know they make floors and tiki huts with it. This root system seems pretty solid. The branches up there are in pretty good positions to support floor joists ... " he trailed off thinking of the possibilities.

"Okay, well, I don't know what a floor joist is, but I'm sure you'll figure it out. Let's go back and tell Kevin and Candi what we found."

She moved to take a couple of steps. "Ooh, ah, shit. My heels are killing me."

"Here, lean on me." Jonathan came up next to her and offered his shoulder. "Sorry I stink."

"Don't worry about it, I need the crutch more than I care about your pits."

They worked together, slowly making their way back to the beach where Kevin and Candi were waiting, eager to share their discoveries with their siblings.

*****

"Oh, you're awake. How do you feel?" Candi set down the bits of wood she had been gathering for a fire and reached over to feel Kevin's forehead. "You're not as warm as you were."

"I feel weak, but better, actually."

"Let me see your hand."

Kevin held up his bandaged hand for Candi's inspection.

"It looks better. I think this sickness that you've had has been some sort of ... "

Kevin put his hand on his stomach and moaned, "Oh god, don't say it, please!"

" ... sort of bad tummy thing, that I'm sure will be gone soon," Candi finished with a smile.

Kevin rested the back of his hand on his forehead. "Bad tummy thing. That's good, I hope you're right."

After a minute, Kevin sat up slowly, taking his time in case he felt dizzy or queasy again. "Where is everybody?"

"Well, Jonathan and Sarah left a couple hours ago to see if they could find some water or more food. I expected them back already, but I'm not worried. Not yet anyway."

"Probably the only thing we need to worry about is them killing each other. No biggie."

Candi laughed.

"So, what have I missed?"

"Oh, not much. We were kind of waiting for you to wake up before we decided to do anything. We have some decisions to make."

"Yeah," Kevin said, noncommittally. He was watching her as she got up and walked around their campsite, organizing and preparing for their next big meal of bananas and water.

She stopped when she realized he was watching her. "What? Do you want some water or something?"

"Nope."

"Okaaay." Candi continued organizing the wood she had gathered in the fire pit they had made with rocks and shells. "Tonight I want to try and light a fire. I'm hoping the smoke might keep the bugs away. They were a serious pain in the butt last night." She looked up and caught him staring at her again. "What? Why do you keep staring at me? Do I have something on my face?" Candi self-consciously wiped at her nose and mouth.

"No, there's nothing on your face. Does it bother you that I'm looking at you?"

She shrugged. "A little bit."

"Why?" Kevin was curious and also still pretty dizzy, so he wasn't sure where he was going with this.

"I don't know, it just makes me feel self-conscious I guess."

"You have no reason to be self-conscious."

"Yeah, right."

"Seriously. Why would you think you do?" He seemed genuinely puzzled.

"Um, well, first of all, I look like a sand fairy, as you said earlier. I have no makeup on. I don't even have any shoes on right now, since they're making my feet sweat and smell bad."

Kevin smiled. She was shy. Something in him liked to tease her about it. He liked getting her riled up, even when he was feeling like crap. In fact, now that he thought about it for a second, it was kind of making him feel better to spar with her.

"I like sand fairies."

Candi snorted but said nothing.

"What? I do, I think they're cool. And cute." He was purposely egging her on now.

"Shut up."

"No." *Let's see how far I can push her today.*

"Yes," Candi said firmly, seeming surprised herself a little at her serious tone.

"Why?" Kevin answered her with a challenge in his voice. Now things were cookin'. This was just what he needed. He missed rugby. On the pitch he could issue challenges and then follow them up with some good, bone crunching tackles. He'd just have to settle for a little harmless flirting here on the island.

"*Because*, that's why." She was getting cross now.

"'Because' is not an answer. Tell me why I can't like sand fairies."

"Stop being stupid."

"Okay, now them's fightin' words, girl. Come on over here and say that." He was trying to decide if he'd be able to stand without falling over. He braced his arms behind him, getting ready to stand up.

"Get your big, lazy butt off the sand for a change and come on over here." She never expected him to take her up on her challenge or have the energy to do it, but suddenly he was up and standing over her. She looked up at him to see him grinning mischievously.

"Hello, little sand fairy. The island troll has come to collect his toll."

She squeaked and jumped to the side, scrambling through the sand to get away from him. He heard her giggle as he let out a roar behind her.

"No! Get away from me!" she yelled, racing down the beach.

Kevin tried to keep up, but he was too weak from his stomach issues to make it very far. He felt his stomach lurch and his vision went gray around the edges. He fell into the wet sand and tried to catch his weak and shallow breath.

He could hear her coming back. "Oh, beautiful sand fairy, why do you try to escape my clutches? I just wanted a little kiss on the cheeeeeek." He could see okay now, but his head was spinning, spinning, spinning ...

"You're delirious. This is what you get for being dehydrated and sick, running around like a maniac. Come on." She reached down to help him up. "I'll help you back to the shelter. You need to eat something and drink more water before you pass out again."

Kevin accepted her help, but refused to be put off. He felt like he'd drank a few too many beers. It's probably what made him keep talking and saying things he was normally too cool or wise to say out loud. "I really do think you're cute, you know; why is that so hard to believe?"

"Because you, Kevin Peterson, don't date cute sand fairyish girls. You date supermodels."

"Pfffft!" was his inelegant response. "Supermodel, poopermodel. They're all the same, no fairies, no magic."

"Man, what is it with you and the fairies today, anyway?" Candi shook her head. "You don't seem to be the fae fan type."

"I don't know. When I was younger, I used to read that kind of fiction stuff. Lots of dragons, elves, fairies. It reminds me of this island, like a secret world." He held his finger up to his lips conspiratorially. "Shhhh, don't tell anyone."

"Ah-haaa. So the big, bad rugby stud is a fantasy nut. Don't worry – your secret is safe with me. Don't you know that fantasy is cool now?"

He got a slow, drunken grin on his face. "You just said I'm a stud."

"I also said that fantasy is cool now."

"Yeah, but I was reading that stuff way before it was cool. I wouldn't want to damage my rep as a stud and all." He wiggled his eyebrows at her.

Candi unceremoniously deposited him in the sand near the fire pit and started organizing the wood again. "Yeah, your rep. So valuable here on this middle-of-nowhere, shit island."

Kevin acted shocked at her profanity. "Naughty, naughty, using those bad words. What would your parents say?"

"Screw 'em." Candi was too cranky right now with Kevin's empty flirtations to think about what she was saying.

"Ha!" he agreed. "That's what I say. Screw 'em all."

He stopped talking for a second to take another appraising look. "I don't know why you think it's so crazy that I'd be checking you out. I've noticed you in school before, you know."

"No you didn't, don't lie."

"Seriously, I'm not. You have this purple fuzzy sweater thing you wear sometimes ... " His eyes went off into the distance as if recalling a particularly fond memory.

"Oh my god, shut up."

"But now that I think about it, I think I like you more in what you're wearing now."

Candi looked down at herself. Her long, green shirt hung off of her like a rag. Her once white capris were covered in smudges and who knows what else.

"Now I know you're delirious."

Kevin became serious. "Really, Candi ... all joking aside. I know I've kinda been what a lot of girls might consider a dirtbag at school – you know, focusing on getting laid and having fun." He had the grace to look embarrassed when Candi shot him a scolding look. "I probably should've put more thought into who I was hanging out with. I kinda knew that then; I guess I just ignored it, blocked it out. But now we're here, and, well, things feel different."

"Yeah," responded Candi, bitterly. "I'm the only girl in town, so now you're suddenly noticing me. No thanks."

"Hey, that's not fair. I'm being honest here, and you're just shooting me down without even giving me a chance."

"Yeah, right."

"What do you mean, 'yeah right'? The more I say, the more pissed you get. I don't get it."

Candi threw down the last pieces of wood she had in her hand and turned to face him directly.

"Kevin, I'm going to be straight-up honest with you right now because, what the hell, we're stranded on a deserted island in the middle of who knows where, and all the high school bullshit might as well be a million miles away."

"Good. Now we're getting somewhere. Give it to me, I can take it."

"Fine, you want to know what I'm thinking? Here it is: I've had a stupid crush on you for two years. Two *frigging years*. I've watched you slobber all over supermodel after supermodel. I watched you walk the halls with girls hanging on to your every word. I've listened to girls fight over you in the bathroom, for crap's sake! You charm the pants off everyone you come near: teachers, parents, coaches. I never had a chance with you then, and to tell me I have a chance now, when I'm literally the only girl in your world, is frankly kind of insulting." She paused for a breath and then continued, "So there, that's it. The truth in all its ugliness. Now I'm going to go walk into the ocean and drown myself."

Candi stood to get up and start walking to the water, mumbling to herself.

"Wait! Don't drown yourself yet, sand fairy! You like me! You said it yourself! Come back here!"

Kevin came up from behind her and grabbed her by the elbow, spinning her around to face him. A clump of her knotted hair fell into her eyes. He tried to move it aside gently, but it resisted his efforts and kept falling back into her eye.

Candi broke away in frustration and started walking again. "I'm more like a sand *beast* than a sand fairy."

Kevin walked quickly to catch up to her. They continued on together, walking side by side down the beach.

"Okay, if you insist, sand beast."

Candi turned partway and punched him in the arm.

"What? I'm just trying to make you happy."

"Shut up."

"That's it." Kevin all of a sudden grabbed Candi in a bear hug and lifted her up and spun her around.

"Put me down, you troll."

"Not until you agree to give me a chance."

"No way."

"Okay then, I hope you like bear hugs."

"Put me down! Seriously, I can't breathe."

"I can't either. You've taken my breath away with your sand beastiness."

Candi started laughing in spite of herself. "God, you're annoying. Fine, put me down and we'll talk." She struggled a little before saying, "I know you know how charming you are. You're not going to be able to manipulate me like you do everyone at school."

"Just don't try to run. I'm getting my energy back, and I'll take you down like the cheetah takes down the weak-ass antelope on the Serengeti."

"Okay fine, I won't run. I don't want you passing out again."

"I'm putting you down now, so behave yourself."

"You behave *yourself*."

Kevin put her down. Candi stood staring out at the ocean, her arms folded.

"Look at me."

"No."

Candi felt Kevin lay his arm across her shoulders, pulling her to his side.

"I'm sorry."

"Sorry for bear hugging me to death?"

"No."

"Sorry for sweating on me all night for the past two nights?"

"No."

"Well what are you sorry for, then?"

"I'm sorry I was so stupid and blind before."

Candi had nothing to say to that.

"Forgive me?"

"No."

"Okay then ... "

"Okay then what?"

"Okay, now I'm apparently gonna have to bear hug you into submission, since you won't see reason."

Candi yelped and took off running, laughing.

Kevin came up behind her huffing and puffing. He still was no match for her, since he hadn't eaten in about four days and was seriously dehydrated. He called out, "Just wait! I'll get you, little sand beast ... as soon as I get my ... energy ... back." He could barely get the last words out, he was so out of breath. "You're mean, stop running away from me. I'm weak. Aren't you supposed to be taking care of me or something?" He reached the campsite and collapsed in the sand where he'd been lying earlier.

"Come on, you need to get something to eat and drink, tough guy." She peeled him a banana and held it up with the remainder of their last bottle of water.

"Eat. Drink."

"Yes, boss."

"That's more like it."

They smiled at each other in companionable silence. A line had been drawn in the sand, and Kevin had stepped over to her side. It felt good for both of them, even if Candi didn't want to admit it. Their worlds had changed. The old world was behind them; this new world was going to be something else entirely.

"Oh, and for the record ... " said Kevin with his mouth full of banana, "I don't 'slobber' on girls, okay?"

Candi laughed. "Whatever you say."

*****

As Jonathan and Sarah broke through the trees and headed towards the campfire, Candi immediately knew something was wrong. As they got closer, she saw that Sarah was limping and Jonathan had a cut on his forehead and terrible, bleeding scrapes on his hands and arms. Strangely enough, even with this new batch of injuries, both of them looked happier than they had when they left.

"We found water!" yelled Sarah, a triumphant grin splitting her face.

"*I* found water," corrected Jonathan.

"Like I said – *we* found water," said Sarah sweetly, shooting Jonathan a challenging look.

"Fine, we found water. Just through the trees about thirty minutes that way."

"And it runs over a rock like a shower, Candi. A shower!"

"I'm totally jealous, no wonder you look so refreshed," said Candi as they drew near. "But what the heck happened to you? And you? You guys look like you got in a fight." Her eyes narrowed. "You guys didn't get into a fight with each other did you?"

She was instantly dismayed at the thought. *How could they have? We're all we have now. We're family.* Just as she was admitting this to herself, Candi realized how true it was. *Oh, the irony.*

"No, don't be silly. What happened was that Mr. Know-It-All here decided he had to do some exploring without my recommended safety precautions in place, so, of course, he nearly fell to his death, and it was only my quick thinking and awfully powerful, if I do say so myself, physical prowess that saved his life. Isn't that right, my little pookie pie?" Sarah reached over and touched Jonathan's chin with her finger.

Jonathan looked at her, a horrified expression on his face.

Candi looked at Jonathan in shock.

Kevin looked up from the ground where he was lying, instantly amused.

"No, that is *not* what happened. What happened was that I made an error in judgment with regard to the angle of the slope of the rock I was on, failing to take into account the friction coefficient between the sand, my shoe, and the rock, which resulted in my having to make alternate arrangements for ... "

" ... getting his ass back up on the rock in one piece," Sarah finished for him. "Lucky for him, I was there to save his cute ass." She looked around the campfire and put her hands on her hips. "So, what's for dinner?"

"Bananas."

"I'm getting tired of bananas, bananas, bananas for every meal," said Sarah. "'This shit is bananas ...'"

"STOP!" the other three yelled in unison.

"Geez, sorry. No need to be Gwen haters."

Candi stared at the banana she was having a hard time choking down. "She's right, we need to find other food. We're surrounded by the ocean. Maybe we could catch some fish or octopus ... or clams even."

"Oh, sick. Octopus." Sarah shivered for effect.

"Well, you could always stick with the bananas," suggested Jonathan.

Sarah nudged him with her foot and he smiled back.

Kevin didn't appear to be nearly as tired of the bananas yet as everyone else. "I ate at least four bananas a day at home. They're good for the muscles – all that potassium." He looked down at his bicep muscle as he flexed. "Damn. I'm already losing mass."

Candi sat mesmerized by the muscle that was slowly bulging up, out and then down again on Kevin's arm.

Kevin looked up and caught her staring.

She looked away quickly, but not before she saw him smiling at her. *Busted*.

"Okay, so let's make a list of everything we need to do," said Jonathan.

Everyone just sat there looking around.

"Shit, we don't have any paper," said Candi.

"Did Sugar Lump just say 'shit'?"

"Yes, she sure did," said Kevin happily.

"Don't call me Sugar Lump."

"Okay, stop fighting," said Jonathan. "We'll have to remember the list then. Each one of us will remember part of it. So what do we need to do?"

"Decide where to live. I think it should be near the fresh water," suggested Kevin.

"Agreed, but I also think we need to be able to see the shoreline from where we are."

"Yeah, you might have missed this while you were hanging over the edge of the cliff, but where we were, we had a perfect view of the entire island – which by the way is shaped like a giant peanut if anyone wants to know. Aaaand, there wasn't a single biting insect up there either, probably because of the deliciously refreshing breeze."

"Okay, so unless anyone has any problem with it, I think we should build our permanent camp near the fresh water."

"But it's not a camp, it's a home," said Candi.

"Whatever."

"No, not whatever. It's not a camp, Jonathan." Candi was looking at him seriously, but he obviously didn't see what the big deal was because he just rolled his eyes.

Sarah chimed in. "No, I get it, she's right. We have to stop acting like this is just a couple day thing. We could be here for a really long time. I mean, so far we have seen zero signs of any other people, either here on the island or out there in the water. I looked out over the island when we were up on that rock. The whole thing looks the same. Maybe we're going to be here a long time. I don't know about you guys, but I'm not going to continue to freak out about it, 'cause if I do, I'm gonna get zits." She finished firmly, "We need to find a *home*, not a camp."

Kevin looked at Jonathan and they exchanged knowing looks. Candi was certain both of them were thinking about PMS. *Whatever. So long as it kept them from arguing.*

"Okay, we'll find a *home* to live in. We can build it out of bamboo and palm fronds."

Sarah sat up excitedly, "Oh, and we had the most amazing idea. The place by the water and the bamboo and the view – it has a huge, huge elephant leg tree, and we were saying we should build our home in the tree – a treehouse like they have at Disney World, Swiss Family whatever. Tree, breeze, view, no bugs ... heaven!"

Candi couldn't help but join in. "That sounds perfect. I want to see it right away! And what is an elephant leg tree?"

"I think we need to wait for Kevin to feel better. Maybe tomorrow," cautioned Jonathan.

"Of course, yeah, we can wait for Kevin." Candi felt a little bad that she had just blown off his condition so easily.

"Why, thank you, sand beast."

Candi ignored him. "So, elephant leg tree? Anyone?" She looked from Jonathan to Sarah, waiting for an explanation.

"Oh, I don't know," said Sarah. "It's a giant tree that has a trunk about the size of a car, grayish and kinda wrinkly and thick ... like an elephant leg or a group of 'em all stuck together."

"I think the tree is a banyan tree or a ficus or something. It really is huge – wide enough to support a pretty big structure. Our biggest problem is going to be the bamboo. We have a hatchet from the boat supplies, but I think bamboo is pretty tough to cut."

"Leave that part to me," said Kevin, mocking a weight lifter's pose. "Fire power!"

"Ugh," said Sarah.

Candi tried not to stare but couldn't help herself. Kevin caught her looking again and winked. At this point he was doing all of his flexing for her benefit, and she knew it.

"So what else? Kevin, you remember the house thing on the

list. What else do we need to do?"

"Find another water source," reminded Sarah.

"Right. You remember that. What else?"

"Figure out how to catch fish or whatever."

"Yes, definitely. Candi, you remember that."

"I also think we should put together some transportation for the island as we explore," said Jonathan.

"What do you mean? Like a railroad?" Kevin said jokingly.

"No, not exactly, but maybe we could find a way to travel through the jungle quicker, in the trees or something, rig up some platforms. I'm just thinking maybe we could move from tree to tree instead of on foot down there with the critters."

"Ah-ha, like Tarzan or something. I like the way you think, Jonathan," said Kevin. Then he let out a wail that was supposed to be a Tarzan call but sounded more like wounded water buffalo.

"Um, yeah, I think you'd better work on that, Kevin," said Candi.

"What? Not ready for prime time?"

Everyone shook their heads no.

"Fine, I'll work on it. You guys are just jealous, I know."

"What else? Anything else?"

"Smoke signals."

"What do you mean, Kevin?

"I mean, we need to have some giant bonfire we can light if we see a boat ... something to signal rescuers."

"Absolutely.   Excellent idea.   That one is also yours to remember. So let's review. What are we going to plan for and do starting tomorrow?"

"House, bonfire."

"Good."

"Fish."

"Operation Tarzan."

"Fine. Good. What else? Oh, collect more water." Jonathan looked around the camp at the faces staring back at him. "There's one other thing."

"What?" they all answered in unison.

"We need to name the island."

No one said anything at first. It was as if naming it made it all the more real, like it wasn't temporary anymore.

Kevin was the first with a suggestion. "How about B-F-E Island?"

Everyone laughed.

"No, seriously."

Then the ideas came flooding in.

"Bug Island."

"Skeeter Beach."

"Hellhole Island."

"Life's a Beach Island."

"Armpit of the World Island."

"SuckySuckLand."

"I Wish I Was Somewhere Else Island."

"Runaway Island."

"Nowhere Island."

"Sandineverycrevice Island."

"The Sand Lot."

"Peanut Island."

Everyone stopped after that one. It had come from Sarah.

"What? I told you the island is shaped like a peanut, you can totally see it up on the rocks."

They all looked at each other and made the decision, nodding their heads.

Jonathan slapped himself on the knee as if banging a gavel. "Peanut Island it is."

"And today, Jonathan is the king of Peanut Island because he found the water!" said Sarah.

"Hey!" said Kevin, in mock injury.

"Don't worry," Sarah assured him, "a new king will be crowned each day, depending on his contribution." She smiled sweetly at him and then at them all.

"And I suppose you're the queen of the island?" asked Candi.

"Of course."

"And what does that make me?"

The question hung in the air above their heads. There was a challenge in her eyes; there was an answering challenge in Sarah's.

They all knew this was a game changing moment here on Peanut Island. Even though it was going to pass in a mere second or two and seemed kind of silly, the answer Sarah chose to give would have far-reaching consequences. Would she answer as the old Sarah – the Sarah that never deigned to even acknowledge Candi's existence at school? Or the new Sarah – the one who had started to let her guard down? The one who had begun to form a delicate connection with Jonathan ...

"Well, you are the other queen, of course. There are two queens on this island – permanent queens. The kingship, on the other hand, is a rotating crown." She smiled serenely out at her subjects.

Candi grinned, satisfied with the outcome. Something had changed in her too. She wasn't going to take the back seat anymore. Going to this faraway place at the ends of the earth had shown her that reality was not the reality created for her by other people at high school; it was what she created for herself. There was something much bigger at play here, and she was going to be a player. No more getting played for Candi Buckley.

*****

As they finished dinner, talk turned to their parents, a subject they had all deliberately avoided discussing. There were plenty of tears all around as they wondered aloud what had happened to them, wondered if they had gotten off the ship okay. They assumed they had – they had to in order to avoid the pain of the alternative. Even Sarah, who wasn't her father's biggest fan, didn't like the idea of losing him to the depths of the ocean. They had seen firsthand those swarming sharks, and the idea of people they loved in the midst of something like that was too much.

As they were talking about their parents, Kevin started to feel uncomfortable. He couldn't help but think about what his father had been planning to do with the Buckleys' dad. He wasn't sure that it would have hurt them, but if it had been entirely on the up and up, his dad wouldn't have been such a jerk about it when the subject came up or tried hiding what he was really doing.

He knew his dad was under a lot of pressure, and he wasn't the nicest or fairest of guys in those circumstances. Kevin wanted to share his thoughts with the group, but he was ashamed. He was embarrassed for his dad and didn't want to hurt the relationship they had all started to build together here on Peanut Island. *Besides*, he thought to himself, *who knows if we'll ever get off this island?* Maybe they wouldn't, then it would never matter what his father did or didn't do over in the real world.

Kevin's reverie was broken up by Sarah calling out to Candi across the fire Jonathan had made.

"Candi, so what are your plans for your hair?" she asked,

innocently.

"What do you mean, 'plans'?"

"I mean, it kinda looks like a giant knot on your head, and I was thinking I might have some thoughts on what we can do with it."

Candi eyed her suspiciously. "Like what?"

"Like dreads."

"Are you serious? No way."

"Why not? We're on an island. You have frizzy hair, which is nearly impossible to keep combed with no conditioner. Besides, it would look good on you."

"You're nuts." She shook off the comments. "I'm more worried about clothes."

Sarah thought about that for a second. "That is a problem." She looked down at her leopard print dress that had definitely seen better days. "I think you and I should see what we can find out there in the jungle that might be useable as a cloth or something that can be woven. We don't need it yet, but eventually we will if our rescuers take their sweet time getting here."

"You guys should see if there is any hemp growing here," suggested Jonathan.

"What's hemp?" asked Candi.

"It's a member of the cannabis family – a very fibrous plant that makes excellent cloth, rope and other useful things. I saw a special on it on TV once."

"Of course you did," responded Sarah with only a little sarcasm in her voice this time. "Do you remember what it looks like?"

"I think so. I could probably draw it in the sand tomorrow when we have light."

"Perfect. The Queens of Peanut Island will forage for clothing and rope material on the morrow. And now, I'm off to bed." She dipped her head towards Candi. "Your Highness."

Candi dipped her head in return. "Your Highness."

Jonathan and Kevin just shook their heads but were smart enough to stay quiet.

Candi joined Sarah over on the sheet that was their makeshift bed for one more night. Both of them fell asleep instantly.

A New Home

"OKAY, EVERYBODY UP! LET'S GO! Rise and shine! Time to get the lead out and get the dead out! Time for our morning workout!"

Candi was having a nightmare; a nightmare where her life's biggest crush had turned into a drill sergeant and was planning to make her do jumping jacks until she died of exhaustion.

She felt something touching her ear. She reached up to brush it off and her hand bumped into a face.

She opened her eyes to see Kevin's face about an inch away. He was staring at her, unblinking. She didn't move a muscle – she just closed her eyes and wished him away, groaning.

"Wake uuuup sleepy head, time to exercise!" He snuck a kiss onto her forehead, making her mad and happy at the same time.

Then from above her head she heard, "Okay, crew, you have exactly one minute to meet me on the beach for sunrise calisthenics. After that, if you don't show, better be prepared to take a bath in the very cold and very sharky morning ocean! Come on, team, up you go!"

And then the sound of retreating footsteps could be heard.

"Is he frigging kidding me?" asked a sleepy Sarah.

"He sounded serious," said Jonathan.

Candi peeked her eyes open and watched him sitting up and wiping the sleep out of his eyes.

"Actually, this is probably a good idea. We should stay in good physical condition, it'll keep us from getting bored and going nuts."

"Speak for yourself," said Candi. "I'm perfectly happy being unhealthy and bored. Good night."

"I second that motion, Queen Candi. Good night."

Both girls turned over and went back to sleep. They missed the whispering that went on above their heads for the next two minutes.

Suddenly, Candi felt herself being picked up and carried at a fast pace down the beach.

"Whaa ... ?"

SPLASH! ... SPLASH!!

Both girls came up out of the water, sputtering. Candi was still not exactly sure what had happened.

"My hair! My hair!" wailed Sarah.

"Holy shit, you did NOT just pick me up while I was sleeping and throw me into the ocean!" yelled Candi.

"If you say so!" yelled a maniacal Kevin.

Sarah and Candi jumped up, minds set on seeking revenge. The boys ran away as fast as they could, easily outrunning the wet and still groggy girls.

"That's it, ladies! Hup, two, three, four! Get those legs out the door! First exercise: a one-mile run up and down the beach!"

"Screw you!" yelled Candi.

"Okay, if you say so!" responded Kevin, making an immediate u-turn. He fixed Candi with his gaze and started bearing down on her. She took one look at him and turned around, running in the other direction.

Candi heard Sarah scream from behind her. "Oh no you don't, Jonathan, you know I have bruised feet! *Jonathan!*"

Now both girls were screaming and running down the beach – but not out of fright. It was more from the rush of being chased. Candi couldn't keep the crazy anxiety from rising up and bursting out of her lungs.

Kevin finally caught up to Candi, wrangling her around so he could pick her up. He carried her complaining over his shoulder back to where Sarah and Jonathan had finally given up the chase, Sarah holding her side, trying to ease the running cramp there.

He set Candi down and put his hands on his hips in a determined stance. "I decided last night that just because we're on this stupid Peanut Island, it doesn't mean I need to lose all that I've worked for in my rugby career."

Sarah made a scoffing sound, which looked to be about all she could manage since she was so out of breath.

"Mock me if you will, but you don't get a body like mine," he paused to flex one of his biceps and wink at Candi, "by sleeping in and eating bananas all day."

They all looked at Sarah as she opened her mouth to get ready to sing, and yelled in unison, "Don't!"

Sarah closed her mouth and looked at them crossly. "Damn Gwen haters."

"I agree with you in principle, Kevin," said Jonathan. "I just think maybe your methods could use a little work. I'm used to running a lot, but maybe we could not get up at the crack of dawn. Say, more like, I don't know, eight o'clock?"

"It's too hot then, we'll get exhausted."

They all looked at each other and shook their heads.

Kevin looked a bit defeated. "Come on, guys! This is important to me, seriously, don't make me do it on my own." He turned his most powerful puppy dog eyes on the girls. Then he turned to Jonathan with his tough guy look.

"Come on, man, don't leave me hangin'. Besides, I can get your rubber band arms looking like this in no time." He flexed for emphasis, and Candi felt her heart leap once again at the sight of his bulging muscle.

"Really? You think I could get muscular like you?"

"Well, maybe not *as* muscular, but pretty close. Look at you, man – you've only been out here in the sun a few days and you're already looking leaner and tanner. Now we just need to get some protein into that body and start doing some workouts; you'll be big in no time. Chicks like big muscles, don't you, chicks?"

Sarah just raised her eyebrow at her brother.

Candi's face turned red, but she nodded her head. *No use denying it,* she thought. *They are impressive.*

"That's my girl! Now, Jonathan, whaddya say, are you in?"

Jonathan thought about it for a second. He looked over at Sarah who caught his eye and gave a very slight shrug of her shoulders.

"Fine, I'm in. But I prefer not to wake up at the crack of dawn if you can manage it."

"I'll see what I can do. Don't worry – you'll be very happy with your decision. Exactly one month from now you will be well on your way to being the second biggest stud on Peanut Island."

Jonathan frowned. "Aren't I already in that position?"

"Nope, Jonathan, you're not." Kevin clapped him on the back and then went running down the beach, turning some pitiful cartwheels on the way.

"Where does he get that energy? Wasn't he on his death bed yesterday?" asked a mystified Candi.

"I have no idea. I think he sucks it out of us. I'm feeling more tired already."

"Yeah, me too. Let's go eat some bananas; and please, for the love of God, don't sing the bananas song."

"Fine."

The girls made their way back to the campsite, deciding that their energies were better off channeled into packing up to move to their new home rather than doing crazy cartwheels down the beach.

*****

Jonathan watched everyone go in different directions as he mulled over the idea of getting buff. He'd never considered it before; not because it was a bad idea – it's just that he never saw himself that way.

He looked down at his arms, noticing for the first time that he was getting tanner. All his life when he had looked down at them, he'd seen the lily-white, freckled skin of a kid with distant Irish ancestry. Today he saw something else. The idea that he could be something different, someone other than who he'd always been, was intriguing.

The fact that he had looked to see Sarah's reaction to his decision of whether to commit to working out was also interesting. She was a girl that was so far out of his league, he never would have considered he could be a part of her world. But now here they were, in a very small world, indeed – but he was in it and she was in it. And if he played his cards right, pretty soon he would be the second biggest stud on Peanut Island. *And that could be pretty hard for someone like Sarah to resist.* Or at least, he hoped so.

Jonathan walked up to the campsite just in time to hear Candi say, "Well I think we should do it."

"Do what?" he asked.

"Candi thinks we should each be in charge of some sort of activity. Become an expert in it and train the others."

"I was thinking about figuring out the fishing thing," said Candi causally.

"You? Fishing?"

"Yes. Me. Fishing. I can do it."

"Oh, yeah, sure you can." Jonathan wisely kept his mouth shut. He was thinking back to the fishing misadventures they had taken with their father when they were younger, where she would cry whenever a worm got put on the hook.

"You'll see," said Candi casually.

"No, I think it's a good idea. I wonder what I could do."

"Jonathan, you're a brown belt in karate. Why don't you teach us that?"

"Whaaaat? You're a brown belt? How come I didn't know that about you?" asked a suddenly interested Sarah.

Jonathan shrugged his shoulders. "I don't know, I guess it never came up."

"I'll bet Kevin would be interested in that."

"In what?" asked Kevin as he came jogging up to the group, sweating like crazy and breathing heavily.

"Did you know Jonathan has a brown belt in karate? He could teach us to kick some butt."

"Seriously? Jonathan, that's cool, I'd like to learn some moves."

"Sure, if you guys want, I guess I could teach you some things."

"Awesome. I'm down. I'm in. When do our lessons start?"

"In the evening, when the sun is just about to set. That's a good, peaceful time."

"And Sugar Lump is going to teach us how to fish," offered Sarah.

"All riiiight. I'm looking forward to seeing her in action." Kevin gave her a knowing look while he jogged in place and did some boxing moves in the air in front of him.

"Mock me if you will, guys. You'll be sorry when I'm eating delicious steamed fish, and you're still eating bananas for every meal."

"Aw, come on Gumdrop, you're not going to leave us out to starve, now are ya?"

"Only if you don't respect my skills; if you want to eat my catch, you *have* to respect the skills."

"Okay, I solemnly swear to respect you in the morning," said Kevin with feigned soberness, stopping his manic exercising to put his hand on his heart in a mock pledge.

Candi threw the banana peel she'd been in the process of burying at him. "Pig."

Kevin looked around at what the girls were doing. "So, what's going on here?"

Sarah responded, "We're packing up and moving out. Start helping. We want to get to the new site and clear a spot for a temporary house before it gets dark tonight. I want you guys to see the view – it's really cool."

Within thirty minutes they had collected all their things and secured them in backpacks and slings made out of the sheet and tarp. They discussed moving the lifeboat, but it had already started to sink into the sand; it would be impossible to move without either a crane or a lot more people to help. They decided to just leave it there. They had removed anything that could be of use that wasn't permanently fixed to the inside of it.

Jonathan began erasing any sign of their campfire.

Sarah shook her head at what she was seeing. "Jonathan, why are you being so anal about hiding the fire stuff? It's not like the fire marshal is going to come along and give us a ticket."

"I'm worried about pirates."

Sarah snorted. "Are you feeling okay?"

"I'm feeling fine, and I'm serious. There are pirates out in these waters around islands like these; they kidnap people and steal from them and sometimes worse. I don't want to attract any unwanted attention, that's all."

The group exchanged uneasy looks. They had forgotten some of Jonathan's earlier cautionary statements. They moved to help him cover the evidence of their existence. After they were finished, they started hiking through the trees, following Jonathan's lead.

*****

Forty-five minutes later they arrived at the elephant leg tree. Kevin and Candi immediately understood why Sarah had described it that way.

"Wow, that's a big friggin' tree," was all Kevin could think to say.

"Amazing," added Candi.

"Wait, you haven't even seen the best part yet." Sarah led the way to the water.

They oohed and aahed, watching it pour off the rock to the ground below. Candi held her hand out, stepping towards the water as if in a trance.

Jonathan grabbed her shoulder to get her attention, but Sarah told him to let her go. She knew exactly what Candi was feeling at that moment. Sarah had already had her 'shower' and knew that this was what Candi wanted right now, more than anything.

While Candi let the water drip over her body, the rest of them started surveying the immediate area.

"So, what do you guys think?" asked Jonathan.

Kevin nodded his head in appreciation. "It's great. We can set up our temporary house under the roots of the tree, in the elephant legs or whatever, and then we can start work right away on the treehouse. I think there's plenty of support here. I mean, I'm no engineer or anything, but it looks solid to me."

"That's what I was thinking, too. Did you notice the stand of bamboo? We can use that for the floors, walls, and roof structure. We can use palm fronds for the filling in between the poles, the tarp can be our waterproofing for the top. I'm not sure we'll even need it though, with enough layers of palm fronds."

Sarah was slowly walking around, envisioning how to arrange their things in the tree roots so that they could maximize the space and be comfortable.

"Put my and Candi's things over there. You guys will be over there." Sarah was gesturing to two separate areas of the root system.

"Oh, so you're in charge of the house now?" asked Kevin.

"Yes, I've decided that this will be my activity. I will be the house decorator and arranger; I will be in charge of making our house a home." She fixed Kevin with a challenging look. "You got a problem with that?"

Kevin held his hands up in mock surrender. "No, not at all, you're good at that stuff, go for it. Just don't expect me to do any of it."

"Well, then, don't expect me to join your workout group,"

Sarah challenged.

Kevin looked at her with a fake hurt expression on his face. "So it's gonna be like that then, huh?"

"Yep. It's a tough world out here on Peanut Island, deal with it."

"Alright, fine, I'll weave a tablecloth or something."

Sarah smiled at him. "That's the spirit."

"So, Jonathan, when do our karate lessons start?" asked Sarah.

He answered her from around the other side of the tree. "Tomorrow, an hour before sunset."

"Excellent," said Kevin, rubbing his hands together. "Morning calisthenics, housekeeping, then karate. What a schedule."

"Don't forget fishing!" added Candi enthusiastically, now back from her mini shower.

"What do you plan to fish with?" asked Jonathan, coming over to join the group.

"I was thinking we could take some of these bamboo poles and sharpen the ends and make spears. Then we could try to find a shallow area of the water that has some rocks maybe and see if there are any fish to spear ... or whatever."

Kevin nodded his head appreciatively. "That might work; I'm willing to give it a shot."

"You guys can skip the fishing lessons until I've figured it all out. I'll get started in the morning after our exercising is done."

"What kind of spear do you want?" asked Kevin.

"I was thinking I'd like to try two types – one that's just straight and sharpened at the tip, the other one with three forks at the end, like a trident. Can you guys help me make 'em?"

Kevin looked over at Jonathan for confirmation. "Sure, we could probably give it a shot."

Candi gave him a winning smile. "Excellent. Maybe we'll have fish for dinner one of these days."

*****

They spent the next few hours setting up their temporary household. The tarp was used as a floor for the girl's bedroom area, and the boys used the now very dirty sheet. Candi and Sarah got to work gathering fallen palm fronds from the beachfront and jungle areas and dragging them to the big tree. They worked on layering them across the tops of the large roots, trying to create a waterproof roof.

"I think if we have enough of these things on top of each other, maybe even tied together somehow, we'll be able to keep out any water."

Candi looked out through the treetops to the darkening sky above. "I think we're going to find out tonight whether your theory is true or not. It looks like a storm is coming in."

"Oh, great. I'm not sure if we have enough here; maybe we should hook up the tarp instead."

"I'll do whatever you say," said Candi. This was Sarah's territory, and she wasn't going to step on her toes.

Sarah stood eyeing the structure that was slowly going up. "Let's just keep putting these palm fronds together. Angle them all the same way so when the water hits them it will follow the path of the leaves and drip down in the same direction."

Candi did as she was told. When they were finally finished and stood back to admire their handiwork, they were impressed with what they saw.

"There. If any rain gets through this, then I'm just going to have to Google how to do this roof stuff."

Candi laughed. Oh, how she missed Google. What she

wouldn't give right now to Google 'spear fishing'. It's funny how something that meant nothing to her before, like stabbing a poor fish with a stick, had now become one of the most important things in her life. She shook her head, thinking about how much her priorities had changed in just four days.

Jonathan and Kevin came back from the bamboo grove to see what the girls had done.

"Nice work!" said Jonathan enthusiastically. "It actually looks like some kind of island hut."

"Thanks," said Sarah, trying not to sound too proud of herself. The true test of her skills wouldn't come until later when the rain fell.

"Kevin and I rigged up some temporary rain catchers. Looks like we're going to get a storm later."

They all cast their eyes to the sky, noticing that the dark clouds had gotten thicker and were moving faster in their direction.

"Maybe we'd better eat early in case it's a real downpour," said Candi, nervously.

"Good idea. And I have a treat." Jonathan pulled out a few cracked-open coconuts from the backpack he had over his shoulder.

"Hey! How did you get those damn things open?" asked Sarah, moving forward to claim a half.

"I tried to use the hatchet but it wasn't working so well, so I slammed the husk over and over again against the rock and eventually it started giving way; then I just tore it off ... "

"Ahem ... "

"Okay, so Kevin tore it off, and then we slammed the nut against the rock and presto – it opened right up. We lost the water inside, but the coconut is really tasty and very moist."

Candi was having a hard time getting the coconut meat out to taste it. "How do you get the white stuff out?"

"Ah, well, since we don't really have a knife we can afford to use and possibly break, we've been just breaking off pieces of the nut and then biting the white stuff off with our teeth."

Candi shrugged her shoulders. "That works, I guess." She thought for another second. "This is giving me ideas for dinner – if I ever catch a fish, that is."

"Oh, yeah?" asked Kevin, "like what kind of ideas?"

"Well, we can take fish and cook it in the coconut over a fire. Maybe the flavor of the coconut will go up into the fish and make it taste more interesting."

"That sounds awesome, Candi, I can't wait to try it." Sarah was in such a good mood from her success at hut building, she couldn't help but be enthusiastic about Candi's ideas.

Everyone looked at her funny. She didn't sound like Sarah.

"What? ... What'd I say?"

No one answered. They just looked at each other. The island was working some strange voodoo magic on Sarah, making her actually act nice, even considerate.

Jonathan and Kevin starting walking over to the stand of bamboo.

"Hey, wait up!" said Candi.

Candi and Sarah joined them, walking through the bamboo until they reached the waterspout.

"Sarah, you mentioned you wanted to show everyone the view from the rock. Still interested?" asked Jonathan.

Sarah jumped at the chance to see the view again, her earlier confusion forgotten. "You guys are going to love this; but be careful. Failure to properly calculate your exponents and shit could cause you to fall on your ass."

"It's not exponents, Sarah, it's friction coefficients, and I didn't just fall on my ass; I nearly fell to my death."

"Whatever. Don't slip and fall, Jonathan, otherwise I'll have to rescue you again."

They all scrambled up, being careful to stay away from the sloped edge.

Once they reached the top of the rock, no one said a word. Sarah had not been exaggerating; the view was really incredible. They could look out over the island in all directions and see where it met the ocean on the south end. Even under the darkened sky, the water was a beautiful blue-green, fading to turquoise and then light brown as it met the beach. Turning northward, they were able to see over the treetops to the far end of the island. The tree cover was too dense to see through. They could see what Sarah meant when she said the island was shaped like a peanut – not a shelled peanut but a whole one with a couple of nuts inside.

"Wow ... imagine all the stuff that's out there under the trees that we haven't seen yet," said Kevin.

"Maybe we'll get lucky and get rescued before we have a chance," added Candi.

"Well, I for one think this is a good spot to light a signal fire," said Jonathan.

"You're right. Tomorrow I'll lug some wood and stuff up here and get it ready. No point in doing it now since it's probably going to get soaked."

"Speaking of which," Jonathan continued, "I think there's some sort of rainy season here, and if it's like the other areas in the tropics, it comes up in the next couple of weeks or so and lasts all summer. I think we'd better make it a priority to try and find a sheltered area, or maybe we could make one, where we can store firewood and stuff. I know it's hot here, and we really don't use the fire much, but later in the year it will probably get cold, at least at night."

Candi was too engrossed in the view to respond. She was straining her eyes as hard as she could, trying to see an island, a boat – anything at all other than Peanut Island. There was nothing.

"I agree," said Kevin. "I guess we have our work cut out for us. Tomorrow, workout on the beach, signal fire building, firewood storage, and then we start on the treehouse. Did I forget anything?"

"Karate practice in the late afternoon," added Sarah.

"Yeah, a little kung fu action, too, that's right." Kevin practiced some slow motion martial arts moves.

"It's not kung fu, that's another discipline. We'll be doing karate," corrected Jonathan.

"Whatever, dude. All I know is, I'm gonna judo chop some of those bamboo trees down."

Jonathan climbed down the rock, sighing. "It's not judo either, it's karate."

Kevin smiled. He clearly loved messing with Jonathan. "Yeah, okay, are we gonna do some tai chi moves then?"

Jonathan looked up at Kevin. "Are you kidding me?"

Kevin feigned innocence. "What?"

"Never mind, you're messing with me."

"Ah, I can't put anything past you anymore, Jonathan, you're onto me." Kevin joined him back on the ground next to the waterspout, putting his hand on Jonathan's shoulder. They both watched the water coming out over the rock.

"Man, could I ever use a shower."

"No kidding. You go ahead, you smell worse than me. I'll go

after." Jonathan walked away, leaving Kevin standing there.

"Wait a minute ... Did he just mess with me?"

"Yep," said Candi as she walked by.

"Well, I'll be damned," he said, a smile in his voice.

"Hey, what are you doing?" asked Sarah as she came down from the rock.

Candi turned to see what the fuss was all about.

"Taking a shower, what does it look like?"

"Well, before you strip down to your birthday suit, maybe you want to wait until we've gotten outta here."

"Doesn't bother me if you guys see me naked."

Sarah looked at him like he was crazy. "Well it bothers me. Ew."

Candi stood there panic stricken, speechless. Kevin was standing there without a shirt on, about to be totally naked.

"Ah ... um ... yeah ... I'm ... I'm gonna go now," was all Candi could say before the heat in her face made her feel like her head was going to explode. She turned and walked away as quickly as she could, back to the base of the tree and out of sight of the Peterson twins.

*****

"I think it bothers her too," said Sarah, as she turned and walked away, smiling.

Kevin chuckled to himself. The pained look on Candi's face was priceless. She was a virgin, he was nearly sure of it. The thought made him excited and worried at the same time. Here they were on this deserted island. He was the only guy in sight; she was the only girl. It was probably inevitable that they would eventually get together if help didn't come for a while. Normally he wouldn't give having sex with a girl a second thought – he'd just do it, so long as she was willing. But he knew for some reason that he couldn't and shouldn't be that nonchalant about it with Candi. She was different. Not to mention the fact that there was no birth control out here in the middle of nowhere.

Candi was already different from how she'd acted on the cruise ship. These few days away from the world in a place where they had to fend for themselves had already made its mark on her. Somehow she had gone from mildly cute to kinda sexy. *Maybe being stuck on this island with the little sand beast won't be so bad after all.*

He wondered if this experience had done the same for him – changed him at all. He felt the same, but he was starting to notice things he'd never noticed before, and he was feeling really relaxed for some reason, which really didn't make any sense.

As he rinsed the grime from his body as best he could, he thought about how he should be really freaked out and worried right now. Worried about surviving, worried about his team back home, worried about his parents – his life. But he wasn't. It's as if all that stuff had ceased to matter for now. *Oh well.* He shrugged it off. *Might as well enjoy it while it lasts.*

*****

The next few weeks were spent using the lifeboat hatchet to cut down bamboo poles of varying lengths and widths. They used the widest ones to create support poles and joists for the floor of the treehouse which they wedged against various parts of the tree trunk and its root system.

The guys spent a lot of time on the jungle floor and in the tree, studying it from every angle. They didn't want to spend too much time or waste materials on something that wasn't going to be secure or that would have to be re-done. They'd already made that

Elle Casey

mistake once, and they were still kicking themselves over the wasted effort.

The girls, in their explorations for cloth and other items that could be used to make things for the treehouse, found a group of plants in the jungle that came from what Jonathan thought might be hemp. They were very fibrous and so far were turning out to be very useful. Jonathan had the girls pull the plant fibers off in long strips; they used these strips that were braided together to make a plant rope to wrap around and bind the bamboo poles to one another.

Kevin and Jonathan also did their best to make corresponding notches in the wood so it would join together like puzzle pieces on the ends. It was difficult because the wood was very strong and hard to cut with just the hatchet. Each notched joint was fitted into place, then tied with several lengths of plant rope. Next, it was tested by Kevin bouncing up and down on it. Anything that had too much give or seemed loose was re-done. No one wanted to come crashing down out of the tree to the ground below.

The rock next to their tree was good for sharpening the hatchet, which was a good thing, since the bamboo was so thick and strong and dulled the blade pretty easily. They couldn't believe their luck at having a whole stand of it right near their water source. Now that they'd cut quite a bit of it down, they were seeing how the poles that remained were going to act as a wall that could close off a section of the bottom of their root system, giving them ground storage areas they could protect from animals. Not that they'd seen any animals on the island yet – but they had heard stirrings in the night, so it was highly likely something was out there somewhere.

Sarah's roof building and weaving skills had proven

themselves over and over. From the first night when they got a downpour until today, they had been able to sleep in relatively dry quarters. Once they were off the jungle floor, it was going to be perfect.

Sarah had been weaving floor mats, roof materials, bed materials and all kinds of things in anticipation of the treehouse finally being finished. She'd convinced the guys that the girls needed cots to sleep on, so they had cut some thinner bamboo poles to her specifications; she put the frames together, tying them at the corners using the fibrous plant rope. Now she was working on woven palm fronds as the slings to put between the bamboo pole frames. She had a feeling once the guys saw what she was doing, they would want sleeping cots of their own, so she made extra.

Candi was gone every day, always down at the water trying to figure out how to spear fish. She had found a spot on the south side where there were some large rocks spread apart in the shallow water. The tides and water currents had created small pools where the fish loved to look for food. She'd stand on the rocks and try to spear the fish from above. She claimed that she got close once, but so far had come back each day empty handed. She was determined, though, and no one had the heart to give her a hard time about it or tell her to give up.

The morning exercises organized by Kevin now included a rugby scrimmage at the end. They used a coconut with the husk still on as their rugby ball. It was about the right size and weight. Kevin was determined not to forget his moves or lose his agility.

Unfortunately for him, his team was pretty lame – although he had to admit, they'd come a long way in three weeks. Now they could all run around and do what he told them without getting side cramps or collapsing on the beach, gasping for air. He'd even felt

Jonathan's strength improving as he tried to tackle Kevin to the ground.

Jonathan's muscles had really started to noticeably develop with the combined work of morning exercise and treehouse building. The coconuts they were eating had natural fats and protein, which gave their bodies the fuel they needed to put on the muscle. Kevin told them that as soon as they had fish added to their diet, they could really amp up their improvements.

With just the coconuts and bananas, Jonathan wasn't able to eat enough calories to get really big muscles, and Kevin could feel himself losing weight. His torn and ragged shorts were getting looser and looser. He'd already had to make a belt out of the plant rope just to keep them up. This would have bothered him more a month ago when rugby was his life. Now he didn't care so much. He looked down to admire his six-pack abs from time to time, which before had not been as sharp or defined because he'd had more body fat. And if the surreptitious looks he kept catching from Candi were any indication, she was happy with what she saw, too.

The karate lessons Jonathan had been giving in the evening were helping all of them with their flexibility and balance. Kevin wondered why he hadn't thought of doing that kind of workout before. When and if he ever got back home, he was going to be unstoppable on the field.

Kevin stopped his musings when he heard a loud whooping coming from the direction of the beach. He could hear Candi crashing through the trees on the path from the beach to the treehouse.

"That's right, bitches, I caught us a fish! Whoot! Whoot!" Candi came skipping out of the trees, dangling a fish from its gills and grinning from ear to ear.

Sarah came from around the back of the tree where she had her weaving and building workshop.

"Awesome, I can't believe you did it! You totally rock. How'd you do it?"

Jonathan came down from the treehouse where he had been securing a wall Sarah had designed.

"Is that a fish I see there? Holy crap, Candi, you did it!" He walked up and gave her a big hug. "I'm so proud of you. You stuck with it, and you did it."

"Yep, I finally did it. Man, I was ready to quit too, you know? But then I just said, no dammit, everyone else is pulling their weight – I have to do this. And then I started working more on my technique. It's hard because the water kind of warps the position of the fish, so you think you're stabbing in the right place and then it misses the fish entirely. For the longest time, I thought the fish was moving and that's why I was missing, but I finally figured out that it was the distortion of the water. Duh."

"Uh, yeah, I might have forgotten to mention that little issue of optical refraction to you."

Candi brushed her brother's guilty comment aside. "Doesn't matter, I figured it out. At least, I think I have." She held the fish up in front of her face to look at it closer. "I hope this guy is edible."

"I think as long as it doesn't puff up, have a beaky mouth, or have really bright colors, we should be okay."

Sarah frowned at the fish. "I wish we had a monkey that we could make taste our food to see if it was poisonous. I saw some berry looking things in the trees that might be good, but I'd be afraid to try them."

"You know, Sarah, that's not a bad idea," said Jonathan.

"Uh, yeah, except that we are minus one monkey, which is

kind of the key to the whole plan, unless you're volunteering yourself for the job?"

"Stop. No, I know that. But we could use another animal, like a rat maybe."

"Ew! There are rats here?" asked Sarah, looking around her and moving closer to Kevin.

"I don't know, probably. They can swim and they used to stow away on boats all the time. I think at this point they're everywhere. We should try to set some traps, see if we can catch any."

"Well, you're on your own with that one, Jonathan. I don't want anything to do with rats." Sarah shivered.

"They're really not bad, Sarah. We had them as pets at home for lots of years. Jonathan used to do behavioral experiments with them for extra credit in psychology class. They're very sweet and lovable. Smart too."

Sarah just stared at Jonathan. "That's just some weird shit, Jonathan. Why do you guys tell me this stuff?" She shook her head and walked away.

"What?" He followed behind her to her workshop. "What?"

Kevin couldn't hear him anymore as he rounded the corner. "Good work on the spear fishing," he said, quietly.

Candi smiled shyly. "Thanks. Do you know if we have any open coconuts lying around?"

"No, but I can get you some. We have a pile of rugby balls over there." He gestured to the pile of coconuts they had gathered from some trees earlier. Jonathan, with his newfound fitness, had become quite adept at shimmying up the coconut palms and pulling the nuts down.

"Okay, I need one broken up coconut and a couple of banana palm leaves. Try to keep the coconut water if you can 'cause I want to use that too."

Kevin was psyched to finally have something new on the menu. "Okay, Chef, coconuts and banana leaves coming right up!"

A short while later he came back and found Candi stoking the fire she had made. He handed her the ingredients, and she set to work arranging them together. "Oh, I also need some saltwater, can you get me some?"

He came back a few minutes later with the water and was immediately impressed by what he saw. Candi had taken the fish and laid it in a double layer of banana leaves. Under the fish were broken pieces of coconut with the white meat still attached, facing up. She carefully poured the coconut water that Kevin had saved over the top, and it was resting in the coconut pieces that were slightly concave. She sprinkled a bit of the salt water over the top, then curled the banana leaves over the whole package, handling it very carefully.

"Hand me some of that rope stuff, would you?"

"Sure."

He watched as she tied the package up in several spots, making what looked like a neat, fish-shaped, green birthday present.

"Won't the rope just burn off?"

"Probably, but by the time that happens, maybe the leaves will be dry enough that they'll stay put. Or the fish will be cooked by then. We'll see, this is just an experiment."

Candi gingerly set the fish aside until the fire was going well and the coals were hot. She carefully set the fish over the top of the coals, using two high rocks on either end to suspend the fish above the heat.

"Now we wait about twenty minutes or so. I think."

Kevin and Candi sat there staring at the green package over the fire.

"You're pretty amazing, you know that?" said Kevin, looking up at her.

"Yeah, I know, right?" Candi shot him a winning smile.

"And modest too."

"Maybe not so much, at least not today."

"Hey, you deserve to be proud of yourself. Do you have any idea how sick I am of bananas? I never thought I'd say that. I mean, I used to eat bananas like crazy back home." He paused as he thought about memories that were not as sharp as they had been just a few weeks ago, then continued, "Let's just say that I'm looking forward to eating the catch of the day."

"Well, I hope it cooks okay, because I'm burned out on bananas too."

About fifteen minutes later, Sarah and Jonathan came back around from the other side of the tree, laughing at something Jonathan had said.

Candi smiled and it made Kevin happy just to see it.

Sarah squatted down to admire Candi's handiwork. "Wow, what do we have here? Emeril Lagasse in da' hizouse!"

"Hey, that looks really professional, Candi," commended Jonathan. "What's inside? Besides the fish I, mean."

"Oh, a little of this, a little of that."

"Kevin?"

"Hey, my lips are sealed, man. I can't give the cook's secrets away, or she'll kick me out of the kitchen."

"Well, I think it's probably done by now," announced the chef. "We just have to get it off the fire."

"Here," said Jonathan. "Use these."

He handed Kevin a couple of short bamboo poles with the ends cut off halfway, making a flat, scoop-like surface. Kevin used them like giant salad forks to grab the wrapped fish and drop it over to the side of the fire, where they could pull it out of the wrapping without being burned.

Candi carefully pulled on the strings, which gave way easily since they were completely dried out and burned most of the way through. She pulled the dried banana leaf to the side to see what the fish looked like inside.

A cloud of steam came up from the opening in the leaves. The smell was nice – very faintly coconutty.

"Mmm, that smells gooooood," said Kevin, enthusiastically, rubbing his hands together.

"I'm not sure what to do now," confessed Candi.

"Just reach in there and pull a hunk off," suggested Kevin.

Candi reached in and touched the fish but pulled her hand back quickly. "Too hot."

"Here, let me try."

Kevin took the edge of the leaves and pulled the fish towards himself. He gingerly touched the fish, and slowly teased a hunk of flesh away from the body. He popped it into his mouth after pulling the skin off.

The other three searched his face, looking for a sign.

Kevin closed his eyes, opening his mouth to let cool air in so his tongue wouldn't burn. "Mmmm ... heaven."

They all dove towards the fish, completely forgetting any manners or concerns about temperature. They each got a chunk of fish and shoved it into their mouths, not caring whether they got all the skin off first.

"Holy shit, Candi, this is really good," said Sarah, shock in her voice.

"Hey, don't sound so surprised."

Sarah tried to respond around a mouth full of fish. "I don't mean that you're normally a bad cook or anything, it's just, I didn't realize you were like a professional." She smiled as fish juice ran down her chin.

Candi blushed with the compliment. "It's pretty good, isn't it?"

A couple minutes later, they all looked down at the carcass that was sitting on the remains of the banana leaves. "Um, I think next time you should take the guts out," said Jonathan.

"Ew. Yeah, I second that idea," agreed Sarah.

"Yeah, you're right. I was just so excited to have you guys see it and eat it, I didn't even think about that. Next time I'll take the guts out."

They were all satisfied, even full. The fish was flakey and light and had a nice coconut taste that went perfectly with the light salting Candi had added. Even the chunks of coconut had cooked through and easily separated from the nutshells.

Kevin patted her on the back as they walked toward the waterspout to wash off his face and hands. "You can cook for me any day of the week and twice on Sunday, Gumdrop. That was amazing."

"Me too," agreed Jonathan.

"Me three," chimed in Sarah.

Candi smiled as she followed the others to the water. Success at last. "Maybe now I can teach you guys – now that I've finally figured it out."

"Sounds good to me," said Kevin.

That night they all went to bed content and satisfied. It was an especially good night after Kevin and Jonathan announced that the treehouse would be ready to live in by the next day. It wouldn't be completely finished for another few weeks, but the floors and roof were in; it was solid enough for a trial run. All four of them fell asleep dreaming of the beds and the night breezes they were going to be enjoying very soon.

*****

The next morning, Jonathan was the first one up. "Well, I think we can officially verify that we have rats on this island with us."

Kevin walked up to join him. "What's up?"

"Well, obviously something came and took what was left of the fish guts. Plus they left some pellets behind; and I know rat poop when I see it."

"I'll trust you on that one, buddy," said Kevin as he walked to the water spout. He shouted over his shoulder, "I want to get a jump-start on the last bit of flooring we need to put in, so the treehouse could be ready for tonight."

The girls walked over and stood by Jonathan.

"Candi, can you help me today with a few things?" asked Sarah.

"Sure, what'd ya have in mind?"

"Just a couple things for the treehouse. It'll go faster if you help me, and I'd love to have it all done for our first night."

"No problem, just tell me what to do. I'm going to go fishing first if that's okay, but I don't think it will take me as long this time."

"Yeah, that's fine, I'll see you later then, after lunch."

Candi begged to be excused from exercise for the day, and Kevin decided to let everyone off the hook. They were all excited about getting the treehouse ready to live in.

They worked hard the entire day, stopping only for five

minutes to eat a lunch of bananas, coconut and water.

Candi came back from her fishing trip without any fish. "I think it was too early in the day or something. I usually go later when the sun is lower."

"You can go again later. Come help me with my projects," said Sarah, glad to have an assistant.

Jonathan and Kevin worked harder than they'd ever worked in their lives, that day. They made a good team, choosing the right materials together and easily agreeing how everything should fit together. With Jonathan's added muscle, it got easier and easier to transport the materials and get them in place.

"What do you think, Jon? Is she going to be ready?"

"Yeah. We just need to finish that part of the floor and that one wall, and that'll be good enough for temporary living space. What do you think?"

"Yes, definitely. Let's get this mother done."

*****

"Wow, I'm totally impressed with the progress you've made." She walked through Sarah's workshop. "Cots!" She laid down on one. "Oooh, comfy. Is there one for me?"

"Of course. You're laying on it right now."

Candi sat up and looked around. "I love the table. How cool is that? It's like a Japanese restaurant table. We're going to sit on the floor around it, right?"

"Yes. I made cushions to sit on by weaving a big pocket out of palm fronds and then stuffing it with crumbled up palm frond leaves and palm canvas." The canvas was a material that naturally came off the palms around the coconut bunches. It was pliable and thick and made good cushion innards.

"What else? I feel like I'm at Pier One Imports, shopping for my new house."

Sarah smiled.

"I made shutters to go over the window holes that will eventually be in all the treehouse walls. Right now since we only have one wall, I have only one set of shutters. I need you to help me finish that project."

"Sure, no problem. What do we need the shutters for?"

"The rainy season. I think the rain is going to come in at an angle. That's how it was when we took a vacation to Miami one year, anyway – the rain came down and the wind blew it sideways."

Candi held up a rectangular-shaped woven mat. "What's this?"

"It's a placemat."

"Why do we need placemats?"

"We don't *need* them. It's just ... I don't know. To make our little treehouse more like home." She flipped one back and forth, flicking the edge with her fingers. "My mom was always a placemat fanatic. She loved a formal dining table setting. I miss her. This is kind of my way of having her here with me, even though I know she can't be." Sarah looked at the ground, hiding her face.

Candi reached over and stroked her arm. "I'm sorry. I didn't mean to sound critical. I think it's nice how you're making everything so comfortable for us. It's going to make a big difference in our lives. Seriously. Thank you."

Sarah nodded, fighting the sadness and pushing thoughts of missing her mom to the back of her mind.

Candi walked over to admire one of Sarah's roof panels. It was several layers thick, secured with a complicated weaving technique that looked like it would last a long time.

"Man, Sarah, you are seriously good at homemaking."

Sarah shot Candi a suspicious look.

"No, I mean it. I know in this day and age that sounds like an insult – but here on Peanut Island, it's a major compliment. If it wasn't for you, we'd still be sleeping on a dirty sheet in a swarm of bugs."

"Thanks, Candi, that's very sweet of you. It was a team effort." She looked around at her handiwork. "I am good at this, though, aren't I? I think if we were back home, I would never have appreciated what it meant to make a home. Now I do, I really do. I'm not ashamed of that. Even when we get back, I'm sure I'll still feel the same way. This is important." She stopped for a moment to consider what she had just said. "Holy shit. Shoot me now, would you please? I sound just like my mother."

Candi laughed.

The girls both went quiet then, thinking about home, wondering what their mothers were doing. Neither wanted to consider what it might be like for them, home alone, thinking they had lost all of their children. Or worse – that their parents wouldn't be home at all.

Moving In

FINALLY THE END OF THE afternoon came. The guys announced that the floors were totally done. Under Kevin's direction, all four of them formed an assembly line to get their new furnishings into the treehouse. They used a ladder they'd made of bamboo and rope; it was designed to lean against an opening on the edge of the treehouse and could be pulled up and stored above, making it impossible for anyone below to come up if they didn't want them to.

They spent an hour putting the cots away, laying down woven sleeping mats for the guys, working on securing the roofing materials better, and attaching the one set of shutters. The guys put the table in place, and Sarah carefully placed the cushions around it.

The last item Sarah put up was a small mirror that had come from her makeup case. She had framed it with a palm frond border. This she hung by its plant rope loop on a splinter of bamboo that had been implanted into the side of one of the poles of the treehouse in the area she had designated as the bathroom. They couldn't actually use this area as a toilet – that place was still deep in the woods as far as they could reasonably make it from their water source. This bathroom was for brushing teeth and doing hair.

Not that there was a lot of hair doing going on these days, but maybe in the future, when all the building was over, there would be time for beauty again. Sarah sighed. What she really needed was running water.

"What are the chances you guys could get some running water up here?" Sarah asked of no one in particular.

"I don't know about running water, but we could probably rig some sort of water in a pulley system kind of thing," suggested Jonathan.

"Yeah, but not until we get everything else done," said Kevin. "We still have walls that need to go up, platforms to build, extensions to add. The water pulley thing comes after that stuff." He stared at Jonathan, giving him one of those looks that said, 'Don't even think about it.' He knew how easily Jonathan was influenced by Sarah these days. If Kevin let her have her way, Jonathan would build her a fully functioning bathroom with a spa tub before they had the damn walls up. *How and when did Jonathan get so wrapped up in my sister, anyway?*

When they were finally done and the sun was lower on the horizon, they gathered around the south side of the treehouse, in what was the guys' bedroom, looking out over their rock to the treetops, beach, and water below. There were a lot of branches and leaves hanging down in front of the wall, providing an effective screen against the sunlight and the intruding eyes of anyone approaching the island from the south – but there was enough space between the branches and leaves to see out over the water. The view was simply magical.

Candi stood next to Kevin. He reached out, putting his arm around her. She didn't resist. It was nice to stand there and feel the breeze on his face and the warmth of Candi's body next to his.

*****

Jonathan watched Kevin and his sister out of the corner of his eye. He wasn't surprised to see them getting closer. He turned the other way and saw Sarah standing off by herself. She didn't seem to be aware of what was going on. He wondered if she would approve of her brother and his sister together.

Jonathan stepped over to stand next to Sarah and began speaking quietly with her, at a volume only she could hear.

"What are you thinking about?"

"I was just wondering if we're ever going to get off the island."

"What do you think?"

"I'm not sure. I don't even know how badly I want to be rescued right now."

"Why do you say that?"

"I don't know. I'm conflicted. I do miss my old life – but not as much as I probably should."

"I don't get it."

Sarah sighed. "School's always been so easy for me, you know? I had lots of friends, a boyfriend, lots of things to do on weekends ... but there are a lot of things I don't miss, too."

"Like what?"

"I feel guilty saying it."

"It's just us here. I'm not going to judge you."

"My parents for one," she said, looking down at the bamboo floor. "I should miss them more, but I don't. I miss my mom a little. But shouldn't a girl miss her mom more than that?"

Jonathan shrugged. "I guess it depends on the mom."

"And my dad. I really don't miss him at all. Whenever he was home, I tried not to be. Now I don't have to work at avoiding him."

"So being on this island is easier."

"Yeah. I guess. It's almost like a relief, not to have to deal with all that negativity. At home and at school. The drama got old."

"You do seem happier here."

Sarah gave him a narrow-eyed look. "That sounds like a nice way of saying something else."

Jonathan held his hands up in surrender. "No, not at all. I mean it. You're more relaxed. Just less ... stressed."

She stared out at the water again. *"Water, water everywhere, nor any drop to drink."*

"That's weird. That's exactly what I was thinking when we were on that lifeboat."

"Thank you, Language Arts class. I can't get that stupid poem out of my head. At least here there *is* a drop to drink."

"That reminds me, wanna go check the water catchers with me? We had some good rain last night, so they might be full."

Sarah shrugged. "Sure, why not."

Jonathan and Sarah moved away from the back room and climbed down to the ground. They strolled toward the rainwater catching basins that Kevin and Jonathan had rigged out of banana leaves and bamboo cups they had made.

It turned out that each bamboo pole had several cups in it. Each one of the rings that was visible on the outside was actually an internal divider that ran completely through the cane. All they had to do was make a cut just below each ring, and they instantly had a sturdy cup that would hold water. Not only were they using these cups to store water around the treehouse, they were also using the cups at mealtimes.

They arrived at the water-gathering site a couple minutes later.

"Looks like we're full. Here – take some of these water bottles and fill them up from the cups."

Sarah took three bottles from Jonathan and started emptying the cups into them.

"Do you think we'll ever get off this island?" asked Sarah.

"Yes, I think so. I don't know that it'll be soon, but eventually humans will move in this direction. The planet is already suffering from overcrowding."

"Have you thought about what life will be like when we get back?"

"Not really, have you?"

"I have been lately."

"You don't sound very happy about it."

"I guess I'm not."

"That's strange."

"Why?" Sarah stopped filling up her bottle and looked at Jonathan.

"I don't know. I heard what you said earlier, and I get it; but I still can't discount how popular you were in school. You had lots of friends, a nice car, a nice house. You're beautiful. I guess, what I'm saying is, you had it all there. Why wouldn't you want to go back to having it all? Even if there's drama and stuff – it's got to beat being here with just three other people and not a lot to do other than survive."

"Well, I could say the same about you."

Jonathan smiled. "That's really nice of you to say that, but you know it isn't true."

"Well, sure it is. You had friends in school. You had your own transportation, a decent house. Your parents seem pretty nice. What's not to miss?"

"First of all, comparing our lives is like comparing apples to oranges. I was invisible in that school. You were the homecoming queen. You're a supermodel, and I'm – well – I'm me. My friends were just as invisible as I was. Your friends are the who's who of our town. You live in a mansion, I live in a saltbox." Jonathan shook his head, not agreeing with her assessment. "There's no comparison, really."

Sarah walked over to where Jonathan was standing, filling up a water bottle.

"I've had some time to reflect on my life back at school, and I've decided after hearing you say this stuff that our lives back there were seriously effed up."

Jonathan chuckled. "In what way?"

"Well, every way really. I mean, you defined us and our positions in school by our looks and the status of our friends. It's like who we are, deep inside, really didn't matter at all. That's just ... bullshit."

Jonathan nodded his head. Logically, what she was saying made sense, even though he knew high school life wasn't necessarily based on logic. "Go on, I'm listening."

"And your assessment of my home life is so far off – I mean you have no idea. My father is a complete douchebag, and my mother is a drugged-out airhead who can't even open her mouth to protect her own children."

Jonathan stopped what he was doing and looked at her. She was staring at him intently.

"Why do you hate your father so much, and what do you mean your mother's drugged out?"

Sarah walked over and sat down on a nearby log. "My father and I have a long history of mutual loathing. When I was a little girl, I thought he was awesome; he was my dad, you know? But then, when I was about thirteen or so, he just turned into this monster. One day I was getting ready to go to school, and he didn't like what I was wearing, so he just tore into me. He actually told me I looked like a slut. It, like, totally came out of the blue."

"Wow. That's pretty harsh."

"I know, right? No matter what I did after that day, he just wouldn't let up. Every day it was like he had a new insult – for my hair, my clothes, my brains or lack of them. He used to say that someday my personality was going to get me into a lot of trouble, that no one liked people like me."

"God, what a jerk."

"No, the word is 'douchebag'. I decided after hearing his insults for years and trying unsuccessfully to change his attitude towards me, that I might as well just be full-on me. When I was sixteen I told him to go suck it. That kind of sealed the deal between us."

"Holy crap, you told your own dad to suck it?" Jonathan laughed in spite of himself. This was serious stuff, he shouldn't have laughed, but he couldn't help himself.

Sarah giggled too. "Yeah. I told him to suck it and to get off my friggin' back, only, I didn't say 'friggin'.'"

"Man, Sarah, you have balls. What did your dad do?"

"Thank you, Jonathan. I consider the fact that I have balls to be a compliment – even if the idea is kinda gross. To answer your question, my dad slapped me across the face and then chased me through the house. I locked myself in my bedroom and he punched a hole in the door."

"Holy crap, your dad isn't just a douchebag – he's a psycho. What did your mom do?"

"That's the thing – she did *nothing*. She takes pills for anxiety and stress, so whenever my dad starts being a jerk, she says she has a headache, pops some pills, and goes to bed."

Jonathan couldn't think of anything to say. He couldn't imagine what he would do if his mother was like that. He'd always just assumed she'd be there and always be, well, a mother. No wonder Sarah didn't really miss her parents.

"That's ... well ... that's just horrible Sarah. A girl should be able to count on her mother; at least, it seems like that should be the case."

"Yeah, well ... " she shrugged her shoulders.

"If you're interested, I have some thoughts on this matter that you've shared with me, but first I have another question."

"Okay, shoot."

"What does Kevin think about all of this? I mean, he seems to get along with your dad pretty well, but I can't see him just sitting there and letting all this happen to you."

"Kevin actually doesn't know about a lot of it. Most of the incidents happened when he was out of the house. My mom covers everything up, and I'm threatened with everything under the sun to keep my mouth shut. My dad is fond of reminding me that it wouldn't surprise him if I ended up breaking up the whole family."

Jonathan shook his head in sympathy. "Well, in my humble opinion, your dad has mental problems and your mom is missing some critical DNA – the part that causes a mother to protect her young against dangerous predators."

Sarah smiled at him as he continued.

"Whatever happened with your dad, whatever happened at school, that doesn't change the fundamental, irrefutable facts: you're smart, you're beautiful, you're sexy, and there's absolutely nothing wrong with your personality, you're just bossy. But lots of bossy women end up being chief executive officers of large, successful corporations, so I think you shouldn't look at it as a negative."

Jonathan turned around to grab another water bottle. He turned back towards Sarah as he continued to talk. "And another thi ... "

Suddenly, he found himself face to face with Sarah. She was mere inches away.

"Um, hello," the sweat instantly started breaking out in his armpits. "I, uh, ... "

"You just said I'm smart."

"Yeah ... because you are."

"And you said I'm beautiful and sexy too."

Jonathan cleared his throat. It felt like there was a frog in it. "Ahem ... yes, I did."

"So, why don't you like me?" She raised her eyebrow, a challenge clearly being broadcast.

Jonathan felt the sweat bead up on his upper lip. Then he felt it break out on his scalp, slowly trickling down his back. He fought against stepping back – for one reason, he knew that rejecting Sarah now would cause her to not believe anything he had just said, and he really did mean it. For another reason, he liked being this close to her, he just didn't have the guts to make the move himself. But for some reason, right now, in this moment, Sarah didn't seem as intimidating as usual. *She seems vulnerable.*

"Sarah, I do like you."

"No, I mean *like me* like me."

Jonathan rolled his eyes up to the heavens for inspiration. This was his moment. Now or never. Tell her now or lose her forever, like in Top Gun.

"I do *like you* like you." His voice raised up at the end like he

Elle Casey

was back in seventh grade when his voice cracked all the time.

Sarah got her cocky look back on her face. "So, what are you going to do about it?"

Jonathan dropped the water bottle he had been holding, ignoring the water spilling out of it onto the ground. He gently raised his hands and placed them on her upper arms. He pulled her towards him, slowly, and as he did, he lowered his head. He moved his eyes from hers to look at her lips, and felt the heat rise up everywhere in his body.

Sarah's lips parted ever so slightly, in anticipation. He could smell her. It was making him crazy, her salty, wind-scented skin. She was several inches shorter than him, which made him feel powerful. She was beautiful and delicate.

Jonathan knew this moment was going to be one of the most important ones of his life. His first real kiss with the most beautiful girl in the world. He could feel her breath on his mouth, a split second before his lips finally touched hers.

It was dizzying. Her whole mouth was sweet, her lips soft. This was nothing like the kiss on the cruise with that other girl whose name he couldn't even recall. This was something entirely different, intoxicating. He felt the tip of her tongue against his lips, and he opened his mouth to deepen the kiss.

She pressed closer to Jonathan's body, telling him she wanted to feel all of him. His hands moved from her arms to the middle of her back. Then they stroked down until one was on her lower back and one was pushing on her butt. She sighed in pleasure.

Her body was exquisite. She was soft in all the right places. He could feel her breasts pressed against his chest. He felt them rising and falling with her quickened breaths. He reached a hand around to take one in his hand. She let out a whimper, or maybe it was a moan. He didn't know what it was, only that it meant he was doing something she liked.

A crashing through the underbrush and the sound of Candi's voice snuffed out the flame that had begun to grow in an instant.

*****

"Hey, where are you guys? Did you get that water yet? We were thinking we should go over to the ... "

Candi came through the trees into the water collection area, just in time to see Jonathan and Sarah hastily break apart. Both of them had very flushed faces and seemed very distracted. They instantly started acting very busy, collecting bottles from the ground and making excuses.

"Wow, look at that, I dropped one of the bottles. I'm so clumsy sometimes," said Sarah.

"Yep, we're done here, got all the water. Look – three full bottles. That's one for each of us."

Sarah smiled nervously at Candi, looking nervous and unsure of herself.

Candi smiled. She was pretty sure she'd just broken up a serious lip lock between her brother and Sarah. It's about time the two of them worked out their differences. "Cool. Yeah, Kevin and I were saying tomorrow maybe we should go over and look into the jungle farther, see if there's any reason to put platforms up in that area. Also, Kevin thinks we should try to catch some rats one of these days. Not sure I agree with him, but ... " She trailed off, giving them an opening to start talking again. It looked like they were back on solid ground now.

Jonathan took the water bottles that Sarah was holding and gestured for her to walk in front of him.

"I think both of the ideas are good ones," said Jonathan. "Now that we have a lot of the treehouse done, at least the basics, I think we need to start planning for the platforms. And having the rats is good for testing food, like you suggested, Sarah."

"I still wish we had a monkey."

"No, you don't want a monkey. They bite and they get into trouble."

"And rats don't?"

They started walked back to the treehouse as they discussed the pros and cons of different food tasters.

"Well sure, but they don't take off fingers when they bite, and they get into little rat trouble, not nearly-human trouble."

Sarah wasn't ready to give in. "Monkeys are cuter."

"Not when they're throwing monkey poo at you, they're not."

Sarah got a disgusted look on her face. "Monkey poo? Are you kidding? Monkeys don't throw poo; you're nuts."

"No, really. Candi and I were at the zoo one time, and ... "

Candi laughed as their conversation faded in the distance she put between them, walking faster so they could be alone. She remembered that trip to the zoo, when the monkeys had started slinging monkey poo on the zoo visitors. It seemed like Jonathan's inability to stop sharing every detail of his knowledge had not turned Sarah off, if that lip-lock she caught the end of was any indication. *Good for them. They're good together, even if they are a bit of an odd couple.*

Actually, now that she thought about it, she realized Sarah and Jonathan weren't such an odd couple after all. Maybe in high school they were, but out here, in the real world – the most real world she'd ever been in – they were perfectly matched, like yin and yang. He was quiet and she was outspoken, but it worked. They had a lot of similarities too. They were both smart, both athletic, and nowadays, both pretty good looking. She had always thought Jonathan was cute, but now with his tan and growing physique, he was what most teenagers would consider pretty hot, actually. *Huh. Weird.*

Candi reached up, self-consciously touching her hair. She knew it looked terrible. Sarah had suggested dreadlocks, and so far Candi had resisted. But she knew if she didn't make an effort to do something soon, she'd just have a matted mess and nothing to fix. She decided then and there to have Sarah put it in dreadlocks. When she got back home she could just cut them all off and start over.

When she reached the treehouse, she found Kevin chopping thin stalks of bamboo into short lengths. He already had about ten of them on the ground.

"Whatcha makin'?" asked Candi.

"I'm making the materials for a rat cage. I found more rat crap down here by our fire. I thought we should try to trap some of them and see what's what."

Jonathan and Sarah came through the trees to join them.

"Sarah, do you think you can make rat traps if I give you some specifications?" asked Jonathan.

"Probably, if you ask nicely."

Jonathan just looked at her and raised one eyebrow.

Candi watched as they exchanged a look that told her things were getting steamy in the jungle. She looked over at Kevin, but he seemed oblivious.

The group spent the next hour debating the best rat trap design while Sarah built the box that was going to serve as a cage.

"I think the Wiley Coyote Looney Tunes style is the best," said Jonathan.

"What the heck are you talking about?" asked Kevin.

"You know ... Looney Tunes? They're classic cartoons. Old-school."

"I don't remember an episode with rat trips ... sorry."

"It was a Road Runner trap. Anyway, you have a box that's propped up by a stick that has a string tied to it and food attached to the string. The idea is that a rat will grab the food and run away with it, pulling the string, causing the stick to fall, thereby causing the box to fall down on top of the rat, trapping him inside."

Kevin thought about it for second and then started nodding slowly. "You really think that could work?"

"Yes. We've got the box." He gestured to Sarah's newly finished project. "So, now we just need to tie some fish guts to a string that's attached to a stick, and we'll be all set."

"Well, I was going to go fishing again anyway, so maybe today's a good day for all of us to have a lesson – I've gotten pretty good at it, if I do say so myself," said Candi.

"Yeah, maybe us men can give you some pointers down there while we're at it."

Candi scoffed at Kevin's comment. "Yeah, we'll see about that. Come on, let's go now."

Everyone stood up and went over to grab a fishing spear from the collection Candi kept handy and sharp. They waited for Sarah to stow her rat box and then headed down to the shallows as a group.

Candi had found an area that had several rocks scattered in shallow pools of water that deepened around the base of the rocks. These spots seemed to be the favorite haunts of the fish.

"Okay, first lesson – don't let them see your shadow. And don't sing. I found out eventually that they don't like noise."

Everyone got up on one of the big rocks in the water with Candi.

"Now you have to sit and wait for a fish to come. Sometimes they're hard to see, since they're basically the same color as the sand most of the time. Just look for movement. The only thing you can really see is the black of their eyes."

"I can't see shit," said Sarah.

"Yeah, me neither," said Kevin.

Jonathan was staring so intently into the water, he looked like he was in a trance. "Yeah, sorry, Candi. I can't see a thing."

"Well, it's not like there are a million of them out here, you have to be patient. Oh, wait! Look. One's coming now."

She gestured a little to the left, to an area that was near the deeper water.

"I still can't see shit."

"You will. Wait until it's closer." Candi had lowered her voice to a whisper. "Now, when it's close enough, slowly raise your spear – slowly – they don't like sudden movements. And remember, the water distorts their actual position, so you have to aim kind of behind where you actually think they are."

Candi stood poised on the rock, spear raised above her head. She was staring intently at the water. She could feel Kevin watching her from the other side of the rock.

She lunged. The spear flew out of her hand and sliced neatly into the water. Candi jumped in after the spear and quickly picked it up, lifting the tip towards the sky.

She shook the water out of her eyes and hair. "You have to get the spear turned upside down pretty quick, otherwise they wiggle off the end and you lose 'em – or you have to go running all over the place to chase them down."

A shiny fish was flipping back and forth about five inches from the end of her spear point. Candi was smiling up at the group on the rock. "See? Easy! Now you guys try."

She climbed back up easily, the well-toned muscles in her arms and legs flexing with the well-practiced movements. "We have to spread out, though. I've just scared the fish from this pool, so we have to move. You guys make sure you have at least one empty rock between you, that way you won't scare each other's prey away."

They followed Candi's directions and spread out, examining the water for potential dinner candidates. The first one to try their hand at spearing was Kevin.

"I see one," he said in a loud stage whisper.

"Okay! Remember to spear a bit behind where you think the fish is."

"Raaah booyah!!!!" was the next thing they heard, then a big splash.

"What the hell?" Jonathan turned around to see what Kevin was doing.

Kevin came up with an empty spear. "Dammit, missed that sucker. Hmm." He looked confused, staring into the water and then at the top of his spear. "I think there's something wrong with my spear."

Candi laughed. "There's nothing wrong with your spear, it's your technique."

Kevin looked hurt. "What's wrong with my technique?"

"Maybe next time use a little less Rambo and a lot more stealth."

Kevin frowned at her but didn't say anything.

Jonathan was next up, but he didn't have any better luck, even though he was less enthusiastic with his war cry.

"This isn't as easy as I thought it was going to be."

Candi looked at him crossly. "Of course it's not easy. Why do you think it took me two weeks straight to figure it out?"

Jonathan shrugged his shoulders, "I don't know. I guess because you're a girl."

Jonathan never saw it coming. *WHACK!*

"Owww, Sarah! What the heck was that for?" He bent down to rub the welt that was coming up across his calves, staring daggers at a very satisfied looking Sarah.

"That's for being a chauvinist pig. Sex has nothing to do with it. It's skill and determination, something we girls have tons of, right Candi?"

"Right." And with that, she turned lightning quick and speared another fish, holding it up for everyone to see while shaking the water out of her hair. "That's two for me!"

Kevin just grumbled to himself, staring out into the water.

Jonathan kept rubbing his legs, shooting dangerous looks at Sarah. Sarah pretended she didn't notice. She had already given up on mastering the art of spear fishing, now focusing all of her energy on her cuticles.

"I think two fish is enough, if you guys are ready to go back ...
"

"Fine. I need to go rest my bruised calves anyway."

"Yep, I'm ready to go back. I want to work on another rat cage," said Sarah, already climbing down from her rock, heading for shore.

"You guys go ahead. I'm going to stay here and work on this some more," was Kevin's reply.

"Oh boy," said Sarah, as the trio walked back to the treehouse.

"What?" asked Candi.

"He's going to be out there for hours. Right now, I guarantee you, it is making him crazy that you can do this and he can't. This will now be his number one project – becoming the best spear fisherman in the northern hemisphere."

Candi laughed. "Good. I'd like the company."

*****

Once back at the treehouse, Candi cleaned and prepared the fish for cooking. They took the guts she had removed and put some of them on the end of a piece of plant rope and hooked it up in the cage, the rest they buried far from the treehouse. They put the contraption off into the bushes, deciding they'd leave it alone until the next morning. It seemed like the rats came out at night anyway.

Kevin came back an hour later, very sunburned and without any fish. He was grouchy until dinner, refusing Candi's offer of help. She laughed to herself. Either he'd figure it out like she had, or he'd break down and ask for her help eventually. She was just glad she wasn't going to be the only one out there anymore.

The group sat on their cushions around their dinner table and had their first almost normal dinner since they arrived a month ago. They laughed at the jokes Kevin told. They giggled at factoids that Jonathan shared, and as usual, he wondered what was so funny. Sarah was as relaxed as Candi had ever seen her, and it made her unable to stop smiling. She missed her parents a lot – sometimes unbearably so – but this new family she had wasn't bad. In fact, it was pretty awesome. She'd never felt this comfortable with someone outside of her real family ever before.

"We need to find something else for our bed covers," said Sarah as she popped the last hunk of cooked coconut into her mouth.

"I know, those ponchos make me sweaty," said Candi.

"Yeah, you're right," said Jonathan. "I assume it's going to get colder at some point. I mean, I'm not sure what latitude we're on, but judging from the angle of the sun, I'd say we're farther north of where we were on the cruise ship, so it's probably going to get cold here in the winter."

"Do you guys hear that?" asked Kevin. His head was cocked at a funny angle as if he was listening to something out in the trees.

"What?" asked Sarah, whispering.

"It sounds like ... a squealing or something or a very pissed off bird."

He looked at Jonathan, and Jonathan's eyes lit up.

"The rat trap!"

They all scrambled up from the table and rushed over to the ladder. Kevin was the first one down, followed by Jonathan. They rushed over to the trees where the girls had put the trap, Sarah and Candi right behind them.

"I can't see anything," said Jonathan, frustrated.

But now they could all hear the squealing; they had definitely caught something.

Candi came over with a piece of bamboo that had palm canvas wrapped around it, tied in place with thick layers of plant rope. She had dipped the end in the hot coals left over from dinner, catching it on fire so it burned brightly. It made a decent torch, although it wasn't going to last very long.

"Here, does this help?" She held it up to illuminate the area where the trap sat.

There, under the bars of the now overturned bamboo box, sat a very unhappy brown rat. Its tail had somehow gotten caught between a rock and the edge of the cage. It sat glaring out at them, the light of the torch reflecting off its shiny, red eyes.

"Holy shit, it worked!" yelled Sarah. She held her hand up for a high-five, which Kevin immediately returned. Jonathan realized what was expected of him a split second later and gave her an awkward high five too.

"So cool ... Sarah, you are an expert builder of furniture and rat traps," congratulated Candi.

"Yeah, well, he ain't no monkey, I can tell you that," said a critical Sarah, staring at the small, scrappy-looking rodent who was giving the distinct impression that he was not happy with his circumstances.

"So, what do we do now?" she asked.

"Well, we have to bring him over to the fire so we can see him better. Then we have to figure out how to hold him permanently."

"I made a cage I think will work."

"A cage? When did you do that?" asked Kevin. "I thought this was the cage."

"When you were out there playing Poseidon," responded Sarah, a little too casually.

Kevin gave her a suspicious look but didn't say anything in return.

Sarah went to her workshop, returning with a cage that was made of bamboo, held together at all of its joints with the plant rope. It had a lid that lifted and latched using plant rope ties.

With some coaxing from a small bamboo stick and some clever maneuvering, they transferred their guest from the trap to his new home.

"What do we feed him first?" asked Candi. She was anxious to find some new ingredients to cook with. She was getting tired of steamed fish with coconut.

"Give him some of those berries we found yesterday. They look yummy," said Sarah.

Candi went to a basket hanging from the tree roots where she kept her cooking ingredients, locating a small palm canvas packet of the berries that they'd been finding everywhere.

"Here you go, Ratatouille," she said, as she dropped them through the bars into the cage.

They all leaned over, watching the rat ignore the berries.

"Well, that was exciting," said Sarah, sarcastically.

"Come on, let's go to bed. He's nervous; he's not going to eat in front of us. Leave him down here on the ground and we'll check on him in the morning," said Jonathan, yawning for effect.

"Okay, everybody up, so I can get the ladder secured." Kevin waited until they were all in and then climbed up himself. He muscled the ladder up onto the rope loops attached to the side of the treehouse that caught the poles on each end, securing the ladder sideways against the side of the treehouse.

The breeze made their new home cool and comfortable. Sarah and Candi had done their best to clean the one sheet they had. They placed it over a pile of cushioning fronds and palm canvas for the guys' bed. The girls had their bamboo cots, which for now they had put next to each other in their room, sharing a poncho as a cover to keep warm.

"G'night, Sarah ... g'night boys," called out Candi.

"Night, Candi and Sarah," said Jonathan.

"Ditto," said Kevin.

"Good night, subjects; Queen Candi," said Sarah.

Candi snickered.

Sarah giggled.

Candi felt an uncontrollable urge to laugh out loud and gave in to it. It was infectious. Sarah started laughing too – softly at first and then more loudly. Soon they were both hysterical, their laughs quickly degenerating into snorts and cackles.

"They're nuts," said Jonathan.

"You don't have to tell me that," responded Kevin.

The guys fell asleep before the girls had quieted down. Soon a light snoring could be heard coming from their end of the treehouse.

Candi slowly calmed down, now completely out of energy and slightly dizzy from all the deep breaths she'd been taking. Sarah sighed long and loud, as if trying to calm herself down.

"Man, I needed that," said Sarah.

"Yeah, I guess I did, too. I feel like I just drank one of those margaritas again."

Sarah was quiet for a minute, thinking about that fateful night. "Remember that? The night we had margaritas and then went dancing? That was fun."

"Yep," said Candi. "That was the last day of our lives as normal teenagers."

"Do you miss it? Being a normal teenager?" Sarah asked in a more subdued tone.

"Actually, no." Candi was surprised at her own answer, but it was true. She didn't miss being unsure of herself. She didn't miss constantly trying to impress some nameless, faceless person or group. She didn't miss always trying to reach some unattainable goal – to be accepted by the people who she thought were better than her. Just acknowledging that this was something that used to be important to her was kind of embarrassing.

"Me neither. I was just thinking about how much easier life on this island is – which is kinda effed up when you think about how every day here it's pretty much life and death. I mean, it's not 'am I going to win homecoming queen' or something empty like that ... you know what I mean?"

"Yeah, in a way. I mean, whether I was going to be homecoming queen was obviously not on my list of worries, but there were other things. Like how can I start hanging around with the cool people? How can I improve my social status?"

"Who are the cool people at our school, anyway?" asked Sarah.

"Are you being obtuse?"

"No, I'm serious. I mean, all the people I knew were pretty fake. I thought Gretchen was my friend and then she went and slept with my boyfriend – who I also thought was a good guy. Seriously, when I think about it, the only cool people that I knew at our school were you guys – and I didn't even really know you."

"That is so sad," said Candi.

"Why is that sad?"

"Because to me, the cool people were you and Gretchen and Barry and all those people who you now tell me are fake a-holes. I've spent I don't know how much of my time obsessing over or worrying about how I was going to get those jerks to like me. And now you're telling me that I never should have bothered in the first place, and that apparently, I'm the coolest girl in school."

"Well, yeah, except for me of course. I'm maybe just a little bit cooler than you, but you're pretty cool too."

Candi reached over and smacked Sarah on the arm.

"Ouch, what'd ya do that for?"

Candi could hear the smile in Sarah's voice.

The conversation stopped, but the contemplation didn't. Each girl was lost in her own world, thinking about the fundamental shift they'd come to make – when it had happened and how it had happened, neither of them knew. But that it did happen was certain. The question was, what were they going to do with this newfound knowledge? And would it last when they got back to the 'real world'?

*****

"Son of a bitch!" yelled Kevin. He could hear the almost instantaneous response to his frustration coming from the treehouse above his head.

Candi called out, "Kevin? Are you okay?"

"Yeah, I'm down here with our rat cage."

"Is there something wrong with it?"

"Well, only that it apparently doesn't really make sense to design a rat cage that's held together with something a rat can chew through in about five seconds."

"Dammit," said Sarah. "Now I don't know if we can eat those stupid berries or not."

"Back to the drawing board," said Jonathan as he climbed down the ladder. "If any of you has any ideas for a new design on our cage, let me know. I'm tapped out right now."

"I'm not going to worry about it," said Kevin. "I think we need to get going on those platforms. Maybe there are some other fruits or nuts or something over on other parts of the island. We need to start doing some exploring."

"Yeah. Why don't we all gather together this morning over breakfast and talk about our plans. We have lots to do, but I want to make sure we're all in agreement on priorities and stuff," said Jonathan.

"Priority one," announced Candi, "is Sarah dread-locking my hair."

Kevin could hear Sarah scrambling around above. "Really?!

Yay! I'll go get my stuff right now." She was going into the bathroom area where she kept her makeup case. He could tell by the banging of her feet on the floor.

Kevin looked over at Candi, watching her reach up to feel her hair.

"Nervous?" he asked, smiling.

"Maybe a little. But it needs to happen. Goodbye frizz-head. Hello Rasta girl."

"It'll look great," he encouraged. He knew now that Candi could look beautiful not matter what she did with her hair. None of them had access to shampoo or brushes, but it didn't stop her from being one of the most attractive girls he'd ever seen. His thoughts were interrupted by Sarah coming down the ladder and grabbing Candi's hand.

"Sit." She pushed Candi down onto a chunk of palm tree that they used as a seat near the fire.

Kevin sat back on his heels, watching his sister take charge of Candi's hair.

"Now, we have to first try and get the existing knots out. It's going to hurt, but trust me, when I'm done, you're going to look *awesome*. Seriously. You have the face for this, and now with your tan and those adorable freckles ... you are gonna have the boys all over you."

Candi didn't say anything, but Kevin caught her looking over at him. It made him feel warm inside to think that maybe she was trying to be pretty for him.

"Ouch!"

"I'm trying to be as gentle as possible, but getting the matted knots out is hard. Please don't cry!" Sarah begged.

"I'm not." She sniffed.

"I'm sorry – I'm almost done," promised Sarah. A few more rips of the comb, and she was ready.

"There! Now I'm going to section it off and start dreading it. That won't be as painful. It will be a little, but not as much, okay?"

"Yes, I'm fine, I can take it. Just get it over with."

Kevin was totally engrossed in his sister's hairstyling process. He'd never thought about what went into making those hair rope things before. It was actually pretty cool. And he could see now, as they started to appears, why Sarah had suggested it. Not only was it going to be perfect for life on the island, but it really suited Candi's face.

An hour later, Candi's hair was carefully divided into even chunks around her head. Sarah had carefully tied each chunk at the roots with the plant rope and then back combed them until each of them turned into a tight dreadlock. She tied off the ends with more plant rope to keep her handiwork from coming out.

"Now, you have to keep the rope ties in for a while until we're sure the dreads are staying, but don't worry, it won't be long. I'll have to make sure they stay tight for you, but not having any conditioner and all this salt everywhere will help the dreads get solid pretty quick. Now turn around so I can see my finished product."

Candi did as she was told. Her eyes were red-rimmed from crying but that didn't keep Kevin from seeing how amazing she looked.

"Holy shit, Candi," said Sarah, "I knew this was going to look good on you. Man, if the people back at school could see you now, you'd be in the running for homecoming queen."

Candi gave her a critical look.

"I am dead serious, Candi. Here, look." She handed Candi the mirror that had been hanging in the bathroom.

Candi took the mirror from her and held it up so she could get a full view. She moved the mirror from side to side, trying to get a full reflection.

Sarah was right. It did look good. Kevin had never considered himself a dreadlock lover before, but he was definitely liking them on Candi. They made her look a little rebellious and a little bit wild.

"Oh, this feels so much better than all those matted clumps. I can feel a breeze on my scalp for the first time in ... well ... ever!" She smiled and grabbed Sarah in a big hug. "Thank you so much! I *love* it. I wasn't sure if I was going to, but you were right; it's cool."

"Okay, girls, breakfast is served!" said Kevin, grinning mischievously.

Candi and Sarah looked at each other with question marks on their faces.

He pulled out two bananas from behind his back.

Sarah and Candi rolled their eyes.

"I should have known," said Sarah.

Candi stuck her tongue out at him as she took her banana and said, "Tease."

He raised an eyebrow at her. Apparently her new hairdo made her not only sexier, but bolder too.

"Okay, we have to decide what we're going to focus on next," said Jonathan. "It *was* the treehouse. It still needs a lot of work, but we can focus on other things if we want now since it's livable at least. I would suggest we walk through the middle of the island to see if there's any reason to install some platforms in the trees."

"I agree, it's worth a shot. What do you girls think?"

"Sure."

"Yeah, I'm game. Maybe we'll find some other food we can add to our menu," said Candi.

"Okay, so that's settled. What else do we need to get done in the next week or so?"

"Well, I'd like to finish the walls for the treehouse because if there's some sort of major rainy season here, I don't want to be trying to build stuff when it's pouring; and I don't want to sleep with rain going all over my bed," said Sarah.

"Yeah," agreed Candi. "I think that makes sense for sure. I'd also like to find something to use as blankets or covers ... something other than that plastic poncho."

"What I wouldn't give for a Pottery Barn right now," said Sarah wistfully.

Candi nodded her head vigorously in complete agreement. "I totally love Pottery Barn sheets. They are the softest ever."

Kevin thought about it for a second and then said, "I don't know about Pottery Barn, but I'm kinda thinking I'd like one of those cots like you girls have."

Sarah smiled. "Yeah, I had a feeling you'd say that. Cut the bamboo for me, and I'll make you both one. I already have the sling parts done."

"Okay, so we have to finish the treehouse and explore the option of platforms. What else?"

"I want to start a band."

Everyone stopped chewing their bananas and just looked at Candi like she was nuts.

"What? I'm serious. I miss music and I'm tired of Sarah's banana song. I think we should each make some sort of musical instrument and one night a week we can sit around the campfire at night and make some music. I always wanted to be in a band," she confessed.

Kevin got a big grin on his face. "I get to play the drums."

"I can make a shell shakey thing with little shells and coconuts tied together," said Sarah gamely.

"Well, if you want to do it and everyone else is on board with it, I can probably figure something out for myself. I'm in," said Jonathan.

Candi smiled. "Great. This is going to be fun!"

The others just looked around at each other and shrugged their shoulders. If it made her happy ...

"You know what?" asked Jonathan.

"What?" answered the other three in unison.

"We never just go in the water for fun. I mean, why don't we? When we went to the beach for vacation and stuff, we spent the entire day in the ocean. Now we live at the ocean and we never go in. Seems stupid. I vote that we have a picnic at the beach before the weather changes."

"Works for me," said Kevin, shrugging.

"I think it's a great idea, Jonathan. It reminds me of when we went to Myrtle Beach that summer," said Candi, wistfully.

"I'll be there. Maybe by then we'll have food from some other part of the island, and we can make it a really good picnic," said Sarah.

"So we have lots of things on our agenda. We have the treehouse to finish, platform exploration, ummm, music night, and a picnic on the beach. That should keep us busy for a while." Jonathan stood up. "No better time to begin than the present. Anyone up for a trip to the center of Peanut Island?"

Everyone volunteered. They left the fire ring to gather supplies, each taking a backpack with a full water bottle, rope, bananas, and cracked coconuts. Jonathan carried the flint and the telescope. They each picked up a spear from Candi's fishing tackle.

They started walking straight towards the center of the island and were soon in an area that they had never been to before. The trees were dense, birds were chirping and screeching in the canopy above.

"Man, it's louder here. I can't hear the ocean anymore," said Sarah.

"If we could figure out how to spear a bird, we could have chicken for dinner," said Kevin, only half joking.

"It took me two weeks to figure out how to spear a fish that was two feet away from me – I don't think I'd be able to do the bird thing anytime soon," said Candi.

"Well, you know, guys, where there are birds, there are eggs ... ," said Jonathan.

"Hey, what's that?" asked Sarah. On the ground, in a clearing where the sun was able to shine through pretty strongly, was a round, green fruit of some sort. Sarah walked over and picked it up. The tree she was standing next to had several of the same things still attached to its branches. "Is this a lime?"

"Let me see," said Jonathan, holding out his hand.

"Hmm, I don't think this is a lime. It doesn't look or feel right. Kevin, do you have the knife with you?"

"Sure, hand it over."

Jonathan gave him the fruit and Kevin sliced it in half. The inside was a bright pink.

Jonathan smiled at Candi. "You know what that is, don't you?"

"Is it guava?" she asked.

"Yep, I think so." He looked at Sarah and Kevin. "We used to have Mexican night at our house once a week. Our mom would make tacos or enchiladas and we would drink guava juice. The container had a picture of a guava fruit on it. We loved it. I think it has a lot of vitamins too."

"How did a guava tree get all the way over here if it's a Mexican fruit?" asked Sarah.

Jonathan looked up into the trees. "My guess is it came here in a bird's butt."

Sarah looked at Jonathan like he'd just grown two heads. "I'm sorry. I thought I just heard you say a bird brought a fruit tree here in its butt."

"I did. What I meant was, the birds eat the fruit in Mexico, which means they get a seed or two in their bellies, then they fly around in their migratory pattern over to an island, they poop, and the seeds come out and start growing. That's how fruit trees that were native in one place start growing in other places – when it's not man transplanting them, that is."

Kevin cut the fruit up into four pieces. "Let's give it a try. Bird's ass fruit. Yum."

They each took a hesitant bite into their piece. All of them smiled, although Sarah not as enthusiastically as the others. "What's the matter, Sarah, don't you like it?" asked Candi.

"It's okay. It's not my favorite thing in the world; plus the whole bird's ass thing isn't very appetizing. But it sure beats the heck out of bananas right now. I'm happy to have a banana break."

"Me too. And I think I could use this to cook with the fish," said Candi.

"You know, guys, we should keep our eyes open for sugar cane," said Jonathan.

"What's it look like?" asked Kevin.

"Actually, it looks a lot like the bamboo we've been cutting down, only it's shorter and the stalks are thinner, and most of the leaves are at the top."

Sarah looked at Jonathan with a frustrated expression on her face. "How can you possibly know that? Did you download Wikipedia into a hard drive in your brain?"

"Well, about four years ago, in middle school, I did a science experiment about sugar cane. See, I was in the grocery store with my mom, and there were these sticks in the produce department – I asked her what they were and she told me they were sugar cane. She bought a cane for me and told me to peel off some of the fibers and chew on them. I did it and it was sweet, like sugar kind of, but different. So then it was time to do a science experiment for school, and I had the sugar cane sitting there. I decided I'd do an experiment about making sugar."

"And how'd that work out for ya?" asked Kevin, smiling.

"Well, I put together a diorama of the process with pictures and stuff. I tried to actually make the sugar at home, but I wasn't very successful."

"Well if you couldn't do it at home with a kitchen and everything, I don't know that we'll be able to do anything with it here," said Kevin.

"Yeah, but I was trying to make refined sugar – like the whole deal with white crystals and stuff. To make things sweet, you just need to squeeze the crap out of the fibers. Cane juice is like sugar water kind of. It just still has the brown sugar molasses in it, so it has a stronger flavor."

"I think I could work with that. We could actually make like a dessert or a sweet coconut drink if we had some sugar cane juice." Candi was obviously getting excited about the idea.

"Mmm, sounds like party time. Island coconut daiquiris,

minus the ice and pineapple," said Sarah.

"Okay," said Kevin. "Add it to the list of things to do this week – find sugar cane."

The group continued moving through the trees. "I think it would be worthwhile to build some platforms going from the treehouse to the guava area. It took us about forty-five minutes to get here walking on the ground. If we had some sort of platform system and used ropes or something to swing from one to the next, we could move a lot faster," said Jonathan.

Kevin looked above his head into the tree canopy. "We really wouldn't need to do too much, I don't think. I mean, there are tons of wide tree limbs that wouldn't need a platform at all."

Candi eyed the trees suspiciously. "I don't know about the whole idea, guys. I was never very good at climbing the rope in gym class."

"Yeah, me neither," said Sarah.

"Well, we at least need to do a tree climbing class," said Kevin. "Who knows when you might be out in the jungle and need to get up off the ground? We still don't know what other animals are out here."

"That's a good point, Kevin," said Jonathan. "Let's put that on the list too – tree climbing. Maybe if we get good at tree climbing and rope swinging, we won't need platforms. I guess we won't know until we get up into the trees."

They walked on, debating the pros and cons of moving through the trees like monkeys. After a while they stopped for a lunch of bananas and coconut.

"I need to start heading back soon if you guys want fish for dinner," said Candi.

"Oh, man, I definitely want that," said Kevin.

The others agreed.

"Let's get moving then," said Jonathan. "I suggest we loop a little towards the west side of the island, see if there's maybe some sugar cane over there where it gets full sun most of the day."

"Might as well," said Sarah.

"Let's do it," said Kevin.

"Lead the way, Jonathan," said Candi.

The group made a turn, heading towards the west side of the island. They reached the line of trees near the water, but it looked much the same as the east side of the island where they had landed in the lifeboat.

"Well, this is a bummer," said Jonathan. "I had hoped there'd be something else over here."

"We haven't gotten all the way around, Jonathan, don't give up hope yet," said Kevin, clapping him on the back as he took the lead.

*****

Kevin's stride hadn't let up, even though they'd been walking for a few hours. The others started to fall behind a little as the humidity and lack of energy caught up with them.

They didn't see exactly what happened next, but they heard Kevin's yells.

"Holy ... shit ... what the ... hey guys! Need a little help here!"

The others followed the signs of his tracks – broken leaves and branches, along with footprints in the soft ground – and found him standing in what looked like a sandy bog. He was sunk in up to his ankles.

"What are you doing, Kevin? Quit messing around, get out of there," Sarah insisted.

"I would if I could."

"What is that? Sand?"

"Try *quicksand*."

"No friggin' way," whispered Candi.

Sarah looked at Candi, who appeared to be as stricken as Sarah felt. Her eyes went back her brother again, unable to compute in her mind what was obviously playing out in front of her.

"Don't struggle," ordered Jonathan.

"Yeah, I know. That's what got me in this deep – trying to get out."

Kevin was twisting his body around trying to see them behind him. All that did was manage to sink him in up to his calves. "Don't get too close! You'll get stuck too."

"Kevin, stop moving!" Sarah panicked as she watched the lower part of his legs disappear under the gelatinous-looking sand. He was now in up to his knees. "I'm going in there to get him," she declared, brazenly.

"No! Stay right where you are," ordered Candi, holding out her arm to block Sarah from walking any closer to her brother.

"We can't just stand here and watch him get swallowed up in that quicksand! *Shit*, I didn't even know quicksand was real! I thought it was just in the movies!" screeched Sarah, on the edge of hysteria.

Jonathan was staring at Kevin and the bog, tapping his fingertips on his chin.

"Kevin?"

"Yes, Jonathan?"

"I need you to trust me on this, okay?"

"Sure, man, I trust you. What are you thinkin'?"

"Okay, what I need you to do, is lie down in the quicksand."

"Ummm, no thanks, Jon. I think I'll just stay right here

standing up like this."

Sarah looked at Jonathan like he was a madman. "You must be out of your freaking mind!"

"Shhh, no, I'm not out of my mind. You just have to trust me. I'm pretty sure this will work."

"Pretty sure?" asked Kevin. "You're *pretty* sure? Couldn't you be more like 'really sure' or 'almost one hundred percent sure'?" He laughed nervously.

"Well, I've never actually tried this before, so I can't be totally sure, but according to the laws of physics, this should work. You and I will just have to trust in those laws together."

Kevin barked out a short burst of bitter laughter. "See, though, the problem is, Jon, that physics and I have never really been on the best of terms. I got a C in my last physics class, and I'm pretty sure it's because the teacher liked the firepower a little more than she should have, and not because I actually had a friggin' clue what she was talking about all semester, sooo ... "

"You don't have to understand physics to be its bitch. Now either do what I say, or sink. It's up to you."

Everyone looked at Jonathan like he was totally off the range.

"Great," Sarah threw up her hands, "he's finally cracked. Now. When we need his brain the most." She walked over to Jonathan and snapped her fingers in his face. "Hello! Is there anybody in there? Jonathan? We need you to come back to us, babe."

He brushed her hand away from his face. "Listen, this is what's called tough love. Now, Kevin, lay your butt down horizontally in that sand and then roll over here to where we're standing. It's the only way out."

Kevin sighed. He looked around, as if trying to find another solution but coming up empty. "Okay, Jon, you win. So far you've never let us down, so I'm going to trust you. I'm putting myself in your hands. Brothers?"

He held up his hand ceremoniously.

Jonathan held up his hand at Kevin. "Brothers. Now throw me your backpack."

Kevin obeyed and then leaned forward so that he could get his body horizontal in the muck. It was difficult at first – his legs didn't want to come out, but eventually the weight of his upper body pulled him down. Then he began to float on the top of the surface.

Sarah clasped her hands together and squeezed for all she was worth. She began bouncing up and down on her toes, chanting, "Come on, come on, come on ..."

"Now roll over here!" yelled Jonathan, in an excited voice. "Ha, ha! It's working!"

Candi looked at her brother in horror. "You act like you're surprised!"

Jonathan shrugged, smiling. "Well I am, kind of. I mean, I suspected it would work, but I didn't know for sure until he actually did it." His face was alight with the joy of the discovery he'd just made.

Sarah shook her head at him and swallowed the lump in her throat. She turned back to Kevin just in time to see him roll out of the muck at Candi's feet.

He moved to get up, but before he was completely vertical, Candi grabbed him in a huge bear hug. She was so small compared to Kevin, it didn't look very effective, but he seemed to get the idea behind the gesture.

"Hey, little Gumdrop, are you happy to see me?"

"Yes," she answered from his shirtfront. "Don't *ever* do that again."

Sarah, now much more in control after seeing her brother safe and sound, walked over and slapped him on the arm. "Yeah, don't ever do that again. You scared the crap out of me. Can you imagine what Dad would say? 'Oh yeah, sorry Mom and Dad, but Kevin sank in a pit of quicksand while I watched ... sorry 'bout that.' Yeah, that would go over really well."

Jonathan reached out and touched Sarah's arm. She nodded at him, acknowledging his support.

Sarah caught Kevin watching what was going on between them, a mystified expression on his face for a moment, before he turned back to address Candi's attentions. "Hey, little sand fairy. Rasta girl. I'm okay, you can let me go now."

"Oh, yeah, right." Candi let go and stepped back quickly. "Sorry about that. I was just happy you weren't, you know, dead."

Kevin chuckled. "Yeah, well, me too. Let's go home. And here's a tip everyone ... put your spear out in front of you while you're walking, and poke it in the ground. If it pokes in too easy, don't step there."

They laughed, letting Kevin's humor help wash away the fear and stress that lingered over their heads. It was all too easy to forget how dangerous this island could be if they lowered their guard too much.

*****

They eventually reached the point where Jonathan said they had to turn in eastward so they wouldn't end up taking the long way back around the whole southern end of the island.

They arrived at the treehouse with about an hour of daylight left.

"I'm going to go try and get us some dinner," said Candi, grabbing two spears.

"Mind if I come along?" asked Kevin.

"No, not at all. I'd like the company."

They made their way over to Candi's favorite fishing spot in companionable silence and climbed up on the rock together. "Aren't you going to fish?" she asked him.

"Nope, I'm just gonna watch you. I'm not very good at it. Yet."

Candi laughed. "Okay, suit yourself." She got quiet, her eyes scanning the water for telltale signs that a fish was nearby. She didn't have to wait long, noticing movement in the shallows below her.

Kevin squinted at the place he saw her focusing on. It was more difficult to see with the sunlight fading, but Candi looked like she had her target locked in her sights.

Kevin watched as she poised on the balls of her feet, her right arm cocked back. She was holding the spear in her fist and he could see her grip was solid. The muscles in her forearm were bulging. He looked down at her legs, admiring the way her quadriceps, hamstrings and calf muscles were flexing, showing off their lean definition. All those morning workouts, rugby games, and karate lessons were really making a difference. *Sweet.*

He thought back to how she had looked in school versus how she looked today. She was super tan now and had some really cute freckles across her nose and cheeks. *Who knew freckles could be so sexy?* Her hair was nearly blond with all the sun streaks. She had those cool dreadlocks, that for some reason really worked for her, making her look all badass and, well, different. He'd never seen anyone but a professional athlete look as lean and fit as she did standing here on the rock in front of him today. All in all, her look had changed and Kevin approved, even though admittedly, she had looked pretty fine even before they got to the island.

Probably the biggest difference he saw in her was not in her appearance, though – it was in her self-confidence. She walked differently. She had a stride now, when before she'd had just a plain old walk. Before, she'd been afraid of her own shadow; she was always hiding behind her shyness or something – like she wanted things but didn't have the guts to go get them. Now, she was different. Sexier. Funnier. Cuter. More powerful or something. The more he studied her, the more he realized he was seriously attracted to her, and it wasn't because she was the only girl in his world.

He thought about his last three girlfriends. Compared to her, they were empty shells. They had nothing going on upstairs and there was nothing different or special about them that he had ever noticed. They were like cookie cutter girlfriends – they all looked and acted the same. He couldn't imagine any of them standing here on this rock, wearing dreads, and spearing fish to feed his family. Not a chance. And yet, here was Candi, his little sand fairy. The girl who today couldn't stop herself from grabbing him when she had thought he was going to die. *Man, am I stupid or what? What am I waiting for with this girl?*

"Candi?"

"Shhh."

He whispered back. "Oh, yeah, sorry. I'll wait."

No sooner had he said that than she sprang into action. Two seconds later she was standing in the water with a huge fish on the end of her spear, up in the air wiggling around, trying to break free.

"Woo hoo, that's a big mother!" she yelled, smiling wide as she climbed back up onto the rock. She pulled it off the spear and ran a string through its gills and mouth, passing the knot that closed the string through the loop at the other end.

"You were saying?" she asked Kevin, sitting down across from him. Water was dripping down her face so she gave her head a quick shake, spraying him with water.

He squeezed his eyes shut.

"Oops, sorry about that." She reached up to wipe a drop off his cheek.

Kevin opened his eyes, grabbing her hand midway, holding onto it.

Candi looked at him in confusion.

"You really are amazing, you know that?"

Candi looked down at the rock, instantly appearing self-conscious and embarrassed. "Stop."

"No, I'm serious. Look at me." He used his other hand to take her chin and gently force her face up. "I was watching you. You've changed since we came here. You were pretty and cool before, but now ... now you're even more amazing. You take care of all of us. You're a good person. And you're hot as hell with your dreads and your tan and that rockin' body."

Candi breathed out a single note of laughter. "You're crazy."

"No, I'm not. I consider myself very observant of the female form, actually, and you have the whole package. Not only do you have a killer body, you're also a really nice girl and super smart. Normally I'm scared to death of girls like you, so I go another route, but I'd like to think I've learned a few things since we came here." He took her hands in his and continued. "I don't want to screw up what we have here, but if you're willing to seriously give me a shot, I'd like to ask you to be my girlfriend. Like, officially."

Candi's face got redder and redder, the more he said, but she didn't respond right away.

"What are you thinking? I can tell your brain's going a million miles an hour right now," he said, smiling at her encouragingly.

"I'm not sure. My head is pretty much spinning right now."

"In what way? A good way or a bad way?"

"Both, maybe. I don't know." She sat there staring at him, occasionally glancing down at his arms and then back up to his face.

He'd give anything to be in her head right now and know what she was thinking. She wasn't letting any of her inner thoughts show on her face.

"I'm waiting for your answer ... but hey, if you need more time, just tell me. I mean, I'm not going anywhere, you know?"

Kevin was trying to make her laugh to ease her stress.

"I guess I'm wondering if you'd still want to be my boyfriend if we weren't on this island."

"I'd say yes, I would want to, but would you even believe me? And does it even make a difference? This island is where we are now. This is our life for the foreseeable future."

Candi bit her lip for a few seconds and then said, "Oh, what the hell ... why not?" A huge grin split her face.

Kevin was taken aback by her sudden and unconventional answer. "Well, that's good, right? I mean, that's a yes, isn't it?" It sure looked like a yes, her eyes sparkling with humor.

Candi laughed. "Yes, that's a yes. Sorry about that. Just fighting some inner demons."

"Ah," said Kevin knowingly, "my reputation has preceded me, I think."

Candi smiled at him and squeezed his hand. "I'm not who I was, and you're not who you were. Let's just be us – who we are, right now on Peanut Island."

"Good idea," said Kevin softly, as he leaned in closer to Candi, his eyes moving to her lips.

They met halfway, the fish on the rope and the spear completely forgotten. Kevin released her hand so that he could reach up and touch her face while his lips met hers. He immediately tasted the salt there. They were so soft and delicate, barely touching his. He turned his head to deepen the kiss, sliding his tongue into her mouth, finding it warm and inviting. Her tongue was soft and wet, moving over and around his in a way that made him instantly aroused.

He moved his hands under her arms and picked her up to put her in his lap. She moved her legs so she was straddling him on the rock. Now she was up higher than he was, and she took control.

*****

Candi surprised even herself with her boldness. She angled her head to deepen the kiss, putting her hands on the back of Kevin's head and neck. She ran her fingers through his hair, then down his back, feeling his huge muscles bulging as he balanced himself and moved his arms down to her butt. He squeezed it, making her moan with the hot flashes it sent charging through her body. She was getting very hot, very quickly.

Unfortunately, they weren't in a very romantic spot, which became apparent when Kevin's calf muscle decided to get a cramp in it from the odd angle it had been holding. He immediately stopped kissing her.

"Ouch, *shit.* Oh, man ... pain!"

Candi sat back to look at his face which was screwed up in a grimace of pain. "What? What'd I do?" She was mortified that she might have done something wrong.

"No, not you ... calf muscle ... charlie horse!"

"Oh, no, oh, those hurt. Here, let me help." Candi jumped off his lap and grabbed the leg he was reaching for. She felt his calf and found the big knot of spasming muscle.

"Okay, this is going to hurt for just a second. Hang on." She grabbed ahold of it and squeezed it as hard as she could.

"Arrrggh!!! Holy *shit* woman, whatareyoudoingtome?!"

"Shush, this works, just sit still."

Sure enough, the muscle slowly relaxed and she could see that the pain had subsided almost immediately. Kevin's face relaxed as the tension left his body.

"How's that for red-hot romance?" he gasped out, giving her a weak smile. Sweat that had broken out across his upper lip glistened in the light of the setting sun.

Candi laughed, reaching up to wipe the droplets from his face. "That's hot alright. I guess maybe next time we decide to, uh, you know, we should not do it on a rock in the middle of the water."

"Yeah, right. Romantic make-out session, not on a rock. Gotcha."

Candi stood up, holding out her hand. "Come on, let's get going. It's getting dark."

Kevin accepted her help, and together they made their way back to the treehouse, Kevin limping only slightly. There they found Sarah and Jonathan busy making tiki torches out of bamboo poles, palm canvas, and mounds of plant rope.

"Hey, tiki torches. Cool idea. This will work perfectly with music night," said Candi.

"That's the idea," said Sarah. "What took you guys so long?"

Candi laughed nervously, causing Sarah to look up from what she was doing. "What?" Her eyes narrowed in suspicion.

"Oh, nothing. Fishing. You know. With a spear. Catching fish. In the water. Got one, see?" She held up the fish for Sarah's inspection.

Sarah didn't say anything; she just looked from Candi to Kevin and then back again. Candi could almost see her putting pieces of a puzzle together in her head. A slow smile spread across her face just before she winked behind her brother's back at Candi.

Candi's heart fluttered, and she looked away. The last thing she wanted was Sarah getting involved in her fledgling love life. She kept herself busy for the next half hour preparing the fish she'd caught, hoping Sarah would take the hint and leave her alone.

She squeezed some of the guava fruit they had collected over the fish to see if it would change the taste a little bit, putting more pieces of the fruit in with the fish too, wrapped up in banana leaves for cooking.

She tried not to think about what had happened on the rock as she worked, but she was beyond thrilled with the idea that she was Kevin's official girlfriend. She wasn't even really sure what that meant here at the treehouse. *Is he going to keep it a secret? Will he tell the others, or just let them come to their own conclusions?* She wasn't sure which one she preferred. It's not like they could keep secrets on the island for long, so either way, Jonathan and Sarah would eventually find out.

"So, what's up?" asked Sarah, walking up and sitting down to watch Candi prepare the fish. She and Jonathan had finished the torches and he was putting them away up in the treehouse.

"Nothing much, just making dinner. What did you do while we were fishing?"

"Worked on the tikis. What about you? What did you and Kevin get up to out there ... by yourselves ... on the beach?" she asked, a sly tone in her voice.

Candi could feel the blush rising up in her face. Sarah was no dummy. Somehow she'd already sussed out what had happened. *How does she do that?*

"Just caught a fish." The half-truth sounded false even to her own ears.

"Yeah, right. Fess up, girl. I saw the looks on your faces when you got back. Kevin couldn't stop smiling; neither could you, plus, you're a terrible liar."

Candi let out a big sigh. "If you want to know what happened, just go talk to your brother."

"He won't tell me jack shit; so, no – I'm asking you. You and me are girls, we girl-talk ... so start talkin' girl."

Candi continued in silence with the dinner preparations, not sure that she should say anything. She didn't want Kevin to think that as soon as she got back she went running to Sarah gushing about her new boyfriend. How dorky could a person possibly be? ... Even though that's exactly what she'd wanted to do.

Sarah took her silence for stubbornness. "Candi, come on, I thought we were like sisters. Sisters share stuff. Or maybe I was wrong ... "

The guilt was like a knife through Candi's heart. She looked up at Sarah, ready to pour her guts out, until she caught the sneaky look in her eyes.

"Wow, Sarah, you're good. I almost fell for that."

"Shoot, how'd you figure me out?"

"Well, let's just say, next time ... don't use your devious wicked witch of the west look right after you give your bleeding heart line."

"Yeah, okay, I'll work on that. But seriously, we are like sisters, so you should tell me stuff. Come on ... who dreadlocked your hair? Me, your big sister, that's who! Who saved your brother's life? Yep, me again, big sister Sarah."

"Okay, wait, so let me get this right ... you being my big sister makes Jonathan, like, your brother?" asked Candi, innocently.

"*Ew*, no, that is totally gross – don't even say that." Sarah had a disgusted look on her face.

A few weeks ago, if Candi had seen this expression, she probably would have been offended, thinking Sarah didn't like the idea of being associated with her brother; but now, she knew Sarah's disgust was for an entirely different reason. Sarah wanted to be *with* Jonathan, so seeing him as a sibling was like incest, which was totally eww. Now it was her turn to do some digging.

"What's the matter, Sarah? The idea of making out with your brother a little too creepy?"

"I have *no* idea what you're talking about."

Candi stopped what she was doing with the fish and banana leaves and looked Sarah in the eye. "We're girls. We girl talk. So start talkin', girl."

Sarah sounded less sure of herself when she answered this time. "There's nothing to talk about."

"Okay, well, then there's nothing for me to talk about either." Candi put the wrapped fish on the fire with a self-satisfied smile. *That should keep her at bay for a while.*

"Fine," said Sarah, shrewdly, "I'm going to make out with your brother, get him naked, and then show him a little slice of heaven. *That's* why I don't like thinking of him as a relative."

Candi gasped in surprise and a speck of saliva went flying down her windpipe. She choked and wheezed, barely able to breathe.

Sarah started whacking her on the back, and Jonathan came over to see what was going on.

"What's wrong with her? Candi, are you okay?"

Candi looked up and saw Jonathan and Sarah both squatted down looking at her – Jonathan with concern in his eyes, Sarah with a triumphant gleam in hers.

Candi waved him away, "I'm fine ... I ... just inhaled some drool."

Jonathan got a disgusted look on his face. "What'd you do that for?"

"I didn't do it on purpose! I just inhaled really sharply and down it went. Go away, I'm fine."

"Fine, I'm leaving." He shook his head and muttered as he walked away, *"Girls."*

"Your turn," said Sarah, smiling sweetly after Jonathan had left.

Candi rolled her eyes. *What the heck. She'll find out eventually anyway.* "Alright, I'll tell you, but you have to swear to keep your big mouth shut about it. I don't want you to screw it up." Candi looked from left to right, checking to see where Kevin and Jonathan were. Jonathan was back in the workshop area of the tree roots and Kevin was nowhere to be seen. *Probably at the waterspout taking a shower.*

Sarah mimicked zipping her lip and then throwing away the key. She forgot the locking the lock part, but Candi let it slide. She knew the chances of Sarah keeping it a secret were pretty slim anyway, but on this little island it didn't really matter. It's not like high school where it could make or break your social life.

"Kevin asked me to be his official girlfriend today." Candi watched Sarah's face to judge her reaction.

Sarah didn't say anything, she just smiled.

"So? Aren't you going to say something?"

Sarah shrugged. "There's not much to say. I knew it was

something like that. So, did he seal the deal?" Sarah wiggled her eyebrows to emphasize the hidden meaning of her words.

Candi looked aghast, "No, of course not! Like I would just have sex with Kevin on a whim like that because he asked me to be his girlfriend?"

"Well, there's more than one way to seal the deal ... maybe a promise of future deal sealing, perhaps?"

Candi's face got hotter than it already was. "We kissed."

"Ah-*ha*! I knew it." Sarah stood up and started dancing around the fire, chanting in a stage-whisper, "Candi and Kevin, sittin' in a treehouse, k-i-s-s-i-n-g ... mouse ... "

Candi couldn't help but laugh. "I think your rhyme needs a little work."

"Yeah, you're probably right." Sarah sat back down next to Candi and stared into the flames. Without looking at Candi she continued, "I'm happy for you, I really am. Honestly, I know we don't have a lot of options out here on The Peanut, but you guys make a good couple. If I could pick anyone in the world for my brother to be with, it would be you. Here or anywhere."

Candi felt tears come to her eyes. That was the nicest thing Sarah had ever said to her. She leaned over quickly and enveloped Sarah in a bear hug.

"Whoa, Sugar Lump, ease up on the P-D-A," said Sarah, trying to laugh off the seriousness of the situation.

"That's so sweet of you, Sarah. Thank you." Candi sat back down and wiped her eyes, taking a couple of deep breaths to calm herself.

"Were you crying? Man, you're a softy," teased Sarah.

"Yeah, so? When the wicked witch of the west says she loves you it's a big deal, okay? Don't you cry at happy parts in movies?"

"Sure, I cry. I'm just not sure if I should be insulted at that second wicked witch reference or not."

"Don't be. I know it's your way of expressing your affection, so I'm good with it."

Sarah smiled. "Don't tell anyone I cry at happy parts in movies or it will ruin my rep for being a hardcore bitch."

Candi laughed. "I think I know better than that."

Sarah looked at her thoughtfully. "Yeah, I know you do. Sisters keep secrets, though, you know that, right?"

Candi looked at her, all laughter gone from her eyes. "Yes, I do." She held out her hand. Sarah looked at it confused.

"Secret sister handshake time," responded Candi to Sarah's questioning look.

"Oh, yeah, the dorky secret sister handshake. Let's see ... " she reached out and the two of them tried to maneuver through a series of slaps, snaps and other things to come up with a secret handshake. It was pretty pitiful.

"Geez, you suck at this," said Sarah.

"I'm pretty sure it takes two to suck at this," responded Candi.

"Ok, obviously we need to work on it. I'm going to take a quick shower before dinner. I'll catch you later on this ... handshake stuff."

"Okay, see you later. Dinner will be ready in about fifteen minutes."

"K."

Candi watched Sarah walk away. She was so happy right now, she couldn't keep from grinning ear to ear. She had a boyfriend and a big sister like she had always wished for; one who didn't take any shit and would have her back no matter what. *This is so much better than trying to ingratiate myself by shopping in a gift shop for a bathing suit.*

The memory of those first days with Sarah came rushing back. Candi was amazed at how much things had changed. She couldn't decide if it was her perspective that had become so different or if was just the things *in* her perspective that had caused this evolution. She shrugged her shoulders; it was a philosophical question for another time – she just remembered she had planned to try to make a coconut guava drink, and she needed a couple more coconuts.

Candi tracked Jonathan down and had him crack open six coconuts, saving the water that was in the nut. She used several of their bamboo cups and worked on mixing the coconut water with some of the guava slices. She used a bamboo stick with a small, round, conch-like shell tied to the end of it to mash the guava pulp into the coconut water. When she was finished, she took a taste, immediately spitting it out. *Eww, that's pretty gross.* She set the cup down next to the others on the shelves Kevin had built – bamboo poles lined up next to each other between two tree roots and secured together, side-by-side. *Maybe after they sit for a while they'll taste better.* She went back to the fire and took the fish off, completely forgetting her experiment.

"Dinner time everyone!"

The others filtered back to the campsite to join her. Kevin immediately took the space next to Candi.

"Hello, girlfriend," he said, winking at her.

Candi smiled and looked at the ground. *Okay, so he isn't going to hide it.* She looked up to find Sarah smiling at her. Jonathan was waiting for his piece of fish, having completely missed the import of the word 'girlfriend'. Candi sighed at his innocence. He would catch on eventually.

She passed out portions of the steamed fish, coconut and guava to everyone. After they'd all had a taste, they agreed that the guava was a nice change. It was better than what they'd eaten every night since the fish started making up the main part of their dinner meal, and that was the goal – consistent improvement.

"I think tomorrow I'd like to try smoking some fish," said Candi.

"What do you need to do that?" asked Sarah.

"Well, some sort of chamber that will hold smoke inside for as long as possible. The fire would be at the bottom. There would need to be shelves up above the fire, high enough not to burn. And we'd need lots of both dry and damp wood, and things that smoke a lot when they burn."

Jonathan and Kevin thought about it for a minute. Kevin was the first to speak. "Can we use the tarp? Because if I build a bamboo chamber in a box or teepee shape, I could drape the tarp over it and that would keep the smoke in. Or we could use palm fronds probably."

They all looked at each other and shrugged their shoulders in agreement.

"Good. I think with everyone's help, we could do this, no problem," said Kevin.

"Excellent," said Candi, smiling. "Smoked fish is really yummy. We used to get it around Christmastime every year. I hope I can make it taste okay; I think the smoke does most of the work though."

Jonathan nodded. "Yeah, I love smoked fish. I'm surprised we didn't think of this sooner."

"Actually, I've been trying to block out thoughts of home." Candi didn't want to finish her thought – that she really missed their parents – because she was afraid she was going to cry in front of everyone.

"I think I've been doing the same thing," said Kevin.

"Me too," said Sarah, suddenly very sober.

Jonathan raised his hand, "Guilty."

Kevin started to squirm. Candi watched him and got the distinct impression that he was uncomfortable. She reached over and touched his arm, a question in her eyes.

He looked at her briefly and then took a deep breath, letting it out in one long short burst. He looked at each of their faces in turn and then began to talk. "Listen guys, I have a little confession to make."

Candi looked at him with alarm, wondering if he was going to confess something about her. She didn't know why it suddenly made her nervous. These guys were her family; she had nothing to worry about with them. She was only a little embarrassed about how she'd let that kiss get away from her earlier. But she soon found out this little confession had nothing to do with the kiss.

"Before we left on the cruise, I found out some stuff that I haven't told anyone, not even Sarah." He looked over at his sister, and Candi followed his gaze. Sarah reacted in a confused way, confirming she had no idea what he was talking about.

"It's about Mr. Buckley." He looked at Jonathan and Candi. Candi sat very still, just waiting to hear what he was going to say and trying to ignore the sick feeling that rose up from her stomach.

Kevin sighed, continuing. "My dad was making all these phone calls in the weeks before we left on the cruise. He was talking to these guys I know he used to work with, real assholes. Sarah, you know who I'm talking about ... that guy, Mr. Summers, and his buddy Mike Holder."

Sarah nodded her head. "Yep. Assholes. I can confirm that part of the story."

"Anyway, I overheard some of the things he was saying, so I was kind of able to put some things together. I also read an email on his computer when he left it sitting on the dining room table one afternoon." Kevin paused and looked at Jonathan.

"Jonathan, your dad had invented some sort of software that was for telephone stuff, right? And no one had ever solved some sort of problem like this software did if I understand correctly ... "

"Well, the software is for telephone relay systems which are all completely computerized now. His software more efficiently routes the signals that go through those systems, which saves energy, time and resources. It has pretty far-reaching effects, particularly when one considers how relay traffic has steadily increased year over year for the past, I don't know, twenty years."

"Exactly. Well, my dad knew of some other uses for the program that I'm pretty sure your dad didn't – some sort of military uses I think. So he had hooked in with some guys through these a-holes that he knows, and once he signed your dad to a contract, he was going to cut your dad out and work the commercialization himself ... and I got the impression it was for purposes that your dad wasn't so crazy about."

Everyone was dead silent around the campfire. Kevin looked at the ground, clearly ashamed.

Candi was the first to speak. "Is this why you asked me to be your girlfriend today? So I would be more inclined to forgive you?" Her heart had gone cold, and all she could think about was being betrayed. He had been so smooth out on that rock today.

"What girlfriend? You're his *girlfriend?*" Jonathan stared at them in shock. "Since when?"

"Kevin, excuse my French, but what the *fuck?*" said Sarah, seriously pissed. "Why didn't you say anything to me?" She looked around the campfire. "Why didn't you say anything to *us?*"

Kevin started to look panicked. The looks he was getting from around the campfire were none too friendly. Candi was happy to see that everyone was supporting her dad.

"I'm so, so sorry guys. I know, I should have said something earlier. Believe me, I started to so many times; but I was just too much of a wimp. I knew it was wrong, what my dad was doing, and I wanted to tell you; but since we've been here, I don't know, it's just seemed so far away – like it was a bad dream or something."

Candi gave an inelegant snort. "Sha, like that's an excuse." She shook her head silently in disappointment, letting his story and lame excuses confirm the realization that he'd asked her to be his girlfriend to try and get some sort of alliance going to cushion the impact of his treachery; and that's exactly what it felt like – *treachery.*

"Oh, shit, Candi, not *you!* Don't be mad at me! I asked you to be my girlfriend because I like you, I want you to be my girl! It has *nothing* at all to do with this crap. Nothing at *all*, I swear."

Sarah spoke up. "Kevin, you may think you're right about that, but the truth is, we can't have secrets from one another. For now and until the foreseeable future, we're family, all four of us. We're all we have. We are totally connected by what we do and say *and* what we don't say. Without each other, we won't survive this island. And the shit that happened before we came here, and the shit that will happen when we leave, it's all *real*. It all matters, because it's going to impact us as a family now." She looked at all the faces around the fire; they were all listening to her intently. "I don't mean to be overly dramatic here, but really – I consider you guys my family. We live together, we eat together, we sleep together, we survive together, we are building a *life* together ... Candi and Kevin, you are my brother and sister. Jonathan, you're my, um, I'm not exactly sure yet – but whatever, we're family. And that's all I have to say."

Jonathan cleared his throat and looked at Kevin as he spoke. "I'm not sure that I can speak for Candi on this one, since she, uh, apparently has a different relationship with you than I realized, but anyway, speaking at least for myself, I can say that over the past few weeks, I have learned that you are not your father. You may look like him a little, but that's where the similarities end. I know you've got my back, and you've got my sister's back. I know you wouldn't do to us or to our parents what your dad is doing or trying to do. So I, for one, am not going to hold it against you that your dad is a douchebag." He paused before continuing, "However, I do have a problem with you keeping secrets of the type that are bad or could hurt us; so if we're going to continue to live on this island together, like a family as Sarah said, we have to have an understanding. No more secrets. Secrets are like lies as far as I'm concerned, and I need to be able to trust my family."

Candi nodded her agreement. "I have nothing to add to that. I agree with Jonathan and Sarah."

Kevin's eyes were bright with unshed tears. His voice was hoarse when he said, "Thanks guys. Like I said, I'm so sorry that I didn't tell you sooner. I should have. I know that. From now on, no more secrets. No lies. We are a family." He stood up and held out his hand over the fire.

The group knew this was Kevin's call for a team huddle, since he'd done it enough times during their morning rugby games. The others slowly stood and put their hands out, silently stacking them in the middle over the fire, looking into each other's eyes. "Family," said Kevin.

"Family," said Sarah.

"Family," said Jonathan.

Everyone looked to Candi to see if she was ready to forgive. She sighed heavily.

"Fine. Family."

"Whoot!" yelled Kevin, before turning and lifting her up, grabbing her in big bear hug and spinning her around.

"Put me down, you troll!" she yelled.

"No! You're my girlfriend, and I'm dancing with you!"

"Oh, my god, you need some serious dancing lessons if this is what you call dancing." Candi looked over at Sarah when the spinning had finally stopped to see what she thought about her brother's public display of affection. Sarah was watching them with a pleased expression on her face.

"I miss school dances," Sarah said wistfully.

Kevin put Candi down and hugged her hard, before letting her go to begin cleaning up around the fire. Candi pretended to help him, but listened carefully to the conversation Sarah and Jonathan started to have, sneaking glances over as often as she could without being too obvious.

"Not me," said Jonathan, a note of horror in his voice.

"Why don't you like school dances?" Sarah asked. "I thought everyone liked them."

"First, I can never get a date; and second, I can't dance ... so that kind of destroys the only two things that make a dance worth going to."

"Well, we could have a prom here on the island, and I could be your date. That is, if you want me to be your date." Sarah looked at

Jonathan, the bait dangling between them.

Candi smiled as she looked at the expression on her brother's face – hope mixed with fear.

"That doesn't solve the dancing problem," responded Jonathan, appearing neutral to her invitation.

Very cool, bro, very cool. Candi was impressed with her brother's handling of Sarah, who she knew could be intimidating as heck to any guy, let alone an inexperienced one like Jonathan.

"Well, I could teach you to slow dance and then after that, maybe you could just speed it up for the fast dances. Besides," she continued, as she moved closer to stand in front of him, "we don't really have any music, so we'd just be swaying from side to side. What could be easier than that?"

Jonathan held his ground, looking down into her eyes at the invitation that was definitely being issued from them. "If we were back home, would you go to the prom with me?"

Candi held her breath as she waited for Sarah's answer.

"Yes. In a second."

And Candi could tell she meant it.

Jonathan smiled. "I wish I could believe that."

"Believe it," said Sarah, just before she reached up on tiptoe and gently kissed him on the lips.

Jonathan moved his hands to rest them on her hips. "Do you have any idea what my friends back home would do if I walked into the prom with you as my date?" The idea made him nearly glow with happiness.

"Well, I don't know about your friends, but my friends would be jealous."

That comment made Candi smile. She could totally see it. Jonathan had changed, as had Sarah.

Jonathan chucked. "That's funny. Your friends would probably refuse to eat lunch with you ever again and you'd be banned to the chess club table with me for life."

"You underestimate your charms, Jonathan." She ran her hands up and down his upper arms, which by now had become quite well-muscled and very tan. "I'd have to work, I think, to keep my old friends from trying to steal you away from me."

Jonathan pulled her closer. "So, will you go to the Peanut Island prom with me, then?"

Sarah put her arms up around his neck, "Yes, I would love to."

They leaned in and gave each other a hot, wet kiss that threatened to turn into more – until they started hearing catcalls from across the clearing.

"Woo hoo, get a room, you two!" they heard Kevin yell.

"Wow, hey ... rated G, please, guys," from Candi.

Jonathan and Sarah instantly broke apart, both of them acting a little embarrassed.

Everyone moved away and began picking up their dinner mess, avoiding the awkward moment that threatened to overwhelm them.

Sarah was the first to speak. "Jonathan and I were talking, and we think we should have a prom on the island."

"A prom?" asked Candi, pretending she hadn't just listened in on their entire conversation.

"Yes, a prom. The Peanut Island Prom. We can have a dinner, some dancing, and then whatever. We'll have to get creative."

Kevin looked at Candi; she shrugged her shoulders.

"I'll go to the prom – on one condition," said Kevin.

"What?" said Sarah.

"That I can get a date." He looked at Candi and raised an

eyebrow.

"Hey, that's not fair, you're putting me on the spot."

"All's fair in love and prom dating, Gumdrop. So what do you say?" He walked over to her and took her hand in his. Then he started going down on one knee.

"Oh, my god, what are you doing?! Get up! *Stop!*"

"Candi? Candace Buckley? Will you go to prom with me?"

Candi felt her eyes start to water. Her heart was in her throat. Kevin had no idea what this meant to her. She hadn't even thought of dreaming about this, even in her wildest fantasies about him. The furthest she ever got in her make-believe world was hoping that he'd like her back ... even just a little bit would have satisfied her. But now he was offering more.

She cleared her throat. "Fine. Yes, I'll go to the prom with you."

Kevin stood up and pulled her to him for a hug. "A wise choice," he said in her hair, leaning down to kiss her head. "I was ready to start begging and that would have been embarrassing for all of us."

Candi laughed. "You're a dork."

"Don't tell anyone."

*****

All of them were exhausted. It had been a long night, filled with confessions of guilt and love and future intentions. They climbed up the treehouse ladder and went to their rooms, each of them thinking of the upcoming event and what they were going to do to make it as much like the real thing as possible.

In all of their planning, none of them thought to consider the possible consequences of bringing the outside world's version of the prom to their protected, isolated Eden.

Prom Night

PROM PREPARATIONS TOOK OVER THEIR activity schedule, ahead of the completion of the treehouse and the building of platforms. The girls put themselves in charge of food and the guys were managing the entertainment and setup. They all decided as a group to hold the prom on the beach where they first arrived on the island. The guys had checked it out and reported back that the lifeboat was still there, but now mostly buried in the sand at the water's edge.

They kept their planning and efforts secret from one another. The girls spent time making skirts out of palm frond strips that they secured around their waists with rope. They planned to use island flowers to add decoration, but had to wait until the afternoon of the prom to pick them.

"What are you making?" asked Sarah, frowning as she tried to figure out Candi's design.

"I'm making a second skirt that's going to be shorter and thinner than the first, to wear as a type of grass tube top. I'm just not sure yet how I'm going to keep from exposing myself, since I don't want to wear my dingy-white bra underneath."

"Huh," responded Sarah. "You could always do what I'm

doing ... the classic Hawaiian hula-girl style. I just need to work out the mechanics of securing these two coconuts over my boobs. I was going to use a plant rope surrounded by flowers, but so far I'm having a hard time getting holes in the coconut halves that didn't split the entire shell." She threw down her latest failures. "Oh well. I have two more days to get it done. If I don't figure it out by then, I'll just go topless."

Candi looked up in alarm. "I hope you're kidding."

Sarah just winked and said nothing.

*****

The day of the prom arrived. Sarah was putting the finishing touches on the coconut top she had finally managed to put holes in. It wasn't the most comfortable prom dress she'd ever worn, but it was island chic for sure. She had picked about a hundred tropical flowers in whites and pinks and was in the process of sticking their little stems into spaces in the plant rope part of the halter-top. She had already secretly made a flowered head wreath for Candi.

She reached up to the bamboo shelf to take a sip of water from her cup that was resting there. She had her eyes on her project and didn't notice that she grabbed the wrong one. She took a big gulp of what she thought was water, gagging and spitting it out when she realized it was something entirely different.

"Oh my god," she said to the air around her. "What the hell was *that?*" She looked into the cup and saw a cloudy liquid with something floating in it. There was a slight taste of it still on her tongue. She made a bitter face as she tried to figure out exactly what the taste was.

"Hmmm, tastes like ... wine?" She looked into the cup again. The contents were too murky to tell what it was or what it had been, but it had to be something that Candi had cooked up. She was the only one who messed with ingredients like this.

"What's up?" came Candi's voice. She approached with a fish dangling from a looped plant rope that was hanging down by her side.

"You tell me," responded Sarah, thrusting the cup out at Candi with a disgusted look on her face. "What the hell is this?"

Candi came over to look inside. "I don't know, what's in it?"

"If I knew, I wouldn't be asking you, duh."

Candi looked down into the cup again and then up at the shelves where the other ones sat. "Oooh ... oops!" She smiled sheepishly.

"Oops? What does *that* mean?! What did I just drink?" Sarah put her fingers to her lips, a stricken look on her face. "Was it lizard balls or something? Was it poison?" she asked in a meek voice.

"No, don't be silly," said Candi, laughing. "It's not poison, it's coconut water and guava." She took the cup from Sarah's hand, putting her nose to the edge to sniff it. "What does it taste like?"

Sarah shrugged her shoulders, relieved to find she wasn't going to be dying a painful death by poison lizard balls anytime soon. "I don't know, wine maybe?"

"It smells like wine too." She took a tentative sip. "Yep. Tastes like wine. Not very *good* wine, probably, but I wouldn't know. The only stuff I've ever tasted was at my parents' holiday parties."

A grin slowly spread across Sarah's face. She stared at Candi, waiting for her to make the connection.

"Why are you smiling like that? Stop it, you're making me nervous."

"No, no need to get nervous, get happy! You just made some prom punch!"

Candi thought about it for a second. "Prom punch. Hmm. It

probably is alcoholic. I remember in science class that alcohol is created through fermentation – and to start fermentation all you need is sugar ... and wild yeast."

"I totally remember that," said Sarah, enthusiastically.

"I can still picture Mrs. White running around the classroom, touching all the surfaces and saying how there was probably wild yeast sitting right there."

"Yeah, and that many wild plants had it, and it got blown by the wind to all kinds of places, right?"

"Exactly. Wow. I can't believe we're actually using science class to make alcohol on a deserted island."

"And we thought all of that education was going to be totally useless," said Sarah, grinning from ear to ear.

"Okay, prom punch it is. But I think we'd better filter it. That gook in there doesn't look so good."

"I'll go get the sheet." Sarah took off to the treehouse, thinking that the bed sheet currently serving as the boy's bed cover would make a pretty decent filter. She came back a minute later holding it in her hand.

"Here's a clean spot. I just washed this thing two days ago, so if you use the corner of it, I'm sure it'll be fine."

Candi had a grossed out look on her face.

"What? It's alcohol, no bugs can live in it. The sheet is clean, don't worry about it; I doubt we'll drink much of it anyway. It's pretty gross. It's just the idea that we could have alcohol at our prom. Pretty cool, right?" She looked at Candi for confirmation.

Candi acquiesced. "Yeah, pretty cool. Hold up the sheet, I'll pour the stuff over it and catch it in this other cup."

After they finished filtering the punch, they each took a shower, using sand to scrub the stink off their bodies as much as they could. Sarah had gathered a few very fragrant flowers, and they each rubbed the petals on their bodies, doing their best to wear perfume for their big dates. The Peanut Island Prom was less than an hour away, and they were as nervous as they would be if they were home putting on satin gowns and professionally made corsages.

*****

"No, dude, you have to put it up like this," said Kevin. He was holding up a bamboo pole at an angle on the beach, trying to set up a limbo rack. They'd had to veto the volleyball game idea since they had no good ball substitute. Kevin had been bummed for a while, but Jonathan was able to convince him that the limbo rack was a decent second choice and probably something the girls would like better.

"Oh, yeah, okay, I see what you're saying." Jonathan grabbed the pole and held it at the angle Kevin had specified.

"Keep it there while I get the other one – then we can tie them together."

They had been working for an hour, setting up a fire pit and the limbo area. They had also gathered anything they thought could be used as a musical instrument. Candi said before that she wanted to start a band, but they hadn't yet gotten around to doing that. Tonight was going to be their first performance.

"What do you think the girls are going to say about our outfits?" asked Jonathan.

"I think they're gonna want to get us naked," said Kevin, smiling at the thought. "I'm not gay or anything, Jonathan, but even I have to admit you look hot in a grass skirt."

Jonathan laughed. "I don't know about that, but I do like the headband and the arm things. I feel like a native warrior or something."

"Yeah, it's like the All Blacks rugby team. I wish I had memorized their Maori chants. These outfits would be perfect for that. Too bad we don't have tattoos ... "

"We *could* have tattoos," said Jonathan, cryptically.

"Uh, not sure I want to stab myself with something sharp out here in the middle of no-antibiotics-land."

"No, I mean temporary tattoos. Using berry juice or something. We can just wipe it on in patterns."

Kevin thought about it for a second. "I like it. Find us some tattoo stuff. I'll totally do it."

Jonathan disappeared in a flash. He knew exactly where to find the materials. He'd already seen them in the trees before.

Kevin yelled after him, "We only have another hour or so before sunset, so hurry up!"

"Yeah, okay!" Jonathan ran but not as fast as he could. He didn't want to sweat too much before the big night. And it was big too – tonight would be his first date *and* his first dance. And he was going with the most beautiful girl he'd ever known.

*****

Sunset came and the girls were in the workshop area in the roots of the trees, putting on their finishing touches. They had used makeup from Sarah's precious stores in her makeup case. Sarah did a classic nighttime sultry look for herself, using dark blues and purples with heavy black eyeliner. For Candi she went with a more natural look, using browns and a hint of green. She used dark brown liner to outline her eyes and then used it to fill in Candi's freshly plucked eyebrows to emphasize their delicate arch.

They loaded all the food they'd prepared into woven baskets Sarah had made, preparing to carry it all to the beach.

"Wait one second," said Sarah. She went back to the workshop, returning with what looked like a pile of flowers.

"I made this for your hair." She held up a string of flowers, designed to sit like a crown on Candi's head.

Candi got tears in her eyes. "Sarah, that is so sweet! And they are so pretty!" She grabbed Sarah in a hug, careful not to squish the flowers. "Thank you so much," she said over Sarah's back. "You are an awesome sister, you know that?"

Sarah felt herself go a little misty, too. "Shut up, you're going to ruin my makeup. Now sit still so I can put this on you."

Candi stood in front of Sarah and waited while Sarah secured it amongst her dreadlocks.

"Perfect. Exactly like I imagined it would look. You're going to knock Kevin's socks off tonight. Well, not his socks, since he won't be wearing any. You know what I mean." Sarah wiped away the tear that had tried to escape her eye.

Candi wiped under both of her eyes too. "We are the hottest chicks on this entire island."

Sarah laughed and Candi joined her. "Yes we are. Look out bitches, the Queens of Peanut Island have arrived." She held out her hand, and the two of them executed a perfect secret sister handshake.

"Come on. I wanna get to the party and get my drink on. The guys are going to be totally shocked when they see this punch."

Candi smiled as she bent down to grab her pile of baskets. "I wonder what they're going to be wearing."

"I have no idea. Probably the same old shorts they've been wearing for the past six weeks."

"I'm surprised we haven't seen what they've been up to."

"They found a good hiding spot, because I've been watching

out for it and I haven't seen anything," said Sarah, a little miffed that they'd outsmarted her.

The girls made their way through the trees. As they got closer to the beach, they started hearing sounds.

Sarah slowed down until Candi drew up next to her. "What's that sound? Can you hear it?"

Candi stopped and cocked her ear towards the beach. "It sounds like ... drums?"

They looked at each other and then started walking at a fast pace, finally breaking through the trees and finding the source of the noise.

The guys were each sitting on tree trunks they had dragged to the edge of a big bonfire, playing musical instruments they had made.

Kevin was using thin bamboo sticks topped with tied-on seashells to bang on a set of sawed-off, upright bamboo poles, in a very danceable rhythm. There were several poles of different widths and heights stuck in the ground in front of him. Each pole had been cut at a joint, creating flat surfaces for the bamboo drumsticks to hit, like mini drums.

Jonathan had two sets of coconut shells that had been broken in half, cleaned out, filled with tiny shells inside, and then secured back together with cords wrapped around them. They made perfect maracas.

Together, the two of them were putting out a hell of a native dance mix.

"Woo hoo!" shouted Sarah, coming into the clearing with her baskets. She quickly set them down and began dancing around the fire. Candi set hers down too and joined in. They swirled their grass skirts around, dancing to the rhythm of the boys' beat.

The guys shouted out their encouragement, laughing as the girls tried to do some Tahitian belly dance moves. The girls soon dissolved in laughter, so the guys quit playing and joined them around the fire.

Kevin was the first one to speak. "Wow, you guys look great." He took Candi by the hand. "Come over here, I have something for you."

Sarah watched her brother with interest, wondering what he possibly could have up his sleeve for Candi.

He pulled Candi over to the log he'd been sitting on and bent down, reaching behind it to pull out a string of flowers and green leaves. "This is for you. Wanna get lei-ed?" He winked at her suggestively.

Candi smiled and giggled a little bit. "Sure, lei me." She followed the lei with her eyes as he put it over her head, settling it between her breasts.

Kevin looked in her eyes. "Beautiful."

Sarah nudged Jonathan, gesturing over at Candi and Kevin with her chin. He looked over at them and then down at Sarah, smiling at her. She warmed not only at his approval of whatever their siblings had going on, but also the connection she felt, sharing it with him.

"Thank you." Candi looked up at Kevin, her face all aglow. "Wow, you look great too." She laughed. "That is like the coolest prom suit I've ever seen."

Kevin backed up a little bit and bowed. "Thank you, girlfriend."

"And I love your warrior paint." She reached up to touch his face and the paintings that he'd done down his arms. They looked very tribal.

Sarah looked at Jonathan, very much admiring his tattoos and the grass skirt he was wearing, which had the same effect on her as a Scottish warrior wearing a kilt. *Totally hot.* The skirt ended just above his knees. She loved the look of his bare legs at the bottom. He had tied braided cords around his now pretty well-muscled upper arms, the ends of the cords hanging down to his elbows. He had a similar braided cord wrapped around his head. His hair had gotten longer and the cord added to the slightly wild and savage warrior look he had going on. All in all, it was pretty damn sexy. Sarah looked at him with hunger in her eyes, willing him to look over at her.

"She's going to kiss him," he said, not even noticing the come hither looks Sarah was sending his way, he was so busy watching his sister and Kevin.

Sarah looked over in time to see it happen. "Wow. And not shy at all about it, either."

"What was that for?" Kevin asked, looking a little dazed by the passion she displayed in that kiss.

"I don't know. I like your tux."

Kevin laughed. "What do you think about Jonathan's?" He gestured across the fire.

"Yeah, Candi, what do you think about our dates?" asked Sarah.

"Not bad," said Candi, a smile in her voice.

"Should we show them what we brought?"

"Yep." Candi moved away from Kevin to join Sarah at the baskets. Her skirt made swishing sounds as she moved and Sarah noticed that Candi couldn't help but put a little extra sway in her walk.

Sarah held up the first basket. "First, we have, of course, a fruit salad, made up of bananas and guava. Everyone please hold your applause. We also have some smoked fish, compliments of Candi and Kevin, our chef and smoker builder, respectively."

Candi and Kevin took a bow.

Then Candi took the lead. "And last, but not least, we provide coconut wine for your drinking pleasure!" She held up two very large bamboo cups filled with the fermented juice.

"What?" asked Kevin, as if he hadn't heard correctly.

"Did you say 'wine'?" asked Jonathan.

The guys went over to take a look at what was in the cups. Candi explained, "Yeah, it was kind of an accident. I tried to make coconut guava drinks a few days ago, but it tasted awful, so I just kind of left it sitting there and forgot about it. A few days later, *poof*, we had alcohol."

"Wow, that is so cool," said Jonathan. "Natural fermentation using wild yeasts and fruit sugars – of course." He was staring into the liquid when he absent-mindedly wondered aloud, "I wonder how many hydrogen dioxide atoms that released into the atmosphere?"

Kevin shook his head and rolled his eyes. "Never mind the science, Jon. We have wine at our island prom. What could possibly be cooler than that? Good job, girls." He took a breath and then continued, "And now, I will present to you our entertainment for the evening. What would you girls like to do? We have a choice of music or games. Or both, it's up to you. You have already seen some of our amazing percussion skills. We have instruments for you too."

Candi set down the drinks. "What games?"

"Well, first there's limbo, just over there," Kevin gestured to his right. "And then, here on my left, we have a game that neither of us can remember the name of, but we remember playing in gym class in seventh grade."

Candi and Sarah looked over to where Kevin was pointing. There were two long poles, laying parallel to one another, each resting at the ends on short poles that held them slightly off the ground.

Sarah smiled. "I remember that game. You bang them first on the thingies and then you slide them towards each other and bang them together, and whoever is not banging the poles is in the middle jumping in and out of the poles trying not to get their ankles smashed."

Candi grimaced. "Yeah, I remember that game too. I'm the one who always had the smashed ankles."

"Limbo it is!" announced Kevin. "But maybe we should eat first."

"Yeah, let's eat," agreed Jonathan.

They sat down around the roaring fire and passed the food baskets. The girls had brought bamboo mini-troughs for everyone to eat out of. The boys had discovered days earlier that they could hack one of their bamboo cups in half, making a pretty good plate in the shape of a trough for their dinner meals.

Candi poured the coconut wine. They each took a sip from their cups, grimacing when the wine hit their tongues.

"Whoa," said Jonathan, "that stuff is potent."

Candi wiped away some that had spilled onto her chin. "Yep. Nothing but the good stuff for my peeps."

"I can't remember when I've had something that tasted this bad," added Kevin.

They all started laughing.

"I don't know what your problem is," said Sarah, "I think it's pretty good."

"Well here, you can have mine," said Kevin. He poured his portion into her cup. She finished it in several long gulps.

After they finished eating, they put their dishes in the baskets and began the limbo game. The ones who weren't limboing played out beats with the instruments. As the alcohol began to work its way through their bloodstreams, those who had drank more of it, namely Candi and Sarah, really started to feel the effects. They weren't able to limbo very well because they kept losing their balance.

They tried the bamboo pole game next, but the girls either fell next to the poles, got their ankles whacked, or couldn't keep a rhythm for the boys to do their jumping. The guys gave up, calling it quits after the two girls collapsed in giggles and then tried to pick up the game poles and use them as javelins.

"Okay, I think it's time we wrapped this prom up," said Kevin, holding onto Candi's shoulders to keep her from wandering off.

"Oh, poo, I haven't even had a chance to dance yet," said Candi, pouting.

"I'm not going anywhere 'til I've had a dance," insisted Sarah. "Jonathan, dance with me sweetie, I'm beggin'." She looked at him and started batting her eyelashes, sticking out her lower lip.

"Fine, one dance. Then you're going to bed," said a very sober but tired-sounding Jonathan.

"Whatever you say, mister bossy cow." She held out her arms.

He walked over and stepped into them, putting his hands around her waist.

"We don't have any music," he said, a little bit self-consciously.

"We don't need music, just come here." Sarah pulled him

close, putting her head on his chest. She could hear his heartbeat and feel the warmth coming from his skin. He smelled so good ... like smoke and sweat and ocean ... like ... Jonathan. She inhaled deeply.

"You're not going to sleep are you?" he asked. She could tell he was smiling when he said it.

"Nope. Just smelling you. You smell nice. Sexy. Like Jonathan."

"I thought normal people didn't smell other people. That's what you told me on the cruise ship, anyway."

"Shush."

"You smell nice too." He rested his chin on her head. "I love the feel of you in my arms. When I'm all dressed up like this, I feel like a warrior or something. Wild. Protective of you, even though you really don't need protection."

"That's nice," said Sarah, feeling all warm inside. Any other time or place, his words might sound corny. But here, they were perfect and exactly what she wanted to hear.

*****

Kevin looked over at his sister and Jonathan and decided that they needed some privacy. "Wanna go for a walk?"

"You're one of those guys who likes long, moonlit walks on the beach?" Candi asked teasingly.

"Yes, under certain circumstances, I am."

"And what would those circumstances be?"

"When I'm with my hot girlfriend, she's tipsy, and I want to get her alone."

Candi's eyes opened in mock offense. "Well, then, let's go, since you're going to be all romantic like that." She smiled, taking the sting out of her teasing.

Kevin reached around and smacked her on the butt as she tried to run away. He caught up to her just a few yards later and grabbed her hand. They walked together, hand in hand, down the beach until they could no longer see the firelight.

Candi was feeling brave. "Now that you have me out here in the middle of nowhere, what are you going to do with me?"

"This," was all he said, before pulling her into his arms and leaning down to put his lips against hers.

Her body instantly responded. She pulled herself in close to him, feeling his need and moaning happily. He was kissing her deeply, dancing his tongue across hers, while his hands roamed all over her body.

"Do you want to lie down?" he asked. "I don't want to scare you away, but I'm going to keep going until you say stop."

"Yes," she gasped out. "Let's lay down."

They lowered themselves together down to the sand. Kevin was on top of her, between her legs. He began kissing her neck and then her chest. She was breathing heavily.

"You smell so good. I can't get enough." He stopped for a second and looked her in the face.

Candi could see him in the light of the moon and wanted to faint from how gorgeous he was.

"I don't want to do anything you don't want me to do. If you want me to stop you have to tell me. I'm serious."

"I don't want you to stop at all, I *want* to do this."

"Do you mean ... "

"Yes, that's what I mean. It. I want to do *it.*"

"Are you sure? Have you done this before?"

"Yes, I'm sure, and no I haven't, but I really want to. With you. I have for a long time. I'm just worried about ... you know ...

getting pregnant."

"Me too. But I'm having a hard time stopping. What do you want me to do? I can't guarantee you won't get pregnant. We don't have any birth control out here, other than just me pulling out, which isn't the most effective way, as you probably know from sex ed with Mr. Tanner."

She could hear the teasing in his voice and smiled at the memory of that uncomfortable class. "Just um ... finish ... um ... outside ... like you said. I think it will be okay." She tried not to let her embarrassment ruin the mood.

"I'll do my best."

Kevin was gentle with her, and Candi was carried away by the passion and feelings that rushed through her body and mind. She knew she would never forget this moment, never regret it.

Later they stretched out on their backs in the sand, staring at the stars above their heads. Neither one of them said anything. The night was too perfect to spoil with talk right now.

But soon enough, Candi started to worry about getting caught. "Come on, we'd better get back. We don't want Jonathan and Sarah to worry and come looking for us."

Kevin chuckled. "I don't think you need to worry about that. I'm sure they're keeping each other busy. But come on, we can go. I don't know about you, but I'm pretty tired."

"I am completely covered in sand," said Candi.

"We'll take a shower when we get back."

"But it's so late," whined Candi.

"Yeah, but it's our island. If we want to take a shower in the middle of the night, we can, right?"

Candi smiled back. "Right. Showers it is."

"No, not showers. *Shower*. Singular. We're going in together."

Candi felt herself get all warm again. She didn't say anything; she just kept walking back to the treehouse, hand in hand, with her boyfriend, Kevin Peterson.

*****

"What do you think they're doing out there?" asked Sarah. She had moved to sit next to Jonathan on the log next to the fire. After they kissed, they took some time to clean up the dishes and put everything back in the baskets. They disassembled the limbo game and stacked all the poles near the tree line to put away when it was light out again.

"I don't know, taking a walk?" suggested Jonathan. He really didn't want to think about what his sister was doing right now. He knew she was safe with Kevin, but the thought of her and him together? That was, just, *eww.* He didn't want to go there.

"Well, we're here together. All alone, you and me. What do you think *we* should do?"

Her suggestion was undeniable. She got off the log to kneel in front of him, scooting over so that she was between his legs. She reached up and ran her hands from his knees, slowly up his thighs towards his hips.

Jonathan inhaled sharply. She was barely touching him, but it was making him crazy already.

This was nuts, he decided. She was hot for him, he was hot for her ... *I have no idea what I'm doing, but I might as well figure it out.*

Jonathan put his hands on either side of Sarah's face and drew her towards him. Their lips met and it was instant passion. Their kisses turned feverish. Jonathan didn't have a plan, all he knew was that he wanted to be with her right then, right there in front of the fire. He didn't even think about being seen by his own sister. Something about Sarah made him forget to worry.

"Oh my god, Jonathan, I want you so bad!" Sarah gasped desperately.

"Me too," he said breathlessly.

Sarah pulled him down on top of her and within seconds, they were both caught up in the frenzied pace of their lovemaking. They were both crying out, unable to stop the freight train that was leading them over the edge.

Jonathan felt a piece of his life force ebb out of him and into the warmth that was Sarah beneath him. His breath was coming in gasps, the sweat pouring off of him. Some of it dripped from his face and landed on Sarah's.

"Sorry about that, I'm sweating on you."

"Mmmm, I like it." Sarah wriggled a little under him.

Jonathan looked down at her face, glowing in the flickering flames of the campfire. "You're really sexy, you know that?"

She suddenly seemed very vulnerable and shy. "Really?"

"Hell, yes."

"You just said a bad word."

"Yes, I did. Something about you makes me want to do bad things."

"Oh reeeaaallly ... "

"Ah, don't move," he said, "or you're going to have to do that all over again."

"Man, do you have staying power, or what?" she asked, sounding impressed.

"Sarah, I've been storing up this energy for about, oh, maybe six years or so; so whenever you're ready to go, just tap me on the shoulder, and I'll be ready to go too."

"But what do I do when you're all tapped out?"

"I'm pretty sure that couldn't possibly happen when I'm with a girl as beautiful as you."

Sarah said nothing, but lifted her head up to give him a kiss on the lips.

"What was that for?" he asked.

"Just because. Now let me up so I can go rinse myself off. I have sand in every crevice, and I mean *every* crevice. Plus, we got a little nuts there and failed to take one little detail into consideration. And I'm not sure there's anything I can do about that, but I'm going to try."

"What's that?"

"Failure to employ any method of birth control."

"Oh, *crap*," said Jonathan, the heat rising up in his face. *What have I done?* "I can't believe I didn't even think about that until just now."

"Well, I thought about it, but decided to say *what the hell.* Hopefully we won't regret it later. I'm going down to the water to rinse off."

"Are you sure you're okay? You had a lot of that wine. I could go with you."

"Yes, I'm tipsy, I admit it, but I'm fine. Stay here, I'll be back in a few."

Jonathan eased back onto the sand, watching her walk out of the ring of light, heading towards the water. He tried to keep his eyes open, but the little bit of alcohol he'd drunk, the warm fire, and the contentment of losing his virginity to the most beautiful girl he had ever known was a very potent sleeping pill, even more potent than the thoughts of having unprotected sex. He fell asleep within seconds, the waves breaking against the shore the last thing he remembered hearing.

*****

"Jonathan, get up. Get *up*, Jonathan."

He could hear Candi's irritated voice in his dream. He wished she'd go away so he could keep on dreaming about his beautiful girlfriend, Sarah Peterson.

Then he was jerked awake by the feeling of cold water tossed in his face.

"Sorry, buddy, but you need to get up." This voice was Kevin's and it sounded stern.

"What the ... ?" Jonathan sat up and looked around him. "Where am I?"

"You're still at the prom, now where is Sarah?" demanded Kevin.

"Sarah?" He was momentarily confused. *Where is Sarah? How should I know where Sarah is?*

Then it all came flooding back to him. Sarah at the campfire. Sarah underneath him. Sarah so beautiful. Sarah going to rinse off in the ocean ...

"Oh my god," he jumped up in a panic. "Last night she went down to the water; I was supposed to wait up for her, but I must have fallen asleep!" Jonathan started running his hands through his hair in agitation. "Do you mean she didn't come back to the treehouse last night?" He was hoping for an answer he knew he wasn't going to get.

"No, Jonathan, she didn't. That's why we're here with you asking where she is." Candi was pissed. "How could you have fallen asleep and left Sarah, who was drunk, to wander around by herself? This is so unlike you."

"Don't get angry just yet, Candi, let's think this through," said Kevin. "Sarah wouldn't just walk into the water and disappear. Maybe she tried to get to the treehouse and then got lost; you know there was no moon out last night, and it was very dark."

"Yeah, okay, that makes sense," said Jonathan, taking deep breaths to calm himself. "We just need to find her trail and follow it."

Candi nodded her head in agreement, frowning in obvious disapproval at her brother.

"Let's split up, see if we can find her footprints anywhere on the beach," said Kevin. "Focus on the tree line area."

They all walked down the beach, Kevin and Candi going one direction and Jonathan going the other. After less than a minute, Candi yelled out, "I think I found something!"

The other two came running over. Sure enough, there were small, girl-sized footprints in the sand, leading into the trees about twenty yards down from the campfire.

"Why would she go into the trees here?" asked Jonathan, confused.

"Who knows? Maybe she was too drunk to realize what she was doing."

That comment made Jonathan feel twice as bad as he already felt. He responded meekly, "She seemed to know what she was doing before she left."

Kevin gave him a narrow-eyed stare. "Oh, she did, did she?"

Candi put her hand on Kevin's arm to calm him down. "Not now, guys, we need to track her down. Can you tell which way she went?"

"Luckily, she walked through here like a wounded elephant," said Kevin. "Look at all the broken leaves."

"Do you think she's wounded?" asked Candi in a worried voice.

"No, it's just an expression. I mean, she wasn't walking very delicately. Come on, let's follow her path of destruction."

They all followed Kevin single file through the trees. The route they took turned left and right indiscriminately. If Sarah had been following some sort of path, they couldn't see it. She seemed to be wandering, not knowing where she was going, heading in the opposite direction of the treehouse.

They continued on for an hour. It was hard to walk quickly in some of the areas because the trees were so dense. Eventually it started to thin out; they could see sun coming through the canopy above. They could also hear the ocean again.

"I think we're getting near the northern coast of the island," said Jonathan.

Just then they stepped into a clearing, and sitting in the middle of it was a very bedraggled and tired-looking Sarah, still wearing her coconut bra top and grass skirt. The top sat on her chest, slightly askew.

"Well, there you are," she said impatiently, standing up and brushing herself off, trying to adjust her coconut cups so they were straight. "Finally. I thought I was going to have to light a friggin' signal fire or something." She walked over to meet them at the edge of the clearing.

Jonathan stepped over to stand in front of her. "Are you okay?" He searched her face for clues of her mood.

Sarah reached up and stroked his cheek, then slapped it lightly. "Fell asleep, didn't ya?"

Jonathan ducked his head in shame. "Yes, I did, I'm *so* sorry, Sarah. I left you out here alone. I don't know what to say, but I totally understand if you hate me right now." His heart squeezed in his chest at the idea of her not wanting him anymore.

"No, I don't hate you. You and I both had too much to drink, and we have bigger problems to worry about right now, anyway."

"What do you mean?" asked Kevin, looking over at Jonathan with an expression that said he wasn't going to let him off as easy as Sarah had.

"Follow me, peeps.   You are not going to believe the shit I found."

Interlopers

SARAH LED THEM THROUGH THE trees until they reached an area about thirty yards wide that seemed to be cut into the jungle with a giant cookie-cutter. There were no tall trees here. The entire squared-off area was filled with plants, none of which were more than five feet tall. They also weren't palms or guavas or any of the other plants and trees they were used to seeing on the island.

Sarah held out her arms, presenting the plants with a flourish of her arms. *"Voilà!"* She stood there silently waiting for someone to make the connection.

No one said anything. They just looked at the plants, then back at her.

She tried again, throwing her arms out more theatrically. *"Voilà!"*

Then she saw Kevin's eyes nearly bulge out of his head. "Holy shit. Is this what I think it is?"

"Yes, hello, finally the light bulb comes on," said Sarah sarcastically.

Jonathan and Candi stood there with their light bulbs still off. "I don't get it," said Jonathan. "It's a field of short plants."

Kevin smiled. "Look a little closer, Wikipedia guy, see if those plants look familiar to you at all."

Jonathan moved closer and took one of the large, seven-pointed leaves in his hand. "These look like ... "

He didn't finish. He just turned to look at Sarah and Kevin. "Are these what I think they are?"

"What?!" yelled Candi. "Why am I the only one who doesn't get what's going on here?" She looked from Jonathan to Sarah to Kevin. All of them were just staring at her expectantly. "*What?* Is this like alien landing fields or something? Crop circles or whatever? What?! Tell me!"

Kevin put his hand on her shoulder. "Babe, this is a giant field of marijuana."

"Yeah, and there's more," said Sarah, all seriousness now. "It has watering pipe things everywhere and just farther that way is some camping equipment."

Candi was finally putting all the pieces together. She put her hand up to her mouth and whispered, "Oh my god ... oh my god ... there are *people* here." Then she started jumping up and down, "THERE ARE PEOPLE HERE!!" She was smiling and laughing, beside herself with excitement. "We're going to be rescued!"

The others just stood there, looking serious. They weren't excited at all.

"Why aren't you excited about this?" She stopped jumping and stood there, looking confused again and a little bit deflated. "Guys, what's wrong? Aren't we going to be rescued now? Isn't this a good thing?"

Sarah went over and put her arm around Candi's waist. "That's what I thought when I first saw everything. I was like, 'Yay! We're going home!' – but then I realized that the people who planted these *drugs* are criminals ... and these criminals probably wouldn't be very happy about a group of kids, who are already assumed to be dead, knowing about their massively illegal operation here." Sarah waited a second for what she said to sink into Candi's brain before continuing. "So we are not going to be rescued by these guys. We are probably going to be *killed* by these guys, unless we can come up with some kind of plan."

Tears sprang into Candi's eyes. "Oh, my god ... killed? We're going to be *murdered?*" She looked around her in fear, suddenly whispering, "Are they here on the island now?"

Kevin glared at his sister. "You didn't need to be that harsh, Sarah."

"Well, sorry, but it's true. And no, they're not here now, otherwise I'd already be dead. I found this crap as soon as the sun came up, and I've been freaking out about it ever since. You've only had to freak out about it for five minutes. Talk to me at one o'clock, and we'll see where *you* are with it."

Jonathan held his hands up. "Okay guys, this is not the time to fight. We need to assess the situation and figure out what we can do. We're a team; we can figure something out, I know we can. We didn't come all this way to give up now."

"Jonathan's right," agreed Kevin. "Let's look around and see if we can gather some intel from what we see here and at that campsite Sarah mentioned."

They all spread out, looking to see if they could find any other trails, footprints, or signs of the interlopers who had planted the pot. Their search turned up nothing helpful.

"Sarah, why don't you show us the campsite you found," suggested Kevin.

They walked for about five minutes until they reached the spot. There was a tent, some pots, and a tarp.

Candi stared at the pots enviously. "I don't suppose I can take any of these things, can I?" she asked.

"No," said Jonathan. "We have to erase all evidence of our presence here. We don't want them finding out about us and hunting us down. Our treehouse is hidden, but it wouldn't be too hard to find. We've practically cut paths leading from the south side of the island right to it."

"I think the one thing we have to do right away is figure out where they're landing on the beach – where they park their boat. Then we can spy on them when they come," said Kevin.

"I agree," said Sarah.

"Okay, Kevin, lead the way."

*****

Kevin headed off in the direction of the west coast of the island, realizing quickly how close they had actually come to this spot the day they had gone out into the trees to explore and found the guavas. He was kind of glad they hadn't found the drugs until now. They would have never had such a fun prom night if they had known about this threat to their lives.

They easily found the place where the drug dealers, as they were now calling them, anchored their boat. There was a protected cove not five minutes from the pot plants, and the beach held evidence of old campfires.

"Now what?" asked Candi.

"Now we go back and put our plan together," answered Jonathan. "We have to stop off at the prom beach to clean up our stuff there. That area would be very easy to see from the water. I'm not sure what side they approach the island from, but we can't assume anything. We don't even know where this island is on a map, so we don't know if these guys are coming from the north, south, east, west ... ." He stopped for a second and then continued with a frustrated look on his face. "There are just too many variables to accurately estimate anything; it's making me crazy."

Kevin grabbed a few palm fronds from a nearby pile. "Take one of these, each of you. Use it to wipe our footprints away, if you see any."

They all walked together in a line back to where they had come from, doing their best to swish palm fronds around the ground, erasing their footprints and hiding the evidence that anyone had been there. They broke some branches in other areas around the pot grove, in case someone saw the other ones, hoping maybe it would throw the criminals off the trail of where they had originally entered the area.

They got to the prom beach after lunchtime and spent an hour cleaning it up. They stowed the bamboo poles deep in the trees and buried the campfire leftovers.

"What are we going to do about the lifeboat?" asked Candi.

They all looked out to the water where they had left it weeks before. Only the tip of the bow was still visible above the beach's surface. The ocean, tides and sand had nearly finished claiming it as their own.

"I don't think we need to do anything, the sand will continue to cover it. Within two weeks it will be completely buried and invisible," said Jonathan.

They went back to the treehouse. A somber mood hovered over their heads, turning the rest of the day into one filled with anxiety and fear. Each was lost in thought, worried that they might have gone through all of this, only to lose each other at the hands of modern day pirates.

*****

Candi, unable to take the stress anymore and needing to clear her head, went fishing. She came back with two decent sized fish. She hung them on the tree and stowed her spears in the workshop, calling out to everyone as she reached the bottom of the ladder.

"Hey, guys, I want to talk to all of you for a second. I'm coming up."

She climbed the ladder to the treehouse, finding them all sitting at the table together.

"I was thinking about our situation, and I think I came up with an idea."

"We were just talking about that, but we couldn't come up with one that didn't involve death," said Sarah morosely.

Candi sat down and began to outline her plan.

"When these drug dealers come to the island, they're either going to come just to check on their plants, or they're going to come to harvest them. Either way, it's going to be more than one guy probably, maybe even several, and they're obviously going to come by boat; so, maybe when they come, we can hide at the edge of the trees, and when they're in the forest with the plants, we can swim out and get on their boat radio and call for help."

They mulled her idea over in their heads for a minute. Sarah was the first one to speak. "Why don't we just steal the boat?"

"Yeah, I say we steal the boat and get the hell outta here," said Kevin.

"Boat radio, eh? Hmmm," said Jonathan.

"Well, I thought about stealing the boat, but then I realized: one, we don't know how to drive a boat; and two, even if we could drive it, we have no idea where we are, so we won't know where to point the damn thing. We could try to rescue ourselves and end up going towards Africa. It'll probably be a powerboat that'll just run out of gas before we get anywhere, anyway. And I don't know about you guys, but I don't want to die out in the middle of the ocean." She thought about it for a second and then added, "Gee, I hope it's a powerboat because I have no idea how to sail."

"What you're saying makes sense, but what if there are guys who stay on the boat?" asked Kevin.

"Well, if that happens, we're screwed. We need to get to the radio and do it without them seeing us, because once they know we're here, we're dead. They'll hunt us down and find us ... and then, well, you know what happens next."

They all sat there letting her words sink in. Now all of Jonathan's dire warnings of pirates didn't sound so crazy. These guys might not officially be called pirates, but it was the same concept.

"You know, *Pirates of the Caribbean* is *very* misleading," said Sarah angrily. "I saw those pirates as being all sexy and funny ... I was rooting for them; but they were criminals, and they killed people and stole crap! Why was I rooting for the bad guys?"

Jonathan laughed. "That's Hollywood for ya. They can convince us to do anything, I think. I was a big Jack Sparrow fan too."

"Yeah, well I'd like to have a word or two with Johnny Depp, that's all I have to say," grumbled Sarah.

"So what's the deal then, what's our plan?" asked Kevin. "Jonathan?"

"Well, if I hear you all correctly, we've agreed to keep our eyes out for the bad guys to come. We wait for the boat to anchor. Then one of us swims out to the boat and gets on board to use the radio and call for help."

"Yes," joined in Candi, "and when we get on the radio, we say who we are and explain that the night of the ship sinking there were huge rogue waves that pushed us very far away and so they need to search outside the normal area. And we tell them that the island is shaped like a giant peanut with rocks on the south side."

"Anything else?"

"Yes," said Sarah, "tell them there are drug dealers here and to hurry the hell up and rescue us."

Kevin and Jonathan nodded at each other. Kevin added, "I suggest we add long distance swimming and holding our breath under water training to our morning exercises."

"Agreed," said Candi.

"Fine," sighed Sarah.

*****

Kevin took charge of their new exercise regimen, which included not only swimming over and under water, but also tree climbing. They all agreed that the best place to hide when they were watching out for the bad guys was up in a tree. They took shifts every day, watching the beach where they thought the drug dealers had probably anchored their boat before. Whoever saw the boat on their watch was supposed to run back and tell the others, putting their radio contact plan into action.

"You guys are doing great," said Kevin, treading water next to Jonathan and Candi. "That was a full two minutes for you, Candi. Jonathan, you did two minutes and twenty seconds."

"Holy crap, Jonathan, I didn't know a person could hold their breath for that long," said Candi, still a little breathless from the strain of not breathing and then treading water for so long.

"We need to be able to tread water for at least twenty minutes," said Kevin.

"What?!" complained Candi, "I can barely do it for ten!"

"It's just a matter of training, Candi, you can do it," encouraged Jonathan.

"Let's go back now, I have to go relieve Sarah anyway," said Kevin. Even he was a little tired of treading water for so long. He had thought before they started this that he was in the best shape possible. Now he realized there was always room for improvement.

They swam back to the beach, each of them practicing cutting a clean line through the water with a freestyle stroke and then swimming underwater making no surface disturbance. They were getting pretty good.

*****

While Kevin headed off to relieve Sarah, Jonathan and Candi cleaned themselves off and prepared for lunch.

"They haven't come in the three weeks we've been preparing," said Candi. "Do you think they're coming at all?"

"Yes. I don't think drug dealers go to the trouble of putting in all those plants and installing an irrigation system just to walk away and leave all that money in the ground."

Candi sighed. "I know, I was just hoping you would say something else."

Jonathan chuckled. "Just because I say it, doesn't make it true."

"Yes it does," argued Candi. "You're smart and you tell the truth. What you say always comes true."

She was feeling sorry for herself – for all of them. She was in love with Kevin, and she knew he was in love with her too. Knowing that they were in mortal danger had caused them to come together much quicker than they probably would have in another time and place. They were even sharing a room now, while Jonathan and Sarah shared the other. Candi couldn't imagine what she would do if something happened to Kevin – or Sarah or Jonathan for that matter.

Sometimes she and Kevin lay awake at night talking about it, and about their lives together. He was even more worried about her than she was about him. He told her that he had an overwhelming need to protect her that was instinctual. If she didn't stop him, he'd serve his own guard duty and then go with her while she served hers, getting almost no sleep. She had to remind him over and over that they needed him well-rested and ready to fight if necessary.

Jonathan put down the cups he was carrying. "Listen, Candi ... we are going to get out of this. We are going to win, I promise." He went over to her and hugged her close. She hugged him back fiercely.

Just then, Sarah came crashing through the trees. "They're here!" she yelled in a frantic voice. She stopped at the campfire ring, bent over trying to catch her breath.

Candi's heart was in her throat. "What?! They're here? *Now?*"

"Yes," gasped Sarah. "One boat. Two guys. They're anchoring in the cove now. Kevin is there, in the tree. He said to come and get you right away."

Jonathan released Candi from his embrace and strode over to where they kept their fishing spears. He grabbed four of them. "Come on. Let's go." He didn't hesitate – he just started striding through the trees towards Kevin and their designated lookout tree. He increased his speed to a steady jog, and the girls kept pace with him, stride for stride. All those weeks of exercise and healthy eating had built up their endurance.

As they approached the tree, they looked up to see Kevin. He noticed them below and motioned for them to be quiet and to come up and join him. They all climbed with well-practiced motions, moving silently through the leaves and branches.

"What's going on?" whispered Jonathan, once they were all gathered near the same branch as Kevin.

Kevin merely pointed out towards the water.

There was a medium-sized powerboat anchored in the cove. No one was on it.

"Okay, guys, this is it," said Kevin. "Let's review the plan. Candi?"

"Alright. First, Jonathan goes around and gets as near the pot plants as he can to get eyes on the dealers. How many are there, Kevin?"

"Two. A black guy and a white guy."

"Okay, Jonathan, you find them and first signal to us through Sarah that it's okay for Kevin to go out to the boat. Then you keep watching them. If you see them going back to the beach, you signal Sarah again and she will signal me in the tree." She turned to Kevin. "Kevin, after you get the first signal from me, you swim out to the boat, get on the radio, and send our distress signal. You remember everything you have to say, right?"

"Yes. I say that we are the Petersons and Buckleys, there are four of us, we are from the cruise ship *Columbus*, that rogue waves carried us very far on the lifeboat, and we don't know where we are but that it's an island shaped like a peanut with rocks on the south side. And there are drug dealers on the island too and we need to be rescued."

"Right. Then you swim back as fast as you can. You will check the lookout tree from the boat to see if you can swim above water or if you need to go into underwater stealth mode. If I get Sarah's signal that they're coming back, I will put up the signal for you. That means 'get the hell out of there.'"

The signal was a piece of the white sheet they had torn off to hang on one of the branches, visible from the water and hopefully *not* visible from the jungle where the pot plants were.

Sarah's signal would be sent using a slingshot they had made out of bamboo and a ponytail rubber band she had found in the bottom of her makeup case. She would be waiting on the ground in a spot where she could hear Jonathan, who was spying on the bad guys, and still be close enough to Candi's lookout tree. If she got the birdcall signal from Jonathan indicating that the drug dealers were moving back to the boat, her job was to shoot a series of hard berries into the leaves below the lookout tree so Candi would know to tie the white strip to the tree for Kevin to see.

Jonathan had been practicing his birdcall for weeks. It was nearly perfect, only barely distinguishable from the bird sounds they heard most often on the island.

"Okay, that's the plan. Any last minute issues?" asked Kevin.

"Just this," answered Candi, reaching up to grab him and plant a huge kiss on his mouth. "Come back safely."

Kevin smiled. "Of course. You guys have my back; I'll be perfectly fine."

*****

They all moved off into their positions, intent on doing everything they could to keep each other alive. No doubt these drug dealers had guns either on the boat or on their persons.

Kevin stood in the tree line, waiting to get the signal from Candi that it was safe to move to the water. A couple of very long minutes later, he saw her waving the white flag, so he quickly sprinted down to the water's edge and slipped quietly into the gentle waves that were hitting the edge of the beach. He swam freestyle, confident that he could get to the boat before they moved from wherever they were near the pot plants. There was no time to waste.

*****

Jonathan kept his eyes on the drug dealers from a safe distance up in a tree that had a good view of the pot grove. He could hear them talking, but couldn't make out what they were saying. They seemed to be walking around, bending down, looking at the grove. *Probably checking their irrigation lines.* After they stood in one place conferring about something, gesturing to the area around them, they started heading back in the direction of the beach. Jonathan's heart started beating three times faster than normal.

He put his hands to his mouth, getting ready to make his birdcall signal to Sarah who he could not see from where he was sitting. All of a sudden he realized that the drug dealers weren't going back in the direction he expected them to. They were angling to the left, heading right towards Sarah's hiding place.

"Ke-ke-ke-caw!" burst out Jonathan, but the sound was all wrong. He was so panicked, and his blood pressure was so high, it was affecting the sound of his voice. His birdcall sounded like an island bird being strangled to death.

The two guys stopped walking and turned around. They whispered to each other as they looked at the surrounding trees. Jonathan held his breath and hoped that his cover was good enough that they wouldn't spot him up above. *Don't look up, don't look up, don't look up,* he chanted inside his head. *And don't run into Sarah.*

The two guys shrugged their shoulders and then turned back towards Sarah's hiding place, continuing on. Jonathan didn't want to risk another strangled bird sound, so he climbed down the tree as quietly and as quickly as he could. He was going to follow the two guys to make sure they didn't run into Sarah. He was prepared to kick some serious butt if they did.

*****

Sarah heard Jonathan's mangled-sounding call, and immediately pulled back on the rubber band to send the berries off towards Candi's hiding place. But the rubber band snapped, managing only to send the berries into a pile at her feet and put a welt on the back of her hand.

Oh no! was all Sarah had time to think, before she took off running as quietly as she could to the lookout tree. She reached the base of it in less than a minute and signaled Candi with a loud *"Pssst!"*

Candi looked down and saw Sarah gesturing with her broken slingshot. Candi got a look of horror on her face as she realized what this meant. She scrambled to tie the white flag up in the branches. Sarah stood below, praying Kevin would see it before it was too late.

*****

Kevin made it to the boat and climbed up on the platform next to the motors. He was dripping wet but didn't have time to worry about whether the drug dealers would notice the puddles on their boat or not. Hopefully they would be so wet when they came on board they would blame themselves.

He saw the radio attached to the console near the steering wheel. He ran over and grabbed the handset. He pushed the button on the side but heard nothing. He looked at the front of the radio, noticing immediately that it wasn't on; the lights were all off, the screen black. He jiggled the first switch he saw up and down, trying to get it to power up, with no luck.

Shit! He thought to himself. *Where is the friggin' power on this thing?* His eyes were scanning the console when he noticed a white and fluorescent orange, miniature buoy-looking thing hanging from the console; attached to it was a key that was sitting in a keyhole.

Duh, he admonished himself. He turned the key partway, hoping it was like a car and would turn just the power on to the radio and not actually turn the engine over.

It worked.

The console lit up, and the radio suddenly had power. Kevin pressed the button on the side of the handset, putting it into transmission mode. He began speaking.

"Hello?"

He lifted his finger off the button and waited for a response. Then he pressed it again. "Hello? Is there anyone out there?"

He waited again, the silence deafening.

"Hello? Mayday, mayday, is there anyone out there?"

He turned to glance at the lookout tree, expecting to see nothing, but instead saw the signal. *Holy shit.* Then he heard some static on the radio and a voice.

"Hello, Juan? Is that you? Who is this?"

Kevin didn't hesitate. "This is Kevin Peterson ... me and three others are stuck on an island ... our cruise ship the *Columbus* sank about two months ago and we were thrown by some rogue waves way off course in our lifeboat ... the island we're on is shaped like a big peanut, there are rocks on the south side ... we need to be rescued, there are drug dealers on this island ... please come help!"

He waited for an answer, but none was forthcoming, and he knew he had to leave. He put the handset on the hook and ran to the edge of the boat. Just as he was getting ready to jump into the water, he heard some static and remembered the key. He had left it on position.

He was turning around to go back and turn the key to the off position, when he suddenly heard voices coming from the trees. He ducked down and peeked over the edge of the boat toward the beach. The two drug dealers were walking out of the trees, heading towards the water.

I'm trapped! The panic began to rise up and made it hard to breathe.

He crawled over to the console, reached up, and turned the key back to the left. Then he scrambled on his hands and knees over to the side of the boat facing the ocean and carefully slipped over the edge, into the water, trying not to make a splash as his body hit the surface.

*****

Candi couldn't tell from where she was sitting in the tree if Kevin had been able to get on the radio or not. She saw him go to the console area but that was it. Then the bad guys came walking out onto the beach towards the boat. *Ohmygodohmygodohmygod.* Sarah appeared at her right elbow, now able to see what Candi was seeing.

She whispered in Candi's ear, "What the hell! They're going to see him! My damn rubber band broke."

"Get out, Kevin, get out, get out, get out," whisper-chanted Candi.

They watched as Kevin turned back around from the console area and crawled to the edge of the boat.

The bad guys had started walking into the water and were only about twenty feet from where Kevin was hiding.

Kevin slipped over the edge of the boat and entered the water. Candi and Sarah looked at the drug dealers who were now swimming breast stroke style, about five feet away from the swimming platform near the engines. They gave no indication that they had seen Kevin.

Candi could see the outline of Kevin's body beneath the surface of the water. He was swimming parallel to the shore, underwater, away from the boat.

"What's he doing?" asked Sarah. "Why isn't he coming to the shore?"

"I think he's trying to get as far away from them as possible before he comes in, just in case they look back at the shore or whatever." She nodded her head in silent approval. "I hope he can hold his breath long enough," she added, worrying he wouldn't be able to; none of them had held their breath for longer than two minutes and thirty seconds.

Soon, Jonathan joined them at the base of the tree. He climbed up in seconds, getting as close to them as he could.

"What's going on?" he whispered.

Candi said nothing – just pointed out into the water where Kevin's form was barely visible beneath the water.

"Smart. He's going to surface far away from the boat. That's brilliant."

At least, it looked like a brilliant plan – until the boat started up and headed directly towards him.

"Holy shit, do they see him? Are they trying to kill him with the boat?" asked Sarah, horror coloring her voice.

The boat wasn't moving fast; it was just trolling along, as the two on board seemed to be moving around, getting things out of cabinets and stowing the anchor they had just pulled up by hand.

The three watched in fear as the boat closed in on Kevin's submerged form. Closer and closer it got. Kevin had been underwater at least two minutes by now, according to Candi's estimate. There was no way he was going to survive this.

"We need to get down there, right now!" said Candi frantically. "Move!"

They all scrambled out of the tree. Candi was deathly afraid of what they were going to see when they got there, but knew they had to do whatever they could to help Kevin.

By the time they reached the tree line, the boat was heading out of the cove. Jonathan held up his arm, stopping them from moving out of the trees. "Wait until they're farther away."

"I need to get in the water and find Kevin!" insisted Candi. He still hadn't surfaced yet that she could see.

"Look, they're hitting the gas, they'll be out of sight in ten seconds. Just wait. Kevin wouldn't want you to blow our cover after all he's been through."

It was the longest ten seconds of her life.

As soon as the boat left the cove and turned the corner out of sight, Jonathan lowered his hand and said, "Go!" They all took off running to the shoreline, Candi diving into the water and swimming over to the place where she'd last seen him. He wasn't there.

"Candi! Look!"

Candi was treading water when she heard Sarah's cry. She saw Sarah standing on the beach, pointing off to Candi's left. There, she saw Kevin's head surfacing above the water.

"Kevin! I'm coming, hang on!" Candi and Jonathan both raced over to where Kevin was treading water. Candi was so happy, she couldn't stop smiling. The sense of relief that she felt nearly overwhelmed her. Then she noticed that the water around Kevin was turning a darker color – dark red.

Candi's heart went into her throat. *He's bleeding ... a lot.* She reached him at the same moment Jonathan did.

"What happened?" Jonathan asked.

Kevin was gasping for air. "I went under and stayed there. I opened my eyes and saw the boat coming in my direction. I tried to dive down farther, but I didn't go down far enough. Propeller caught my arm."

Kevin's water-treading was awkward, Candi could see that now. He was only able to use his legs and one arm.

"We need to get out of the water, ASAP," said Jonathan. "This blood is going to attract sharks.

Candi nearly passed out. *Sharks.* Kevin was injured badly – she didn't even know how badly - and now they had to worry about sharks. The fear gave her renewed energy. She grabbed Kevin's t-shirt and started heading for shore. "Kick your legs, Kevin. I'll drag you in," she gasped. "Come on, Jonathan, grab his shirt with me."

With the two of them pulling and kicking with adrenaline-fueled muscles, they were able to get Kevin to the shallow water where he could stand and walk the rest of the way. He held his injured arm close to his chest where it quickly covered the front of his body with blood.

Sarah was waiting for him as he emerged from the water, wearing only her bra and underpants. She'd already taken off her leopard dress, ready to use it to help stop the bleeding.

The others waited as Kevin pulled his arm away from his body. Sharp intakes of breath revealed what none of them wanted to say – it was bad. A deep, vertical slice laid open his skin and muscle, down the length of his forearm. It was bleeding freely, pouring down into the sand.

Candi felt queasy, but she took charge anyway. Jonathan immediately sat down in the sand, putting his head between his legs. "Sorry, guys! Vasovagal response again. Gotta get my circulation back under control, I'll be with you in a minute."

Sarah rolled her eyes. "Tell me what to do."

"Get me some plant rope. We need to tie this thing closed."

Sarah was back with some plant rope in less than a minute. Together the two girls worked to get the wound closed up as best they could, securing it with Sarah's dress on top and ropes holding it all together. "This will do for now," said Candi. "When we get back to the treehouse, we'll figure out something more permanent. Can you walk okay, Kevin?" Concern filled her eyes.

"Yeah, I think so. Nothing wrong with my legs, I'm just a little lightheaded."

Jonathan spoke from his sitting position on the beach. "He's lost a lot of blood, better get him back before he passes out. He'll be hard for us to carry."

Jonathan joined them and they managed to get Kevin back to the treehouse and up the ladder before he did pass out. They all stood over Kevin's bed, discussing their next move.

"We need to get that wound cleaned and closed," said Candi, sick to her stomach over the idea that they didn't have the supplies to do any of that properly.

"How do you propose we close it?" asked Jonathan. "We don't really have any stuff for that."

"How about a needle and thread?" asked Sarah.

Candi shot her a disgusted look, angry that she would be so glib at a time like this.

"What? I'm serious."

"Yeah, okay, great idea, except that we have neither a needle nor any thread, Sarah. Don't be so thick."

"Yes we do." She turned and left the room.

Jonathan and Candi exchanged questioning looks. *What did Sarah have up her sleeve this time?*

Sarah returned in less than a minute with her Louis Vuitton makeup case.

Jonathan stared at it with suspicion. "That friggin' makeup case. I should have thrown that thing overboard with the radio."

Sarah opened it, rummaging around inside. "Ah-ha!" she said, holding up something in her hand, a triumphant look on her face. "Then you would have gotten rid of a perfectly good sewing kit!"

Candi's face registered the shock she was feeling over Sarah's announcement. She held out her hand, wordlessly.

Sarah placed a small, plastic packet in it. Inside was a single, thin needle and five different strings of various colors. It was the kind of sewing kit you get at a hotel for button that fell off.

Candi couldn't think of anything to say. It's as if a miracle had just happened in their little treehouse, compliments of an angel named Sarah.

Jonathan grabbed Sarah in a bear hug. "You are the most amazing woman. I am so sorry I almost made you leave that stupid case on the ship."

Sarah smiled over his shoulder. "You're welcome. I meant it when I said nobody messes with my Louis Vuitton."

Candi smiled. Sarah was always going to be Sarah, no matter what, and that was okay with her.

Candi turned back around to Kevin, mentally psyching herself up to do what she had to do. She began issuing instructions. "We have to move quick while he's still out of it. Get lots of salt and regular water up here, the sheet, scissors, the antibiotic cream, gauze and tape from the first aid kit."

She was interrupted by Sarah who had already gone down the ladder and was busy following Candi's instructions. "Check my Louis for the scissors!" she yelled from below.

Jonathan opened the case and quickly located a pair of delicate fingernail scissors. He handed them to Candi and then continued his search. "What else is she hiding in here?"

"Jonathan! Close my Louis!" came Sarah's voice again.

Jonathan got a sour look on his face but shut the case. *"Chicks."*

Candi got to work readying the needle and thread, doubling the thin cotton, hoping it would be strong enough to hold his skin together. Sarah came back up the ladder with the other supplies, joining Jonathan and Candi next to Kevin's cot.

"I need you guys to hold him down. This is going to hurt a lot, and I'm not sure when he's going to wake up."

Sarah went over to Kevin's other side and lay down on his arm and shoulder, trapping them beneath her. Jonathan went down to his legs and held them down from above, leaning over and resting his hands on Kevin's knees.

Candi uncovered the wound. She couldn't help but grimace. It was really gross. She took a bamboo cup with fresh water and used it to rinse out the wound. It started to bleed heavily again. She held the edges of the skin together at the middle. "I'm going to start in the center," she said.

Jonathan was looking up at the ceiling, paying no attention to what she was doing.

Candi was okay with that because she knew he would be no good to them unconscious. She inserted the needle into Kevin's skin on the edge of the wound. Then she went across to stick the needle in the other side, pulling the thread almost all the way through. Then she tied the ends together, using the knot to draw the edges of the wound closed. She put two more knots in that stitch and then cut it off with the scissors. "One down, about a hundred left to go." Her stomach rolled, vomit threatening to rise up. She held it down, readying herself for the next stich.

When she was about half done, Kevin started coming around. He was weak from loss of blood and confused. He started to struggle as Candi was piercing his skin for the second part of a stitch.

"Hold him still!"

The other two held him down as best they could, but Candi couldn't make the stiches and hold his injured arm at the same time. She had to calm him down. "Kevin! *Kevin!* Listen to me! You were hurt. I'm stitching you up, but you have to lie still!"

He stopped moving for a second. "Gumdrop?"

"Yes, it's me. Can you stop moving, please?"

"Hurts," he moaned.

"I know, I'm almost done. I'm stitching your arm up. Please stop moving." She looked at Sarah. "Sarah, come over here and hold his other arm down. I can't have him moving it while I'm stitching.

Sarah said nothing, just followed her instructions.

Candi finished the stitching with only minor struggles from Kevin. He fell unconscious again near the end, which made it go faster.

"There. Done. Thirty-five stitches. He probably needs more, but we are out of thread. The scar is going to be ugly." She didn't want to consider the fact that it might get infected and then there would never be a scar.

"Sarah, can you clean it up real good with the salt water and then clean water? I'm going to go clean myself off. I'll bring your dress with me to the shower and see what I can do about getting the blood out." She looked down and saw that her green top and capris were covered in blood too.

"Sure, you go ahead."

Jonathan joined Candi at the shower. "You were awesome, Candi. You saved his life."

Candi didn't feel any better at hearing his compliments. "He lost a lot of blood, there's nothing I can do about that."

"Yeah, but he's tough. He'll pull through, you'll see. Just stay positive. We still need to deal with these drug dealers who are going to be back soon."

"How do you know they'll be back soon?"

"Well, I assume they will because those plants look pretty big, like they're ready to harvest. I think when they come again, they'll bring more guys and more boats. That's a lot of plants to haul."

"Makes sense." She sighed, not wanting to think about that awful reality.

They finished washing off and then relieved Sarah so she could do the same. She put her soggy and slightly blood-stained dress back on biting her lip before setting her mouth in a thin, determined line.

"Thanks, Candi. You saved him. I'll never forget this."

Candi was embarrassed. "You would have done the same if it were Jonathan."

They gave each other a fierce hug before Sarah left to go wash off.

Kevin slept on, his face a scary shade of white. Even his lips looked pale.

"Can you get our food ready today, Jonathan? I'm going to stay here with Kevin."

"Sure, no problem, Candi. Sarah and I will take care of everything."

The rest of the night passed without incident. Kevin continued to breathe shallowly but with no sign of fever. Candi slept with him, getting up every hour or so, trying to get him to drink and checking his wound.

The next day Kevin woke up for a few hours. He wasn't able to stand for longer than a minute because he was feeling really weak, but the color was starting to come back to his face. Candi insisted that everyone let him sleep as much as possible, while she barely slept at all.

Jonathan and Sarah handled all the housekeeping duties, taking turns watching from the lookout tree at the cove. Jonathan shared his concerns with Candi and Sarah and they agreed – the bad guys were coming back. Soon.

*****

After a week had passed, Kevin was finally able to resume his schedule, minus the strenuous morning workouts. His appetite was back, and he was given double portions at every meal to help him build up his strength. He had a hell of a scab forming on his arm, skinny in some spots, thick and mottled in others.

"Man, I feel like I got run over by a bus," he said one night when he was finally able to join them around the fire. "Cool scar though."

"Well, you did get run over ... by a boat. I'm thinking that's pretty much the same thing," said Candi. She looked at his arm. "That scar is awful. I'm sorry I didn't do a better job sewing you up."

"So tell us again, Kevin, what happened out there on the boat. The last couple of times we asked you, you were still a little fuzzy on the details," said Jonathan. They had held off questioning him too seriously up until now, since the loss of blood apparently made him a little woozy and not so lucid all the time.

Kevin related his experience to them again, including the transmission by someone looking for Juan. They debated whether the message was heard by anyone who could help them. It was disturbing that he hadn't heard any response when he was done; and the fact that there was some guy looking for 'Juan' on the channel was worrisome too.

"Maybe I didn't get a response because I had to get the hell out of there," offered Kevin. "Maybe they responded after I shut it off."

"Yeah, but who wouldn't immediately respond to such an obvious distress call?" asked Candi. "And if they did respond later, that means they responded to the wrong guys."

He switched topics. "By the way, I'm ready to start doing lookout shifts again."

Candi looked at him with concern, but it was Sarah who spoke up. "I don't think you climbing trees is such a good idea right now."

"Why?"

"Because just the other day you were mumbling on about how Candi was Wonder Woman and you were Superman and you were going to make superhero babies together some day."

Candi's face flamed red.

Kevin just looked confused. "I did?"

"Yeah, among other things," volunteered Jonathan, grinning around the food he had in his mouth.

"Fine," conceded Kevin. "Maybe I'll just go with Candi and keep her company." He looked at her for approval.

She knew he was going crazy being in the treehouse all the time. "That's okay with me, if you guys think it is." She looked around at the others and they nodded in agreement.

"So what's the new plan?" asked Kevin. "I assume you've already made those decisions while I was sleeping the week away."

"We figured the next time they come, we need to be ready to get the hell out of here," said Sarah.

"Isn't that too risky?" he asked.

"Well of course it's risky, but at this point, it might be too risky not to. First of all, since the next time they come it will probably be to harvest, they're likely going to bring more than one boat, and more guys too. We need to somehow get to one of those boats and drive it away. We also need to disable the other boat or boats so they can't follow us."

Kevin nodded but said, "Why don't we just hide from them and stay here?"

"Well, we thought about that," said Candi, "but we were concerned that they might already know we're here. They were looking all around the pot plant area, including the place where we had come in and trampled all the plants down. Jonathan saw them gesturing all over the place. Then, instead of going directly to their boat, they started heading to where Sarah had been hiding. Lucky for her, she had already left because her slingshot broke, and she needed to alert me some other way. But they probably saw more evidence of us being there. Now we know that some guy on the radio asked about someone named Juan ... doesn't seem like Coast Guard talk to me."

Sarah joined in, "You didn't get a response from the radio person right away, and that doesn't seem right, especially considering what you said. Why wouldn't they respond back, like, instantly?"

"Well, maybe they did but I didn't get the signal," suggested Kevin.

"Or maybe you transmitted to some of their drug dealer buddies and not a rescuer."

Everyone stopped talking and just stared at each other across the cold fire pit. The only sound to be heard was the ocean.

"We're screwed," said Kevin.

"Yeah," agreed Jonathan. "That pretty much sums it up perfectly."

"Alright, so 'Operation Escape On The Drug Dealer's Boat' it is then," declared Kevin.

They spent the next two hours working out their plan, packing their backpacks with the things they knew they would need to take when the time came. They weren't going to have any advance notice when it was time to execute their strategy, so they had to be ready at all times.

*****

They didn't have to wait long. Three days later, Sarah came running back from her lookout duty to report that two boats and five men had just arrived at the harbor. They had guns too. She saw three of them holding the weapons in front of their bodies as they pulled in, while they looked towards the tree line.

"What does that mean?" asked Candi in a worried voice, as she shoved the last item into her backpack.

"It means they know we're here," answered Kevin, all traces of humor gone from his voice.

Kevin's assessment sent them all into overdrive. They scrambled around the treehouse, securing what they didn't need up above and shoving things they did need into the backpacks.

"Does everyone have at least one bottle of water?" asked Jonathan.

"Yes!" they answered in unison.

"Okay, let's go, guys. I don't want to be sitting ducks up here in the treehouse when they come," growled Kevin.

After they climbed down, Kevin took the ladder and walked off into the trees with it.

"What are you doing?" whispered Candi, going after him.

Sarah heard his answer before he disappeared into the trees.

"Hiding this to keep those assholes from getting into our home."

Candi and Kevin rejoined the others, and they all stood in a tight circle so they could talk softly.

Jonathan began. "Okay. We're probably going to have a hard time getting away on the boat in the daytime. I say we lay low until nighttime and swim out then. Candi, you and I can swim out to the boat we're *not* going to take, and tangle our bed sheet and some plant ropes around the propellers of that boat as much as possible. I'm not sure how much it will slow them down, but we have to do what we can."

"Why don't we just steal the key?" asked Sarah.

"Because I think they know we're here. They're not going to leave their boats unguarded. We can't take the risk of trying to climb onto two boats. We have to take the one that has the least amount of guys on it and disable the other one from the water. I don't know much about boats, but I assume there are no wires or things we can just unplug down there by the engine – otherwise it would constantly break down every time it went fast or touched the sand. I think messing with the propeller is our only option."

Sarah nodded at his reasoning. "Makes sense."

Jonathan continued, "Kevin, you and Sarah will swim out to the other boat and wait until you think it's safe to get on. There will probably be at least one guy on there, maybe more. Wait until you think maybe they're sleeping or whatever, get on board, and somehow neutralize them. Get them off that boat however you can." Jonathan looked at Kevin. "I know you're still kind of on the injured list. Do you think you can handle this?"

Kevin got an offended look on his face. "Handle it? Sheee-it, just don't get in my way."

Jonathan smiled. "That's what I wanted to hear. Any more questions?"

"I just need to go fill my water bottle up a little," said Sarah. "I'll be right back."

*****

The three stood in the clearing waiting for her to come back, none of them hearing the sound of approaching footsteps.

"Well, well, well ... what do we have here?" The sound of the stranger's voice sent shivers up Candi's spine. She turned slowly with the others to see a gun pointed right at them. It was being held by a guy dressed in Bermuda shorts and a muscle shirt. When he smiled, she noticed he had a gold front tooth.

Pirates! was all she could think. She risked a glance over at Jonathan and saw him giving her an 'I told you so' look. She was never going to doubt him again. The only thing the guy was missing was an eye patch or a peg leg.

The guy with the gold tooth glanced up above them, noticing the treehouse for the first time. "Nice place you got here. We're going to like staying in it when we come to the island. Too bad you won't be staying in it anymore." He laughed at his own lame joke. "Now we're all going to go back to the beach and talk to Jean-

Philippe. It's up to him where you die." He gestured with the gun as he moved sideways to make room for them to precede him in the direction from which he had come. "Get moving."

Candi forced herself not to look in the direction that Sarah had gone. She didn't want to let on to this guy that there was someone missing. Just because they were going to die, didn't mean she had to.

They all started down the path, Candi hyper-conscious of the fact that there was a gun pointed directly at her back. She prayed he wouldn't pull the trigger until this guy Jean-Philippe or whatever had his say. Maybe between now and then they could come up with an escape plan.

"*Eeeeeyaaah!!*" came a screech from behind Candi.

CRASH!!

"*Ooopf!*" The sound of a man going down with a grunt reached her ears.

Candi spun around to see Sarah standing over the prone form of their captor, who was now on the ground, surrounded by pieces of broken rat cage. He started to shake off his confusion, raising up his gun to take aim at Sarah.

She didn't hesitate; she kicked the hand that was holding the gun, sending it flying, and then bashed him over the head with the piece of rat cage she was still holding.

He slumped over sideways into the bushes.

They all stood in stunned silence for a second, staring at the unconscious drug dealer and the karate death queen, Sarah Peterson. "Now stay down, you fugly pirate!" she commanded.

Candi, Jonathan, and Kevin all rushed back to surround Sarah and give her a giant group hug. Kevin gave her a resounding high five that echoed in the trees around them.

"Sarah, you are the most amazing woman I've ever known ... thank you for saving us!" Candi grabbed her around the waist in a tight hug filled with the power of her relief.

Jonathan came up on her side and silently gathered her in his arms. "You crazy woman."

Sarah was smiling, if a bit shakily. "No one messes with my family."

Kevin stepped back from the group. "Hey, guys, I don't mean to be a wet blanket on the love fest here, but before we get going, we have to immobilize this jerkoff, or he'll alert the rest of them. We need to keep him quiet at least until we're outta here on that boat. If they get to him first, we won't have the cover of darkness to execute our plan. And obviously, they know we're here somewhere. So let's get moving."

They tore off a couple of strips from the precious bed sheet and used them to stuff the guy's mouth. Then they bound his hands and feet with lengths of plant rope, finishing him off by tying a cord around his head to securing the sheets inside his mouth.

Candi felt a little bit guilty. "What if they don't find him and he dies out here?"

Sarah looked at Candi incredulously. "Candi! This asshole was going to *kill* all of you. He's getting what he deserves. Let the universe sort it out. We just need to survive."

"I hate to admit it, Candi, but I agree with her. We're living out Darwin's theory of evolution, or more accurately, Herbert Spencer's often quoted theory: survival of the fittest. Only the strongest survive. We're a team, and we stick together. It's us against them. If someone has to die today, that will suck for sure – but let it be one of them, not us," said Jonathan, putting his arm around Sarah's waist.

Candi nodded her head. They were right. This a-hole with the stupid gold tooth had pointed the gun right at her back, knowing he was leading them to their deaths. She looked at the jerk on the ground who they had just tied to the stand of bamboo. "Sorry, dude. I guess you should have picked better friends."

They all smiled at her wisdom as they walked away. They hadn't chosen each other as friends, but in that moment, none of them would have chosen any other people in the world to stand against these drug dealers with.

*****

They arrived near the south side of the cove, hiding on the ground in the cover of the trees. It was late afternoon, darkness was just a couple of hours away. They stayed quiet, taking a few minutes to eat a meal of bananas. Sarah started mouthing the words to her favorite song. *'This shit is bananas, B-A-N-A-N-A-S!'* No one had the heart to stop her this time. She found it wasn't nearly as much fun when it wasn't annoying someone, so she stopped.

As darkness fell, they kept a keen eye on the activity surrounding the boats. One of the guys emerged from the trees and set up a tent on the beach. He made a fire and started cooking something. They could catch whiffs of the scent on the breeze, and Jonathan's stomach started growling. They all gave him bug eyes, signaling him to shut up. He mouthed, *What? I can't help it! I'm hungry!* Sarah blew him a kiss, and he smiled back. Candi rolled her eyes and Kevin smiled.

They watched as the group of four men, now missing Mr. Gold Tooth, sat down and finished their dinner. They were talking a lot and gesturing towards the trees, probably discussing their missing friend.

Eventually it got late. The kids' legs were cramped from

sitting still for so long. Kevin signaled that it was time to execute the plan. He gestured for them to all lean in so he could talk quietly.

"Okay guys, this is it. I don't think they can see us now, it's too dark. Jonathan and Candi, you guys are going to swim underwater to that boat on the right. It has two guys on it that I can see. Tie the stuff around the propellers. Don't just twist it around, tie knots in it if you can. Then swim over to the other boat and join us. Sarah and I will take your backpacks with us." Then he looked at Sarah. "You and I are going to swim underwater to that boat on the left. It has only one guy on it. Put Candi's backpack on your front and yours on your back. I'll do the same with Jonathan's. When we get to the boat, we'll hang onto the back, staying silent until Candi and Jonathan join us." He looked around at each of their faces in the dark, barely able to make out their features. "Does everybody know what to do?"

They all whispered in the affirmative. "Okay, let's go. Candi, you and Jonathan first. Good luck." He gave Candi a swift kiss on the lips before letting her go. His heart convulsed painfully in his chest as he watched her slip away.

Sarah reached out and grabbed her brother's hand and squeezed. He squeezed her hand back but said nothing.

*****

After a couple of minutes, Kevin and Sarah slipped from the trees, moving silently down to the water's edge. They listened for signs that they had been discovered but heard none. They crawled on hands and knees into the water and were soon submerged.

The weight of the backpacks made swimming difficult and awkward. Sarah had no idea if she was swimming in the right direction, so she stayed close to Kevin, constantly bumping into his arms or legs, which made her feel better because it meant he was close. She felt him stop, so she stopped too and surfaced, treading water.

Their heads emerged; they were about ten feet away from their target. Sarah couldn't see any sign of Candi or Jonathan. She and Kevin slowly and silently dipped back under the water and didn't come up again until they were at the back of the boat. As soon as they brought their heads up out of the water, they heard a loud belch. From the sound of it, the guy was sitting in the seat by the steering wheel.

They hung onto the platform that jutted out from the back of the boat, just over the two outboard motors. Within minutes, Sarah started to shiver. She didn't know if it was from the coolness of the water, the adrenaline, or just her general nervousness. Kevin reached over and squeezed her arm. She didn't know if it was to offer support or warn her about her chattering teeth. She gritted them together as hard as she could, transferring the shivering to her body instead.

Five long minutes later, Candi poked her head up out of the water silently, next to Kevin.

Then Jonathan arrived.

Kevin pressed his mouth to Candi's ear, and Sarah heard him whisper, "All set?"

Candi turned and pressed her mouth to his. "All set."

Kevin went to each of them, as quietly as he could, and gave them instructions.

They all moved to put his plan into action.

*****

Thirty seconds later there was a splashing sound coming from the water in front of the boat, courtesy of Sarah. Candi heard the boat's occupant get up from where he was sitting and start walking towards the bow. Jonathan and Kevin rose up out of the water as silently as they could and climbed onto the platform.

Candi stayed in the water at the back of the boat, now in charge of holding all four backpacks. They were so heavy she was struggling to hang onto them. She felt her hand slipping and realized she was going to get dragged to the bottom of the ocean if she kept ahold of all the backpacks in her hand. She dropped one, letting it sink down below her.

Jonathan and Kevin were dripping all over the place, the sound like a loud shower to their ears; but Sarah was doing a good job of acting like a deranged dolphin, so the boat guy didn't hear either Kevin or Jonathan coming. They snuck up behind him as he peered over the bow to see what the splashing noise was.

He stood up and turned around, running right into Kevin coming up the tiny set of stairs that led to the bow; Kevin immediately knocked him back with an upper cut to the jaw.

The guy let out a yell as he went down that was heard by the guys in the other boat. Jonathan came racing up the stairs behind Kevin and headed straight for the drug dealer who had recovered from his fall and was getting up to face off against Kevin. Kevin had maneuvered himself so he was on the right side of the bow.

The guy didn't see Jonathan coming until it was too late. Jonathan lowered his shoulder and gave the guy his best Kevin-style rugby-tackling move ever. The guy went flying towards the side of the bow where his leg got caught in the metal bar that ringed the edge of the boat. His leg stayed put, but the momentum sent his upper body over the top. The rest of him followed, and a loud splash signaled his departure from the boat.

In the meantime, Candi had pushed the backpacks up onto the

platform. Sarah joined her, having finished her task of getting the bad guy to the front of the boat, and they both launched themselves out of the water and into the platform. They heard yelling pirates behind them on the beach and next to them in the other boat.

Kevin raced back to the console, turning the key that was luckily sitting in the ignition, trying to get the engines to start. The engines were turning over, but nothing was happening.

"How do you start this friggin' thing?!" he yelled, desperation flooding his voice.

They could hear the sounds of men yelling and engines coming to life close by.

"Hurry up Kevin!! That a-hole in the water is going to get back up here!" yelled Sarah. She ran to the front of the boat and climbed up on the bow, peering into the water below.

"I know! Stop harassing me, I can't start it!"

Jonathan joined him at the wheel. "Give it some gas. Maybe it needs some fuel in the lines."

"Okay, boy genius, how do I do that?" asked Kevin angrily.

"I think you move these two levers. I used to watch Miami Vice re-runs, and they used boats a lot on the show," he explained.

Just then a movement coming from the boat's galley area caught Candi's eye. Suddenly the sliding door opened and a guy emerged. He was holding a gun, pointing it at Jonathan who was standing right in front of him.

Before she could even consider what was going to happen next, Candi saw a black shadow move away from the front of the boat.

"Hee yah!!" yelled Sarah, as she launched herself at him, leg out, giving the guy the most painful karate kick to the head that he would ever experience in his life.

The gun jerked away from Jonathan, a shot ringing out, gun flying from his grip and landing on the floor of the boat. Candi gasped, watching the guy fall to the ground, dazed. Jonathan and Kevin sprang into action, grabbing the guy and sending him overboard to join his friend.

"Where the hell'd that guy come from?!" yelled Kevin, totally freaked out.

He didn't wait for an answer – he just rushed back to the steering wheel and turned the key again. They all listened as it turned over. They heard the other boat turning its motors over as well. It sounded clunky, like the bed sheet and ropes were doing what they wanted them to do.

"Try it again, I'm going to press on this lever," ordered Jonathan.

Kevin turned the key, just as Jonathan was pressing one of the levers forward. Immediately the engine caught, and the boat leapt forward. All of them were caught by surprise and thrown to the back of the boat by the forward momentum, except for Kevin who was stopped from going very far by the seat behind him. He heard the girls scream, and he turned around to see total chaos, outlined by the moon that was now out in full force, no longer covered by clouds.

They were all in a pile at the back of the boat. "Oh my god, someone's bleeding," announced Sarah.

"It's me," said Candi weakly. "I think that guy shot me."

"WHAT?!" roared Kevin, torn between going back there and turning his attention back to the task of driving the boat. "Holy shit!" he yelled. He'd just realized that the boat was pointing the wrong direction and instead of heading out to sea, it was heading towards the other boat.

He grabbed the steering wheel and jerked it to the left, narrowly missing the other boat. He looked at the lever Jonathan had pushed forward and noticed there were two of them, but only one was forward. He pushed the other one forward slowly, seeing what would happen. The boat straightened out and gained more power. The levers were about three quarters of the way to the top. He realized each one controlled one of the motors in the back individually. He had to move the levers together if he wanted full power and the ability to steer properly.

Shots rang out, but the boat kept going. Kevin spared a glance over his shoulder. "Are you guys okay back there?!" he shouted over the noise of the engine.

"Yes and no!" was Sarah's answer. "Just keep going!"

Soon he was joined by Jonathan, who grabbed the handset of the radio and started transmitting.

"Maydaymaydaymayday, we need some help! Somebody out there, please help us!" He turned the dial on the front of the radio to another position and tried again. "Maydaymaydaymayday, someone, anyone out there! We need help!" He tried changing the dial again, stopping for a second to listen to the static that had broken out over the speaker. He started to press the button again and then he heard the growling sound of another engine. He looked out over the back side of the boat and saw lights coming in their direction. "They're coming Kevin!"

"Hold on, guys – I'm going to push this thing as fast as it will go!" yelled Kevin. He pushed the throttle levers to their full forward positions. The boat's tip picked up high in the water, but settled down again. "I don't know what's happening ... it feels like we're going fast but the boat just went down lower," said Kevin, panicking.

"Don't worry about that, it's planing."

"What?!" yelled Kevin.

Jonathan continued, louder. "I said, it's planing! When a boat is just sitting in the water, its weight is being carried by the buoyant force – it has a displacement hull! But as the speed increases to the critical point, the hydrodynamic lift increases to the point that it becomes the predominant upward force on the hull of the boat, which makes it ride more horizontally rather than diagonally! See what I mean?!"

"No!"

Jonathan shrugged his shoulders and then worriedly looked back at his sister and Sarah. Candi was laying down on one of the cushioned benches in the back of the boat, and Sarah was kneeling next to her.

Jonathan pushed the button again. "Maydaymaydaymayday, is there anyone out there? We need help! We're being chased by drug dealers! Please! Someone ... " he trailed off, worried they were never going to be saved. He looked at the gas gauge and saw that they had about a half a tank of gas.

"I'm going to go check on Candi. Keep going that direction."

"What direction?" Kevin asked with a bitter laugh. "I have no idea what direction we are headed right now."

Jonathan pointed to a radar screen that was glowing on the console. "I think this line here is the shoreline of the island. Just point directly away from it, and avoid any other similar looking lines because they will probably be other islands and shallow waters."

He left Kevin to drive and went back to check on Candi.

"What's going on?" he yelled at Sarah, crouching down to look in Candi's face.

"She's been shot in the arm, she's bleeding. I don't think it hit an artery or anything. Not that I'm an expert, but there's not as much blood as I'd expect, like there is in the movies."

"How are you feeling Gumdrop?"

"I've had better days, but I'm okay. Keep trying the radio."

Jonathan stood up to look out the back of the boat. The lights of the other boat were still behind them. He went back to the front. "Candi's been shot, but Sarah says it's not an artery. She's awake and talking, but we need to get her to a doctor."

Jonathan looked at Kevin's face and saw from the lights of the console that Kevin had tears running down his cheeks, his throat moving convulsively as he held back as much as he could. Jonathan awkwardly patted him on the back. "Don't worry, she's going to be fine. We all are, I'm sure of it."

Kevin swiped at his cheeks with the back of his hand. "Yeah," was all he could say. He turned and watched the lights of the boat behind; they appeared to be closer than the last time he looked.

Jonathan pressed the button on the radio handset again. "Mayday, mayday, mayday, somebody please, answer me!"

He let go of the button and heard static on the line. Then a crackling. He looked closer at the radio console. "Hello?" he said into the handset.

Some crackling came over the speaker again and then a voice. "Roger, on that mayday, Captain, state your position."

Jonathan got so excited he dropped the handset. "Oh crap!" He grabbed the cord and followed it down to the dangling handset as the voice came over the speaker again.

"Captain, please state your position and have all passengers don life jackets ... copy?"

Jonathan grabbed the handset and pressed the button, "Hello!

I'm ... I have no idea where we are, but we are being chased by drug dealers at high speed ... Over!"

At first there was no reply. Then some static and the voice again. "Captain, be informed it is a federal offense to make a false SOS mayday over these frequencies."

Jonathan's face blanched. "No! Sir! This is NOT a false mayday! We are currently being chased by drug dealers! We stole one of their boats, and we are being chased by one of their other boats! They have guns, sir! My sister has been shot with a GUN! With a BULLET!!" He paused for a second and then continued. "Come and arrest me. Please. I will gladly be arrested, just get us out of here!"

They all waited anxiously for the voice to come back. It seemed to take forever. "Captain, identify your vessel and location."

"My name is Jonathan Buckley. I am here with my sister Candi Buckley and our friends Kevin and Sarah Peterson. We were on the cruise ship *Columbus* that sailed on February fifteenth from Miami."

Then there was silence for a few moments followed by some crackling. "Copy that ... standby."

None of them could remember ever waiting so long for anything in their lives.

"Captain, provide Loran coordinates or GPS of your location."

Jonathan barked out a bitter laugh. "Sir, I wish I could, but I have no idea where we are. Can't you use your radar or something?"

"Captain, do you have a radar screen on the console of the vessel? By the steering wheel?"

"Yes!"

"Captain, do you see a number at the top of the screen

between the number one and three hundred sixty?"

"Yes, it says one-eight-five."

"Okay," the voice continued, "there should also be some sort of GPS unit on board there. Either built into the console or attached to some holder near the console."

Jonathan bent down to look at the console closer. He saw a black box sitting suspended in a holder near the wheel.

"I see a black box, but it's not on."

"Find the power button and turn it on. It should show you your current latitude and longitude."

Jonathan dropped the handset and felt all over the GPS unit for a button. He found one on the side and pressed it. Precious seconds ticked by as it powered up. It seemed to take forever. Jonathan looked back and noticed that the drug dealers were closing in. "Can't this thing go any faster?" he shouted at Kevin.

"I've got it going full blast, it's going as fast as it can."

The GPS screen lit up. Jonathan saw some numbers in the lower right corner that looked like they might be latitude and longitude coordinates.

"Hello, Sir, are you there?"

"Yes Captain, go ahead, state your position."

"Okay, we are at: two-six-point-seven-three-one-two-two-dash-six-nine-one-nine-one-eight-nine-five."

They waited for a response.

None came.

"Sir? Did you hear me?"

"Son, are you sure you're looking at the right numbers?"

Jonathan panicked, "I think I am! They're the only numbers there! How am I supposed to know, I've never been on a small boat before!"

"Alright now, calm down. We have a cutter in that area. It'll take about ten minutes to get there. I need you to turn the vessel to the left, heading one-one-zero. Do you understand that?"

"Turn the wheel Kevin. Watch that number at the top of the screen."

Kevin focused on the screen, "Yeah, I know. I can figure that much out."

"Okay, we're turning. Now what?"

"Just continue heading one-one-zero, and you'll see our lights. Hold steady, Captain, we are underway toward your position."

"Thank you sir. And I don't mean to be rude, but can I ask you to please hurry? These guys are catching up to us, and I know they'll kill us if they can."

"We're going as fast as we possibly can. You just hold it together. Did you say someone has been shot?"

"Yes, my sister. In the arm."

"Captain ... apply direct pressure to the wound ... have all personnel don life jackets. There is a Coast Guard medic aboard the Coast Guard cutter near you, don't worry. Everything's going to be okay."

The line went silent for a couple of minutes, then the static stopped again and the voice came out of the speaker.

"Buckley vessel, come in Buckley vessel, this is the United States Coast Guard, over."

"Yes, sir, we're here. Over"

"Is this Jonathan I'm speaking to?"

"Yes sir, it is."

"Captain, you parents have been notified of your status. Just thought you'd want to know."

"Oh my god!" burst out Jonathan as tears started streaming

down his face. "Candi! Did you hear that! Our parents are okay!"

He quickly pressed the button on the handset. "What about the Petersons? Did you call them?" He waited desperately for the answer. He looked at Kevin and saw the stern set of his jaw. Jonathan reached out and put his hand on Kevin's shoulder.

"Captain, we were unable to make contact. Your parents and the Petersons will be enroute as soon as the Petersons get home."

Relief washed over Jonathan. Kevin had a relieved smile on his face, but continued to focus on the radar screen to be sure he stayed on course.

"Thank you so much sir, I can't tell you how happy that makes us."

"I have to tell you kids, you sure ended up way out in the middle of nowhere. You have entered large open water far from shore."

Jonathan pressed the button, "Where did we end up sir?"

"In the Bermuda Triangle."

Jonathan couldn't think of anything to say to that. He clicked the button but said nothing. That was so far off course from where their cruise ship had been, it didn't make any sense.

About five minutes later, they heard another transmission. "Coast Guard Station Indian River ... Captain ... our cutter has your position locked. Continue underway at one-one-zero. We also have a visual on the vessel pursuing you. They will likely terminate their pursuit."

Sure enough the lights from the drug dealer boat turned away and quickly faded in the distance. Now that the pirates knew the Coast Guard was locked in and coming, they had to choose between getting revenge and getting caught, or going away and harvesting as many plants as they could before they were discovered.

"Want me to take over for a while?" asked Jonathan.

"No, that's alright, I can do it."

Jonathan gave him a curious look and then headed back to where the girls were. Candi was still awake and seemed okay, even though she was in a lot of pain. Jonathan held her hand and absently rubbed Sarah's back with the other.

Soon Kevin was shouting out that he saw a bunch of lights up ahead. Then a voice came over the radio speaker.

"Buckley vessel, come in Buckley vessel."

Jonathan spoke into the handset. "Buckley Peterson vessel is here. What do you want us to do?"

"Captain ... place your engine in neutral ... stand by to be boarded as we come alongside."

*****

Good to their word, the U.S. Coast Guard cutter arrived and took over the rescue. The kids were transferred off the drug dealer's boat to the cutter. Candi was immediately rushed to the infirmary, Jonathan refusing to leave her side.

Kevin and Sarah sat with the captain and his crew in what looked like the command center of the boat. The boat's cook brought up some food for them; it was the best food they had ever eaten. Neither of them said much. They were overwhelmed by what was happening and didn't know what to think or do.

They arrived at the port; all of their parents were there waiting. Ambulances were there too to take them to the hospital for observation. Candi went into surgery to remove the bullet from her arm. The kids were kept in separate rooms, kept in the dark about what was going on with one another.

Their time was completely consumed by worried parents and

then by the media that had somehow gotten wind of the fact that the four teenagers presumed dead from the *Columbus* cruise tragedy suddenly showed up after spending over two months on a deserted island in the Bermuda Triangle. They found out from the reporters and their parents that their lifeboat was the only one released that night, due to some kind of mechanical breakdown. Everyone else was transferred to another boat that was brought in several hours later. By then, the rogue waves had disappeared and there was no immediate danger to any of the other passengers. The *Columbus* was towed into port over the next two days for repairs.

Search parties had gone out looking for them for a period of two weeks, never finding any clue of their whereabouts. Everyone assumed they had drowned at sea. Even the last of the private party searches had been called off over a month ago. Their parents had held funerals for them and hundreds of kids from their high school had come to their combined memorial services.

After a day in the hospital, Kevin and Sarah were released to their parents' custody. They promptly flew back to North Carolina, not permitted by their parents to visit their friends.

Jonathan was also discharged. He stayed with his parents in a nearby hotel until his sister was able to leave three days later. She'd have a hell of a scar, but she was going to be okay.

In the car on the way to the airport, Jonathan held his sister's hand. She looked so small and frail. His heart was breaking for her, because not only was she dealing with the pain of a gunshot wound, she was also dealing with a broken heart. It had been four days now, and Kevin hadn't bothered to call even once. He hadn't heard from Sarah either.

Homecoming

CANDI WAS LYING IN HER bed, staring at the ceiling. She'd been staring at the same spot for the last two hours. It was four o'clock in the afternoon. She had once again refused to go to school. It had been three weeks since their return. She still couldn't make herself get out of bed.

The doctors said there was nothing wrong with her physically; she was just suffering some sort of emotional trauma from the island experience. They told her parents to leave her alone and eventually she'd snap out of it.

Jonathan knew better. She was in her room dying of a broken heart. There were some days he felt like doing the same thing – just sitting there, not doing anything. Not feeling anything. But instead he got up and went through the motions. It was the only thing he could do and stay sane.

So far he hadn't seen Sarah up close at school. She was avoiding him, he was sure of it. They never had classes together before, but he used to occasionally see her in the hallways. Not anymore. He didn't blame her though; he was a realist. This wasn't their island world anymore – this was the real world where guys like him and girls like her didn't get together.

That wasn't to say that the girls in school were agreeing with Jonathan these days. He'd come back to school a different guy altogether. He was tan, muscular and exuding a confidence that was normally impossible for a high school kid to have. The pretty girls who had never noticed him before found all kinds of reasons to hang around his locker now and walk with him to class. One of the guys on the football team even asked him if he wanted to come to tryouts over the summer for next fall's team.

Jonathan shrugged it off. He wasn't interested in all of that. He was only interested in Sarah, but she wasn't interested in him, so he had to move on. He knew that. He tried to call her on the phone several times, leaving messages. Finally her dad told him to stop calling – that she wasn't interested in talking to him. His now carefully honed survival instinct was pushing him forward, telling him to let her go. If she wanted him, she knew where he was.

Candi, on the other hand, had given up. Kevin's distancing began on the boat and continued with him never contacting her even once since they'd gotten back – not even to find out how her surgery went. Jonathan saw him in the hall, laughing it up with his friends. He had his old girlfriend hanging around him all the time – the one Sarah had said cheated on him before they left. Jonathan shook his head in disgust just thinking about it. He guessed it was a good thing that Candi wasn't there to see it.

Jonathan got home at the end of the day and went up to see his sister. She was lying in bed on her side, facing away from the door. He sat down on the bed next to her. "What's up?" he said.

"Nothing."

"Did you get up today?"

"Nope."

"When are you going to come back to school?"

"Never."

Jonathan sighed. "You have to come back, Candi. You can't keep moping here like this day after day, I'm worried about you."

"I'll be fine, don't worry." She hesitated for a minute. The room was completely quiet. In a soft voice she said, "Did you see Kevin today?"

Jonathan didn't know whether to tell the truth or lie. Normally he would never lie, but he hated to see her so sad. *But if I never get her to face the truth, she'll never get out of this dumb bed.* He decided that even if the truth hurt, he had to tell her.

"Yeah, I saw him. He was with that Gretchen girl."

Candi's voice waivered. "Did he look happy?"

"I don't know, not really. He was kinda smiling, but it looked fake."

"You're just saying that."

"I don't think so. But I really don't care about him, Candi, I only care about you. Apparently we misjudged him. Sarah too. We need to move on. This is the real world, the island wasn't."

"You still haven't seen Sarah?"

"No. Once in the hallway from a distance, but not since. She doesn't return my calls. I think she's avoiding me." He put his head down. It made him sad to say it out loud.

Candi sat up weakly. "How can you go to school and face that every day?" she asked him in an anguished voice. "I just can't do it, Jonathan. I just can't!"

Jonathan took her hands in his and looked her in the eyes. They were red-rimmed and puffy. "Yes you can. You're stronger than this. You survived a deserted island for more than two months! You learned how to spear fish and feed us! You got shot and survived for chrissakes! Dealing with a screwed up high school romance is nothing compared to that."

Candi sighed. "You know it was more than just a high school romance."

"Yeah, I know, but you know what I mean. We need to move on. Survive. That's what we do, right?"

"I guess."

"So," Jonathan continued in his most enthusiastic voice. "What do you say that today, we have a *shower!* And after that, a nice dinner at the dining room table; then we can pick out your outfit for tomorrow." He raised his eyebrows, encouraging her to join in and agree.

"I don't know. Maybe." She released his hands and laid back down.

Jonathan rolled his eyes and stood to leave. "Time to stop feeling sorry for yourself."

Candi got instantly cross. "Get out of my room, you turd!" She launched a pillow at him and watched it hit the closed door, as he jumped out of the room, pulling the door closed behind him.

Candi sat up and put her feet on the floor. She couldn't believe Kevin was back with that girl. *What is wrong with him?* He deserved better than that.

He didn't want to be with her ... fine. But he should at least be with someone with a brain who would appreciate him. She decided it was long since time she had a shower. Her last one was ... three days ago? She still had her dreadlocks and refused to take them out – but they needed a thorough cleaning. She'd been lazy since she'd decided to take up residence in her bed.

As she walked across her room to grab her robe, she heard some commotion downstairs, coming from the front hallway. She opened up her closet, looking for something to wear so she could go down and find out what was going on.

*****

"Your son is in a shitload of trouble, Candace, and I want to know what you're going to do about this problem he's created!" yelled Frank Peterson. He was standing in the front doorway, his daughter Sarah standing behind him on the front porch with her head down, saying nothing.

Mrs. Buckley was standing in the doorway, holding onto the door with a shocked look on her face. "Frank, I know you're upset, but I'm not really sure what's going on here. Do you want to come in to discuss it?"

"No, I don't want to come in to discuss it! I want that little shit to come out here and get what's coming to him!"

"Daddy!" yelled Sarah, stepping forward.

"Shut up, Sarah, and stay out of this! I told you one day you were going to get yourself into trouble."

Sarah's face turned white, and she backed away from him.

Jonathan came running down the stairs, having heard the ruckus through the closed door of his bedroom.

"Hey mom, what's going on ... " he trailed off as he saw Sarah standing on the porch, looking down at the ground like a meek rabbit. She looked as unlike Sarah as he'd ever seen her. "Sarah?" he asked, tentatively.

She looked up at him. "Hey, Jonathan. Long time no see."

Jonathan looked to his mom for an explanation. "Mom? What's going on?"

"I'll tell you what's going on, you little shit, you've impregnated my daughter!"

Jonathan's mother's hand flew up to her mouth, and her shocked eyes looked from Jonathan to Sarah and back to Jonathan again.

Jonathan's eyes nearly bugged out of his head. "Pregnant?" He wasn't sure that he'd heard right.

"Yeah, dumbshit, pregnant. You know how that works, right?"

"Dad, stop." Sarah had moved forward to put her hand on his arm, to stop what was about to come flying out of his mouth next.

"Get off me!" he yelled as he angrily brushed her arm off.

Jonathan instantly lost his cool. It was one thing to be a rude jerk; it was a whole other thing to be abusive to someone he cared about, who was *pregnant* for crying out loud.

"*HEY!*" Jonathan yelled, jumping down the last couple stairs and striding over to the front door. "That's enough, Mr. Peterson. You can't come over here to my house and talk to my family that way. And you *certainly* can't talk to Sarah the way you just did or treat her like that." He paused for a second screwing up his eyebrows. "What's *wrong* with you? Can't you see you're upsetting her?" He gestured towards Sarah.

"Oh trust me, I'm going to do a lot more than just upset her."

"Um, no, I don't think so," responded Jonathan, matter of factly.

Jonathan stepped over, pushing Frank out of the way and walked up to Sarah. "Come here." He took her hand and pulled her into the house while Frank worked to right himself. He had tripped over a rocking chair that was near the front door.

"Sarah, get your ass back out here."

"Nope, sorry, not happening Mr. Peterson. She's staying here until further notice." Jonathan glanced over at his mom who was standing frozen in place. She gave a slight nod of her head, giving her approval, but she wasn't able to find her voice quite yet. The shock of what she was hearing and seeing was too overwhelming.

"Over my dead body," Frank said as he moved towards the doorway.

Jonathan stepped forward and met him toe to toe. Jonathan had him by at least two inches. "That can be arranged."

Jonathan's mom looked at her son's face and nearly fainted. What had happened to her little boy on that island? He looked like a killer right now; she could see he was serious. She knew that look. She just had never seen the threatening part of it – that was definitely something new.

She looked up at Sarah, who had moved to stand on the second stair of the staircase inside the house. Sarah was staring at Jonathan, pride shining in her eyes.

Well, I'll be damned, thought Candace. *Not only did they, well, make a baby together – they actually have feelings for one another.* Candace had to be honest with herself, she never saw that one coming – although she should have guessed it. Jonathan had come back a man from the experience. It's only natural that Sarah would have been drawn to that.

Candace let out a long sigh. "Okay, guys. I appreciate the whole testosterone thing and all, but this is not the way we handle things here, and I don't think this is the right time either. Frank, you need to leave, and I need to call Glen and get him home from work. We'll call you later at the house."

Frank stepped back to the edge of the porch. "You're going to hear from my lawyer, lady."

Jonathan grabbed the edge of the door. "Bring it."

Then he slammed the door in Frank's face.

"Jonathan!" scolded his mother.

"Sorry Mom, but that guy is a serious douchebag."

Jonathan turned his attention to Sarah and took a deep breath.

"Hey Sarah. So ... " Words failed him. For the first time in his life, he had no factoids to help him over the hump.

"Hey, Jonathan." Sarah was also feeling uncharacteristically shy.

They all heard Candi clear her throat at the top of the stairs and turned to look at her as she began speaking, "So, let me get this straight – I'm going to be an aunt?"

Sarah looked at her and shrugged. "Guess so."

Candi stomped down the stairs, brushing past Sarah. She grabbed Jonathan by the hand, dragging him to the staircase.

"Where are we going?"

"Shut up, Jonathan."

Then Candi reached the second stair where Sarah was and used her other hand to turn Sarah around so she was facing up the stairs, urging her forward by gently pushing on her back. "Up you go."

"Where are we going?"

"Shut up, Sarah."

Candi dragged and pushed the two of them up the stairs until they reached Jonathan's room. She let go of Jonathan's hand and gently guided Sarah to his bed, sitting her down. Then she pulled Jonathan into the room until he was standing in front of her. "Sit!" she ordered, pointing to the space next to Sarah.

Jonathan did as he was told.

Candi stood in front of them, hands on her hips.

"You two have some serious talking to do. That includes talking about why you, Sarah, are blowing Jonathan off and not returning his calls ... "

" ... but ... "

" ... no buts! And Jonathan, that includes what you are going to do with Sarah about this baby that you two made together. Obviously Sarah can't go home, so figure this all out. I'm giving you an hour."

She turned and left the room, carefully shutting the door behind her.

*****

The silence descended, neither wanting to be the first one to speak.

Then Sarah burped. Jonathan's eyes nearly crossed. In all the time he'd ever been with Sarah, he'd never heard her burp before.

She started to giggle.

He couldn't help but smile too.

"I burp all the time now for some reason."

"Is that normal?" he asked.

"For me it is, I guess."

"Interesting."

"You would say that."

"Sarah, why didn't you answer my calls? You must have known you were pregnant for a couple of weeks ... "

"You called? Because you could have fooled me. Maybe your phone is broken."

"Seriously Sarah, stop messing around. I've called you every day since the day we got back. I've left a million messages. I didn't have your cell number, so I called your house."

Sarah got a very angry look on her face. Then tears started to fill her eyes. Jonathan misunderstood. "Listen, I'm sorry it bothered you. I did kind of feel like I was stalking you, but I thought ... I thought ... Oh well, I guess it doesn't matter what I thought."

"Jonathan, I never received one message from you. Who did you talk to?"

"Your mom and dad. Or I just left a message on the voicemail."

"Well, that would explain why the phone has never rung more than once at my house for the past month. I was wondering why my mom was suddenly so interested in answering it. She said she had a charity function coming up and that she was on the planning committee. She said that's what the calls were for. And I believed her. That lying bi ... "

"Hey, hey, hey, there Sarah, she's your mom. She was probably just doing what your dad told her to do, and he was probably just worried about you."

Sarah gave him one of her threatening looks.

"Okay, so he's still a douchebag, and we can't guess what his motivations were. It doesn't matter now. What matters is that we talk about this, figure things out." He reached over and took her hand in his.

"So let's figure it out then. I'm pregnant. I can't live at home anymore. I will soon become a major cliché – 'pregnant unwed homeless teen'."

"First, you can live here. If I know Candi, she's not going to let you live anywhere else now anyway – you know how she is. Second, you can be pregnant or not. It's your body, and it's your choice. Either way, I will be there for you one hundred percent. And last, the unwed part, um, well, we could get married." Jonathan's heart was about to explode. He was afraid to look her in the eye.

"A-hem. Okay. So. We're talking now. Okay, um, so as far as the living here goes, I guess that would be a good temporary solution. Then you can help me figure something more permanent out. Second, I think we're on the abortion issue – and I'm sorry if this totally f's up your life Jonathan, but abortion's not really my style. And last, the unwed part, holy shit. Don't ever ask me to marry you like that again or I'm gonna have to punch you in the nose. The day you ask me it better be on one knee and with one hell of a ring, you get my drift?"

Jonathan laughed in spite of the gravity of the situation. He grabbed her in a spontaneous hug. "God, I'm so glad you're here!"

Sarah started crying.

"Now what's wrong?" asked Jonathan, confused all over again.

"Nothing, I just cry all the time. Deal with it."

Jonathan just smiled. "You know Sarah, your estrogen and progesterone levels are going to be very elevated, which will probably cause all manner of issues starting with your moods and ... "

Sarah smacked him gently on the back of the head. "T-M-I, babe. T-M-I. By the way, did you know that I even went to the math club and the chess club looking for you after school?"

Jonathan released her from his hug. "No way."

"Yes way. I kept going every week, hoping you'd show up so we could talk. I never saw you in school. You're not on Facebook. I think I met all your friends though. Someone name Albert showed me some chess moves."

Jonathan smiled wryly. "I'll bet he showed you some moves. Man, a guy can't turn his back for a single second at chess club. They're so competitive there ... "

Just then the door opened. Candi stood in the doorway. "We all square up here?"

"Not quite," said Sarah, standing up and walking over to her. "Why have you been hiding here at your house instead of coming to school?"

Candi shrugged her shoulders. "I'm not ready."

"Well get ready, sister, 'cause you're going tomorrow. Show me to your room so we can pick out an outfit."

"Sarah, I'm not sure ... "

"Bullfarts. Now move. I'm pregnant and you do not want to mess with me right now. Did I mention I get morning sickness when I don't get my way?"

Candi looked at her incredulously. "Bullfarts?"

"Yeah, well, I'm going to be a mother soon, so I have to stop swearing so much ... "

Their voices faded as they walked down the hall and went into Candi's room.

I'm going to be a father? Jonathan couldn't wrap his brain around the idea. He did the calculations. That meant his child would be his age when he would be ... thirty-four. *Geez, that's old.*

He got up and went to his computer. He needed to research family housing at the colleges he had planned on applying to. He had scholarship offers from some already. Might as well see if they still wanted him if he was bringing two others along.

*****

"Listen, Sarah, I appreciate your help and all, but I don't think I'm ready to go back to school tomorrow."

"You're right. You aren't thinking. You're sitting here like a little mouse in a hole instead of going to school and kicking Kevin's ass ... I mean butt."

Candi's face dropped, and Sarah saw it.

"Listen, I know you're sad. I know he's been a total ... turdmonkey. But trust me when I say this: Kevin loves you. He's just scared to death. You rocked his world on Peanut Island. Everything he thought he knew about himself changed. Everything he thought was important changed. You got shot, and believe me that scared the ... doody ... out of him. He cried you know."

"No he didn't."

"Yes he did. Like a baby. When he thought you might die, he was freaking out. That's why he wouldn't let Jonathan drive the boat – he was afraid Jonathan would screw it up, and the Coast Guard wouldn't be able to find us. In the hospital our dad wouldn't let us see you guys. Then Kevin got back to school, and he just got overwhelmed with all the attention. But I know he thinks about you all the time. He sits in his room, holding his stupid bamboo cup all the time."

Candi was skeptical. "Well that doesn't explain why he's not here now, why he hasn't called."

"No, you're right, it doesn't. He's an idiot, but he's a guy. So come with me to school. Do your thing. Show those boys your new look. If it's time to move on, then move on. But don't stay in your room every day feeling sorry for yourself. That's not the Sugar Lump I know."

"Don't call me Sugar Lump."

"I can do what I want, I'm pregnant. Now, let's look in this lamefarts closet of yours and see what we can find."

"God, lamefarts Sarah? Really?"

"Have you ever tried to stop saying 'ass' and 'shit' before? Don't judge me, I'm doing the best I can."

Candi smiled. Sarah was going to be a great mom, even if she wasn't that great at making up rated PG swearwords.

Within ten minutes Sarah had put together a really cute look for Candi and had her swear she would wear it. Then they found something for Sarah to wear since she had arrived with nothing. They called her mom and asked her to pack Sarah a bag that they would come get tomorrow when her father wasn't home.

*****

The next day they all woke up bright and early. Mrs. Buckley gave them a ride to school. They got out of the car and headed into the school together, Jonathan holding Sarah's hand. Candi was smiling on the outside but nervous as hell on the inside. She didn't know what she was going to do when she saw Kevin.

She didn't notice all the people turning to stare at her as she walked by. All she could think about was seeing Kevin. She arrived at her locker and had to think for a minute to remember the lock combination. It had been three months since she had last used it. She opened it up and found everything like she had left it. No one had slipped any notes through the cracks. She sighed and closed it. Standing there, hidden behind the door, was a guy she had seen a few times, but couldn't remember the name of.

"Candi, right?"

"Um, yeah ... "

"Yeah, I saw you come into school earlier. I'm not sure if you and I have officially met. I'm Jason. Jason Hicks."

Candi smiled tentatively, mystified as to why Jason Hicks was introducing himself to her. "Nice to meet you ... ?" Now she remembered where she'd seen him. He was on the rugby team. On the days they had games, they wore their team jerseys to school. She remembered seeing him with Kevin and the other rugby players in the hallways.

"Are you here because Kevin sent you?"

"Kevin who? Peterson? No, man. I'm here because I was wondering something."

"What's that?" Candi asked, still suspicious.

"I was wondering if you have a date to the prom yet."

"Prom?" Candi was confused.

"Yeah. Prom. It's in two weeks. Do you want to go with me, maybe?"

Candi shook her head in confusion, trying to knock the cobwebs out.

"Is that a no?" asked Jason, wondering why she was shaking her head like that.

"Um, no, it's not a 'no'. I was just ... never mind. Um, Jason, thanks for asking, but can I get back to you on that? I actually had totally forgotten about prom. I'm not even sure if I'm going." She gave him an apologetic shrug.

"Forgot about prom? How is that possible?" He gestured around them. All over the hallways and even ceilings were posters and decorations reminding them of the big dance.

Candi smiled and laughed. "Yeah. Duh. I've kinda been gone for a while. Today is my first day back."

"Yeah, I read about your cruise. I even went to your memorial service. It was nice by the way. Bad luck though, eh?"

"Not really," Candi answered. "Listen Jason, it was nice meeting you, but I have to go."

"Yeah, sure. I'll see you around. Here, I wrote my number down, in case you want to text me or whatever, since you haven't officially said no to me about the prom." He flashed her a million watt smile. Candi noticed for the first time since he started talking how cute he was. *Wow*, thought Candi, *he isn't just cute. He's seriously hot.* She took the paper from his hand and walked away smiling.

Candi made her way to chemistry class, arriving right before the bell rang. She walked to her seat, noticing that all the eyes in class were on her. The girls were shooting her rude looks, the guys looked hungry. *What the heck? Everyone sure is acting strange today.* First Jason, now her whole chemistry class.

They had a lab that day. By the end of the class period, two more guys she'd never talked to before had asked her to the prom. She was starting to think there was some sort of conspiracy, but when she questioned them, they all seemed innocent of any subterfuge.

She saw Sarah after class and they headed to lunch together. "Sarah, have you noticed anything weird going on at school today? I mean, is there some mass practical joke going on? Do I have a huge booger on my face or something?"

Sarah laughed. "No, what are you talking about?"

"So far three guys have asked me to the prom. Three! And they're all cute! We've had three formal dances so far this year, including prom, and this is more potential dates I've had than for the other two put together. The first dance, no invites. The second dance, a friend of my brother's from the chess club."

Sarah looked like she was in pain. "Ooh, that's not good."

"No, it wasn't. But so far Jason Hicks, Brice Trawick and Mike Thompson have all asked me."

"Niiiice," assessed Sarah. "Well, it's obvious what's going on. I'm surprised you don't know."

"Well, enlighten me, would you please? Because this is freaking me out."

"Tell me, Candi, have you been having any trouble with the girls in your classes?"

"As a matter of fact, a few girls have looked like they wanted to kick my butt."

"Yeah, that's what I figured you'd say. See, the problem is, you're hot now. You're big league hot. The guys want you, and the girls hate you because they're jealous. Welcome to my world."

Candi laughed. "That's ridiculous."

"Is it? Take a look, sister." They had reached the cafeteria, which had a reflective coating on the large, floor-to-ceiling glass walls. Sarah pointed to Candi's reflection. "Note the amazing hair – dreadlocked to perfection, sun-bleached; the thin, muscular, tanned legs, shown off to perfection thanks to the mini skirt and heels I skillfully chose from your lamefarts closet; and last but not least, the confident air that seeps out of your every pore that says 'don't mess with me, or I will lay you out'. You have it all, babe. Better get used to your new life."

Candi shook her head in denial. "That's ridiculous."

Sarah rolled her eyes. "Whatever. Let's go into the cafeteria and do a little experiment." They stopped outside the main doors. "What usually happens when you walk in here?"

"Nothing."

"By nothing you mean that no one pays any attention to you?"

"Yes."

"Okay, see what happens this time. You go in by yourself. I'll go in first and take a seat at the tables on the far left, last row. You wait one minute and then come in; meet me at the table where we will discuss the results of our experiment."

"Fine."

Candi watched Sarah open the doors to the cafeteria and disappear inside. A minute later, Candi grabbed the doors and walked in. She began walking to the tables that Sarah had mentioned which were across the room and farther back from where Kevin usually sat.

Within ten steps, Candi started feeling the stares. The loud talking that usually overwhelmed the room quieted down a little.

She could see girls leaning in to whisper to each other while looking at her. Their faces didn't look very happy. The guys, on the other hand, sat up straighter and smiled at her, nudging one another with their elbows. One of them left his table to meet her as she walked through the center of the room.

"Hey Candi, remember me? Rick Waznewski? We were in algebra together two years ago?"

"Um, yeah, hi Rick." This guy had never even looked at her once in algebra or anywhere else.

"Do you want to come sit over with me and some friends?" he gestured over to the table next to where Kevin usually sat. Kevin wasn't there yet.

"No, I'm meeting a friend at another table, but thanks."

"Sure, anytime. Uh-oh," he winked at her, "incoming." He walked away as another guy came up. This one she knew played for the school basketball team. He was about six foot four, which meant she came up to his elbow.

"Hey, what's up?" he said as he approached her.

"Um, nothing."

"Yeah, so, I'm in your chemistry class. Greg."

"Hi Greg."

"Hi. I was wondering if you have a date for prom yet."

"No, not yet. But I don't think I'm going."

"How come?"

"I don't know, I just don't know if I want to."

Greg smiled. "Is this your nice way of letting me down easy?"

Candi smiled back. "No, I'm serious. I'm just not sure yet."

"So how much competition do I have?"

"Excuse me?"

"How many other guys have asked you to go?"

Candi smiled, a little embarrassed. "You're the fourth."

"Did Rick ask you?"

"No."

"Well, count him in, because I heard him saying he was going to. Looks like you're going to be the prom queen this year."

Candi laughed. "Don't be silly; I'm no prom queen."

"I wouldn't be too sure about that. Well, anyway, I'll see you around. If you decide you're going to prom, message me on Facebook or something."

"Okay, sure. Thanks."

"Later."

Candi finally made it to the table and sat down. Sarah was waiting with a knowing smile on her face. "So? I'm right, right?"

"Yeah, for some crazy reason I think you are. Two more guys came up to me, and all the girls are staring and talking about me, I can totally feel it."

"Yep. Jealous. You used to be one of those girls, Candi."

"I never talked about people in a mean way, Sarah."

"I know, I'm just kidding. But seriously, you are different and everyone can see it."

Candi looked down at the table. "Everyone except the one who really matters."

Sarah smiled. "I wouldn't be too sure about that if I were you." She looked pointedly across the room at Kevin's usual table.

Candi turned around in her seat to see what Sarah was looking at. She saw that Kevin had arrived and was in a heated exchange with Greg. Kevin looked mad. Greg was throwing up his arms, like he was explaining himself. Then he put his left hand on his heart and held up his right arm for a high handshake. Kevin grabbed it and they pulled each other closer and patted each other on the back.

"What the heck was that?" asked Candi, confused.

"Well, if I'm reading their body language correctly, and I'm pretty much an expert at that by the way, Kevin just went over there and said something like 'get the hell away from my girl', and then Greg was like 'hey man, I didn't know she was your girl' and then Kevin was like 'no harm no foul, man', and Greg was like 'yeah, man, sorry about that, are we cool?' and Kevin was like 'yeah, we're cool' – and then they shook hands and did some man cuddling, and it's all over. Kevin has officially peed on his territory."

Candi looked at her with her jaw dropped open. "You are completely insane."

"Crazy like a fox, baby. Like. A. *Fox.*"

Just then a lunch tray dropped down on their table next to Candi. "Hello ladies. This seat taken?"

"Why hello there, Jason." Sarah looked at Candi meaningfully.

"Hey Sarah, hey Candi, what's up?"

"Nothing much. Still the same as earlier today."

"Got any plans for the weekend?"

Sarah interrupted. "She's helping me move."

"Oh. Well, if you want any help with that you could give me a call. I'm pretty strong, I can lift boxes and stuff." He held up his arm and flexed.

Candi laughed. "I'll keep that in mind."

Sarah grabbed her phone that had just beeped, signaling she had a text. She laughed when she saw it. "Uh, Candi? I have a message for your friend Jason here."

Jason frowned. "For me?"

"Yes. This is a text from my brother." She handed him her phone.

Jason read it and then stood up and picked up his tray, handing the phone back to Sarah. "See you guys later."

Candi watched his receding form and then looked back at Sarah. "What the heck was that all about?"

"See for yourself."

Candi took the phone from her. There was a text on the screen from 'Dipshit'.

"Who's 'dipshit'?"

"That's how I named Kevin in my phone. Read what it says."

Candi read the text. STAY AWAY FROM MY GIRL.

Candi's heart started racing, first with excitement and then with annoyance. "Who does he think he is? I mean, he ignores me for a month, he's sitting across the room from me, but he can't get his butt up to come over here? So he texts a threat to a nice guy who does come over to talk to me? Seriously, Sarah, are you cool with this?"

"Nope. I think he's a dipshit." She held up her phone and waved it at Candi. "Helloooo ... "

"Oh, right. Dipshit is the one who sent the text."

Sarah continued, now talking quietly to herself, "Although I guess I'm going to have to change his name on here since I can't say dipshit anymore ... what should I use? Oh! I know ... " She started typing on her phone keys. D-U-N-G-B-E-E-T-L-E

"Well, he can kiss my butt. I'm not his girl. He's made that perfectly clear."

Sarah continued typing on her phone.

"Don't text him back, just ignore him," said Candi.

"I'm just answering him. He asked me for your cell number."

"Don't tell him!"

"Too late."

The lunchroom was completely full to capacity now. Candi turned to look at Kevin's table. It was loaded with the usual suspects – all the members of the rugby team, cheerleaders, and Gretchen, who was sitting across from Kevin, staring at him and then Candi with an angry look on her face.

Kevin looked up at Candi and stared at her. He was being bumped and jostled by the group at his table and the one behind him, but he just elbowed them off. He couldn't take his eyes off her. He jerked his head sideways, signaling her to come over.

She met his stare defiantly. She shook her head at him, signaling to him that he must be out of his mind. No way in a million years was she going to get up and go over there, just because he told her to.

"He wants you to go over there."

"I know."

"Are you going to go?"

"Hell to the *no."*

Sarah laughed. "Good for you. Make him work for it."

"I'm not making him work for it, I'm just not going to be treated like some stupid girl who has to go running after mister rugby stud."

Her phone beeped in her purse. She sighed loudly as she fished it out. She had a text from an unknown number. The dungbeetle.

COME SIT WITH ME.

"Pfft. Not likely."

NO THX, she texted back.

Sarah laughed as she looked at Candi's face. She was cute when she was mad. She looked over at her brother. He looked frustrated. "What did you tell him? Whatever it is, he looks veeerry frustrated."

"I don't care."

Sarah just smiled.

Candi's phone beeped again.

I NEED TO ASK U SMTHNG.

Candi's fingers flew over the keys.

NOT INTERESTED.

Kevin stood up a couple seconds later, still holding his phone and looking at the screen. He looked over to where Candi was sitting.

"Uh-ooohhhh," said Sarah ominously.

"What?" whispered Candi.

"He's standing up. He looks cranky."

Candi's phone beeped.

DON'T MAKE ME DO IT.

Candi's heart leapt into her throat. She felt butterflies racing around in her stomach. *What is he talking about? Do what?*

She turned around and watched him stand up on his seat.

"Holy horsepuckies, he's standing on his seat, Candi!" said Sarah, mouth wide open, laughing her butt off at what she knew was coming.

"Oh my god, Sarah, make him stop!" whispered Candi as loudly as she could. Her face was nearly catching on fire it was so hot.

Kevin cupped his hands on either side of his mouth, and began to yell. *"HEY CANDI! CANDI BUCKLEY! WILL YOU GO TO PROM WITH ME?"*

The cafeteria was dead silent for a full five seconds.

Then the cheering started, along with banging on the tables and benches. It was mass pandemonium in the cafeteria, everyone cheering and hollering, making as much noise as they could while waiting to see what Candi was going to do.

The words Candi wanted to hear, from the guy she wanted to hear them from. But now she wasn't so sure. Her heart was raw from his indifference over the past few weeks. She didn't know if she should give him another chance.

"He's waiting, Candi," reminded Sarah, trying to be heard over the ruckus. "Everyone's waiting, to see if the prom queen is going to say yes to the prom king." She smiled, riding the wave of craziness.

Candi threw up her hands. "Now that's just ridiculous. Three months ago I was invisible at this school."

"Well, you're not anymore," said Sarah.

Candi's phone buzzed on the table. She sighed heavily. "This is getting old."

I WAS HOPING TO SEE U IN ONE OF THOSE GRASS SKIRTS AGAIN.

Tears came to her eyes. Memories of the island and the night of their island prom came flooding back. She stood up suddenly, throwing her purse over her shoulder. She probably should try to stay mad, but she couldn't. She was happy. He hadn't forgotten. She turned her head and saw that he was moving down the aisle between the tables, staring right at her. Guys were slapping him on the back as he pushed by.

"Where are you going?" asked Sarah.

"Kevin's on his way over here. I'm leaving."

"Are you blowing him off?" Sarah was confused. She knew Candi loved her brother and that her blockhead brother loved Candi back. She could see him coming their way with a determined look on his face and she had a pretty good idea about what he was going to do. He had gone down on one knee for her before ...

"I'm not that easy," explained Candi, smiling confidently at Sarah.

Sarah beamed back at her. "That's my girl! Let me know how it works out. I'll see you at home."

Candi glanced over her shoulder long enough to see Kevin battling the last of the crowd to get to her. He didn't care who was watching – and it seemed like almost everyone was.

"Candi! Candi, wait up!" he yelled.

The crowd picked up the chant banging the tables with every syllable, "CAN-DI! CAN-DI! CAN-DI! CAN-DI! ... "

She walked quickly towards the side exit doors of the cafeteria. As she opened the doors and stepped out into the sunshine, she realized that she liked the idea of a home with Sarah in it. Not because of what it would do for her social status, but because she genuinely loved her like a sister. She laughed to herself about how ironic that was.

Six months ago she would never have imagined herself walking out of the cafeteria with Kevin Peterson shoving chairs aside to come running after her, while she looked forward to an evening spent with her pregnant friend Sarah Peterson and the baby daddy, her brother Jonathan.

Life has a crazy way of working out, even when it's totally wrecked.

The End

... or is it?

Next in Series

RECKLESS ... The much anticipated sequel to WRECKED, the story of four teenagers from different ends of the social spectrum who were castaway on an island together before finally making it back home ... only to be thrown back into high school life with completely different perspectives than they had before. Will they fall into the same traps or forge new paths for themselves? Follow Kevin, Candi, Sarah, and Jonathan as they move into their future - always hopeful, often uncertain, and sometimes even ... RECKLESS.

Other Books by Elle Casey

War of the Fae: Book One, The Changelings
War of the Fae: Book Two, Call to Arms
War of the Fae: Book Three, Darkness & Light
War of the Fae: Book Four, New World Order

Clash of the Otherworlds: Book 1, After the Fall
Clash of the Otherworlds: Book 2, Between the Realms
Clash of the Otherworlds: Book 3, Portal Guardians

Apocalypsis: Book 1, Kahayatle
Apocalypsis: Book 2, Warpaint
Apocalypsis: Book 3, Exodus
Apocalypsis: Book 4, Haven

My Vampire Summer
My Vampire Fall

Wrecked
Reckless

About the Author

Elle Casey is an American writer who lives in Southern France with her husband, three kids, Hercules the wonder poodle, and Monie the bouvier. In her spare time she writes young adult novels.

A personal note from Elle ...

If you enjoyed this book, please consider leaving feedback on Amazon.com, Goodreads.com, or any book blogs you participate in. More positive feedback means I can spend more time writing! Oh, and I love interacting with my readers, so if you feel like shooting the breeze or talking about books, please visit me. You can find me at ...

www.ElleCasey.com
www.Facebook.com/ellecaseytheauthor
www.Twitter.com/ellecasey
www.Shelfari.com/ellecasey

Acknowledgments

No writer is an island, and I am no exception. I'd like to acknowledge several people to whom I am very grateful, including Lady Olivia and Sir Richard who loaned me bedrooms in their apartment in Paris so that I could write in peace – with Lady O even delivering my favorite lunch to me while I typed away. You've supported me since the day I stepped on French soil (in all of my endeavors), and I will never forget it. I also want to thank my editors R.W. Jensen and Beth Godwin who really put a fine polish on my writing – your suggestions were always right on the money; I wish I could write with you hanging over my shoulder! Thanks to Guillermo Flores Jr., my Coast Guard veteran who cleaned up my radio chatter; super big hugs, G! Thank you to all the people who encouraged me over the years to write; you know who you are. Thanks to my extended family in New York, California, Florida, Maine, Illinois, and Colorado for being so cool. Thanks Creative-Club on elance for my cover art and CrashconEddie too for the paperback version. Thanks Apple for my Mac. Thank you France for giving me and my family all that you have. Thanks DDG crew of Sommières; you ladies are amazing ... time for another GNO! Thank you Breaking Benjamin – your music kicks ass; I want to meet you guys some day so I can fawn over you. To those who have taken the time to review my books, thank you; when you see me, introduce yourself so I can hug you. Last, to my fans ... I love you all! Without you I'd still be dreaming of being a writer. From the bottom of my heart, THANK YOU.

To everyone who has bought my book, I hope you enjoy reading it as much as I did writing it!